Etherya's Earth Volume 3:

The Novellas

By

REBECCA HEFNER

Contents

The Dawn of Peace: Page 3

Immortal Beginnings: Page 117

Two Souls United: Page 199

Garridan's Mate: Page 291

Sebastian's Fate: Page 393

The Dawn of Peace

An Etherya's Earth Prequel

By

Rebecca Hefner

This book is a work of fiction. Names, characters, places and incidents are the product of the author's imagination and are used fictitiously. Any resemblance to actual events, locales or persons, living or dead, is coincidental.

Copyright © 2022 by Rebecca Hefner. All rights reserved, including the right to reproduce, distribute or transmit in any form or by any means.

Cover Design: Authortree, authortree.co
Editor and Proofreader: Bryony Leah, www.bryonyleah.com

Contents

Title Page
Copyright
Dedication
Map of Etherya's Earth
Chapter 1
Chapter 2
Chapter 3
Chapter 4
Chapter 5
Chapter 6
Chapter 7
Chapter 8
Chapter 9
Chapter 10
Chapter 11
Chapter 12
Chapter 13
Chapter 14
Chapter 15
Chapter 16
Chapter 17
Chapter 18
Chapter 19
Chapter 20
Chapter 21
Chapter 22
Epilogue
Before You Go
About the Author

For new and seasoned readers of this series. I always wanted to write a prequel for you—it just took me a few years to get around to it! Enjoy the HEA.

THE PASSAGE
PURGES OF METHESDA
Valeria
Naria
CAVE OF THE SACRED PROPHECY
STROK MOUNTAINS
Astaria
PORTAL OF MITHOS
River Thayne
Lynia
Uteria
DEAMON CAVES
Restia
HUMAN WORLD

Chapter 1

Six Years after the Awakening

Kilani, daughter of esteemed Slayer council member Pretorius, clenched her teeth as she swung the sword through the air. Her task required extreme concentration since it was imperative she didn't hurt the person at the other end of the weapon. Although her sparring partner was only fourteen years old, she was already fierce with a sword.

"Use your height to your advantage, Miranda," Kilani said, slicing the weapon low by her hip.

"I don't have any height," Miranda gritted, advancing and thrusting the sword toward Kilani's abdomen. "Damn it, I thought I had you."

Kilani held up a hand, halting their skirmish. "You did well, my princess. You only started training weeks ago. Give it time."

Nodding, Miranda ran a hand over her sleek black hair, secured into a tiny ponytail at her nape. "You know, both our fathers would kill us if they knew we were training. We're not playing the appropriate female roles for the austere Slayer kingdom." Her lips formed a cheeky grin.

"I'm not sure you'll ever fit that mold, Miranda, and for that, I am grateful. The War of the Species rages, and it must end before it destroys both tribes."

"I hate that our species have devolved to this point. Vampyres and Slayers existed in peace for centuries before the Awakening."

Cupping her shoulder, Kilani gave a reassuring squeeze. "Hopefully, all will be well again one day, princess. The war will end, Slayers will live without fear, and Vampyres will walk in the sun once more."

"And they can finally stop raiding us for our blood...the vein-sucking jerks."

Kilani cleared her throat. "I think your father would faint if he heard you speak in such a manner."

Miranda's lips twitched. "Then let's keep it between us."

Kenden, Miranda's cousin and commander of the Slayer army, chose that moment to appear, stepping into the clearing from the surrounding woods. "Miranda," he said in his deep baritone, "King Marsias is looking for you. It's time to return to the castle."

"Fine," she sighed, handing her sword to Kilani, "but we made progress today. I'm getting better."

"One day, you'll be a powerful warrior. Hopefully by then, we can talk your father into rescinding the decree that women can't fight in the army."

"I'm proud you would welcome women into the army, Ken," Miranda said, patting him on the shoulder. "And Kilani should be your first recruit. She's amazing with a sword."

"I only agreed to let her train you when I was unavailable," Kenden said, arching a brow. "I don't want you dragged into an untenable situation, Kilani. If your father or King Marsias learn we're training Miranda, there will be hell to pay."

"Understood," Kilani said with a nod. "Father and I have never seen eye to eye on these matters. Misogyny has reared its ugly head in our kingdom now that war is upon us. It's amazing how people revert to their base beliefs, no matter how antiquated, when they are thrust into harrowing situations. I would worry for the state of our kingdom, but I know Miranda will pull us back to the light one day."

"If Father ever lets me take the throne," she muttered. "Every day, he morphs into someone colder—someone I barely recognize. It's chilling to look into his eyes and see the darkness there. I hope he doesn't lose himself in an effort to win the war."

"Your mother's abduction and death at the hands of Deamon King Crimeous destroyed him. His pain clouds his judgment and fuels his anger. We'll do our best to steer him down the right path," Kenden said. "For now, you must go, Miranda."

With a nod, she waved to both of them before heading into the forest and disappearing from sight.

"Marsias is intent on remaining king," Kilani said softly. "I don't see him relinquishing the throne to Miranda for decades, maybe even centuries. It's possible she'll eventually have to wrest it from him by force."

Inhaling a deep breath, Kenden nodded. "I foresee many obstacles in the dark days that lie ahead. The Vampyre army is vast, and with their self-healing abilities, we lose twice as many men as they do in each battle."

"Which is why women should be allowed to join the army," she said, chin lifting.

"Yes." Kenden kicked the ground with the toe of his boot. "But Marsias will never allow it, nor will the council. Your father is one of the most vocal supporters of an all-male army."

"My father is an old man who is only alive because of our cursed immortality. I swear, the goddess should've bestowed us with finite lives for people like him."

Kenden's features softened. "I'm sorry your relationship with him is so strained. I miss my family terribly since they were killed in the Awakening and have no idea what it's like not to love those most closely related to you by blood."

Pondering, Kilani pursed her lips. Seconds passed before she said, "You just learn to live without love. Some things are more important."

He flashed a compassionate smile beneath his straight nose and mop of brown hair. "You will find a great love one day. Of that, I have no doubt."

"Okay," she said, waving her hand. "Go home to Leticia. I don't have time for frivolous discussions."

"Leticia and I ended things," he said, lifting his shoulder. "I'm just too busy with the troops and the war. I hope she finds someone who can give her what I can't."

"I'm sorry to hear that. If we're not careful, my father and King Marsias will try to push us together as they always do when we're both single. Of course, trying to kiss you would be like kissing my brother, although I do like you a tad more." She grinned and held her thumb and index finger an inch apart.

"I'll take that as a compliment...I think." He squinted. "Speaking of your brother, I hear your father is preparing him to take his spot on the council when he retires."

"He tells Drakor that to appease him, but Father will never give up his seat."

"It should be your seat since you are firstborn."

"Council members have always been men. Hopefully, Miranda will change things when she becomes queen. Having the blood of King Valktor makes her the one true heir. Marsias is just a placeholder."

"A powerful placeholder," Kenden said. "His desire to avenge Queen Rina is vast. Since the prophecy states that someone with Valktor's blood will kill the Deamon Lord Crimeous, and Miranda is Valktor's only living descendant, I feel he will want her to bear a male heir."

Scoffing, she fisted her hands on her hips. "Of course. Because a *female* could never kill Crimeous. Rubbish." She gave a *pfft* and felt her cheeks inflame with anger.

"You are ahead of your time, Kilani. The kingdom is not ready for you, nor will they be ready when it's Miranda's time to assume power. The transition must be handled with care."

"I'll offer my help, although Father likes to relegate me to societal duties. He has no idea you trained me to fight."

Kenden's eyebrows lifted. "Honestly, I was floored when you asked me to train you after the Awakening, but I see the value in teaching those who want to learn. If I have that foresight, I trust others can acquire it too."

"We'll see," she muttered, rubbing her arm. "In the meantime, I should get going. Father is hosting a fundraising dinner for Marsias so he can dazzle the aristocrats into funneling more money into the war. The fight against the Vampyres is costly, especially now since we have to line the compound walls with armed soldiers to protect us from the raids."

"That it is. I assume you organized the fete?"

She nodded. "It's my duty to organize all social functions since Mother died. I hate it with a passion, but it is easier to comply than fight with Father." Her eyes narrowed. "I don't remember getting an RSVP from you."

"I have a night training."

"Lucky you." Sighing, she ran her hand through the blond hair that fell slightly past her shoulders. "Well then, let me get to it. I'd much rather meet you at the sparring field under the moon."

"It will happen one day, Kilani," he said with an encouraging squeeze of her shoulder. "Let's win the war, and then we can drag the kingdom into modernity."

"From your lips to the goddess's ears."

His eyebrow arched. "We renounced the goddess when she withdrew her protection from our people."

Kilani shrugged. "She cursed the Vampyres to darkness, causing their skin to burn if they even step into the sun. Perhaps she did her best to punish both species equally."

"Perhaps."

"On that uplifting little note, I'm off," she said, raising a hand and giving a salute. "See ya."

Kenden's goodbye followed her through the woods as her boots crunched the fallen leaves and branches. Eventually, she reached the clearing that bordered her father's home and trailed across the long meadow.

Once inside, she snuck through the back door, ensuring none of the servants observed her in her black sparring gear. After showering, she pulled the long, flowing red gown from her closet, wrinkling her nose in distaste. God, she hated formal dresses. Dragging it over her head, she smoothed the fabric before applying a bare smattering of makeup. After pulling her hair into a functional yet elegant bun, Kilani headed downstairs to ensure everything was prepared for the fundraiser she was dreading with every cell in her body.

Chapter 2

Four hours later, Kilani lifted her wineglass to her lips, sipping the dark red liquid as she tried not to die of boredom. One of the aristocratic Slayers she'd known for decades was chatting her ear off as they sat at the expansive table in the mansion's ornate dining room. She was pretty sure her father had switched the place seating cards so her seat was next to Friedan's. Pretorius thought he was wily, but Kilani was all too familiar with his futile and transparent matchmaking attempts.

"Kilani," Friedan asked, "did I lose you?"

"No, just enjoying the wine," was her curt reply. "I think I need to take a walk before the dancing begins. Please excuse me." Tossing back the wine, she set the glass on the table and rose, craving fresh air.

Once outside, she rested her hands on the cool stone of the balcony rail, gazing up at the full moon as she shivered in the crisp nighttime air. Vampyres were known to raid Uteria during the full moon since it offered additional light for their conquests. But they'd raided the compound the previous month, thereby decreasing the chances they would attack again so soon. Vampyre King Sathan was known to keep Slayer prisoners alive in his dungeon so he could extract every drop of blood from their veins and bank it for his people.

"Blood-sucking bastards," she muttered, her breath forming a puff in the chilly air. "I'm so tired of this fucking war."

"I hoped you would enjoy talking to Friedan tonight," her father's deep voice called behind her, "but instead, you stand out here talking to yourself. You will never find a husband this way, Kilani."

Closing her eyes, she inhaled a deep breath, silently instructing herself to remain calm. The last thing she needed was another blowout with her father.

"I have no wish to get married or find a mate," she said, lifting her lids. Her gaze bore into his, showing her fortitude. "I wish to be a solider, Father. Once Miranda is old enough to take the throne, I will pledge my skills to the kingdom and fight to protect it."

Pretorius scoffed. "It will never happen. You dream of a future that will never be. I implore you to dismiss these thoughts and find a suitable mate."

Sighing, she shook her head. "I can't have this argument with you again, Father. Let's just agree to disagree, shall we?" Wishing to change the subject, she gestured toward the brightly lit home. "The fundraiser is going well."

"It is." Glancing down, his eyebrows drew together before he lifted his gaze to hers. "I won't have a daughter who defies me, Kilani. If you do not wish to live by my rules, I have no choice but to petition King Marsias for banishment."

Kilani's heartbeat began to thrum in her chest. Surely, he wasn't serious? They had disagreed for centuries, but she at least thought he cared for her, even if he didn't love her as he did her brother and deceased mother.

"Father, if you banish me to Restia, there will be no one here to perform Mother's duties. I thought you at least needed me to fill that role."

"Not to Restia," he said, his tone firm. "I will petition to ban you from the Slayer kingdom. If you wish to be so progressive, perhaps you should cross the ether and live with the humans. Maybe that will teach you our societal rules aren't the prison sentence you insist they are."

Fear coursed through her at the thought of leaving the only home she'd ever known, along with a healthy dose of anger. "You would banish me because we disagree? Because I'm a woman who wants to *choose* her own fate? That's absurd!"

"It's necessary!" he said, slicing a hand through the air. "I won't continue to live with the embarrassment of having a daughter who refuses to adhere to societal rules that have existed for centuries."

"Which means they're antiquated and need to change!" she demanded, exasperated. "Whether you like it or not, change will come to this kingdom. Miranda *will* become queen one day, and it's possible that with her leadership, the War of the Species will also end."

"Slayers and Vampyres will never live in peace again," he said, dismissing her statements as if they were insignificant. "You clutch onto a life and dreams that will never be." Lifting his finger, he cocked an eyebrow. "This is your last warning, Kilani. Find a husband by the next harvest, or I will begin banishment proceedings."

Clenching her fists, Kilani struggled not to punch him in his straight, austere nose. "You understand I will never accept this," she murmured.

"Then you have *chosen* your own fate," he said, using her previous words against her. "I hope it's worth it."

"You bastard!" she hissed, jabbing her finger in his face. "You have never treated me as an equal part of this family—"

"Because you don't do your part," he interjected. "You have a role to fill. If you cannot do it, I have no use for you."

Pain sliced through every pore of her skin, the words searing as if she'd been doused in acid. As emotion swirled deep in her gut, her ears perked, and she gasped before glancing toward the far end of the meadow.

Recognition lit in her father's eyes before he pivoted, staring out across the dark field.

Suddenly, cries of war echoed across the fog-ridden meadow, and Kilani's eyes widened.

"Go inside and inform the guests the Vampyres are raiding."

"Kilani—"

"Go," she said, facing him with disgust. "I have a sword stashed in the garden shed. I will arm myself and do my best to fight them off. Gather everyone in the basement and lock it behind you. Do you hear me?"

Something sparked in his dark orbs as he gazed at her, and Kilani had the strange thought this would be the last time she ever saw her father.

"Go!" she yelled.

His throat bobbed in the moonlight before he pivoted and scurried inside.

Straightening her spine, Kilani prepared for battle. Her faith in Kenden was firm, and she knew he would arrive soon with troops. In the meantime, she would put her training to good use.

Stalking to the shed, she yanked open the door and strode to the sword. Glancing at the small shearers that hung on the wall, she stuck those in the belt at the waist of her flowing dress. And then she marched outside, sword in hand, ready to fight the Vampyres.

Chapter 3

Alrec, son of Vampyre soldier Jakar, crested the hill that overlooked the massive Slayer mansion. Lights burned brightly inside as Slayer aristocrats held the fundraiser to finance the War of the Species.

"The troops are ready to advance, sir," Takel's deep baritone droned beside him. He was an excellent warrior, and Alrec was thankful to have him as his first-in-command.

"Good," Alrec said, scanning the open field and the mansion beyond. "I'm frustrated we're here again so soon, but King Marsias's suicide decree leaves us no choice." The stubborn ruler had commanded any Slayer who was abducted to end his life rather than survive in the dungeon and become food for Vampyres. Ten of the Slayer men abducted in the last raid had somehow secured a toothpick—most likely carelessly tossed on the floor by one of the Vampyre dungeon guards—and they'd used it to fulfill King Marsias's decree.

Sighing, Alrec ran a hand over his face. So much death in the endless war the Vampyres fought with the Slayers. How long could they go on like this?

"Alrec?" Takel asked.

Dragging himself out of the morose thoughts, he pulled the sword from the hilt on his waist and held it high. "Secure ten Slayer men and then retreat," he called to his battalion. "I have no wish to drag out this raid."

The men chimed a united, "Yes, sir!" behind him before he shook his sword and yelled, "Charge!"

Adrenaline rushed through his veins as he surged down the hill, crossing the meadow as his boots crunched the grass below. His battalion of twenty Vampyres followed close behind, ready to fulfill their duty.

Suddenly, a flash of golden hair caught his eye under the silver moonlight, and Alrec's breath lodged in his throat. A Slayer woman stood tall, sword in hand, as her kinsmen scurried behind her, fleeing like ants toward the safety of the bunkers below the home.

"I will confront the female!" Alrec yelled to his men, indicating they should continue past him toward the mansion. "Seize the Slayer men and retreat quickly!"

The soldiers charged forward, scurrying toward the back entrance of the mansion as Alrec approached the woman. As he drew near, he noticed the flowing red gown clinging to her frame as she lifted the sword. Both hands clenched the hilt, her azure eyes glowing under the darkened sky, and Alrec felt his heart clank in his chest.

She was *magnificent*.

Regaining his wits, he trudged toward her, hoping she would recognize the futility of fighting him. As he drew closer, their height and weight discrepancy became clear. He towered over her by at least a foot, and his muscled body outweighed her by several stone.

"Lower your sword, little one," he called, surprised by the protective swell in his voice. "I have no wish to harm you."

"Little one, my ass," she responded, teeth clenched as she lifted the sword higher. "I'll be damned if you abduct my people without putting up a fight."

Halting when he was close enough to strike, he planted his feet and slowly lifted his hand, showing her his palm. "I don't want to fight you. I can kill you in seconds. Is that really what you wish?"

Midnight blue eyes roved over his features. "I would rather die a noble death defending my fellow Slayers than let you abduct us without a fight." Aiming the tip of her sword toward him, she crouched. "Come on, *Vampyre*," she sneered, her tone full of malice. "Let's see how tough you are when you're against a Slayer with the temerity to fight back!" She charged until he had no choice but to defend himself.

The steel of their blades crashed together, the clanking sound ominous against the cries and shrills of war in the background. The Slayer was quick, her movements deft, and a surge of elation jolted down his spine. Alrec relished being a warrior, and there was nothing more thrilling than a worthy opponent.

He thrust his sword through the air, connecting with hers every few seconds before retreating and trying a different angle. The vexing woman seemed to anticipate his every move, and he realized her training was vast.

"Who trained you?" he gritted, pressing his sword to hers as the weapons crossed between their bodies. "You are exceptional."

"Kenden trained me himself, you blood-sucking bastard," she cried before drawing back and rotating. Heaving her sword, she lodged it in his shoulder, causing a surge of pain before he grasped it with his large hand and yanked it from his skin.

"Well done," he mocked, squeezing the blade as she gaped up at him, the small sliver of fear in her stunning irises both pleasing and disconcerting. Blood dripped from his hand where he clutched the blade—and his shoulder where she'd stabbed him—but his self-healing abilities would quickly repair the wounds. Pain rushed through his body as he tossed her sword to the ground. Although he would self-heal, he still felt pain.

The woman gasped, nostrils flaring as she gazed up at him.

"You've lost possession of your weapon," he said, gesturing with his head toward her sword, which now sat several feet away on the soft grass. "Our skirmish is over—"

The blasted woman drew something from her belt that flashed in the moonlight before she thrust it into his abdomen. Sucking in a breath, Alrec realized she'd stabbed him with some sort of pruning shears.

"Good grief, woman!" he bellowed, grasping the handle and dislodging the sharp metal from his body. "Is it your objective to anger me until I kill you? You know your meager weapons will only hurt and my wounds will heal quickly. Only an eight-shooter or a poison-tipped blade can kill me, and you seem to have neither."

"I'll fight you with my bare hands," she cried, balling her fists.

Pain sluiced through his body as he simultaneously fought the urge to laugh and knock the Slayer unconscious. She was a piece of work indeed. Never had he met a woman with her grit and determination.

"We have ten Slayers!" Takel's voice chimed from across the meadow. "Should we retreat?"

"Yes," Alrec confirmed, backing away from the Slayer as she stood crouched in her fighting stance. Overcome with admiration for her, he decided to let her live.

"What is your name?" he asked, backing toward the far-off hill, needing to know before he retreated.

"Kilani, daughter of Pretorius, and you'll regret the day you abducted my kinsmen, Vampyre."

"No doubt," he murmured, rubbing the laceration on his abdomen as he studied her. "We don't wish to abduct your people. Tell Marsias to end the suicide decree. Next time, I won't be so nice, little one. Remember that when you speak to your king." Sparing her one last glance, he pivoted and ran across the field to join his men.

Strangely, the Slayer woman's stunning image remained in his mind long after the new prisoners had been secured in the dungeon. Eventually, after several nights of dreaming about her, Alrec accepted his fierce little warrior would always have permanent residence in the part of his brain it seemed couldn't let her go.

Chapter 4

Kilani's heart pounded as she digested the fact the hulking Vampyre had let her live. Although she'd put up a good fight, he could've easily overpowered her. Mulling over his actions, she turned to face the mansion. Kenden's soldiers were now on the scene, and he jogged toward her, concern lacing his features.

"Are you okay?" he asked, breathless as he approached and rested a hand on her shoulder.

"Yes. I fought the battalion leader, but he let me live." Brushing dirt off her arm, she scowled. "Bastard. Now I'm indebted to a Vampyre." Glancing toward the house, Kilani observed the chaos as soldiers scrambled and Slayers cried over the men who'd been abducted. "It's never going to end, is it?" she asked softly.

"One day," Kenden murmured. "For now, we should get you to the infirmary just in case."

"I'm fine," she said, backing away. Staring at the cold stones of the mansion, a sense of finality washed over her. "I have no place in this kingdom, Ken. I don't want to marry for duty, and Marsias won't allow women in the army. I'm fighting for a kingdom that doesn't want me."

"Things will change, Kilani—"

"When?" she cried, lifting her hands. "Once our men are dead and the Vampyres have depleted their only food rations? In the meantime, will I continue to live a miserable life in a world where my father is intent on banishment?"

Kenden's eyebrows drew together. "He threatened to banish you?"

Kilani nodded, contemplative under the dark sky as a plan formed in her rapidly buzzing brain. "I won't let him dictate my life, Ken."

Chestnut irises darted over her. "What do you want to do?"

Swallowing thickly, she backed toward the darkness of the nearby forest. "Tell them I was killed by the Vampyres, trying to defend our people."

"Kilani," he said, a soft plea in his voice as she inched toward the woods. "You don't have to do this..."

"I'm making a choice. Perhaps the only one I have left."

Sighing, Kenden rubbed his forehead. "I can't let you—"

"Tell Miranda I said goodbye," she said, her voice raspy with emotion. "She has the power to save us all. She will always have my support."

Kenden's expression was soulful and sad under the twinkling stars. "There is an abandoned cabin on the outskirts of the Portal of Mithos, near the foothills of the Strok Mountains. It's secluded, and I doubt anyone would find you unless they knew to look. I used to go hunting nearby with my father before he was slain at the Awakening."

"Who built it?" she asked, curious as she edged deeper into the woods.

"I don't know. It was there long before we hunted but has been abandoned for decades, maybe even centuries. It sits near a lake where fish are abundant."

"Thank you." Barely able to speak since her throat was so tight, she lifted her hand and waved. "Until I see you again, Ken. Thank you for letting me go."

"Goodbye, Kilani," he said with a small salute. "May I see you again when the world is ready for you."

With one last glance at his soulful expression, Kilani memorized her friend's features, hoping the image would comfort her in the life of solitude she was embarking upon. And then she turned and ran deep into the woods, past the walls of the compound, to an eternity where she would be alone but finally able to control her own destiny.

Chapter 5

Five years later

Alrec grunted, slicing his sword through the air as he fought the Deamon. This particular cluster of Deamons who lived at the base of the Strok Mountains were vicious, and Alrec's battalion had been tracking them for some time. Not only had they attacked a Vampyre unit stationed outside Astaria's wall several weeks ago, but they had also raided the Slayer compound of Uteria the previous week.

Alrec's battalion had been assigned to track down the bastards and eradicate them before they could cause more harm—to Vampyres or Slayers. After all, Slayers were their food, and they needed to remain alive.

And he didn't want any harm to befall his golden-haired Slayer warrior.

Yes, somewhere along the way, through sweat-soaked dreams and hazy visions, she'd become *his* Slayer. Alrec had long since realized the futility of trying to rid her from his mind. She lived there rent-free and most likely always would.

It was quite a cluster since Vampyres and Slayers were locked in a war neither side was able to win and romantic love between species was forbidden. Different species couldn't bear children, and Etherya decreed the species remain separate eons ago. Not to mention Alrec's desire for the Slayer he hadn't seen in five long years was unwanted. He'd prayed to the goddess countless times to rid the woman from his mind, but Alrec was also practical.

Erasing the image of her gorgeous face was a futile endeavor, and he was a man who didn't waste time.

So, he carried on, eventually becoming used to the woman's stunning features inhabiting every crevice of his brain.

The Deamon landed a powerful blow to his side, dragging Alrec back to the battle. Thrusting his sword high, he fought the Deamon, edging him closer to the riverbank as the Vampyre battalion fought behind him. Their shouts and cries of war grew softer as Alrec advanced, hoping his men were aware of his location.

Suddenly, the Deamon tossed his sword to the ground and pulled a weapon from his belt. Gasping, Alrec realized it was a mini eight-shooter. The weapon had been developed by the powerful Slayer commander, Kenden, and was one of the few devices capable of killing self-healing Vampyres. If fired, it would simultaneously deploy eight bullets into a Vampyre's eight-chambered heart, killing him on contact.

"You don't want to do this," Alrec said, holding up his hands as he clutched the sword tight in one fist. Searching his surroundings, he looked for high ground where he could retreat and regroup. "I am the battalion leader, and my men won't show mercy if you kill me."

"I don't care, Vampyre!" the Deamon spat. "You are all expendable to us."

Thinking quickly, Alrec decided he would run toward the river and dive in. The current was strong, and he would probably be carried several miles, but he was a competent survivalist and would be able to navigate back home to Astaria eventually. Frustration curled in his gut that he saw no angle to strike the Deamon, but Alrec liked living and was smart enough to know his sword and strength were no match for a direct blow from an eight-shooter. Inhaling a deep breath, he filled his lungs with oxygen and sprinted toward the river.

The Deamon gasped, turning and firing at the same moment Alrec dove into the cold, rushing water. The last thing he heard was a small explosion, followed by a powerful burst of pain in his side. Then he became submerged, and all he saw was darkness.

Takel scanned the horizon beyond the river, frustrated his men hadn't yet found Alrec. After they'd defeated the Deamons and the few left alive scattered in retreat, they spent hours searching for their missing battalion leader. Unfortunately, they had no results and the sun would soon rise, burning them all to death.

"Takel," a deep voice chimed as a firm hand cupped his shoulder, "we have to head back to camp. We can send a battalion to search for Alrec tomorrow night. We won't rest until we find him."

Sighing, Takel nodded. "You're right, Draylock. I'm worried he was injured with a poison-tipped blade or struck by an eight-shooter. I hope we find him alive."

"We'll do our best. For now, our men need rest, and dawn is near."

Resigned to return to look for his friend, Takel pivoted from the river and led the battalion back to their base.

Chapter 6

Kilani exited the cabin, lifting her face to the sky and stretching as the faint sounds of birds chirping pulsed through the air. She'd always loved dawn. Something about it was refreshing, reminding the soul it had another day to get things right. Inhaling the fresh air, she reveled in the crisp tingle in her nose before clutching the spear at her side and trailing to the river.

In the five years she'd inhabited the cabin, it had become her home. When she discovered it, the wood and stone that comprised the foundation were overgrown with brush. The inside had a large bed with pillows and a mattress filled with goose feathers. A handmade sofa and two chairs comprised the only other furniture, and as she'd inspected the abandoned home, curiosity ran rampant.

Running her fingers over the sofa, she'd imagined it had been fashioned for a child or spouse by someone who loved them. Where had they gone? Judging by the sticky cobwebs and thick layer of dust, the home had been abandoned for some time. Never one to shy away from good fortune, Kilani had cleaned and polished the interior, determined to make the place feel like home, for it was the only home she would know until she could return to the Slayer kingdom, and she realized she might not feel safe enough to do that for centuries.

So, she toiled in her new home until it was pristine and learned how to fish. After constructing a fishing pole from a tree branch and some twine she'd found in the closet, she realized waiting patiently for fish to bite the bait wasn't her forte. Patience had never been her strong suit after all. Instead, she fashioned a spear from a stronger branch and taught herself to spear the fish. After some practice, she became quite good at it and now lived on a diet of fish and vegetables she grew in the garden. Some days, she would long for the rich food she'd become accustomed to as a Slayer aristocrat before she remembered food came with a hefty side of misogyny and repression. Upon those cheery thoughts, she would scowl and chew the damn fish, savoring every bite.

It was a solitary life, although she wasn't lonely. Kilani had been lonelier stuck in a life where she had no choice. Here, on her small patch of Etherya's Earth, she could grow into someone stronger. Someone who could possibly return to the Slayer kingdom sometime in the future when Miranda had fulfilled the prophecy and saved them all.

"Hell," Kilani muttered to herself as she traipsed toward the river, "you might be patient after all. Maybe living in the woods has worked miracles."

Approaching the riverbank, she noticed the clouds turn from gray to yellow and knew the sun would soon rise. The fish were always plentiful at dawn, and she gazed into the murky water, ready to catch her breakfast.

Something flashed out of the corner of her eye, and Kilani held her gasp, not wanting to make a sound if danger was near. Gripping her spear, she inched toward the sparkle in the distance. Approaching, a soft cry exited her lips as the image became clearer. The sparkling object was a metal button on a weaponry belt...and it was attached to a very large, very injured Vampyre. Blood trickled from eight small wounds on the side of his chest, and he was immobile except for the slight pulsing of the vein in his neck. Leaning down, Kilani jutted the blunt tip of the spear against his shoulder, confirming he was unconscious.

Grasping his stubbled chin, she turned his face, already knowing he was a Vampyre because of his huge frame but wanting to confirm he had fangs to satisfy her assumption. Glancing at his features, she inhaled a deep breath.

The Vampyre was the man who had spared her life five years ago in the raid at her father's home.

Releasing his chin, Kilani straightened and stared at the sky. As soon as the sun rose, it would burn his body to a crisp. Clenching her jaw, she knew what she had to do. Although she hated Vampyres, she also had an inherent sense of honor, and this man had spared her life once before. Now, it was time to return the favor.

Pivoting, she jogged to the cabin and grabbed the pallet she used to haul wood for the fireplace. After dragging it back to the river, she grunted and grumbled as she maneuvered the Vampyre's injured body atop the slats. Gripping the rope, she hauled the massive Vampyre back to her cabin, ensuring he was inside before the sun rose.

Needing to inspect his wounds, she removed his clothes and shoved him into the bed, covering him with the sheet before she gave in to her curiosity and inspected his more...*intimate* anatomy. After securing his wrists and ankles to each bedpost with her strongest ropes, she stood at the foot of the bed and gazed upon his unconscious frame, wondering how in the hell she'd ended up with a half-dead Vampyre in her bed.

Chapter 7

Alrec climbed toward consciousness, pain pulsing at the side of his chest. Reaching for the wound, he grunted, frustrated his arms wouldn't work. Struggling to open his eyes, he focused all his energy on lifting his eyelids, which seemed fused together. Eventually, they fluttered, and Alrec slowly lifted them, squinting at the dim light that eased through.

Adrenaline surged through his frame as he realized he was naked in what appeared to be a warm bed. Gazing down, he noticed the sheet covering his torso and legs and the ropes that secured each ankle to a bedpost. Tugging his arms, he grunted when he could barely move them. Sensing a presence at the foot of the bed, he glanced down and tried to focus.

A woman stepped forward, and the first thing Alrec noticed was her hair. The golden crown of hair he'd seen in his dreams for five long years, followed by her pert nose, full red lips, and eyes the color of the blue moss that grew atop the lake beside his childhood home at Astaria.

Widening his eyes, he whispered, "It's *you*."

She arched one of those golden eyebrows, her expression sardonic as she gazed at him above her crossed arms.

"Yes," she said with a nod. "I was wondering if you'd remember me. I remembered you when I found you minutes from death by the riverbank. The mercy you showed me years ago is the only reason you're alive."

Alrec blinked several times as he processed everything he knew about his current situation. He'd been fighting the Deamons when one of the bastards cornered him by the riverbank. Alrec had jumped into the river to avoid his eight-shooter blast…and then all had gone dark.

"Am I…?" Glancing down at his wound, which was covered by a white bandage, he cleared his throat. "Am I in the Passage?"

She scoffed and shook her head. "No such luck, buddy. You're stuck here in paradise with me. Who knew it resided between the Deamon Caves and the Strok Mountains? Surprise." She held up her hands and waved them in a mock cheer.

"Okay…" he said, struggling to understand why the Slayer had saved him. "You've been nursing me? Why haven't I self-healed?"

Striding forward, she neared his side and gently ran her fingers over his bandage, causing Alrec to shiver. The sight of her slender hand trailing over his body jump-started his pulse, and his heartbeat thudded inside his injured chest.

"I don't know," she murmured, absently staring at the bandage. "I don't have the proper tools here to test the poison in the bullets that were lodged in your chest. But I removed them, and they were laced with something quite nasty. Eight-shooters with poison-tipped bullets are known to kill a Vampyre in seconds. Even though the bullets didn't make it to your heart, I think they were close enough to circulate the poison throughout your side and chest. You're slowly healing, but it will take time."

Alrec's eyebrows drew together. "Fucking Crimeous. He continues to create deadlier poisons as the conflict worsens. It makes him formidable, which is the last thing we need."

She smirked. "Since you're already in a deadly war with the Slayers."

"Yes," he muttered, annoyance growing with each minute he remained restrained. "Fighting the Deamon King and the Slayers requires extensive time and effort. This is why I was here with my battalion. We were surveilling the Deamon outpost to gather intel. It's imperative we learn their weaknesses."

The woman flattened her lips, appearing smug as he lay in the bed.

"I'm not sure what the shit-eating grin is for, but it would be nice if you would untie me," he said, pulling at the restraints.

Leaning down, the tips of her hair brushed his chest as her warm breath floated across his face. "I know one of their weaknesses," she almost whispered, "and there's no way in hell I'm untying you."

Anger surged down his spine along with a hefty dose of arousal at the woman's scent. It was laced with hints of evergreen and mint as fresh as the wind on a warm spring night. Struggling to keep the desire at bay, he clenched his teeth.

"Do you really think I'm going to hurt the woman who saved me?"

She glanced at the ceiling, pondering. Finally, she shrugged and straightened. "Debatable." Gazing down, her eyes focused on the rather large tenting of the sheet at the juncture of his thighs. Alrec remained still, unwilling to squirm under her scrutiny. "Although, judging by your...*reaction*, you seem more like a lover than a fighter."

"Kilani," he said softly, pleased when she gasped and lifted her eyes to his. "Yes, I remember your name. I couldn't forget the name of such a magnificent warrior." *Or such a beautiful woman.* Holding his tongue, he allowed that sentiment to remain unsaid. "I give you my word I won't hurt you. And if you're willing to share any intel you've gathered on the Deamons, I would be forever grateful."

Tilting her head, she studied him as if he were a bug under a microscope. Finally, she lifted a finger and spoke in a firm tone. "The word of a Vampyre means nothing to me. And I have no wish to help a soldier I met when he was previously raiding my people for their blood. Be careful you don't anger me," she said, reaching for the glass full of murky liquid on the nightstand. "I still might decide to kill you." Touching the rim of the glass to his lips, she whispered in an ominous tone, "Drink up."

Alrec struggled before she slid her fingers through his hair and yanked, holding his head in place and all but pouring the liquid down his throat.

"By the goddess, that's awful!" he exclaimed, coughing and sputtering as he swallowed. "Is it poison?"

"Relax," she muttered, rolling her eyes. "It's an herbal concoction I made that will help you heal...and help you sleep. I have things to do around here and can't entertain an injured Vampyre all day. Sweet dreams." Rapidly blinking, she stood and gave a jeering wave. "See you on the other side."

Alrec opened his mouth to tell her he didn't appreciate the mocking tone...except speaking suddenly felt like a massive effort. Lowering his lids, he felt his head loll to the side...and then he fell down the hole of darkness once again.

Chapter 8

The next time Alrec opened his eyes, he was immediately drawn to the muted curses and whimpers of frustration uttered by the Slayer as she stood over the counter. Struggling to focus in the dim light, he wondered what was causing her pain.

"Kilani?" he called, the words hoarse since his throat was as dry as sandpaper. "Are you hurt?"

Those midnight blue eyes snapped to his as she stood behind the small island counter. It was made of wood, and Alrec found himself wondering if she'd fashioned it herself. How long had she been living alone in the woods? Was she hiding from something or someone?

"I'm fine," she muttered, squeezing her wrist so a small trickle of blood fell into the glass below. "You have to eat, don't you?"

Remaining silent, Alrec admitted she was right. A Vampyre needed Slayer blood every three days to survive. Although they ate food for pleasure, the goddess had made the species interdependent so they would be tethered together for eternity. Slayers offered their blood for sustenance, and Vampyres protected them in return—until the Awakening, when it had all gone horribly wrong.

Kilani poured approximately one ounce of blood into the glass before rubbing salve over the small wound on her wrist and applying a bandage. Grabbing the glass, she sauntered over, the sway of her hips in her cream-colored pants mesmerizing.

"Here," she said softly, sitting on the side of the bed. "I won't force it down like the tea." Her lips twitched as she lifted the cup to his lips. "I think you'll like this better anyway."

Alrec eyed her warily as he drank, immediately becoming consumed with the taste of her blood on his tongue. It was thick and quite rich, indicating she came from a pristine Slayer bloodline.

"You're an aristocrat," he said after swallowing.

"Yes." Gazing down at the empty glass, her expression grew morose. "I was until I realized being a female aristocrat in our kingdom was more a prison than a privilege. I left the night you attacked...and never looked back."

Alrec's eyes roved over her features, curiosity rampant as he longed to ask more questions. Unsure which to ask first, he decided it was best to let her lead. Clearing his throat, he said softly, "I would like to know your story, Kilani."

Her gaze lifted to his, surprise crossing those stunning features. "You would?"

"Yes." Grinning, he tilted his head on the pillow. "Is that such a strange request of the woman who saved me?"

Sighing, she rubbed her arm and stared absently toward the kitchen. "I don't know. I'm not used to men asking for my story. They usually just tell me who I'm supposed to be. Except for Kenden. He was one of a kind."

A strange spurt of jealously flared in his chest. Kenden was the powerful Slayer commander who had built a competent army after the Awakening. It was quite a feat considering Slayers weren't built for war like Vampyres. Narrowing his eyes, Alrec realized he didn't relish the little Slayer's wistful smile. Had they been lovers?

"Oh, no," she said, shaking her head, and Alrec realized he'd blurted the question aloud. "Ken was like my brother and helped lead me here. He's the only person in the immortal world who knows I'm still alive except for you,"—she arched a brow—"and I am grateful he keeps my secret."

"Why do you exile yourself from your people?"

Sighing, she ran a hand through her silken hair. "They're not ready for me yet. I might go back one day. Once Miranda has taken the throne, fulfilled the prophecy, and can foster positive change in our kingdom. Until then, I choose to remain here." Lifting her eyes to his, she murmured, "It isn't much, but it's my choice, and that's enough."

Alrec longed to hear more—to ask her why she didn't have choices in her kingdom and if she ever wished for companionship. Instead, he stayed silent, his eyes locked on her lithe frame as she trailed to the kitchen and washed the glass.

"Do you get your water from the river?" he asked, noting several full basins lining the countertop.

"Sometimes," she said with a shrug as she dried the glass. "And there's a lake nearby too. The house had some old blankets and curtains when I arrived that I made into clothes." Setting the glass in the drying rack, she drew her hand over her shirt and pants. "They're not the fancy silks I wore at Uteria, but they're comfortable."

She toiled in the kitchen, gathering medical supplies before returning to sit at his side. After setting the supplies on the bedside table, she peeled away the bandage covering his wounds, her face a mask of concentration.

"So strange..." she said, examining his wounds. "I've never heard of a Vampyre taking so long to heal. That poison really got under your skin. Literally."

Picking up a wet cloth, she began to gently clean his wounds, her motions methodical and tender. Her honeyed evergreen scent overwhelmed him, and he looked away, understanding he wouldn't be able to control his body's reaction to her. Whether he liked it or not, he was extremely attracted to the little Slayer.

Thick muscles tensed underneath his skin the longer she tended to him, blood coursing through each vein as if they might explode. Closing his eyes, Alrec felt his shaft thicken and pulse, the sensitive skin growing taut, and he ached for release. Kilani's breathing grew shallow, permeating the quiet room, and he opened his eyes to observe the pounding vein in her neck. Her cheeks now carried a rosy blush, and Alrec was relieved the attraction was mutual.

"Do you want to talk about that?" she asked, glancing toward his massive erection now tenting the covers.

Breathing a laugh, Alrec looked to the ceiling and sighed. "There's not much a man can do when a beautiful woman is touching him. Much less when he's restrained." Tugging at the ropes, he latched onto her gaze. "You could untie me, and we could talk about it."

Full lips curved as she finished her ministrations and began to secure a bandage over his wounds. "Good try, but I've been celibate for a long time. Not sure I'm ready to dive back into that rat's nest. Especially with a Vampyre whose name I don't know. Surely, that's blasphemous for a Slayer female, no?" Her eyes glowed with amusement.

"Alrec," was his soft reply as he noted her shiver at the deep tone of his voice. "My name is Alrec. There is one objection you can remove from your list."

"Alrec," she said, gently patting the bandage to ensure it was secure. "A warrior's name."

He nodded against the pillow. "I'm not an aristocrat like you. My father was a soldier, and his father before him. Both were killed in the Awakening along with the rest of my family."

Compassion swamped her features. "And you survived?"

"I was a new recruit and had been stationed at Valeria to receive the barrels from the blood-banking. The assignment saved my life but took everyone I loved. Now, I aspire to be the best soldier I can to avenge them."

Sadness entered her eyes. "So you hate Slayers as much as I hate Vampyres. So much hatred..." The words trailed off as she glanced away and smoothed a hand over her hair. "We have so much vitriol to overcome. I worry we're doomed."

"I don't hate you, Kilani," he said, his tone soothing. "And perhaps that's a good start. I don't have it in me to hate the Slayer who saved my life."

Glancing at him out of the corner of her eye, she pursed her lips. "Well, I hate you. You saved my life and indebted me to a Vampyre. I'll never forgive you." Mirth sparkled in her eyes as she stood, indicating her teasing. "But honor won't allow me to let you die, so we're stuck with each other...at least until you're well. Then I'll send you back to Astaria, and we can go back to hating each other."

Alrec frowned at the thought of never seeing her again. How strange that his heartbeat quickened at the idea. Although it defied logic, he felt a connection to the Slayer who'd saved his life. Her image had been emblazoned in his brain since he met her on the battlefield years ago. Now that he'd experienced her honor, inhaled her intoxicating scent, and been surrounded by her beauty, he couldn't imagine hating her. But by the goddess, he could imagine loving her…and stroking her golden bronze skin as she writhed in pleasure and moaned his name.

The musings made zero sense, but they persisted nonetheless.

Unable to process them, he leaned his temple on his bicep, staring into her eyes in the hopes she would see his genuineness. "I have no desire to hate you, Kilani. Perhaps we'll even become friends. It would be a positive step toward realigning the species."

Scoffing, she rolled her eyes and trailed back toward the kitchen. "Friends," she muttered, washing her hands in one of the basins. "As if I would ever be friends with a Vampyre."

Alrec was disheartened by her words until she glanced over her shoulder and flashed a slight grin. Elation welled in his chest, and he vowed to earn her friendship in the days ahead. It wouldn't come easily, but somehow, Alrec had never looked forward to anything more in his life.

Chapter 9

Alrec awoke to the distinct feel of something sharp pricking his neck. His eyes roved south, trying to determine the threat level. Kilani stood hunched over the bed, pressing a knife into his skin as she assessed him.

"If this is your idea of foreplay, I think I misjudged you, Kilani."

She shot him a droll look. "Funny. Here's the deal: I'm going to untie you and let you get dressed. I washed your clothes, and they're laid out on the bed."

Glancing down, Alrec observed the black pants and shirt, thankful the woman was finally going to let him dress. Focusing back on her, he took note of her black clothing, which looked more tactical than the light linen she'd been wearing before. Maybe she'd fashioned them out of curtains too. The woman was resilient if nothing else.

"Once you're dressed, you're going to slip on these restraints." Holding up a cinched rope with two arm loops, she shook it. "Keep your hands behind your back. And then we're going to go walking. You need to increase your circulation if you're going to heal, and it's dark, so you won't burn to death."

"The restraints aren't necessary," he said, a slight plea in his voice. "I won't hurt you, Kilani."

She cocked an eyebrow. "Considering I met you on a battlefield when you were attacking my people, I'm a bit wary. Come on. The sooner you get dressed and bind yourself, the sooner we can walk. It's a clear night, and I'm craving fresh air. Let's go."

Standing, she tossed the rope so it landed on his clothes. Stuffing the knife in her belt, she untied his wrists and ankles before stepping back and crossing her arms over her pert breasts. Alrec allowed himself one glance at the supple skin that peeked above her neckline and then rose, accepting she was all business. Once he was dressed, he slipped each wrist through the binding behind his back.

"Thank you for cooperating," she said, striding over and tightening the ropes so they dug into his skin. "We're going to take it easy since your body has latched onto the poison. If you start to feel lightheaded, let me know."

He nodded, already craving the crisp night air upon his skin. She led them to the front door, closing it behind them and securing several locks. Then she began to walk toward the gurgling sounds from the nearby river, leaving him no choice but to follow.

They set a slow but steady pace, walking in step along the riverbank as the stars twinkled above. Alrec's muscles were stiff, but he would recover quickly. Such was the way of Vampyres, even with poison still lingering in his chest.

Glancing to the sky, Alrec noted the Star of Muthoni. Since it was the brightest in the sky, he could use it to calculate the distance back to Astaria.

"It's over four hundred miles to the east," Kilani said, gesturing with her head.

"What is?"

"Astaria. Do you think I'm dumb enough not to know you were calculating your way home?"

Grinning, he gazed at the crown of her golden hair, acknowledging the protective swell in his chest as she strode beside him. She was almost two heads shorter, the top of her head barely cresting his pecs. Etherya had created Vampyres to be much larger than Slayers, and he found himself wondering what it would be like to hold her small frame against his. Would she relax and snuggle into his muscular body, or would she remain stubborn and hold back? Would she trail kisses with those red lips over the path of scratchy hair that led to his most sensitive place or take him in her mouth? By the goddess, he could only imagine making love to her. Surely, she would be so tight she would squeeze every last cell of his shaft.

He'd have to make sure his little one was slick and ready if that were to happen—

"Hey, where did you go?" she asked, snapping her fingers in his face.

Drawn from the lascivious musings, his lips curled. "Sorry. I was daydreaming. What did you say?"

"I asked how you're feeling. I have no problem sending you back to Astaria, but I want you to be one hundred percent first. One thing I hate is failing, and I'm not going to fail at your recovery."

"Failing isn't so bad," he mused. "Some would argue it's the best way to learn a lesson."

"Some?" she asked sardonically. "Are we to argue about this then?"

Chuckling, he longed to reach over and tuck away the strand of hair that grazed her cheek. Since his hands were bound, he settled for inhaling her scent, which seemed more intoxicating in the fresh air. "If you like. I think arguing with you would be quite fun."

"Oh, it's an experience all right. Just ask my father."

"Tell me about him," Alrec said, his tone open and curious. "I won't judge you, Kilani. You have my word."

Deep blue eyes studied him as the river gurgled beside them. "For some reason, I believe you," she finally said.

"Then tell me."

Sighing, she began the tale. One of unchangeable traditions and unyielding expectations. One where she had no say in her own life, or whom she would marry, or her destiny. It was a sad tale, and after she'd grown quiet, he understood why she'd chosen to live in solitude rather than live a life that would make her miserable.

"It's a choice few would make," Alrec said, his boots crunching leaves and branches as they walked. "Some would accuse you of being selfish for shunning a life of privilege and skirting your duty."

She stilled, inhaling a deep breath as she gazed at the dim horizon. "I guess some would."

"I, however, would not be one of those immortals." Halting, he turned to face her. "It's incredibly brave to live your truth even if others cannot see your vision. I find it quite admirable."

Turning, she lifted her gaze to his, something smoldering and simmering in the glowing orbs. Slowly lifting her hand, she gently touched his wound, safely dressed beneath a bandage and his black shirt. Her small fingers trailed over his pec, and a labored breath rushed from his lungs at the tender caress. His nipple grew hard and puckered under the fabric, and she lightly flicked it with her nail before gazing into his eyes.

"Careful, little one," he said, the deep baritone of his voice surrounding them. Tiny hairs stood to attention on her forearm, and he was pleased by her body's reaction to him. "I have let you restrain me because it makes you feel safe, but you know I could break free of these restraints if I wished."

Something flashed in her eyes as she skated her fingers up his chest, touching the tips to his pulsing vein and tracing it. "Is that a threat...or a promise?" she whispered.

A low growl exited his throat, causing her to gasp, and his shaft stood to attention at the shocked rush of air. "It's just a fact, little one."

Nodding, she lowered her hand to rest over his heart. The eight-chambered organ pulsed beneath her palm, and Alrec thanked the goddess he'd lived, if only so he could experience this one moment in the moonlight with his beautiful Slayer. Shallow breaths rushed through his lips as his body seemed to melt under her touch.

"I'd almost convinced myself your kind didn't have one," she murmured.

His eyebrows drew together. "Didn't have what?"

"A heart, Alrec," she said, the wistful words sending a jolt through his solar plexus. "I'd convinced myself your kind didn't have a heart."

Standing underneath the canopy of trees beside the gently rushing river, Alrec allowed her to absorb his heartbeats, longing for the day her lips would replace her hand atop the rapidly beating organ.

Chapter 10

Kilani continued to nurse Alrec, pleased he was healing more each day. As his body grew stronger, she knew it was futile to keep him restrained to the bed. He was a massive warrior, and even with his injuries, he could snap her in two without a thought. The fact he let her keep him restrained comforted her, and Kilani had so rarely been comforted. There wasn't much room for that when you were born into a family that put duty before love.

As Kilani continued to care for Alrec, she became quite surprised by his sense of humor. He would often tease her that she'd missed a spot after she changed his bandage or chide her for being so serious. Kilani would just roll her eyes and dismiss his playful jabs, although they brought her great pleasure deep within.

She'd never had an easy friendship with a man—hell, she'd rarely had an uneasy one—and she found it rather refreshing. Although it annoyed her that she enjoyed his company so much, she couldn't deny it made her...*happy*. The word had been foreign to her for so long, but the injured, chiding Vampyre had accomplished that task.

"Aren't you tired of sleeping on the couch?" he asked, dragging her from her thoughts as she smoothed the tape over his clean bandage. "I'm healed enough to sleep there. You'd have to untie me though." He arched a brow, and Kilani felt her cheeks warm at his heated gaze.

"My dear Vampyre," she said, resting her hand over his chest and blinking rapidly, "you should know by now you can't outsmart me. I thought you too sharp to try and outsmart a superior opponent."

Scoffing, he scrunched his features. "Perhaps I let you believe that so you'll keep putting your hands on me. It feels rather nice."

Kilani drew her hand away as if it were on fire and scowled at his resulting chuckle. "I'd rather stick my hand into a rattlesnake's belly."

Deep brown eyes assessed her, complete with the knowing smirk she found extremely sexy, and she struggled not to squirm under his gaze.

Finally, he opened those broad lips and asked, "Are the men of the Slayer kingdom completely daft? If I had the opportunity to court you and win your hand, I would try until my last breath."

A laugh bounded from her chest. "Wow, cheesy much?" Standing, she strode to the kitchen to rinse the cloth and drain some blood for his dinner. "And I'm a lot to take," she said, placing a glass on the island and slicing her inner forearm with a small knife before allowing the blood to fall. "I don't think Slayer men knew what to do with me. Slayer aristocrats anyway."

"Would you consider marrying a soldier or laborer?"

"Sure," she said, squeezing her arm to help the blood drain. "But my father would've had a conniption. That was a no-go as long as I lived in the kingdom."

"I've always found it so strange aristocrats look down on soldiers and laborers. We're the ones who protect them, allowing them to live their fancy lives."

"Hey, not all aristocrats feel that way." Holding a cloth to the cut, she allowed the blood to clot before wrapping it and securing the bandage. "I couldn't care less what station a man holds as long as he lets me fight. The Awakening...well, it *awakened* something in me, for lack of a better term." Clutching the glass, she padded over and sat on the edge of the bed. "I no longer wanted to wait for my life to begin. I wanted to seize the day and fight." Lifting the glass, she studied the blood in the light of the nearby candle as her lips formed a humorless smile. "Female soldiers hold no value in my kingdom, so I can't see myself finding a mate there. Until things change at least." Extending the glass, she shuffled on the bed and lifted it to his lips. "Dinnertime."

"Wait," he commanded softly, causing her to still. "You are a magnificent woman, Kilani. It was the first thought I had when I saw you poised to kill me in a meadow all those years ago."

Her eyebrows lifted. "You may be the only one who thinks so."

"Then I'm glad you never found a mate. It would be a shame for you to be tethered to a man who didn't understand your worth."

Left unspoken between them was the obvious sentiment that *he* understood her worth...and the almost tangible energy that always seemed to sizzle between them when they slipped into these more serious discussions. Uncomfortable, she touched the glass to his lips. "Come on. I can't have you waste away before I kick you out. Drink."

His lips surrounded the rim of the glass, and her throat grew dry as they moved on the crystal as he drank. The motions were erotic, spurring images of him fastening those full lips to her breast and closing them around her nipple. Would he gaze into her eyes—as he was now—while he worked his lips over her sensitive flesh?

Overcome by the vision, she tilted the glass, forcing him to finish so she could return to the kitchen. The heat of his body seemed to envelop her, and she suddenly felt the urge to run.

"Thank you," he murmured when she lowered the glass. "Your blood is the finest I've ever had, but I wish you didn't have to harm yourself to feed me."

"Oh, it's fine," she said, breathless as she stood and ran a hand through her hair. "I'm tough and have handled worse, believe me."

She began to wash the glass, cognizant of his gaze as he stayed mute in the bed. Frazzled, she set the glass on the cloth to dry and glanced around the kitchen, desperate for another activity so she could shift the focus.

"There is a way you could feed me and it won't hurt."

Facing him, she placed her hands on her hips, knowing she shouldn't take the bait. "Like I said, it's fine."

"You could let me drink from you, Kilani," he said, his voice mesmerizing as his gaze drilled into hers. "I would lick your wrist, coating it in my self-healing saliva, which would prevent the pain. Then I would pierce you with my fangs, drink, and lick the wounds closed. It's how we were designed after all. The decree that Vampyres cannot drink directly from Slayers came from immortals, not from Etherya."

"The immortal rulers made that decree because direct drinking allows a Vampyre to read and absorb a Slayer's thoughts and mental images," she said, her tone flat. "And if you think I'm going to let you read my mind, you've definitely lost yours."

His soft laugh filtered through the room. "I won't say getting you to divulge the secret you know about the Deamon weakness hasn't crossed my mind, but I assure you, there's nothing nefarious about my proposal."

"Nothing nefarious," she repeated, her tone droll.

"I'm the one who's restrained here, little one." He tugged at the ropes. "You have the upper hand."

"And I'd like to keep it that way, thank you very much." Finished with the discussion that had somehow turned her knees to jelly, she walked to the closet by the front door and threw on her shawl. "I'm heading to the garden. Need to gather some of my own food so I can keep feeding you. It's a vicious cycle, keeping you alive. I might decide to let you die tomorrow."

"Kilani," he drawled in a teasing, sultry tone that sent shivers of arousal down her spine. "Did I ruffle your feathers, little one? Perhaps you're as excited at the thought of me drinking from your wrist as I am." He waggled his brows. "Or I could drink from your neck. I think that might be even more exciting, no?"

Gritting her teeth, she shot him a glare, annoyed he was calling attention to her unwanted attraction. Vampyres had heightened senses for arousal, and she had no doubt he could smell the slickness that was rapidly coating her inner thighs under his unwavering gaze. Frustrated, she pivoted and stalked outside, slamming the door behind her.

Unfortunately, the sound of his desire-laden chuckle followed her to the garden and lingered as she toiled under the bright sun.

Chapter 11

Kilani fell into a pattern with Alrec as the wounds on his chest healed quicker each day. After a week, the red welts had all but disappeared, and she found herself melancholy at the fact he would soon leave and return to Astaria.

"You know, I'm starting to dig the bondage thing you have going on here," Alrec said, his tone sardonic as she sat beside him, dragging a wet cloth over his chest. "But we both know I'm healed, Kilani." Tugging on the ropes, he flashed a grin, his fangs gently pushing into his lower lip.

Her ministrations ceased as she studied the black hairs on his chest, darker than the thick brown hair atop his head. "I guess you're right. And you've been nothing but gracious on our nightly walks. I would even venture to say we're becoming...*friends*." She mimicked gagging, causing Alrec to chuckle. "It's a tough pill to swallow, being friends with a Vampyre. The world has gone mad." Rising, she trailed to the kitchen to wash the cloth before spreading it over the rim of the sink to dry.

"I am honored to be your friend," he murmured, causing her heart to slam at his genuine tone.

Placing her hands on the sink, Kilani stared out the small window, acknowledging how much she cherished this time of day. Dusk had become the linchpin of her existence, when she would untie Alrec, bind his hands behind his back, and they would take their nightly walks by the river.

In the days that had passed, they had discussed their histories and told each other their stories. She'd learned that he'd never been in love, although several Vampyre women had certainly tried to catch his affection. He spoke of them fondly but took his vow to protect his people seriously, and that had always taken precedence.

Although he was now alone upon Etherya's Earth, as was she, he wasn't lonely. Instead, he revered his family for dying noble deaths in the Awakening and strove to be a great warrior. It was admirable, and Kilani was perplexed at how easily he'd wormed his way into her stubborn heart and earned her respect.

"What's that smile for?" he asked softly from the bed.

Sighing, she padded over and studied him, rubbing her arms as she debated. "It's time for our walk. I'm contemplating not binding your hands tonight. Is that a mistake?"

Laughing, he shook his head. "I'll be a perfect gentleman. You have my word."

Gnawing her lip, she acknowledged unbinding him would put them on even ground. No longer would she have the upper hand, nor could they pretend she was in control. Whether they voiced the obvious or not, it was evident Alrec could overpower her and instantly kill her if he wished.

"I'm trusting you," she whispered, reaching to untie his wrists.

Solemn brown eyes stared deep into hers. "Thank you, little one."

Kilani swallowed, annoyed as the image of him whispering the endearment in her ear as he loomed above her in the large bed flashed through her mind. Making quick work of his binds, she busied herself in the kitchen while he dressed, only sneaking the occasional glance at his magnificent ass. After all, she was a red-blooded Slayer and hadn't been so attracted to a man in centuries. The fact he was a Vampyre should've alarmed her, but since it didn't, she just allowed herself to enjoy the view.

They headed outside and began to trek along the river. Alrec asked her basic questions, and she did so in return, and the conversation flowed as it always did between them. As they strolled, curiosity welled until she could no longer contain it.

"It's hard for me to believe you've never been in love. Don't you want to bond and have a family one day?"

His eyebrows lifted as he grinned. "Have we finally gotten to the point where we discuss our dreams and fears? That seems quite personal for two mortal enemies, no?"

"Forget it," she said, rolling her eyes. "I was just wondering—"

"I'm teasing you, Kilani." His warm fingers ran over her forearm before he slid his palm over hers and laced their fingers. "You are quite serious for a Slayer. I thought you were supposed to be the carefree species."

"We were until the world fell apart," she muttered, unable to stop herself from squeezing his fingers, noting how perfect they felt laced with hers. "It changed my perspective, and now I can't even remember what carefree means."

His gentle laughter washed over her, spurring a reflexive grin.

"Why are you laughing?"

"I was just thinking that perhaps I should remind you what it means to be carefree," he said, the silken tone of his voice causing tiny bumps to rise on her forearms. "I can think of several activities we could try."

"I'm sure you can," she said, arching a sardonic brow. "But let's get back to the question. Are you trying to avoid my grilling?"

His footsteps halted, and he gently tugged her hand, turning her to face him. Stepping closer, he lifted his free hand and tenderly grazed her jaw. Cupping it, he ran his thumb over her cheek, the caress mesmerizing as he spoke softly in the moonlight.

"I always felt I would fall in love with someone both fierce and tender. As a warrior, I need a partner who can understand my calling to protect my people and balance that with affection. Vampyres don't allow females in the army, so I've never met a woman who possesses both..." His words trailed off as his thumb inched toward her lips, gently brushing them as she stood frozen...mesmerized...enchanted...

"Don't say it," she whispered.

His full lips curved. "Don't say 'until you'?" Shaking his head, he leaned closer. "I would never. It's incredibly lame, and I can't chance dousing your attraction to me. Your glances at my ass as I dress are the only thing keeping me going."

Kilani's mouth fell open, and she swatted his chest. "I do not glance at your ass!"

Chuckling, he tilted his head. "Warriors are supposed to be better liars, Kilani. We'll have to work on that."

His hand slid to her jaw again, and she bit her lip, knowing she was busted. Placing her hand over his heart, she noted the strong beats pulsing in tandem with her own as arousal swirled between them.

"We can't," she whispered.

"Why not?" was his silken response, his handsome features laced with mischief and desire.

"Because we're different species—"

"The logistics are the same. Trust me."

"And how do you know? How many Slayers have you slept with?"

Breathing a laugh, he shook his head. "None, but I'm willing to break the streak."

Expelling a breath, she tightened her fingers on his chest as acceptance coursed through her pulsing frame. Hell, she hadn't truly experienced joy in so long. Giving herself to this Vampyre, to this man who'd spared her life years ago, was reckless and impulsive...and perhaps it was *exactly* what she needed. After all, what was the point in living a life you chose if you never felt any bliss? If you never allowed yourself one moment of pleasure or gratification?

"I see your wheels turning, little one," he chimed, gently tapping her forehead. "I don't make this decision lightly either. Never in a million years would I have imagined I'd become consumed with a Slayer. But here we are, and it seems foolish to squander the opportunity."

"Consumed with me, huh?" she teased, her eyes darting between his. "Perhaps you're only placating me because I saved your life."

Releasing her hand, he slid his palm across her lower back, pulling her close until there was nothing between them but desire. Splaying his fingers, he gently cupped her ass, molding his body to hers before lowering his head and grazing her nose with his.

"I was consumed with you the moment I saw you planted in a field with fire in your eyes and a weapon clutched in your hand, ready to defend your people. I never forgot you, Kilani."

"This is insane," she breathed against his lips. "We're supposed to hate each other—"

"For one night, let's forget what we're *supposed* to do and just feel. Can you do that for me, little one?"

Something sticky and stifling coursed through her veins, and she struggled to dissect it until she realized it was...*fear*. All she'd known for years was her solitary life in the woods. If she gave herself to this man, would she suddenly begin to crave more? Living without affection and companionship when you couldn't experience them was one thing. Living without them after you'd immersed yourself in them was daunting...perhaps even dangerous.

"I can't allow myself the luxury of craving something I can never have."

Resting his forehead against hers, he stared deep into her eyes. "Then you'll have to find a way to have everything you desire."

Even as her brain told her she was making a mistake, she slid her arms around his neck and lifted to her toes. "I don't think that's possible," she murmured.

"Do you want me to kiss you, little one? To carry you home and make love to you?" He brushed a tender kiss across her lips. "All you have to do is ask."

Tightening her arms around his neck, she pressed her body against his, reveling in his desire-laden growl. Still unsure, she dug her fingers into his neck, arousal gushing between her thighs at his resulting groan.

"I want you to kiss me," she whispered, closing her eyes as she held on for dear life. "Let's start there—"

The words were consumed by his strong lips and wet tongue as it swept them away with one smooth stroke. Throwing caution to the wind, Kilani relaxed in her Vampyre's arms and allowed herself to enjoy the moment.

Chapter 12

Alrec clutched his little Slayer, disbelief entwining with arousal as it snaked through his veins. Never did he imagine he'd be granted the opportunity to kiss her...to taste her...but now that he'd touched her, he wondered if he could ever truly let go.

Small, wanton purrs exited her throat, igniting his arousal as he reminded himself to go slow. If it were up to him, he'd lower her lithe body to the soft grass and lick every drop of arousal from between her thighs before slicking her up again and burying himself deep inside. Knowing she wasn't ready, he focused on kissing her, thanking the goddess a million times for his good fortune.

Her tongue slid over his, coating him with her taste, and his body shook with arousal at the ardent strokes. Longing to please her, he swiped his tongue over hers before sucking it between his lips. A deep moan rumbled through his belly as he sucked her, overcome with her sultry whimpers and the sharp points of her nails digging into his neck.

Releasing her tongue, he trailed soft kisses over her wet lips and firm jaw before resting his mouth on the shell of her ear. "You taste so good, little one," he breathed, pleased when she shivered in his arms. "I want to lick you everywhere."

"Alrec," she murmured, sliding her fingers in his thick hair and gently tugging, urging him to meet her gaze. "I can't become attached to you." Solemn blue eyes swirled with fear, affection, and longing as she stared back at him.

"Are you so sure that would end in doom, little one?" Delving his fingers into her soft hair, he stroked the silken tresses as their labored breaths mingled. "Even if you're convinced you're smarter than me, you're not a fortune-teller, are you?"

Laughter gurgled from her throat. "Seeing the future is one skill I don't have."

"Then let's take this day by day and live in the moment. Our lives are long, Kilani. It won't hurt to take a small sliver of time to focus on what's between us."

Blue orbs darted between his. "But you need to go back to Astaria. You have a duty."

"I do," he said with a nod, "and I will fulfill it for eternity when I return. But eternity is long, and I want to make sure I carry the memory of you with me."

"Damn," she whispered, shaking her head. "That's so freaking romantic. Who knew Vampyres were so sappy?" She flashed a cheeky grin.

"I'm only sappy for women who save my life and threaten to kill me, all in the same day," he teased, palming her cheek and winking as she chuckled.

White teeth toyed with her lip as she pondered. "How long do you want to stay?"

Alrec's features drew together. "I want to be strong for my trek back to Astaria. It's possible I'll encounter Deamons on the way, and I want to be prepared to fight them. Perhaps I could stay a few weeks and we could train together at night. You could ensure I'm in top form before I leave."

"So, you're only interested in my battle skills?" She wrinkled her nose, adorable as she teased him.

"I'm interested in so much more, but we'll start with the sparring." He chucked her nose, thoroughly enjoying their banter. "But to be clear, I want to make love to you, Kilani. I'm going to employ all my swagger to entice you into bed." He waggled his eyebrows.

The smooth skin of her throat gleamed in the moonlight as she tossed her head back and laughed. Overwhelmed by her beauty, he lowered his lips to the pulsing vein and peppered it with tender kisses. She sighed, clutching his shoulders as he loved her.

"And if you'll let me, I'll drink from you here while I'm inside you, Kilani." The words crackled with lust and affection as he drew the soft skin between his lips and gently sucked. Her knees buckled, and he held her tight, pulling her skin back and forth between his lips as she writhed against him.

"Oh, *god*..."

"Yes, sweetheart," he murmured, licking the spot, now red and tender from his ministrations. "All you have to do is ask."

A low, sexy groan rumbled in her chest, and she lifted her lids to latch onto his gaze. "I'll think about it. In the meantime, I like the idea of sparring with you. I want you to be ready to defend yourself...and I might like the idea of kicking your ass every night."

Alrec scoffed and nipped her nose. "I never knew delusion was sexy until now."

She swatted him as he chuckled.

"But yes, it's smart to retrain my body before I leave. And I can't wait to have you flat on your back with a spear to your throat so I can force you to tell me the Deamon intel."

"Never gonna happen," she said, drawing back and gripping his hand. "You live in la-la land, my friend, but I'll allow it." Threading their fingers, she tugged, urging him to resume the walk. Alrec fell into step beside her and immersed himself in the moment. One day, many centuries from now, he would remember the night he first kissed his beautiful Slayer by the gently rushing river under a ribbon of stars.

Unable to squelch his grin, he strolled with Kilani until they grew tired and returned to the cabin. Alrec undressed down to his underwear and lay on the couch, silently offering Kilani the bed. Hours later, he gazed over, comforted by her gentle snores and the sight of her wrapped in the sheets...determined to earn his place by her side in the bed before he had to make the long journey home.

Chapter 13

Kilani threw herself into training with Alrec, thrilled to have a worthy sparring partner after so many years alone. She'd done her best to keep her skills sharp since there were always looming threats in a world as consumed with war as Etherya's Earth. Although she was far from civilization, a stray band of Deamons could always stumble upon her cabin, and she needed to be prepared.

She also wanted Alrec strong for his trip home since it would be a several-week journey and he could encounter many different threats. Although she'd vowed to stay unattached to her handsome Vampyre, deep down Kilani knew she was fooling herself. His kisses along the riverbank had set her body on fire, and his tender words murmured against her skin had almost melted her heart.

Each day, they drew closer to the point where she would shed her reservations and let him make love to her. Kilani already knew this was a foregone conclusion, but she appreciated the respectful way he kept his distance, showcasing his honor. His respect for her was almost as attractive as those sexy fangs and luscious ass. *Almost.*

A few nights after their first kiss, Kilani stood firm on the soft grass, a spear clutched in each hand as she gritted her teeth. Alrec faced her, breath rushing from his lungs as he held his own spear. Kilani had fashioned them for fishing, but they were also perfect for sparring with a hulking Vampyre. Opening her lips, Kilani emitted a grunt before rushing toward her opponent, their spears held high in the air.

Alrec anticipated her move, blocking her weapons with his own before rotating and swiping at her shins. Reading his movements, Kilani jumped, avoiding the weapon and backing away. Alrec advanced and lunged, and they began a series of deft blows, the wooden spears clanking in the warm night air as the skirmish raged on. Eventually, Alrec's height advantage became too much for her skill, and he caught her wrist, holding it high.

"Yield," he commanded, his warm breaths rushing over her face. "I have the advantage."

"No fucking way!" she gritted, thrusting the spear in her free hand high. Uttering a curse, he dropped his spear and grabbed her other wrist. Holding her still, he gazed into her eyes.

"Yield, little one."

"The Deamons you encounter on your way back to Astaria aren't going to yield," she said, trying to twirl away from his grasp. "So I'm not either—"

Alrec lurched, quick as lightning, surrounding her waist with one arm before slamming her to the ground. Although she knew he took care not to hurtle her too hard, the breath was knocked from her lungs as he loomed above her.

"Yield, woman," he said, yanking both spears from her hands as he shifted over her, pinning her to the ground with his large body. Gripping one of the spears, he held the tip to her throat. Kilani glared into his eyes, equal parts furious he'd gotten the upper hand and aroused as hell at the gorgeous man who now held a deadly weapon to her throat.

"Damn, this is so hot," she whispered, breathless as she lay below him.

Breathing a laugh, he nodded. "So fucking hot." Pressing the spear to her neck, he leaned closer, barely brushing her nose with his. "Tell me the Deamon weakness, little one."

Kilani made a *tsk tsk* sound and shook her head, her hair grazing over the grass. "Not until you earn it." Grunting, she reached for the spear that lay just within her reach and sliced it through the air until the tip rested at his neck. "Looks like we're at an impasse."

Alrec's lips curved before he tossed his weapon aside and slid his arm under her body. Rolling them over, he relaxed on his back as she sat atop him. "Go ahead and stab me," he said, eyes twinkling as he placed his hands beneath his head. "I'm enjoying the view."

A muted chuckle escaped before she threw her spear aside and planted her palms on his chest. "You like the woman on top, huh?"

"Sweetheart, I'll take you in any way and from any direction I can have you," was his silken reply.

Kilani licked the suddenly dry roof of her mouth, wondering if she'd ever met a sexier man. She'd had a few lovers in her past—mostly aristocratic men who were boring as hell and handsome in their regal, austere ways—but her Vampyre was masculine and...*raw*, with those sexy fangs, deep brown eyes, and the thick hair she longed to clench between her fingers as she took him deep inside her body. And that ass... Good lord, she loved his ass.

Glancing toward the sky, she noticed the first trickle of dawn easing over the horizon. Patting his chest, she stood and offered her hand. "Come on. You might have bested me, but I don't think you'll best the sun."

Alrec took her hand, and she pulled him to his feet before they gathered the weapons and trailed home. Once there, they removed their shirts and pants, and Kilani washed away the grime, aware of his heated glances as he did the same beside her in the small kitchen.

Alrec stood silent beside her, a question in his gaze as he waited for her to move. Kilani's eyes darted over his firm chest and thick thighs sprinkled with coarse hair before landing on his erection, which was now pushing against the fabric of his underwear. Swallowing thickly, she debated the consequences of her actions, understanding she would most likely develop feelings for him if they made love. He was everything she would've chosen in a man if she'd had the ability to choose one when living at Uteria.

A warrior who embraced her desire to fight instead of shunning it.

A handsome man with gentle eyes and a kind heart.

A man who made her laugh and feel safe, and desired her even though they were worlds apart.

And...he was a fucking Vampyre. In all her musings, Kilani had never imagined her ideal mate would be a damn Vampyre.

"What are you thinking, little one?" he asked softly, still frozen as he waited for her to choose for both of them.

Stepping forward, she was enveloped by the heat emanating from his strong frame as she slid a hand over his ass, gently cupping him through the fabric. "I'm thinking that you're really lucky you have this ass. Because it's hindering my ability to think logically, and I'm about to make a really important decision."

Desire sparked in his eyes as he drew closer. "What decision, Kilani?"

Spearing her nails into the taut muscles of his ass, she gave a sultry laugh at his resulting hiss. "My dear Vampyre," she drawled, stepping closer and rising to her toes, "I'm going to ask you to make love to me—"

And then, all words ceased to exist as her eager lover cemented his lips to hers and lifted her in his arms before carrying her to bed.

Chapter 14

Alrec carried his little Slayer to bed, gently placing her on the turned-down sheets as she gazed at him with lust and affection. Her blond hair fanned over the pillow, and he took a moment to bask in her beauty.

"Kilani," he whispered, stretching over her and running a finger over the soft skin of her cheek. "You're so beautiful, sweetheart."

Sliding her hands around his neck, she drew him close and brushed a sweet kiss over his lips. "Show me." Her nails impaled his shoulders, causing him to groan. "I haven't done this in a long time. I hope I remember how." Biting her lip, she grinned, adorable in the dim light of the candles she'd lit when they returned home.

"I'll remind you," he murmured, pecking her lips before trailing tender kisses over her neck. Her melodious laughter surrounded them, and Alrec knew he would hear the sound in his dreams long after he returned home. Pressing kisses to her flushed skin, he made his way to the valley between her breasts. Gliding his hands under her back, he unhooked her bra and slid it from her body, dropping it to the floor as he gazed at her pert nipples.

"Careful with the bra," she rasped, closing her eyes as he cupped one of her breasts in his palm. "It's the only one I have."

"Then perhaps I will destroy it so I can see these pretty breasts more often." Grazing his thumb over her nipple, he reveled in her gasp as the tiny bud grew taut. Lowering his head, he murmured, "Open your eyes, little one."

Those midnight blue orbs drifted open, and Alrec felt a jolt of awareness in his solar plexus. By the goddess, he'd never been so consumed with a woman. His only wish was to please her—to imprint their lovemaking in her mind so she would remember him long after he returned to a life without her. Sadness swamped him at the thought, so he pushed it away to focus on his little Slayer.

Opening his mouth, he rimmed her nipple with his lips, mesmerized by the emotion in her gaze and her reddened cheeks. Closing his lips around the taut bud, he began to suck her, the motions smooth and methodic as her nipple peaked against his tongue.

"Oh...*god*..." she moaned, threading her fingers through his hair, clutching tight as he loved her. Alrec smiled around her supple flesh, pleased at her soft purrs of pleasure. Sucking her deep one last time, he gently kissed the taut nub before drifting to her other breast and repeating the same torturous, tender ministrations.

"Feels so good..." she murmured, head tossing on the pillow. "Holy shit, I'm so freaking turned on. From a Vampyre...never would've thought...*aarrgh*..."

Chuckling, Alrec sucked her nipple several more times before drawing back and flicking it with his tongue. The deft motions sent a flush across her pale skin, and her back bowed upon the bed. The scent of her arousal permeated the room, and Alrec's body began to quiver with the intense need to taste her.

Rising to his knees, he stared deep into her eyes as he hooked his fingers in the waistband of her panties. Silently asking permission, a swell of desire rocked his frame when she bit her finger and nodded against the pillow. Gaze cemented to hers, he slid the garment from her body. Placing his palms on her inner thighs, he spread her wide, emitting a low groan at the slick that covered her deepest place.

"Sweetheart," he whispered, gently running the pads of his thumbs over her wet upper thighs. "Look at you."

The little imp grinned and pushed into his thumbs, causing Alrec to grit his teeth. Dying to taste her, he lowered between her legs, pushing them wide with his shoulders so he could burrow into her deepest place. Spreading her wet folds wide, he touched his tongue to her drenched opening. Gazing deep into her stunning eyes, he swiped a broad stroke over her pussy, from her core to the tight little nub at the top of her mound, and relished her deep moan as she squirmed against him.

"Alrec..."

"Yes, little one," he rasped against her trembling skin. "Push against me. I've never tasted anything as sweet. I'm going to lick away every drop."

Her resulting moan enveloped him, urging him on as he lost himself in the most pleasurable moment of his life. Nothing in all his centuries upon Etherya's Earth compared to having his strong, gorgeous Slayer open before him as he feasted. Determined to make her scream, he began a series of deep, sweeping strokes along her folds, imbibing her honeyed-essence.

As her whimpers grew more fervent, he latched onto her gaze and spread her wide, impaling his tongue in her tight opening as he placed two fingers on the swollen nub at the top of her slit. Entranced by her, he surged his tongue inside, back and forth, as he circled his fingers on her clit, applying firm, meticulous pressure.

Kilani writhed upon the bed, tightening her legs around his shoulders, and he knew she was close. Consumed by desire for her, he moaned against her core as her body began a series of deep trembles. Closing her eyes, his little Slayer tossed back her head and began to come. Hoping to send her to heaven, Alrec continued his motions, overcome with lust and emotion.

Violent tremors shook her lithe frame until she began to laugh and constricted her legs around his head. The action forced him deeper against her center, and he began to laugh as well, ceasing the motions of his tongue and fingers so she could experience the high before falling back to earth.

"Holy good grief!" she cried, clutching the covers at each side as her body quaked and shuddered. "Help..."

Chuckling, Alrec placed a kiss on her mound before rising to cover her with his now trembling body. His shaft was painfully erect inside his underwear, and he wanted nothing more than to plunge it inside her satiated body. Palming her cheek, he studied her flushed face, grinning when she opened her eyes and swatted him.

"Why did you do that?" she asked, the words breathless and weak. "I was used to my own hand, and now you've ruined that."

"I want to ruin you, little one," he murmured, pressing his lips to hers and plunging his tongue deep into her wet mouth. Their tongues slid over each other's, Alrec's still coated with her sweet honey, and she uttered a low, satisfied groan. "I want you to remember me after I'm gone."

Gazing at him with eyes full of emotion, she threaded her fingers through his hair. "I think that's a given."

"Good." Placing a peck on her nose, Alrec shifted and drew off his underwear. Aligning himself back over her body, he placed his leg between hers, opening her wide and lowering his fingers to her core.

"Let's get you slick and ready again so I can fuck you."

A ragged breath escaped her lips as she pushed against his fingers, undulating into them as he circled her swollen clit. Unable to look away from her gorgeous eyes, Alrec slipped a finger inside her tight channel, loving her resulting mewl. After dragging it back and forth in the taut vise, he added another, gauging her reaction.

"It's going to be tight," she said, teeth digging into her lower lip as she grinned.

"Oh, I'm counting on it." Sliding over her, he removed his fingers and glided the tip of his shaft to her opening. Inhaling deeply, he glided the sensitive head through her wet folds, closing his eyes at the extreme pleasure. Clenching his jaw, he reminded himself to go slow so he didn't hurt her—a massive feat since his body was ready to mount her and fuck her straight through the headboard.

"What are you smiling at?"

Lifting his lids, he slid his fingers through her hair and softly clenched. "At how hard I want to fuck you. But I'll be gentle. Ready, little one?"

Her chest rose with a deep inhale as she nodded. "Ready."

Lowering his forehead to hers, he gazed into those limitless eyes as he began to push inside. Kilani clenched his shoulders, drawing him deep as the pricks of pain from her fingernails drove him wild. Determined not to hurt her, he went slow, dying a small death each time her wet walls surrounded another inch of his sensitive flesh.

"Open up to me, sweetheart," he whispered against her lips. "You can let go. It will feel better, trust me."

Her swollen lips fell open as her muscles melted beneath him, and Alrec took advantage, surging inside her tight channel. Overwhelmed with bliss, he began to drag his cock back and forth through her core, striving to reach the spot deep within that would make her scream.

"Tell me what you need, Kilani."

"Deeper..." she moaned. "Harder...oh, just don't stop..."

Encouraged by the desirous words, Alrec slid his hand from her hair to her shoulder, cupping to hold her in place. Groaning her name, he began to stroke her deepest place with his cock, his hips undulating at a furious pace as sweat beaded on his brow.

"Yesssss..." she hissed, her body open and trembling beneath him. "You're so far inside me...I feel everything..."

Vowing to hit the spot that would send her into euphoria, Alrec pounded her tight channel, coating his sensitive flesh in her honeyed slick as the plushy folds threatened to wring him dry. Closing his eyes, he felt the tingling at his lower back and the tightening of his balls. Knowing he would only last a few more seconds, he rested his lips on her neck, sucking her fragrant skin deep before murmuring into her nape.

"Come again, little one... Come around my cock..."

Drawing her flesh between lips, he sucked her as she writhed beneath him. The head of his cock jutted against a spot deep within her luscious body, finally sending her over the edge. Piercing his shoulders with her nails, she cried his name before her spine snapped, her body devolving into a furious round of quakes against him. Burying his face in her neck, Alrec tightened his hold before letting go, feeling his release shoot down his cock and begin to spurt into her gorgeous body. Lost in the moment, he flooded her with his essence, marking her as his as pulses of desire leaped from his body to mingle with hers. Groaning with pleasure, he shuddered against her, emptying every last piece of himself into his little Slayer. Unable to focus on breathing or moving or...anything that required energy, he snuggled into her, hoping like hell he wasn't crushing her.

Kilani wriggled against him, their bodies entwined as the sweat from their exertion cooled their sated frames. Sighing, she ran her hand over the welts on his shoulders.

"I think I drew blood," she muttered softly, rubbing the marks that would soon self-heal. "Sorry."

Breathing a laugh, Alrec ran the tip of his nose along her neck, inhaling her fragrant scent. "Don't mind. You can pierce me anytime, Kilani."

Gliding her arms around his shoulders, she clutched him close, sliding a silken thigh over his. Alrec was wrapped in her like the most precious present, and he never wanted to let go. Kissing her temple, he asked, "Do you need me to move?"

She shook her head, snuggling deeper into their embrace. "Feels good. I just want to lie here with you inside me for a while. Is that okay?"

"Mm-hmm." After placing reverent kisses on her silken hair, he rested his cheek on the pillow. Since they were different species, there was no chance of pregnancy or transmitting disease, so he was content to lie with her and commit the moment to memory. Relaxing against her, he softly stroked her hair upon the pillow as their breathing grew heavy.

"It's a vestigial third eye," she murmured against his chest.

"Hmm?"

"The Deamon weakness. They have a vestigial third eye between their eyebrows that never evolved. It's a vulnerable spot that allows them to be killed instantly if struck."

Alrec swallowed the emotion in his throat, understanding the admission was more than just intel on an enemy species. It was proof she trusted him, that she saw him as her equal...perhaps even as her partner in a world where they both were quite alone.

"Thank you," he whispered, kissing her forehead. "I'd like to hear more tomorrow, especially on how you found this out. Do you hang out with Deamons I'm not aware of?"

Chuckling, she licked his sweaty chest, causing him to shiver. "No, but I'm pretty observant and have run into a few Deamons since I left Uteria. I'll tell you everything tomorrow."

Unable to hold his eyes open, he allowed them to drift shut as her evergreen scent filled his nostrils. "Can't wait. I was honored to love you like this, Kilani. Sweet dreams, little one."

Her leg tightened around him as she drew him closer. "I was honored to be loved by you. Good night, Alrec."

Losing himself in the warmth of her sated body, Alrec succumbed to sleep.

Chapter 15

Kilani slid out of bed several hours later, leaving her sleeping Vampyre twisted in the sheets as he snored. After cleaning the remnants of their tryst from her thighs, she dressed and headed outside. The afternoon sun was bright, and she smirked at how well she'd acclimated to Alrec's schedule. Since he could only go outside at night, Kilani had been sleeping during the day and using nights to train with him. As long as he lived in her home, she would adhere to that schedule. There was plenty of time to reverse it when he was gone.

Frowning at the thought, she entered the wooden outhouse that had always existed behind the house. Curiosity still lingered about who'd built the cabin, but so far, Kilani hadn't found any clues. Perhaps it would always remain a mystery. Since her life was rather uneventful—barring the most recent events—she welcomed the small dash of intrigue.

Wincing as she stepped inside and closed the door, she acknowledged the soreness between her legs. After all, Alrec was massive, and he'd certainly stretched her with that magnificent cock. Sighing as she took care of business, she let the memories wash over her.

After picking some vegetables in the garden, she headed inside to find Alrec in the kitchen, clad in his underwear as he ran a wet cloth over his upper body.

"I see you're making use of the poor man's shower situation I have going on here," she teased, setting the vegetables on the counter.

"The basins of water are serviceable, but have you ever thought of searching for a well to tap and installing plumbing?" he asked, dipping the cloth in the basin and wringing it before wiping the back of his neck.

Shrugging, she began to wash the vegetables. "Someday. After all, I have an eternity to figure out how to rig the plumbing."

Brooding eyes assessed her as he finished dragging the cloth over his skin. After laying it flat to dry, he strode over and lifted her hand. "Good evening," he said softly, kissing her knuckles.

"I'm used to 'good morning,' but I guess your kind does prefer 'good evening.'"

"We would prefer to walk in the sun again, but I don't foresee that happening for quite a while. As you noted, there is so much hatred to overcome."

Tilting her head, her lips curved into a sad smile. "Perhaps one day things will change and we can help chart a new path. One where Slayers and Vampyres live in peace again."

"I hope so. Although the species have remained separate, there could even come a day when they choose to intermarry."

Laughter bounded from her throat. "Who knew you were such a dreamer? I can't ever see that happening."

"Stranger things have happened in our world, Kilani," he murmured, winking before releasing her hand and trailing over to the couch to dress. "One day, you might eat your words."

"If the immortal world ever reaches that level of peace, I will happily admit you were right. For now, I'll continue to live in reality. Let me wash these and eat some dinner before the sun goes down, and then we can spar."

Grinning at his optimism, Kilani got to work preparing the food. Two hours later, they strolled to the riverbank to spar under the full moon.

"How did you learn about the vestigial third eye?" Alrec asked when they took a break.

"Thankfully, my cabin has remained off the radar from Deamons, but when I first moved here, I ventured quite far to survey the land. I came across a cluster of Deamons and listened to their conversation."

Dragging the spear over the ground absently, she mimicked the Deamon's voice, low and gravelly. *"Make sure the Vampyre bastards don't pierce you between the eyes. You'll die instantly."* Shrugging, she tilted her head. "It was good intel. Perhaps there's a weapon the Vampyres or Slayers can create to take advantage."

"No doubt," Alrec said with a nod. "I'll make sure to pass along the intel to Commander Latimus when I return home. Thank you, Kilani."

Lifting her spear, she arched a brow. "Don't think because I gave you the goods I'm going to go easy on you. Come on, Vampyre. I still want to kick that fine ass a few times tonight."

Chuckling, Alrec clutched his weapon and set his feet. "Come on then," he taunted, hooking his fingers. "Show me what you've got, little one."

Blissful laughter echoed along with their grunts under the dark clouds, and Kilani fought with all her might, although her worthy opponent would always best her in the end. After several hours of training, her hulking Vampyre gently urged her to the soft grass, tugging at their clothes until there was nothing between them but the warm night air.

Giving in to her passion, Kilani made love for the first time under a swath of twinkling stars.

Chapter 16

The next night, after a grueling sparring session, Kilani and Alrec headed inside two hours before dawn to rest. Exhausted, she didn't have the energy to make love. Unsure how to tell Alrec, she lay down in bed, feeling her eyes begin to drift closed.

"I'm so tired tonight," she said, yawning as she snuggled into the pillow. "I'm sorry..."

"It's okay, sweetheart." Leaning over, he kissed her temple and smoothed her hair. "Get some rest. I'll be here when you wake up."

She thought he might crawl into bed and hold her, but the thought drifted away as she fell into slumber. Over an hour later, she awoke, snaking an arm over the mattress to search for Alrec but finding it empty. Sitting up, she pushed her hair out of her face as he strode in through the door carrying an armful of what looked to be...sticks? Bamboo?

"What are you doing?" she asked, wondering if she was still dreaming.

"Hello, sleeping beauty. Did you rest well?" Setting the wood in the corner, he stalked over and kissed her forehead.

"Uh...yeah, but...what are you doing?"

"I'm going to use the bamboo to make some piping for you," he said, gesturing with his head toward the pile. "And then I'm going to tap a well and create a well pump for you before I leave. At least this will leave you with a basic form of indoor plumbing."

Kilani's heart all but melted at his genuine expression and lopsided smile. "You're going to install plumbing for me?"

"Yes," he said, chuckling as he nodded. "I know it might not be as romantic as flowers or jewelry—"

"It's perfect," she interjected, rising to her knees and throwing her arms around his neck. Plopping an ardent kiss on his face, she sighed. "My hero. I'll take plumbing over jewelry any day. Thank you."

"You're welcome." Pecking her lips, he grinned. "Had I known plumbing would've garnered this reaction, I would've installed it several days ago."

"Oh, stop," she said, swatting his chest. "This is amazing. I'll help you."

"I'll need to sand the inside of the bamboo stalks to make sure they're uniform and don't leak. I think I can find some makeshift things around the house to use to construct a pump. It's not going to be the most efficient since the pump will be manual, but it will do."

"Let's get to it then," she said, excited to upgrade her home. "Come on."

Once dressed, she all but tore apart the cabin, looking for items they could use in the construction. There were many serviceable things, including some wire, cloths, old nails, and spikes. Remembering the rubber trees that grew along the riverbank, Kilani sprinted outside to gather some of the broad leaves, realizing they could use them as stoppers for the pump.

They toiled for hours, falling into conversation as they worked, and Alrec asked her about the previous owners.

"I have no idea," she said, carving a slit at the end of one of the bamboo stalks so she could attach it to another and bind them. "Kenden found the shed when he used to hunt and fish with his father before the Awakening. Whoever built it must've wanted to hide from the world too."

"I've heard rumors of other immortal species that exist besides the Vampyres, Slayers, and Deamons," Alrec said, smoothing one of the stalks with the sander he'd fashioned from a slab of tree bark. "Do you think it's possible?"

"Anything is possible," she said with a shrug. "I mean, humans exist beyond the ether and have some pretty crazy stories that have outlived their mortal bodies. Everyone is convinced they'll remain separate from us for eternity, but I have my doubts."

"Do you have a soft spot for humans then?"

"No," she said, wrinkling her nose. "They're still heathens. But we can learn a lot from their failures and wars, and their successes and triumphs. My brother always believed we would adopt their technology one day."

"Perhaps, but that day seems far away in an immortal world that clings to tradition."

"Truth," she muttered, snapping the bamboo pieces together.

They tinkered for another hour until they trailed outside to use the remaining hours of the night to spar. Once inside, they fell into bed and loved each other slowly and tenderly.

Kilani opened herself to him, thanking him with her body and soulful moans as he rained kisses upon her heated skin.

Chapter 17

Alrec continued to construct the plumbing system for Kilani, wondering when her excited smiles and heartfelt words of thanks had become the entire zenith of his existence. Every time she would gaze at him with those wide blue eyes, sparkling with gratitude, Alrec's heart would click further into place. It was as if the organ had never fully functioned until he met his stunning Slayer.

He dug a well behind the home, and using the bamboo pipes they'd molded, he managed to create a makeshift plumbing system for her over the next week. At night, they continued to spar, and Alrec knew he was pushing off the inevitable.

He was fully healed, and it was time for him to return home.

Although he was entranced by the woman who'd saved his life, Alrec had a duty, and he felt a calling to fulfill it. Such was the way when your people were at war, and even though he longed to stay with Kilani, honor and purpose ran deep.

After another long night of toiling with the plumbing system, Alrec placed the final touches on the manual pump, testing it out before declaring Kilani should give it a try. Under the light of the moon, she pumped the mechanism by the well, emitting a joyful cry when it worked and water gushed through the newly laid pipes to the house. Rushing inside, she turned the knob of the bamboo faucet he'd constructed over the basin. Water trickled into the sink, and she covered her mouth, exhilaration sparkling in her eyes as she jumped up and down.

"We did it," she cried before lowering her hands and shrugging. "Well, *you* really did it, but I helped where I could. I have running water. Never thought I'd see the day."

Taken by her genuine delight, he slid his palm over hers and squeezed. "I'm so thrilled it makes you happy," he said, his voice rough with emotion since he knew it was one of the last times he would gaze into her stunning eyes. "I like making you happy, Kilani."

"Alrec," she whispered, stepping closer and palming his cheeks, "you make me so happy. I would choose these weeks with you over an eternity with any other man. Thank you."

Sliding his arms around her waist, he drew her close, aligning their bodies as he gazed deep into her eyes. "Can't we figure out a way to make this work? To stay together even though it seems impossible?"

Compassion clouded her features as she caressed his jaw. "I don't see a way—"

"Would you consider coming to Astaria with me?"

Her mouth fell open as shock laced her expression. Sadness coursed through him as she slowly shook her head.

"You know I can't. Our people are at war, Alrec. I won't live my life under the rule of a species that hunts and drains my people for blood."

"We only abduct men, not women or children, and it's only because your blasted king is intent on extending the war. It's because of his ludicrous suicide decree we must hunt so often."

"I'm no fan of Marsias, but he does what he believes is just. Your people are not innocent, Alrec. How many Slayers have been abducted from their families and died in your dungeon?"

His eyebrows drew together as his mind raced to find a solution. "I would protect you—"

Laughter sprang from her throat as she covered his lips with her fingers. "Do you really think I'm the type of woman who will sit home and wait for a man to protect me?" Arching a brow, her lips curved into a sad smile. "I would hate that life. Plus, we could never bear children together. It's an eternity I would never push you into."

Forming a slight pout, he spoke against her fingers. "How can I accept this is the end? I'm not sure of much, little one, but

I'm certain of one thing..." Resting his forehead against hers, he brushed a kiss on her lips. "I will never care for another woman the way I care for you. *Never.*"

Tears glistened in her eyes as her lips wobbled. "Nor I for you. Now, show me. Love me for the last time, so I can remember. And then, when dusk arrives tomorrow, you must begin the journey home. You can always hold the memory here too." Placing her palm over his heart, she squeezed. "We'll treasure them together even when we're apart."

Overcome with despair at the unfairness of the world, Alrec lowered and lifted her, clutching on for dear life as she wrapped her legs around his waist. Thrusting his fingers in her hair, he crashed their lips together, plunging deep inside, unable to control his desperate need. She moaned, writhing against him as he carried her to bed.

And then, he tore away their clothes, determined to imprint every single detail so they would never forget.

Chapter 18

Kilani clung to Alrec, intent on pushing away her heartache and sadness so she could lose herself in his fervent kisses and warm embrace one last time. Once he dragged off their clothes, he placed her on the bed, crawling over her, the movements slow and protective. Looming above her, he pressed his lips to hers and drew her into a smoldering, desperate kiss.

"Wait," she said, placing her palm on his chest.

Confusion crossed his expression as he pulled back. "Sweetheart?"

Grinning, she wiggled underneath him before sliding off the bed. Grasping his shoulders, she urged him to lie flat on his back as his eyebrows drew together. With a sultry glance, she sauntered over to the corner and picked up the ropes that lay on the small table. Trailing back over, she encircled his wrist and lifted it to the bedpost.

"I remember you saying you were into the bondage thing," she rasped, securing his wrist before trailing to the other side and securing the other one.

Alrec smiled and tugged on the ropes. "It seems we've come full circle."

A hoarse laugh bounded from her throat. "My dear Vampyre, you have no idea."

Sliding one leg over his massive frame, she straddled him, aware of the wetness that seeped from her deepest place onto his abdomen just above his hard shaft. He shimmied under her, his cock searching for her warmth, and she lifted a finger before shaking her head.

"No rushing," she commanded, leaning forward and brushing her lips against his. "We're going to take this one slow."

Alrec's eyes glazed with lust as his breathing grew heavy. "Do your worst, little one. I can't wait."

Her lips curled into a sexy grin as she slid up his body and touched her nipple to his lips. "Suck me, Vampyre—"

The words were abruptly cut off as she gasped when he drew the taut nub into his wet mouth. Kilani moaned, writhing above him as he lapped and licked the puckered bud. Staring into his deep brown orbs, she eventually withdrew from his tender ministrations and slid her other breast to his mouth, longing for more. Her sexy Vampyre gazed at her as he loved her, and Kilani realized she might be embroiled in the most erotic moment she would ever experience. Yearning to give him pleasure, she popped her breast from his mouth and began to trail kisses down his body.

The prickly hairs of his chest tickled her nose as she worked her way down, reveling in his hushed moans and the reverent way he breathed her name. Stopping at his navel, she dipped her tongue inside, pleased when he shivered in response.

"Sweetheart," he whispered, shaking his head on the pillow. "This is so sexy, but I want to touch you too."

"Soon," she murmured, her lips carving a path to the juncture between his thighs where his erection stood firm and proud. Resting on her knees, she cradled him in her hands, moisture gushing between her thighs as he groaned when she squeezed.

"You're *very* swollen here," she said, biting her lip as she began to work his flesh between her hands. "My poor, injured Vampyre."

"There's nothing injured in that area," he muttered, his body bowing atop the bed. "Goddess, Kilani...please...don't tease me..."

Lowering, she ran the tip of her nose over his sensitive flesh, closing her eyes to memorize the feel of his taut skin and musky scent. Extending her tongue, she ran it over the length once...twice...before staring deep in his eyes and lifting the engorged head to her lips.

"I'm honored to love you like this," she whispered against the quivering flesh, repeating the words he'd spoken the first night they'd made love.

"I'm honored to be loved by you...*my beautiful Kilani*..."

Connected with him through their gaze and deep-rooted emotion, she opened wide and slid over his throbbing cock. Alrec groaned, hips surging high on the bed as he uttered a curse. Determined to please him, she worked her wet mouth over the straining flesh, pumping the base with her hand as she lathered him with her tongue.

His passionate moans grew louder...deeper...and his shaft surged in her mouth, claiming every crevice as she gave herself to him, body and soul. Popping him from her lips, she ran her palm over the strained shaft, arching a brow as she silently asked him if she should continue.

"It feels so good, but I need to be inside you, little one," he rasped from above. "Please, untie me."

Taking pity on him, she snaked up his body, straddling his stomach and removing the binds. His hands flew to her hips, grasping firmly as he pushed her down his body. Sliding her wet core over his cock, he glided himself to her entrance. Kilani reached between them, aligning his tip to her center, and then she slowly enveloped him between her sensitive folds, overcome with the deep, full sensation.

"There you are," he whispered, hips jutting back and forth as he dragged himself through her taut channel. "So tight...so wet...made just for me..."

Kilani tossed her head back, whimpering at the possessive words.

"*My little Slayer.* Yes, that's it...keep riding me...goddess, you feel so good..."

She worked her hips tirelessly, undulating against him in the hope he would remember this moment centuries down the road, when they were both far removed from this place and time. Suddenly, his hands tightened on her hips, and he jolted forward, flipping them so she lay on her back as he loomed above her. Gazing into her, he threaded his fingers through the hair at her temple as his cock worked her quivering body.

"Kilani..." he whispered, love blazing in his deep orbs. "I have to tell you—"

"Don't," she interrupted, tears burning her eyes as she covered his lips with her fingers. "If you say it, I won't be able to let you go. Please, Alrec…"

With a ragged groan, he lowered his face to her neck, kissing the trembling skin as his cock thrust deep inside her. Encircling his broad shoulders, she dug her nails into his back and offered the last thing she had to give: "Drink from me."

His head snapped back, and his worried gaze studied hers. "Are you sure? I'll be able to read your thoughts and feelings—"

"I'm sure," she rasped, nodding on the pillow as their bodies vibrated with unsaid emotion. "The words are too much, but I need you to know."

Groaning her name, he lowered his lips to her neck, licking the soft flesh to coat it with his self-healing saliva and shield her from the pain. Kilani closed her eyes, her fingers clutching his flesh as the tips of his fangs scratched her delicate skin atop her pulsing vein. Bracing, her muscles tensed before he growled—sending jolts of desire through her heated body—and plunged his fangs into her neck.

Pleasure unlike anything she'd ever known coursed through her frame as blissful laughter leaped from her throat. Alrec's lips worked the flesh at her neck, sucking the life force from her vein as his thick cock dragged against every cell of her wet core. Clutching him to her ravaged body, stars exploded behind her eyes as her hips thrust at a furious pace. Screaming his name, her body arched beneath him, and she began to come, joy consuming every thought and every inch of her shuddering frame. Alrec moaned against her neck, and she knew his violent trembles meant he was close. Opening to him, she held nothing back, needing him to know how special he was to her…and would always be.

Her magnificent Vampyre lifted his head, eyes glazed with passion as he stared at her, lips red and swollen from her blood and their heated kisses. Pressing his forehead to hers, he growled low and deep in his chest, surging his fingers into her hair and latching tightly. Resting his cheek against hers, he came, shooting pulsing jets of release inside her, claiming her one last time.

Kilani held him, grateful to give him such pleasure…understanding he was *everything*. Her one true mate. Regardless of the fact a future between them was impossible, she would always carry him deep in her heart and acknowledge him as *hers*.

"Good grief, woman," he muttered, kissing a trail down her cheek to the puncture wounds on her neck. Extending his tongue, he began to slowly lick them closed, healing them with his saliva, and she reveled in the smooth, silken strokes.

Once the wounds were closed, they lay entwined, sweaty and sated, until he slowly rose to wet a cloth. Returning to the bed, his lips formed a lazy grin as he cleaned the evidence of their loving from between her thighs. After cleaning himself, he slid between the sheets, drawing her to his side.

Resting her cheek on his chest, she cursed the tears in her eyes, vowing not to let them fall. The conclusion of their affair had always been carved in stone, and she wouldn't allow sadness to pervade their last night together. Snuggling into him, she took comfort in the rise and fall of his chest as his breaths grew heavy.

"I feel the same," he murmured, kissing her hair as his hand softly stroked her back. "I need you to know, Kilani. It wouldn't be fair for me to know your feelings and you not to know mine in return."

Her heart slammed at his admission, knowing he didn't have to return the sentiment he'd absorbed through her blood: she loved him with her whole heart and always would.

"A Vampyre with a sense of fair play," she teased, unable to acknowledge the deeper feelings that clogged her throat. "Who knew those existed?"

His deep chuckle rumbled against her, and she closed her eyes, inhaling his heady scent. God, she would miss it when he was gone. There were so many things she would miss about the honorable man who'd spared her life so she could spare his in return.

"Sweet dreams, little one."

"Sweet dreams, Alrec."

Comforted by the silken caresses upon her back, Kilani clutched him close, fighting sleep since it brought her one step closer to his departure. As his warmth surrounded her, the emotion she'd held at bay tightened her throat to the point of pain. Unable to control it, she nuzzled into his hand when he swiped away the tear that trailed down her cheek.

"*Shhh...*" he soothed, kissing her forehead. "I know, sweetheart."

Somewhere between dawn and dusk she eventually slept, knowing she would have to rise with the moon and tell her Vampyre goodbye.

Chapter 19

Alrec rose at dusk, a sense of melancholy dragging every bone and muscle in his body as he dressed. Kilani watched him from the bed, her eyes sad and morose, before she rose and tugged on her clothing.

Kilani packed a bag for him filled with three containers of her blood, a small knife, and some cloths he could use to bathe with when he reached the River Thayne. Stepping outside, she trailed to the back of the home and located her finest spear. Returning, she offered it to him, arms outstretched, and he smiled.

"I thought you enjoyed stabbing fish with that one the most. Or perhaps stabbing me when we sparred."

Breathing a laugh, she nodded. "It's definitely my favorite. Take it and use it to fight any Deamons who get in your way. I don't like their chances against you with my spear."

Alrec took it, sliding it through a loop on the bag now secured to his back. Stepping forward, he cupped her face, sliding his thumb over her lips as her eyes shone in the moonlight.

"Thank you for saving my life, little one. I'll never forget your kindness."

"Well, you saved mine first," she said, lifting a shoulder, "so we're even. Can't be indebted to a Vampyre. Told you that from the beginning."

His eyes roved over her face, memorizing every freckle and dimple as he recalled the rush of feeling he'd experienced when he drank from her only hours ago. Her love for him was pure and true, and he returned the sentiment a thousand times over. It didn't matter they'd had only weeks in the cabin; he'd begun his descent into love with her in a meadow under a full moon five years ago, and their time together had only exacerbated the emotion. Doubt crept into his slowly breaking heart, and he wondered if he was truly making the right choice.

"It's the only way," she whispered, lifting to her toes and pressing a kiss to his lips. "We both know it. Travel safely, Alrec. Be kind to my people. Perhaps one day, centuries from now, I'll see you again when we're at peace and the world has evolved to embrace me. It's my greatest wish."

"I think you're magnificent," he rasped, leaning down to give her a blazing kiss. "I accept you exactly as you are, Kilani."

Nodding, she stepped back, breaking their embrace since he didn't have the strength to. Lifting her hand, she gave a slight wave. "Give 'em hell."

Alrec's throat bobbed, so clogged with emotion he could barely breathe. Returning her wave, he flashed one last somber, poignant smile. And then, he slowly turned and left the woman who owned his heart.

It took Alrec weeks to navigate back to Astaria. At night, he would travel across the grueling landscape, making the most of the darkness to find his way home. During the day, he would find a heavily covered area or cave to sleep in to shield himself from the sun. He was always cognizant that Deamons could be lurking in unseen alcoves and remained on high alert.

Fortunately, he only ran into one Deamon cluster. It was a group of five Deamons that began trailing him as he approached the River Thayne from the foothills of the Strok Mountains. They were sloppy and quite easily observed by his honed skills, so he continued forward until the glow of dusk began to paint the horizon. Locating a dense thicket of trees, he pretended to set up camp as the Deamons surrounded him. Grasping his spear, which lay hidden on the ground, Alrec whirled and began to fight the creatures, thankful for his sparring sessions with Kilani. They had certainly increased his stamina, and training with someone so skilled only enhanced his abilities.

Eventually, four Deamons lay dead on the ground, and Alrec fought the last one, besting him after several minutes and thrusting the spear between his eyes. The creature died instantly, confirming Kilani's intel. Pleased, Alrec vowed to speak to Latimus as soon as he returned. The commander would want to know about the weakness, and his younger brother, Heden, was a genius at creating new weapons to maim their enemies. Perhaps he could create a device designed to injure the Deamons in their vulnerable sp ot.

When he eventually crested the hill that led to Astaria, Alrec trekked across the meadow to the imposing Vampyre compound, expecting to be thrilled he'd made it home alive. Instead, he felt rather numb as he approached the outer wall. Stopping outside the thick stones, he lifted his hand to his mouth and shouted.

"Hello? Is anyone guarding the wall? It's Alrec, son of Jakar."

"Alrec?" a deep voice called. "We don't have a lot of men stationed here due to the protective shield Etherya placed on the wall, but I hear you! It's Takel. Give me a moment."

Stepping back, Alrec waited until the stones began to slide open. Walking inside, he noticed the soldiers pushing the door closed as Takel approached and patted him on the back.

"My god, Alrec. We thought you were dead! I sent a search party out for two weeks, but we never found you."

"I ended up floating several miles downriver," Alrec said, cupping the man's shoulder with genuine affection. "It's an unbelievable story and one I can't wait to tell you. For now, I'm exhausted and need my warm bed."

"Fair enough, my friend. Commander Latimus will want to hear your story, I'm sure. I'll set up a debrief tomorrow night."

Following his friend, Alrec headed farther into the compound before striding down the dirt road that led to his cabin near the far wall. Once inside, he inhaled a deep breath, hoping he would gain comfort from the familiar surroundings. Instead, as he unloaded his pack and stashed the remaining container of Kilani's blood in the ice box, all he felt was loneliness.

Chapter 20

Alrec threw himself back into fighting, assuming that if he performed the duty he was born to fulfill, the loneliness would soon abate. After all, he'd lived alone for centuries before the Awakening, and when his family died in the tragic event, his solitude had only grown. Although he missed his parents terribly, he'd made his peace with their deaths and vowed to avenge them. That vow had always been enough.

Until *her*.

Now, Alrec ached with a yearning so vast he sometimes wondered if he was slowly going insane. Kilani's image had flashed through his mind with fair regularity ever since he met her on the Slayer meadow. But after their time in the cabin, where she'd graciously saved his life and welcomed him into her embrace, he was fairly sure he was addicted to her melodious laughter and tender soul.

Was it possible to be addicted to another immortal? If so, what did it mean for his future? Alrec took his duty as a soldier seriously and didn't want his skills to become compromised because he was distracted by thoughts of a fierce Slayer with gorgeous blue eyes...

The first few weeks he returned home, he found himself listlessly wandering throughout his tiny home. Dazed and unfocused, he constantly knocked his shin against the chest at the base of his bed or banged his elbow on his bathroom doorknob. Even though he healed quickly, the clumsiness was a nuisance he could only attribute to his fixation on the woman he missed so vehemently.

Sometimes, when he rapped his knee against the bedpost, Alrec's hand reflexively stretched to stroke the wood. Lost in memories, he remembered how Kilani bound his ankles to her bed before he earned her trust. Caressing the wood, he would recall her upturned face in the moonlight the night she finally kissed him. Then he realized he was stroking a goddamn bedpost and told himself to get a grip.

A month after his return, Latimus ordered a raid on Uteria. Alrec did his duty, abducting three Slayer men as he cursed the war and hatred between the species. If things were different, perhaps he and Kilani could build a life together. Although the species had never intermarried before the Awakening, the kingdom was vastly in need of change, and loving a member of the opposite species would certainly mean progress to some.

But Alrec was smart enough to know deep-rooted change took time—most likely centuries—so he carried out his duty, understanding there was no guarantee he or Kilani would survive long enough to see such progress. It was just the way of their war-torn world.

Every day at dawn, Alrec reentered his cabin, situated in a cul-de-sac filled with other laborers and soldiers' dwellings on the outskirts of Astaria. After completing the mundane task of filling his goblet with Slayer blood, he winced at the bitter taste. Now that he'd tasted Kilani's rich blood on his tongue, the life force of a Slayer soldier was a stale, tasteless substitute. Longing for her, he lolled on his bed each morning, lightly clutching the sheets, wishing it was her soft hair or silken skin.

After several months of existing in his listless state, Alrec admitted his existence was becoming quite pointless. Unfortunately, there was no resolution to his predicament in the foreseeable future.

One night, three months after he returned home, Alrec was sparring on the training field alongside his battalion. Takel rushed him, sword held high, and Alrec took a sloppy swipe, attempting to knock his weapon free. Takel laughed and knocked Alrec's weapon from his hand, glaring down at him as Alrec took a knee.

"By the goddess, Alrec," he said, nicking his neck with the sword and spurring a reflexive, angry growl from Alrec's throat. "What happened to you? You can't fight worth shit anymore. You never used to yield. I'm worried."

"That's enough," Commander Latimus's deep voice boomed behind them. "Sheathe your sword, Takel. Alrec, I'd like to speak to you privately."

Sighing, Alrec took Takel's offered hand and rose before silently stalking up the hill behind Latimus. Once they stood side by side, Latimus crossed his arms over his chest and kicked the grass with the toe of his boot.

"This can't go on, Alrec," he said softly. "Your mind is elsewhere, and I have no need for a soldier who can't fight."

Expelling a breath, Alrec glanced at the ground as shame washed over him. "My one duty is to avenge my family as a soldier, and I am failing. I'm sorry, Commander."

Latimus's jaw ticked in the silver moonlight. "You told us of the intel you gathered while you were gone. You said you learned it when you killed some Deamons on your journey."

Nodding, Alrec acknowledged the white lie. He hadn't told anyone about meeting Kilani because he didn't want to jeopardize her safety or tell her secrets. Instead, he told everyone he'd washed down the river and found the cabin when he regained consciousness. Then he nursed himself back to health and traveled home.

"Your story technically makes sense, but I find myself wondering how you stayed alive without consuming Slayer blood."

Alrec pursed his lips. Latimus was shrewd, and the question was valid. "As I told you, I found a barrel full of blood near the cabin. It must have been left there from the blood-bankings before the Awakening."

Latimus breathed a laugh before harshly rubbing his forehead. "You know, you're a terrible liar, Alrec. Probably because you're an honorable man who lies infrequently."

Alrec pursed his lips. "Perhaps."

Wide nostrils flared as Latimus inhaled a deep breath. "If there's one thing I recognize on a man, it's the look of being in love with a woman he can't have."

His gaze whipped to Latimus as he studied his stern expression. "Don't tell me you're in love with someone you can't have. You're the most powerful soldier in the realm and brother to King Sathan. You can have any woman you choose."

Scoffing, Latimus kicked the ground. "I'm a bastard who doesn't know the first thing about loving a woman I'll never deserve."

"Who is she? Perhaps I can help—"

"It's not meant to be," Latimus interjected, his tone firm. "And I urge you to never speak of it again." Facing him, Latimus's ice-blue eyes drilled into his. "But my situation is not yours, Alrec. I don't want you to live in misery as I do. At least one of us should be happy."

Feeling his eyebrows draw together, he pondered. "I won't shirk my duty. And I wouldn't be a man worthy of her if I did."

Placing his hands on his hips, Latimus studied the ground, appearing deep in thought. Finally, his gaze lifted, and he spoke with resolution. "I've been wanting to create a new position in the army for a while, but it's daunting and requires much sacrifice. There's never been anyone I could see filling it."

Slightly confused, Alrec swallowed. "Okay."

"The soldier would have to leave Astaria behind and live a solitary life near the Deamon caves. Essentially, I want a full-time scout to keep a constant eye on the growing Deamon threat. The soldier would have to surveil the area, gather intel, and travel back to Astaria every six months to give me a report."

Alrec worked his mouth, trying to form a response. Was Latimus offering him a chance to return to Kilani and continue to fulfill his duty to the army?

"It's not an easy assignment. The soldier won't be able to see his family at Astaria except when he returns to gather supplies and report to me. Since you don't have any family here, I anticipate that won't be a problem."

"No, sir."

"I'll expect detailed reports and trust you to work autonomously. This is not a vacation, Alrec. It's an important role I need filled. There are very few soldiers I would even consider assigning." Cupping his shoulder, he squeezed. "*You* are one of those soldiers. Know this assignment will require you to live near the Deamon caves until we have eradicated Crimeous and the Deamon threat. It could be centuries."

Rising to his full height, Alrec saluted his commander as blood pulsed through his body. "I understand and accept your assignment, sir."

Chuckling, Latimus arched a brow. "You didn't hesitate. Holy shit. You've got it bad, my friend."

Grinning, Alrec shrugged. "I don't want to divulge her secret, but since you're trusting me..." Leaning forward, he whispered, "Sir, I can't explain it. I've never felt this way before. It's...*consuming*. She's taken residence in my head and my heart, and I can't escape her."

"If she is a Slayer, you will never be able to bear children," Latimus said softly.

"No." Alrec ran the sole of his boot over the grass. "I can't speak for her, but that doesn't bother me. In a world as consumed with war as ours, there are always children that need parents. If we decided to choose that path in the future, I would be honored to adopt a child with her."

"I don't want to pry, but if she lives separate from her people, as I assume since you told me the cabin was far from Uteria, her only option to adopt a child would be to take in a Vampyre. Would she be open to raising a child who is not her own species?"

Glancing toward the horizon, Alrec debated the question. "Well, she saved me, so I guess saving another Vampyre or two wouldn't be out of the question." He held up his hands, showing his palms. "I wouldn't want to speak for her though. She's tough as nails. It would have to be a decision we make together."

"If she's that tough, you'd be smart to have her accompany you on your scouting missions."

"Sir," Alrec said with a deep smile, "I wouldn't have it any other way."

Chuckling, Latimus nodded. "Then it's settled. How much time do you need to wrap things up here?"

"I'll sell my cabin as quickly as possible, and I'd like to say a proper goodbye to Takel and the other men before I leave. Otherwise, I can probably begin the post in a month."

Placing his hand on his hip, Latimus's lips curved into a genuine smile, which was rarely seen from the gruff, stoic commander. "You're a good man, Alrec. Be happy. You deserve it. Come see me before you leave, and we'll choose a date for you to return home and give me your first report." With a salute, he began walking down the hill.

"Latimus!"

Pivoting, he called, "Yes?"

"You deserve to be happy too."

A moment passed before he softly replied, "It's not in the cards for me, my friend, but I'm certainly thrilled for you. Go seize it for both of us. See ya."

Alrec watched his broad shoulders as he strode away, feeling a strange sense of comradery for the strong, enduring commander. Gazing toward the sky, he uttered, "Thank you, Etherya." Closing his eyes, he imagined returning home to Kilani, hoping she would welcome him as her mate and partner...for as long as they both shall live...

Knowing there was only one way to find out, Alrec trekked down the hill, ready to tie up his affairs at Astaria so he could return to his little one.

Chapter 21

Kilani's mood progressively devolved from bad to worse to catastrophic with each day that passed after Alrec's departure. Of course, she'd known it would take some time to get over him—after all, how many times did you meet the love of your damn life? Only once, if the soothsayers' tales rang true—and deep in her heart, Kilani knew Alrec was her soul mate.

Since having a Vampyre as a soul mate was a futile endeavor, she tightened her bootstraps and pushed through each day, determined to make a life for herself in the place she'd chosen. The first task she set out to accomplish was revising her sleep schedule so she slept at night again like a normal damn person. Intent on retraining herself, she lay down in the lonely bed each night only to feel her eyes well with emotion that her lover wasn't by her side. Most nights, she would rise and walk along the river, remembering the spots that held such meaning for her.

The clearing by the old oak tree where Alrec first held her and pressed those broad, firm lips to hers under the twinkling stars.

The grassy knoll where they'd sparred, strengthening his muscles so he would survive the journey home.

The soft grass where he'd gently urged her down and eased away her clothes...as calmly and steadily as he'd eased her reservations about loving a Vampyre. Trailing to the spot, Kilani lowered and crossed her legs before running her palm over the grass. It tickled her skin, reminding her of Alrec's prickly hairs when she'd caressed his chiseled chest.

Sighing, Kilani stared at the stars and cursed every god she didn't believe in for sending her the perfect companion only to rip him away when she'd finally given every last piece of her soul.

"I know we disowned you after the Awakening," she murmured, addressing Etherya although she knew the goddess cared naught for Slayers anymore. Not since her species had devolved into war, breaking the goddess's heart until she withdrew her protection. "But you could throw me a bone, you know?" Kilani continued, sitting back and resting her palms flat on the grass. "You're a badass woman too, right? Female goddesses are way cooler than men. You see the logic in letting me win at *something*, right?"

Silence was her only answer as the soft breeze flitted through the treetops.

Suddenly, a branch snapped in the distance, and Kilani lurched to her feet, crouching in a defensive stance as she perked her ears. Was it a Deamon? Had they finally discovered her cabin? Of course they wouldn't discover it when a hulking Vampyre soldier was in residence.

"That would be too much good fortune for your unlucky ass, Kilani," she muttered, rising and stalking toward the sound. Eyes wide, she picked up a branch, pleased when she noticed its sharp edge. If the bastards were going to kill her, she'd at least go down fighting.

"This is my home, and you're trespassing," she said, frustrated at the slight waver in her voice. "I'm prepared to defend it till my dying breath."

A soft whimper echoed between the trees, causing the hairs on her nape to rise. Slowly walking forward, she passed a row of ferns to see a white wolf standing in the clearing. His sky-blue gaze locked onto hers, and she realized he was as terrified as she was.

"Whoa," she said, showing him her palm as she gingerly approached. "I'm not going to hurt you. Where's your pack?"

The wolf uttered a soft, high-pitched wail and looked off into the distance before reclaiming her gaze.

"They left you, huh?" Inching closer, she assessed his mangy ears and the gray fur along his back that swirled with the white. "From your size, I assume you're the runt. You're big, but not as big as some wolves I've seen around here. Believe me, I get it. Sometimes, you just don't fit in."

The wolf harrumphed before lowering to the ground. Tilting his head, he began to pant, his long pink tongue shining under the moonlit clouds.

"Oh no," she said, holding up her hands and backing away. "I'm not in the market for a pet. Don't look all cute. It's not happening." Gesturing with the stick, she urged him to run along. "Go on, now. Some rabbits live in the bushes over there. I'm sure they'll make a fine dinner."

Turning, she trekked back to the house, noting the branches and leaves that crunched behind her. Frustrated the animal was following her, she roughly closed the door and attempted to sleep.

The next night, consumed with thoughts of Alrec, she headed out for a walk since sleeping was futile. As she crested the bank of the river, the wolf was waiting for her as if he knew she would appear.

"Nope," she said, shaking her head as she pointed to the far-off mountains. "Not happening. I don't want a mangy mongrel around here. Got it?" Stomping down the riverbank, she repeated the mantra in her mind that she was *not* adopting a pet.

The nightly walks continued, and eventually, Kilani became used to the sightings of her furry friend. They were a welcome distraction from her obsession with Alrec and gave her something else to focus on.

A few weeks after first seeing the wolf, she decided to bring it some dinner.

"Here," she said, tossing him one of the fish she'd cooked for dinner. "I even cooked it for you, you lucky bastard."

The wolf uttered a series of excited yelps before resting on his laurels and devouring the fish.

After a few weeks and much deliberation, Kilani accepted she was going to adopt the damn mutt. The last thing she needed was another mouth to feed, but loneliness was slowly eating her away as it pervaded her soul, and the only person who could fix that was never coming back. So, she grabbed a rope one warm, balmy night and headed to the river, intent on laying down the ground rules.

"You're going to do your part around here," she said, sliding the rope around the wolf's neck as she patted his soft fur. "And we're going to take lots of baths in the river. I won't have fleas in my home, do you hear me?"

The wolf chortled, panting with obvious affection, and Kilani led him home with the makeshift leash. Once there, she filled a basin with water and brought it outside before scrubbing the creature so thoroughly she thought his fur might molt. He rang himself dry, spraying droplets of water across the yard, and Kilani experienced her first moment of joy since Alrec's departure.

"Good boy," she said, petting his wet fur as she sat beside him. "Wait...you're a boy, right?" Peeking, she confirmed with a nod. "Yep, a boy. Now, what are we going to call you?"

The mongrel just stared at her before craning his head and uttering a high-pitched sound.

"Well, you're more a dog than a wolf, aren't you?" Standing, she scratched behind his ears. "I'll think of something. In the meantime, come on inside. I'm going to dry you off, and you're going to cuddle with me. You're going to be a poor substitute, but you'll have to do."

His paws echoed on her wooden floor as she brought him inside and toweled him dry. After crawling into bed, she patted the covers, and he jumped in with her, barking before shimmying against her legs atop the sheets.

"I miss him so much," she whispered, slowly stroking the wolf's head. "Will it always hurt like this?"

Her new friend only whimpered before placing his chin on her thigh and closing his eyes. Sighing, Kilani blew out the candle and did the same.

Chapter 22

A few weeks later, Kilani finally began sleeping at night. Although she wasn't sleeping through the *entire* night, there were times when her brain allowed her to let go of her yearning and recharge. Having a warm body next to her was comforting, and she cherished her new companion even though she inwardly chided herself for capitulating so quickly. Perhaps Alrec had softened her. Regardless, she loved the little bugger and was extremely thankful for his presence in her small home.

One night, she was jolted from a deep sleep by the wolf's low growl. Swiping her hair from her face, she rose and pointed at his nose.

"Don't bark, okay? I'm going to go look around, and I'll leave the door cracked. If I need you, I'll call you, but otherwise, stay inside."

The wolf whimpered.

"I don't want you to get hurt." Placing a kiss between his ears, she grabbed the spear by the door placed her hand on the knob. Inhaling a deep breath, she slowly pulled it open.

Broad shoulders trekked toward her, illuminated by the full moon, and Kilani's breath caught in her throat. Stepping onto the soft grass, she whispered, "Alrec?"

His large frame continued to advance, and she rubbed her eyes, telling herself she was still asleep and dreaming. Holding up her hand, she shook her head. "No."

He froze, his features unreadable in the dim light as her chin slightly wobbled. "Don't come any closer. Please..."

Lifting his hand to the back of his neck, he massaged the weary muscles. "Uh...I was rather hoping for a more receptive greeting."

Shocked laughter exited her throat as she shook her head. "This is a dream, Kilani. You're going to wake up and it will be morning..."

"Sweetheart," he called, sliding the pack from his shoulders and dropping it to the ground before continuing to walk forward...one tentative step...then another... "It's me. You're not dreaming."

"Don't give me hope," she rasped, closing her eyes as she tried to discern reality from the surreal. "I just learned how to function without hope...I can't go back..." Lifting her lids, his handsome features came into focus as he stopped several feet away.

Lowering to one knee, he extended his hand and beckoned to her. "I learned to live that way too, but it was no way to live, little one. We deserve better. We deserve *more*. Let me give it to you." He shook his hand, and Kilani felt her heart swell with love.

"Alrec," she whispered, taking a hesitant step forward. "You came back to me?"

"I came back to you," he said with a nod. "Come on, little one. I don't want to live one more moment without touching you." Extending his fingers, he smiled. "Goddess, I missed you."

A strangled cry left her lips as she threw down the spear and broke into a full-on sprint. Alrec's deep laughter echoed off the trees as she bolted into his arms, knocking the wind out of him as they both tumbled to the ground. Straddling him as his back splayed over the grass, she rained ardent kisses over every inch of his face.

"*Oh my god*," she breathed in between the heated kisses. "I never thought I'd see you again. How did you...? Where did you...? Why did you...?"

Chuckling, he thrust his fingers in her hair, lifting her head so he could smile into her eyes. "There's time for that, little one. Let's just say I was miserable without you—and a pretty terrible soldier—so Latimus secured another position for me."

"Another position? Out here?"

"Out here, Kilani. In the home where we fell in love and where we'll create our future. If you'll have me." Embracing her, he rose to sit on the grass, and she wrapped her legs around his waist, determined to hold on for dear life so he'd never leave again.

"I'll have you," she murmured, resting her forehead to his and brushing a kiss over his broad lips. "But will you have me? I feel like you're sacrificing so much to live with me in a secluded cabin in the woods—"

His lips consumed hers, cutting off the words as she groaned with desire. Opening, she let him plunder her, sliding her tongue over his in return, reveling in his taste. His tongue swept every crevice of her mouth before he pulled back to place a trail of soft kisses over her bottom lip.

"I can't live without you, little one," he murmured, the words vibrating against her swollen lips. "You're stuck with me. But we're going to have to expand the house and improve the plumbing. Thankfully, I can restock on supplies when I return to Astaria."

Her pounding heart turned to stone in her chest. "When you return?"

"Once every six months, sweetheart. That's all. Otherwise, I'm yours for eternity."

"Alrec…" Stroking his face, her eyes darted over his austere features, deep brown eyes, and the sexy growth of stubble along his jaw. "My very own Vampyre. Perhaps I *did* do something right in my godforsaken life after all."

Tossing back his head, he broke into a blissful laugh. "Perhaps you did, sweetheart." Running his hand over her hair, affection swam in his eyes.

A bark sounded behind them, and Alrec arched a brow, craning his neck to look at the wolf.

"I…uh…" Clearing her throat, she shrugged. "I adopted a wolf. He was the runt and abandoned by his pack. It seemed fitting."

Eyes sparkling with mirth, he asked, "What's his name?"

Kilani bit her lip. "Dog."

Laughing, Alrec shook his head. "Creative."

"Hey, it was the best I could come up with since I was stuck here in this lonely cabin with a broken heart."

Reverently gazing at her, Alrec drew the pad of his finger across her jaw. "I thought you never got lonely."

"Not until I fell in love with a Vampyre with a fantastic ass who installed mediocre plumbing. It was all downhill after that."

Narrowing his eyes, he planted his hand on the ground and pushed to his feet, holding her tight as her legs clung to his waist.

"Mediocre plumbing, huh?" he teased, nipping her nose as he strode toward the house. "I'll show you mediocre, woman. I'm going to install the best damn system you've ever seen."

Sighing, she rested her cheek against his chest, inhaling his scent as he carried her inside. "So romantic. And if you do it naked, I'll be even happier."

Alrec's laughter bounded through the home as he tried to close the door. Dog uttered some high-pitched cries, and Kilani peered over Alrec's shoulder.

"You've got to stay outside for now, boy. My Vampyre's going to give me some hot, sexy lovin'. We'll let you in after."

"The dog is *not* sleeping on our bed," he muttered, closing the door as Dog whimpered outside.

"Um, yeah, I said that too, but he grows on you like a bad fungus. Trust me, he's going to end up sleeping with us."

Striding to the bed, Alrec lowered her before sliding over her and aligning their bodies. "Honestly, sweetheart, I just don't care right now." Cementing his lips to hers, he thrust his tongue inside her mouth, drawing her into a dizzying kiss.

They tore at their clothes, tossing them aside until all that remained was their unsated lust and unwavering adoration. Staring deep into her eyes, Alrec cupped her shoulders, anchoring her as his shaft searched for her wet core. Gliding the tip of his cock through her slickness, he began to press inside. Kilani's swollen lips fell open in a silent cry, so thankful to have him home.

"I love you," she whispered, arching to meet his careful thrusts.

"I love you, little one."

Undulating his firm hips, her magnificent Vampyre took her to the edge of ecstasy and beyond as she accepted she would spend the rest of eternity with her soul mate after all.

And once they were sated and spent, Kilani padded to the door and let Dog inside...where he promptly carved out a spot at the foot of their entwined legs and fell asleep.

For Kilani, the possibility of the future they would build was brighter than any she could've imagined all those desolate years ago at Uteria. She'd had the strength to make a choice one night after a hard-fought battle, and the Universe had rewarded her with more than she'd ever dreamed.

It was the first of many happy endings upon Etherya's Earth.

Epilogue

Two weeks after Alrec's return, he held Kilani's hand as they strolled toward the river. Dog trotted by their side, tongue lolling from his mouth as he panted. When they reached the spot where they'd shared their first kiss, Alrec drew to a stop and pulled her close.

"Ready, little one?"

Her vibrant beam all but melted his heart. "Ready."

Staring into each other's eyes, they repeated vows written long ago—some by Slayer soothsayers, some by Vampyre archivists—all meaningful to the two immortals who spoke them so reverently. After promising to love and cherish each other, they spoke the final declarations.

"I, Alrec, take you as my bonded mate, for all eternity."

"I, Kilani, take you as my husband for as long as we shall inhabit the realm."

Although each species had different terms for mates—"bonded" for Vampyres, and the more traditional "husband" and "wife" for Slayers—they each expressed the same sentiment. The promises were solemn commitments to be honored with care.

Leaning down, Alrec kissed his bonded mate, sealing their vows as Dog barked beside them. Giggling, she broke the kiss to tell the dog to hush before rising to her toes and drawing Alrec into another tender kiss.

"I swear, he really is a sweetheart. You're going to fall in love with him. Trust me."

Chuckling, Alrec pecked her lips before threading their fingers and squeezing. "We'll see." They resumed strolling along the river as he prepared himself to bring up the topic weighing on his mind. "You know, raising a dog is good practice for having a child."

Her eyes sparkled as she grinned up at him. "Is that so?"

"Mm-hmm." Their hands swung between them as he pondered how far to push. "I'd like to have one with you, sweetheart...if you're open to it. Latimus could help us adopt whenever we decide to take that step."

"A Vampyre child," she murmured, eyes narrowing. "I never imagined that for myself."

Disappointment coursed through him before her lips curved. "But I never imagined falling madly in love with a Vampyre, and that's turned out pretty well, so I'm definitely open."

"Yeah?"

"Yeah," she said with a nod. "Let's settle in here for a few decades and let you get comfortable with the new assignment. I'm *obviously* going to accompany you on your scouting missions. It's the perfect opportunity to use my skills, and I can protect you since I'm the superior warrior between us."

"Obviously," he droned, rolling his eyes.

She snickered as he winked.

"I still have no desire to help Vampyres, but I have a desire to help *you*, so I see the benefit. Deamons are a threat to Slayers too, and if I can help defeat them, even at the hands of Vampyres, I'll do it."

"I'm honored to have you by my side," he said, drawing her close and placing a kiss on her hair. "We make a formidable team."

"That we do. And once we're settled, I'd love to adopt a child with you, Alrec." Halting, she faced him and rose to her toes. "We're going to have a family. It's more than I thought I'd ever have. Thank you."

Embracing her, he allowed himself another kiss before they both turned to face the river. Drawing her into his side, he rested his cheek against her temple as they gazed at the gurgling water. Dog sat beside them, nuzzling Kilani's leg as she burrowed into his embrace, and Alrec felt a moment of vivid harmony.

Their lives together had truly begun.

Dog's place at Kilani's side during their nightly walks remained constant until he grew old and crossed the Rainbow Bridge into the Passage.

And until Kilani adopted another stray a year later. And another after her.

Such became their pattern as they settled into their new lives.

Until the day they adopted their son, and he became best friends with each new pet they welcomed into their quaint, loving home.

Alrec and his Slayer had so many milestones to accomplish, and he couldn't wait to conquer every single one with Kilani as his partner and one true mate.

∞

The goddess Etherya floated behind the dense thicket of trees, her white robes billowing in the soft wind as she observed the Vampyre soldier and the Slayer aristocrat. Never in her vast wisdom did she believe it possible two immortals from her now war-ravaged species would navigate their way to love so quickly. It was a much-needed omen of hope in a world that had devolved into evil and chaos.

Encouraged by the obvious affection shared between the two souls, Etherya closed her eyes and transported back to the Passage. She would clutch onto their affection as a beacon of faith and focus all her energy on manifesting reconciliation between Slayer Princess Miranda and Vampyre King Sathan.

The current state of war in their kingdoms resulted from the actions of previous generations, and perhaps the new rulers could be the ones to repair the damage. Only time would tell, and one thing Etherya possessed in her infinite providence was great patience.

So, she sat by the magnificent fountain in the misty, magical realm beyond her Earth and plotted...and waited...eager to observe—sometime in the not so distant future—the end of hatred between her beloved species.

Before You Go

Thank you so much for reading **The Dawn of Peace**! I've always wanted to write a prequel to this series and I hope you loved Kilani and Alrec as much as I did. Speaking of: would you like to read an *extra bonus epilogue* where you can meet their son? I wrote one for my newsletter subscribers. Just follow the link below to sign up for my newsletter and *you can download the bonus epilogue right away*. Happy reading!
Bonus Epilogue Download Link: https://BookHip.com/XGZWPKL

If you have a moment to leave a review for this book on your retailer's site, BookBub, Goodreads, or anywhere else you review, this indie author would be eternally grateful. Thank you!

Immortal Beginnings

Etherya's Earth, Book 4.5

By

Rebecca Hefner

Contents

Table of Contents
Title Page
Copyright Information
Dedication
Map of Etherya's Earth
Chapter 1
Chapter 2
Chapter 3
Chapter 4
Chapter 5
Chapter 6
Chapter 7
Chapter 8
Chapter 9
Chapter 10
Chapter 11
Epilogue
Before You Go
Also by Rebecca Hefner
About the Author

This book is a work of fiction. Names, characters, places and incidents are the product of the author's imagination and are used fictitiously. Any resemblance to actual events, locales or persons, living or dead, is coincidental.

Copyright © 2021 by Rebecca Hefner. All rights reserved, including the right to reproduce, distribute or transmit in any form or by any means.

Cover Design: Anthony O'Brien, www.BookCoverDesign.store
Proofreading & Editing: Bryony Leah, www.bryonyleah.com

Because you all know I love a sweet, steamy story about a male virgin...

Chapter 1

Four years after Evie defeated Crimeous...

Dragos smelled the smoke and stilled, the saw in his hand frozen against the wood he was cutting. His shed sat behind his modest one-bedroom cabin, and he liked to do projects there on his days off. Sometimes, he carved little trinkets. Other times, he built furniture when the need arose. Last week, he decided he needed another end table to compliment the one that already sat beside his couch, so he'd come to his shed to fashion it on the warm, sunny day.

Sniffing, he set down the saw and trailed outside, squinting against the rays of the bright sun. He'd lived in the Deamon caves for centuries and was used to squalid darkness. Perhaps one day his eyes would adjust to the freedom he now experienced. For now, he waited for his pupils to focus as he searched for the source of the smoke.

He kept a woodpile several feet from his shed, and his head snapped when the cut logs creaked before the pile toppled to the ground. Rushing toward the scattered logs, he observed orange flames envelop the pile of wood. Eyes widening, Dragos realized a little boy was trapped under the burning logs.

"Help!" he cried, his hand waving as he struggled to get free. "I'm stuck!"

"Hold on, son," Dragos called, rushing toward the blazing pile of wood. "I'm going to pull you out!"

Dragos reached between the logs, pulling them apart and tossing them aside as he dug toward the boy. Adrenaline surged as he blocked out the pain, feeling his skin burn as he inched closer to the child. As a former Deamon soldier, Dragos had felt pain many times and barely noticed the sensation. Grunting, he slung the wood pieces aside until he was standing over the boy. Recognizing him, Dragos extended his hand.

"Grab onto me, Galen," he said, reading the fear in the boy's ice-blue eyes. "I'm going to create leverage so I can wedge you out, okay?"

The boy nodded, his black hair swishing as he grabbed Dragos's hand.

"One...two...three!" Dragos cried, tugging him as he pushed the heavy log covering the boy's leg. Galen whimpered before dislodging his leg, and Dragos snatched him from the burning pile of wood. Lifting him, he jogged from the pile, carrying Galen as the boy coughed against his neck. Finally, Dragos felt they were far enough from the blazing embers to set Galen down. Resting him on the ground, he ran his hands over his neck, stomach, and legs, looking for burns.

"You're already healing," Dragos said, relief washing over him as the burned skin on Galen's leg transformed before his eyes. The skin turned from angry red blisters to a pale, smooth color in the span of moments. "Thank the goddess for Vampyres' self-healing properties. You're going to be fine, son."

"Galen!" a woman cried, and Dragos turned to see his neighbor Raina sprinting toward them. She fell to her knees, clutching Galen in a tight hug as she patted her hands over his back. "By the goddess, what happened? Are you okay?"

"I'm fine, Mom," he mumbled, drawing back and wiping his arm over his nose. "I'm sorry."

Dragos noticed the tears shimmering in his eyes and wanted to soothe him. "It's okay, son," he said, rubbing his shoulder. "I can always cut more wood."

"Oh, your arm," Raina said, concern in her tone as she touched his burned skin.

Dragos hissed and withdrew from her touch. The act went against his base instincts since he'd dreamed of Raina touching him almost every night since he purchased the plot of land next to her home, but the visions he had of Raina's soft fingers touching him weren't visions of pain. No—they were vivid images of her running those pink-painted nails over his skin as he moaned beneath her. Or above her. Hell, anywhere beside her as long as they were both naked. Clearing his throat, he shook his head to banish the images.

"I'll be fine," he said with a curt nod, hating to be short with her but uncomfortable with his body's reaction. His skin was more heated from her brief touch than from the flames that still burned on the nearby woodpile. His reaction to her was visceral, and his body hardened as she gazed at him with concern. "I'm just happy I was able to help Galen. Although Vampyres are self-healing, they still experience pain, and I didn't want him to suffer."

"Thank you, Dragos," Galen said softly.

"You're welcome."

"You have burns on both arms," Raina said, her blue eyes roving over his frame. "Are you hurt anywhere else? I don't have any salve, but I can get some from Sadie and apply it to your burns. Unfortunately, you won't heal as fast as my mischievous little boy here," she said, soothing Galen's hair as her expression grew stern. "Were you playing with matches again, young man? Do you remember what I told you would happen if I ever caught you with matches again?"

His lips formed a pout. "I can't play with my friends for two weeks."

"That's right. You're grounded for two weeks so you can think about your actions."

His eyes darted to Dragos before he sighed. "Okay. I'm really sorry, Dragos. I didn't mean to set your woodpile on fire."

"It's okay, and I'll be just fine. If you're bored while you're grounded, you can help me. That might be a fitting punishment for the crime." He smiled, attempting to reassure the boy. Hell, he was only a kid, and kids made mistakes. Replacing the wood he'd destroyed was an acceptable recompense for his mistake, and Dragos wouldn't mind the extra help. Glancing at the still-burning pile, his eyes narrowed. "I need to go grab my hose and put out the fire. It's contained to the pile, but I don't want it to ruin my grass."

"Oh, of course," Raina said, rising and helping Galen stand before extending her hand. Dragos clutched it and rose, cognizant of her soft palm against his calloused one. "I'm terribly sorry and still want to help you with those burns. It's the least I can do for saving my son."

"I'm fine, Raina," he said, lifting a hand. "But thank you. If you'll excuse me, I'm going to go hook up the hose. You stay away from those matches, Galen."

"Yes, sir," he called softly.

Dragos waved before pivoting and stalking back to his shed to find the hose. Once he located it, he hooked it up to the spigot attached to the back of his cabin and trailed to the burning pile of wood. Turning on the spray, he put out the fire, noting he'd have to insert some time into his schedule to replace the now-singed pieces once his arms healed. After the fire was out, he rolled up the hose and stuck it in his shed.

Glancing down, he observed the burns on his forearms. Second-degree, if he had to guess, which meant they would take a few days to heal.

Dragos was a laborer who worked in the weapons factory on the outskirts of the main square of Takelia, the compound he'd inhabited ever since Governor Evie fulfilled the prophecy and freed the Deamons from the rule of the Dark Lord Crimeous. He would still be able to use his singed arms and hands to assemble the weapons, although it would hurt like hell. Perhaps on his way home from work tomorrow evening he would pass by the clinic Sadie ran and see if they had any salve. Thanking the goddess he was only burned on his arms, Dragos admitted it could've been worse.

Glancing at the half-finished table in his shed, he decided he'd resume working on it once his arms healed. For now, he was going to let the adrenaline subside and relax on his day off.

After closing the shed door, he slowly trekked toward his cottage. Sensing a presence to his left, he glanced toward Raina's home. She stood on the grass where their properties connected, arms crossed over her chest as she slowly rubbed them. Although she was several yards away, he felt her gaze as if she were close enough to brush against him. Her curly light brown hair flitted in the breeze, making her look stunning in the late-afternoon sun. Lifting his hand, he gave a slight wave.

Her hand slowly lifted, waving back as she stood tall and firm. Dragos's throat bobbed as he stood frozen, wondering if she was going to approach him—perhaps to thank him again. It was the only reason he could fathom why the pretty widow would approach him. Never would she cross the chasm between them and tilt those full lips to his before begging him to kiss her. No matter how hard he dreamed or willed it to happen, it was impossible for a myriad of reasons.

First, her husband had been killed by Deamons in the war against Crimeous. By the very Deamons that comprised the army he used to fight for. It didn't matter that Dragos's position in the army was against his will or that he hadn't believed in Crimeous's cause. Dragos had been a Deamon soldier, and he'd been on the wrong side.

Queen Miranda and King Sathan, with their generous hearts and desire to unite the species, had offered Deamons the chance to live in their kingdom if they repented and disavowed any allegiance to Crimeous once he perished. That was an easy task for Dragos, and for his compliance he was allowed to hold a job in the immortal realm, although not as a soldier. Deamons weren't allowed to fight in the immortal army since it afforded them access to weapons and inside information the king and queen didn't want their former enemies to possess. But Deamons could hold jobs and exist in society as long as they embraced the kingdom and followed the law of the land. For a man who had never tasted freedom, those were small penances to pay, and Dragos was thankful to the royal leaders for their graciousness.

Still, Vampyres and Slayers—the original species of the immortal kingdom—needed time to accept their reformed enemies. Dragos understood peace took time and was happy to live on his small plot of land. Governor Evie assured repentant Deamons were able to get loans, and he'd secured one with his meager salary from the factory.

When he'd built his cottage and met the beautiful widow next door, along with her two boys, she informed him her husband was a soldier who'd been slain by Deamons in the final battle against Crimeous. Dragos had fought in that battle, and it was gruesome. Remorse washed over him as he'd stared into her eyes, wishing he could change his violent history. It would always be a stain upon his soul, although he'd had no other choice. Crimeous bred the Deamon race for the sole purpose of destroying the immortals of Etherya's Earth.

Returning to the moment, Dragos flashed Raina a soft smile before turning back to his cottage. Even if she could somehow get past the fact he'd been a member of the army responsible for her husband's death, there was another reason he could never have her: Dragos had no idea how to please a woman. Even though he'd lived centuries, Dragos only knew war and death. The women who had lived in the caves had also been prisoners of Crimeous and were kept separate from the soldiers. In fact, Dragos didn't have the first idea of how people connected sexually in their world. Of course, he understood the male penetrated the female with his cock, but how did the logistics truly work? He didn't understand the first thing about seduction or courting, and he had never kissed a woman. How did one go about initiating a kiss? It seemed extremely uncomfortable to him since he was rather shy and a bit stoic.

Sighing at his ineptitude, he stepped inside the cabin and located the half-drunk bottle of whiskey. It was a gift from Lila, the altruistic Vampyre aristocrat who'd taught him to read. She held literacy classes for all the reformed Deamons, and he was grateful to have acquired the skill. When he purchased his home, she'd given him the whiskey as a gift, and he'd thought her so kind. Pouring two fingers into a glass, he strode to the window and pulled back the curtain.

Raina no longer stood frozen atop the grass, and he closed his eyes, wishing she were still there. Wishing he could reach for her and slide his palms over her arms, drawing her close so he could bury his nose in her curls and kiss her soft hair. Lifting his lids, he held the whiskey, slowly sipping as he ran a finger over the smooth glass of the window.

"Raina," he whispered.

Her name was sweet upon his lips, and he doused it with a hefty sip. Wasting time daydreaming of touching someone who would never be his was futile. Tossing back the glass, he set it on the counter before heading to his tiny bathroom to see if he could scrounge up some sort of salve or lotion to squelch the stinging nerve endings under his burned skin.

Chapter 2

Raina, daughter of Tarth, widow of Soran, sat beside her son on the twin bed, gently stroking his arm. All signs of damage were healed, and she thanked the goddess he was okay.

"I'm not mad at you for grounding me, Mom," he said softly. His features were so much like Soran's, and her lips curved as she imagined how her bonded mate would've reacted to their son's transgressions. He would've reminded her boys were mischievous and must learn to navigate the world after making mistakes.

"Well, I'm glad to hear it. But you're still grounded." She winked to soften the blow.

"You're in trouble," her other son, Ekon, chimed from the twin bed across the room. He sang the taunting words before Raina shot him a glare.

"That's enough, Ekon, unless you want to be grounded too."

Ekon pulled the covers over his head and burrowed into the bed.

Pursing her lips to contain her chuckle, she smoothed her fingers over Galen's cheek. "Have sweet dreams, darling."

His lips formed a pout. "Ekon is annoying."

"Am not!" his brother called from across the room.

"Neither of you are annoying," Raina said, standing. "And you need to be nice to your little brother, Galen. He looks up to you."

"No, I don't!"

Raina grinned at Galen and leaned down to kiss his forehead. "Yes, he does," she whispered in his ear. "Remember that, dear. Good night."

"Night, Mom."

Raina strode to Ekon's bed and tugged down the covers to smack a kiss on his head as he giggled. "Good night, sweet boy."

"Night, Mama."

Her heart swelled at the tender tone of his voice, and she exited the room, making sure the door was cracked so she could hear them if they called her. They lived in a modest two-bedroom home Raina had purchased with her bonded mate's pension after he was killed in the war against Crimeous. Before his death, they had lived on the Vampyre compound of Naria, but the house held too many memories for Raina to bear. Moving to Takelia had offered a fresh start, and she'd jumped at the opportunity.

She'd known the possibility of living among Deamons would be high since Queen Miranda and King Sathan had offered reformed Deamons refuge at Takelia. It was a tough pill to swallow since her bonded had been killed by Deamon soldiers, but the need for a fresh start outweighed her aversion to Deamons. Her former home was filled with so many memories, and she felt she might drown in them if she stayed.

Her bonded's pension now supported them, and the monthly stipends were enough to keep them afloat. One day, Raina would consider getting a job—perhaps as a seamstress or servant in Takelia's governor's mansion—but for now, her first priority was being a mother to her eight- and ten-year-old sons. Soran would want them to be raised to become good men, as he had been, and she would ensure it.

Trailing to the small kitchen, Raina cleaned the counter and tidied up before heading to her room. The queen-size bed beckoned to her, and she acknowledged her exhaustion. The adrenaline that had seized her veins during Galen's incident with the woodpile had now worn off, and she longed to fall into a deep sleep. Strange, as she hadn't slept very well since her bonded's passing, but perhaps tonight would be different.

After discarding her clothes, she slipped a comfortable T-shirt over her functional cotton panties and headed to the small attached bathroom to prep for bed. As she slid the brush over her teeth, she studied herself in the mirror, wondering what people saw when they looked at her.

What Dragos saw when he gazed at her with those dark, swirling eyes...

They were mesmerizing, and Raina had been taken with them from the first moment she met her quiet neighbor. He'd been trimming the hedges between their houses, and she'd walked over to introduce herself. Grinning at her reflection, she delved into the memory.

"Hello," Raina called, lifting her hand. "You must be my new neighbor."

Sweat glistened upon the man's forehead, and he wiped it with his arm, bare above his gloved hand. Dark, almost black, eyes gazed at her as he stood silent.

"I...uh, I'm Raina," she said, thrusting out her hand. "I live next door."

His gaze fell toward her outstretched hand, studying it as if he wasn't sure what to do.

"You're supposed to shake it," she teased, reaching toward him. He recoiled slightly, and she stiffened. Perhaps he wasn't friendly and didn't want to be approached. "I'm sorry—"

"Dragos," he almost grunted, shifting the shears to his other hand so he could shake hers. He bit the thick glove with straight white teeth and dragged it off before taking her hand. His palm was calloused and sweaty as it slid over hers, and the contact sent a jolt of awareness through her frame. "Sorry. I didn't learn many manners in the Deamon caves, but I'm trying."

"You're doing just fine," she said, noting the slight tips of his ears that indicated his Deamon heritage. "Nice to meet you. Were you rescued in the caves after the war?"

He released her hand before clearing his throat. "I was a soldier in Crimeous's army. Once we were liberated, I pledged my allegiance to Queen Miranda and King Sathan."

"Oh," she said, feeling the anger and sadness well. So many had survived the war, and yet her bonded mate had perished, reminding her of the fickleness of the Universe. "I see."

His deep eyes regarded her as he slowly blinked several times. "I understand it must be disconcerting to have a Deamon move in next door. I assure you, I only want peace and won't bother you and your family."

Her eyebrows lifted. "You know I have a family?"

"I've seen your boys playing in the yard. Figured you and your husband might worry, but I assure you, they are safe from me."

"Oh, I..." She crossed her arms and ran her fingers over her neck, attempting to still the emotion that welled in her throat. "My husband...well, my bonded, as we call them in the Vampyre kingdom...he died in the battle where Governor Evie killed Crimeous."

Dragos's handsome features contorted with empathy, and he tilted his head as he studied her. "I'm so very sorry, Raina. It was a gruesome battle. Many died that day to secure peace."

Swallowing thickly, she nodded, leaving the obvious unsaid: her bonded had perished, but Dragos had survived.

He emitted a sigh and rested his hand on his hip. "If you or your boys need anything, please don't hesitate to ask. I'm pretty handy and can fix things around the house. Or if you need yard work, I can do that too. Whatever you need."

Tears puddled in her eyes at his kindness, and she struggled with the juxtaposition of the fact the considerate man standing before her was a soldier in the war that had taken her bonded. By the goddess, was this man the one who had fired the fatal blow from the eight-shooter that claimed Soran's life?

"The questions are maddening, but I find they only lead to more questions," he said softly, "and never any answers. At some point, I told myself to stop asking so I wouldn't go insane."

Compassion swamped her at his heartbreaking expression. Recovering from war was never easy, and he likely had his own demons to struggle with, as she had hers. Deciding to be cordial, she smiled and gave a slight nod. "Good advice. I think I'll take it."

His full lips curved, transforming his features into something quite breathtaking. Raina's pulse hammered as she realized something profound: she felt desire for the kind, attractive Deamon who now lived next door. It was the first twinge of desire she'd felt since her bonded passed away several years ago, and it made her slightly uncomfortable. Feeling the urge to run, she cleared her throat and began to back away.

"Nice to meet you, Dragos. The offer is open if you need anything as well. I'm a terrible cook since Vampyres sustain themselves on Slayer blood, but I could always try. And thank you for your kind offer. I'll leave you to your work." Lifting her hand, she waved before pivoting and rushing inside.

Once home, she closed the door and leaned back against it, covering her heart with her hand as it pounded in her chest. "What the hell, Raina?" she whispered.

The house was silent since her boys were at school, and the silence held no answer. Eventually, her pulse returned to normal, but the image of her neighbor's austere features remained emblazoned in her mind long after their encounter was over.

Returning to the moment, Raina gazed into her dark blue eyes in the bathroom mirror, noting how the lighter flecks seemed to glow with desire. Rinsing the toothbrush, she set it aside before inching closer to the reflection. Lifting her hand, she gently trailed her fingers over her lips. She had only ever pressed them to one other man's, and Raina had loved her bonded mate to distraction. But he was gone, and she had learned long ago that living in the past only created heartache and despair.

Clicking off the bathroom light, she padded to the bed and sat on the plush comforter. Reaching toward the nightstand, she pulled open the drawer and dug until she found the letter buried deep in the back crevice. Unfolding the wrinkled paper, she read it in the soft glow of the bedroom lamp.

My Darling Raina,

Life isn't always fair, especially for a soldier in a world as consumed by war as ours. So, I'm leaving you this letter, tucked into a corner of our nightstand where I know you'll find it if I'm gone. Death can never diminish my love for you, even if I am in the Passage and you are still upon Etherya's Earth. Our boys need you, Raina, and if I'm taken from you, please remember that you can only instill them with love if you allow it for yourself as well.

If something happens to me, my love, please find the will to love again. It won't diminish what we had. I can only be happy in the Passage if I know you are happy too. Create new memories and share the ones we had. Both are important and imperative if you are to build a happy home with our sons. Know that I will be the first to cry with joy and hope if you allow yourself to live a full life. You deserve nothing less, and I give you my blessing, Raina.

Until we meet again...

Your first love, Soran

The letter was a manifestation of how well her bonded knew her. Raina would've been content to live the rest of eternity alone had he not left it behind. After all, finding someone new—*loving* someone new—seemed wrong when they'd shared such joy in their close-knit family.

But her bonded had been wise, and even now, only a few years after his death, Raina was consumed by loneliness. She missed being held by someone...missed sharing laughter and pain. There was something so comforting in having a partner, and she longed to have one again.

Placing the letter back in the drawer, she closed it before sliding beneath the sheets and clicking off the lamp. There, under the soft covers, she glided her hand over her stomach, slowly inching her fingers under the soft fabric of her underwear. Once there, she pressed into the supple flesh and bit her lip, admitting in the dark what she sometimes couldn't admit in the light of day: she also missed being touched. Missed being held by a man as he looked deep into her eyes and brought her to the peak of ultimate pleasure.

Raina's eyes snapped open as she gasped, realizing it was Dragos's face she was imagining as she touched herself beneath her panties. Rapid heartbeats drummed throughout her entire body as she pressed her fingers to the rapidly swelling bundle of nerves at the hood of her slick folds. Giving in to the pleasure, she closed her eyes and began to circle the taut nub, allowing herself to envision the handsome Deamon as she brought herself to the edge and plunged into the pleasurable abyss.

Chapter 3

The next day, Dragos returned home from the weapons factory and collapsed on the couch. His arms burned like hell, and he should've stopped at the clinic on the way home to get some salve. But he'd been so tired after work—most likely from gritting his teeth in pain as he assembled the weapons—that he'd beelined straight home, craving peace and solace. Puffing out a breath, he closed his eyes and relaxed before the soft knocks permeated the air.

"Dragos?" Raina's melodious voice called through the wood of his front door. "I saw you return home. I hope I'm not bothering you."

His heart leapt in his chest as he rose, and he steeled himself to be in her presence. After such a long day, and with his arms slightly burning, he was worried he wouldn't be able to control his reaction toward her. Would she sense his desire and be disgusted? Or worse, angry? Vowing not to let that happen, Dragos inhaled a deep breath and opened the door.

"Hi," she said, her white fangs flashing under the late-afternoon sun. "I hope I'm not imposing, but I stopped by Sadie's clinic today." She lifted a white tube and shook it. "This is some healing salve with some fancy chemicals she and Nolan concocted. She says it will soothe and heal your burns expeditiously."

Taken by her kindness, he extended his hand. "Thank you. That's very thoughtful."

"Oh, I..." She held the tube tight and hesitated. "I thought I might rub it on for you. If you want me to."

Dragos felt his throat bob as he stared into her eyes. Disbelief coursed through him at the offer. Although he'd love nothing more than to have her delicate fingers rub salve on his skin, he wondered if she knew he'd never been touched in a moment of healing or kindness. No—Dragos's skin had only felt the crush of war and the slice of weapons.

"Never mind then," she said, offering him the tube. "I don't want to make you uncomfortable—"

"It's fine," he all but grunted, stepping back and gesturing to her with his head. "Come in."

She shuffled inside and glanced around his cabin before grinning. "You have a nice place."

"Thank you," he said, closing the door before trailing toward the couch. "We can sit here."

Nodding, she lowered to the sofa as he sat beside her. Her eyes darted over his arms, and she tilted her head. "I think it will be easier if you take off your shirt," she murmured, eyes narrowed as she assessed. "Your wounds stretch above your sleeves."

"Okay," he said, voice raspy from arousal and fear. Perhaps it was strange to feel fear when one was about to be voluntarily touched for the first time, but he felt it all the same. Tugging the shirt over his head, he lay it on the arm of the couch before facing her.

"Let's do your left arm first," she said, patting her thigh above her knee. "Rest your palm here, and I'll work the salve over your skin."

Dragos slid his palm over the soft fabric of her pants, struggling to calm his erratic heartbeat. Raina opened the tube and squirted a portion on her fingers before setting it on the couch. Smiling into his eyes, she touched her fingers to his forearm and began to gently rub.

Dragos expelled a heavy breath, and her eyes flew to his, a question in them as she froze. "Does it hurt?"

"No," he rasped.

Craning her head, she softly asked, "Is this all right? You seem uncomfortable."

He nodded. "It's just the first time."

"The first time?"

"That anyone has voluntarily touched me," he said, the low timbre of his voice encircling them. "It is…strange."

"Oh," she breathed, her luminous eyes glowing with recognition. "I can stop if you wish—"

"No, please continue," he interjected, licking his suddenly dry lips. "I appreciate your kindness."

Her plump lips curved into a smile before she continued, slowly moving her fingers over his damaged skin. "It is I who should be thanking you. You didn't even hesitate before jumping into a burning pile of wood to help my son. It was very brave."

"I was honored to help him," he said, mesmerized by the feel of the soft strokes against his arm. "I would be honored to help any of you anytime, Raina. I wish you would ask me to do more. I see you carting things around the yard and hauling brush, which I could easily do for you instead."

"Vampyre women are made of stern mettle, Dragos," she said, arching a brow. "You don't think me weak, do you?"

"Of course not," he said, his eyes darting over her broad shoulders and firm frame. Vampyres were well-built creatures, and she was tall and lithe. But he still had a few inches on her, and his muscular body could haul anything she needed. "I just want to help. Since…" He trailed off, not wanting to bring up her husband's death.

"Since my bonded died," she murmured, gaze affixed to his arm as she massaged in the salve. "You can't blame yourself. Hell, I can't blame myself either. It's a lesson that's easy to know here, but not here." She tapped her temple and then her chest before returning to her ministrations.

Aching to comfort her, he slid his fingers under the smooth skin of her chin. She inhaled a quick breath before he tilted her face to stare into her stunning eyes.

"It wasn't your fault, but I can't say the same. I'm so sorry, Raina. I wish I could change my past. I admire you for not hating me. Most people would, I imagine. It exemplifies your kindness, and I am grateful."

Her eyebrows drew together as she shook her head. "We are both the victims of senseless war, but not the transgressors. Hating you would be as pointless as hating the breeze on a rainy day.

Sometimes, one gets stuck in a life they never chose. I cannot blame you for that."

Dragos inhaled shaky breaths as the skin of her chin heated his fingers.

Encircling his wrist, she drew his hand down and placed the palm over her other thigh. "Let's do this one now." Squeezing some more salve onto her fingers, she began to rub it on his other arm.

Dragos watched the smooth motions and did his best not to squirm underneath her touch. Her tender strokes ignited every cell in his body, and he wanted nothing more than to pull her close and press his lips to hers. Would she taste as she smelled? Like blossoming flowers and warm spring afternoons? Feeling his lips twitch, he realized he was now waxing poetic about her smell and almost snickered at his silly words. Yet if anyone represented the freshness and beauty of spring, it was his stunning neighbor.

"There," she said, drawing back and giving a nod. "All done. I think you'll feel much better in the morning. According to Sadie, your wounds should heal by then, and you'll be good as new."

"Thank you, Raina," he said, lifting his arms and scrutinizing his now glossy skin. "I truly appreciate your help."

"It's nothing." Rising, she set the salve on his coffee table. "Keep that for next time, although I hope there isn't a next time. But with my precocious little boys, you never know." She gave a cheeky grin and pulled a tissue from the box to wipe the salve from her fingers. "Should I...?"

"Just leave the tissue on the table. I have to tidy up anyway." Standing, he walked her toward the front door. "How is Galen taking the grounding?"

"Oh, he's fine. I think the worst punishment is being stuck at home with Ekon. The most annoying thing to a ten-year-old boy is forced proximity to his little brother."

Chuckling, Dragos pulled open the door and held it for her as she stepped onto the stoop. "Good to know. My offer for him to chop wood with me was genuine. It might be good for him to learn how, and it would help me replenish the pile."

"Then I'll send him over on Saturday morning at nine o'clock sharp."

"Perfect." Leaning against the frame, he basked in her presence before her departure. "Thank you, Raina—"

Lifting her finger, she pressed it to his lips, causing his body to instantly harden. "One does not need to thank their neighbor for kindness. It should be automatic."

He stood frozen, unable to respond as his pulse throbbed and his cock stood to attention in his black work pants. If her eyes darted south, she'd certainly be able to see his arousal, but they were latched onto his as they stared into each other's souls.

Slowly, she dragged the pad of her finger across his bottom lip, back and forth, as her cheeks flushed under the blue sky. "Soft," she whispered as he stood agonized by her ardent caress. "Somehow, I knew they'd be soft, even if their owner is stoic and firm."

"Knew what would be soft?" he rasped.

"Your lips, Dragos," she murmured, tenderly rubbing them once more before withdrawing her hand. Lifting her chin, she appeared so regal as she stood tall and proud. "Good night. I hope you sleep well."

"Good night," he murmured, stunned he could still speak after she'd so reverently touched his lips.

She trailed away, and he watched her for as long as he could...until she reached her home and disappeared through the front door.

Stepping back, Dragos closed the door and ran his thumb over his lip. It was slightly slick from the remnants of the healing salve left there when Raina had skated her fingers over his trembling flesh. Closing his eyes, he rubbed the wetness, wishing it were her tongue instead of his finger causing the friction. Unable to control his massive erection, he padded to the bedroom and removed his clothing. Lying atop the bed, he gripped his engorged shaft and began to tug. Raina's smiling face appeared beneath his closed eyelids, and he imagined her hands covered in the glossy salve as she stroked his turgid cock.

"Oh, god..." he moaned, the ministrations of his hand rhythmic and fast against his straining skin. "Raina..."

In his vision, she leaned over and took him in her mouth, dousing his sensitive flesh with her saliva as she purred with approval. Gasping, Dragos lost himself in the vision before he began to come, shooting jets of release over his abdomen and chest. Growling with lust, he emptied himself, wishing he could explode in her sweet mouth...or her gorgeous body. Sighing, he threw his arm over his eyes and relaxed on the bed. Exhaustion still claimed him, but now it was from arousal rather than labor.

Yes, desire for the Vampyre who lived next door was rapidly consuming his brain, and Dragos had no idea what the hell to do about it.

Chapter 4

On Saturday morning, Galen scampered toward Dragos as he prepared the wood that needed to be chopped. Grinning at the boy, Dragos tilted his head.

"Are you ready to help me, son?"

"Yes," he said, furiously nodding. "It's way better than being stuck at home with Ekon. He's driving me crazy." He dramatically rolled his eyes.

"Well, I'm happy to have the help, but remember, family is important. I never had a family and always wonder what it would be like."

Galen squinted as he pondered. "It's okay, I guess. Mom is pretty awesome, and Ekon is *sometimes*."

Chuckling, Dragos reached for the axe. "Fair enough." Gripping the handle, he rotated the axe so Galen could assess it. "This is very sharp and I'm going to show you how to use it. It's heavy, but I think you can handle it."

"I can," he said, puffing out his chest. "I'm strong and will be a great soldier like my father one day."

"I have no doubt. Step back and watch me cut a few, and then we'll have you try it, okay?"

Galen nodded and backed away as Dragos faced the wood ready to be chopped upon the stump. It was already a warm, sunny day, so he set down the axe and took off his shirt before beginning to chop. He split several pieces of wood before turning to Galen.

"Ready to try?"

"Yes." Stepping forward, Galen took the axe and Dragos directed him. Eventually, the boy picked up a nice rhythm, and Dragos was pleased.

"You're doing great, son. I'm going to set up another stump and grab my other axe from the shed. That way, we can chop together. We'll chop some for your mom too, so she has it for the fireplace."

"Okay," he said, lifting the axe high and splitting the wood before him.

After grabbing the axe and setting up another stump, Dragos and Galen worked for over an hour to chop enough wood to replenish his woodpile and stock some for Raina's home. When they had enough, Dragos addressed the boy.

"One more log and we're good, I think. Ready?"

Galen nodded before splitting the log before him. Grinning, Dragos lifted the axe high to chop his final piece of wood for the day.

Raina finished her chores around the house and realized Galen had been at Dragos's for over an hour. Wanting to check on him, she made sure Ekon was settled in his room before heading over. As she approached, her breath caught in her throat at the sight before her.

Dragos stood tall, sweat glistening over his solid chest and muscular arms as he held the axe high. A muscle ticked in his jaw before he swung the axe through the wood before him, splitting it as effectively as her heart split in her chest. It cracked and crumbled in a thousand different shards as she realized she desperately wanted to make love to her neighbor.

Swallowing thickly, she cleared her throat, and they both pivoted.

"Hey, Mom," Galen said, waving. "We chopped enough for our house too."

"Oh, that's lovely. Thank you." Stepping closer, she smiled at Dragos. "You didn't have to do that."

"No problem at all," he said, lifting a shoulder. "Galen was a huge help."

Her son beamed, and Raina understood how special it must be for him to receive Dragos's praise. The lack of an adult male influence in his life was noticeable, and although Raina tried her best to fill the void, there was only so much she could do.

"Will you come over for dinner tonight?" she asked before she even realized the words had leaped from her throat. "It's the least I can do for the extra wood."

"Oh, um…sure," Dragos said, wiping his forehead with his arm. "If it's not too much trouble. I know you only drink Slayer blood. I could bring something over—"

"I wouldn't be much of a host if I asked you to dinner and didn't cook, would I?" she teased. "I'm not a great cook, but I can scrounge something up. How about six o'clock?"

"That works. I look forward to it. I'll bring wine if you like. I have red and white in my stash."

"Red would be lovely. Maybe I'll make pasta. That can't be too difficult, right?"

"I love pasta," he said, his lips forming a smooth, sexy smile that made her insides tingle.

"Then it's a date." Extending her hands, she cupped Galen's shoulders. "Come now, let's leave Dragos to enjoy his day off. We'll see you tonight." Ushering her son from their work area, she led him home. Once inside, she placed her hand over her heart, feeling it beat in anticipation. "Well, Raina, you'd better figure out how to cook some damn pasta."

Laughing at her predicament, she gathered her boys to head to the market and purchase the ingredients…along with a cookbook to help her figure things out.

∞

By the time dinner rolled around, Raina was a nervous wreck. She fussed over the pots on her stove, hoping she wasn't burning the spaghetti. Was it possible to burn spaghetti from boiling it too much? She had no idea, but if anyone could manage that epic fail, she could. Realizing everything was ready, she flinched when the knock sounded on the front door.

"I'll get it," Ekon called, sprinting to the door and opening it wide. "Hey, Dragos. Mom is really stressed out, so we have to be quiet and leave her alone."

Rolling her eyes at her son's blatant honestly, she removed the apron and set it on the counter before trailing over to greet Dragos. "My son was *not* supposed to tell you that," she said, gently ruffling his hair. "I wanted you to think I was a magnificent cook who made everything with a snap of my fingers."

Chuckling, Dragos handed her the wine. "I'm sure it will taste just fine. We didn't exactly have gourmet meals in the Deamon caves. The food out here in the immortal world is much better. I'm excited to enjoy a nice meal."

Raina led him to the kitchen as Ekon scampered off to find his brother. "I'll go ahead and open this if you want a glass."

"Sure."

Locating the corkscrew, Raina opened the bottle and poured two glasses. Lifting it, she swirled and inhaled the aroma. "I haven't had good wine in a while."

"Me neither." He raised his glass to hers and asked, "Should we toast?"

"Yes." Gently biting her lip, she pondered. "To my lovely neighbor who saved my son. I'm very happy you moved in next door."

His dark eyes darted between hers. "So am I," he said softly before clinking his glass with hers. "To my magnificent neighbor. I'm honored to be invited to your home."

The words ignited sparks in every part of her body as she took a sip of the full-bodied wine. "Magnificent is a bit much. But thank you anyway."

Amusement entered his eyes, along with a twinge of...lust? "It's the perfect word for you, Raina," he murmured, his deep baritone caressing her skin.

"Mom!" Galen cried, interrupting the intimate moment.

Frustrated, she glanced down. "Yes?"

"Ekon stole my toy soldiers again!"

"Did not!"

"Okay, that's enough from both of you, or we'll skip dinner and go right to bed," she warned in her stern mom tone. "Are we clear?"

"Yes, ma'am," they said in unison.

"Good. Why don't you give Dragos a tour of the house and the back yard while I set the table for dinner?"

"I'll show you my treehouse," Galen said, grabbing his hand. "It's awesome."

"It's *our* treehouse," Ekon chimed, crossing his arms over his chest.

Setting his glass on the kitchen island, Dragos extended his hand. "Show me," he said, clutching Ekon's hand before the boys led him outside.

Raina watched them trail away, pursing her lips at how natural Dragos was with her sons. For someone who'd been raised in the Deamon caves to be a vicious soldier, he was quite gentle and kind. Sighing, Raina realized he would most likely be that way in bed. Tender and thoughtful as he made love to her. As she set the table and loaded the food into serving dishes, she pondered.

When she'd applied the salve to his arms, Dragos said he'd never been voluntarily touched. Did this mean he had never been with a woman? If not, was it by choice or because he truly didn't crave affection? Raina had no idea, but she felt a pressing need to find out. Of course, that was terribly nosy, and she didn't want to make Dragos feel uncomfortable. Fortunately, her boys dragged him back into the kitchen, so she released the musings as they sat for dinner.

According to Dragos, the food was wonderful, which made her chest swell with pride. Pleasing him made her feel...accomplished...worthy...*feminine*. It might be strange, but she felt it nonetheless.

Once they were finished with dinner, the boys retreated to their rooms to play before bed. Raina refilled their wineglasses and led Dragos to the living room sofa. Collapsing on the soft cushions, she grinned at him as he sat beside her.

"Well, you survived family dinner with the boys. You might deserve a medal."

He smiled as he swirled the wine. "It's been a fun night. I'm so used to being alone. It's nice to have some companionship."

Raina studied him, wondering if he wished for a wife and family of his own. "Have you ever been in love, Dragos?"

His eyes grew wide, and she straightened, realizing how uncomfortable the question must be for him.

"I'm sorry. That was quite rude—"

"It's fine," he said, sliding his hand over the back of hers where it rested atop her thigh. "I was just surprised at the question. To answer it, no, I never have. There was no space for love or companionship in the Deamon army."

Raina contemplated as his warm skin covered hers. "But now you have your freedom. Surely, you want to find a mate and create a family."

His gaze lowered as he mulled. "I don't really know the first thing about having a family. I think some people are meant to be alone."

Sadness swamped her at the heart-wrenching statement. She set her glass on the side table before leaning forward and cupping his jaw. "If it's their choice, then, yes, I guess being alone is all right. But you could choose a different path."

His tongue darted out to bathe his lips, and Raina felt a gush of arousal between her thighs. "It's hard to navigate something so unknown," he said softly.

Encircling his glass, she set it on the coffee table before palming his handsome face. Staring deep into his limitless eyes, she asked, "Have you ever kissed a woman, Dragos?"

His throat bobbed, and the pulse at his neck fluttered. "No. As I told you, I've never been voluntarily touched...until you applied the salve."

Her lips curved as she ran her thumbs over his cheeks. "I want you to kiss me," she whispered.

A heavy breath rushed from his lungs as he stiffened. "I don't know how."

Leaning forward, she barely grazed the tip of his nose with hers. "I'll show you."

Dragos lifted his hand and slid his fingers over her jaw. Touching the pad of his thumb to her lower lip, he gently dragged it back and forth, setting her body on fire. "I never dreamed you'd offer to kiss me." His eyebrows drew together. "Actually, that's a lie. I've dreamed of it about a million times."

Emitting a soft chuckle, she inched forward. "Me too. Do it quietly so the boys don't hear, okay?" She waggled her brows. "I need them to stay occupied for several minutes."

Gliding his free hand across her neck, he threaded his fingers through the hair at her nape. It created a slight tugging sensation that shot flashes of desire to her core. Clenching tighter, he drew her close. "Raina," he whispered.

"Kiss me, Dragos," she murmured against his lips.

He groaned, the sound low and primal as it vibrated through every cell in her body. Then he tugged her close and pressed his lips to hers.

Chapter 5

Dragos closed his eyes and touched his lips to Raina's. The darkness behind his closed lids warned him this might be a dream. If so, he never wanted to wake up.

A groan rumbled deep in his chest as he pulled her closer, gently moving his lips over hers. A high-pitched mewl escaped her throat and shot straight to his cock, causing it to rise firm and proud in his pants. Aching to touch every pore of her soft skin, he slid his hand to her thigh and drew her leg across his body. She wrapped around him, inching closer until her mound was pressed against his aching shaft.

"Oh, yessss..." she moaned, squirming against him as he struggled to retain control. For so long, he'd wondered how to navigate a sexual experience. Now, the animal inside roared as biology took over. The desire to tear off her clothes and spread her wide on the couch consumed him. Dragos acknowledged his deep yearning to taste every spot on her quivering frame and understood that, somehow, his body would understand how to make love to Rania. He probably wouldn't be the most prolific lover, but he would cherish her and expend every effort to please her, and that would count for something. Alas, her boys were in the next room, so he maneuvered his lips over hers, grateful to have her lips against his as he'd so often dreamed.

Their lips played with each other until she pressed her fangs into his skin, stilling him as he softly groaned. Lifting his lids, he stared into her eyes as she tenderly bit his lower lip.

"Now bite mine," she commanded softly.

Expelling a ragged breath, Dragos closed his mouth over her bottom lip, sucking her inside and running his tongue over the soft skin. She purred with desire before he gently took the flesh between his teeth and squeezed.

"By the goddess," she whispered. "One day, I want you to do that to my nipple…"

"*Fuck*…" he groaned, feeling his body shudder at the naughty words.

"And maybe even lower if you're open to it." Waggling her brows, she slid her tongue over his lips. "Now lick me back."

Tightening his fingers in her hair, he gently tilted her head, loving the flare of desire in her eyes at the slightly dominant gesture. "You were serious about showing me, weren't you?" he murmured against her lips. "I never knew you were this bossy, Raina."

"Wait till I get you naked," she said, nipping his lip. "I'm going to give you several commands, soldier."

Groaning with lust, he closed his lips over hers and plunged his tongue inside her wet mouth. Raina moaned beneath him, surging her tongue against his and swirling them together. Never had he tasted anything as sweet as her upon his lips, and he thanked the goddess he wasn't killed in battle, just so he could live this one moment upon Etherya's Earth. She wriggled against him, pushing her mound into his turgid cock, and he surged back, showing her how much he desired her. Their tongues slid together, mating in the dance as old as time, until she drew back, breathless.

"My god…" she panted, caressing his jaw as she smiled. "For someone who's never kissed, you're pretty damn good at it."

"I've wanted to kiss you for so long, Raina," he whispered, tucking one of her brown curls behind her ear. "You're the most beautiful woman I've ever seen."

Tears sparkled in her eyes as she gave him a reverent smile. "I think I'm one of the first women you've met since your liberation. You might want to expand your scope."

"I could search all the immortal lands and never find someone so beautiful."

Sighing at the lovely words, she shimmied into him. "That's very romantic. I've missed being held like this...being told I'm beautiful. Thank you, Dragos."

He stared into her eyes, caressing her cheek with the backs of his fingers as their breaths mingled.

"I want to make love to you," she said softly. "Would you consider it?"

Dragos's body shuddered at the thought. "I would give anything to make love to you, but...I'm a virgin, Raina. I can't promise I'll please you although I will certainly try." His gaze lowered in embarrassment.

"Hey," she said, sliding her fingers under his chin and forcing him to reclaim her gaze. "Making love with someone is always pleasurable if there is openness and communication...and chemistry, which we seem to have in spades." Her lips curved as she chucked her brows. "It will be good as long as we're open. Can you be open with me?"

"Yes," he whispered.

"Good," she said, pressing a soft kiss to his lips. "Galen's grounding will be over on Saturday, and he and Ekon have a playdate at their friend's home. They will be gone until sunset. Perhaps we can try then?"

Elation coursed through his veins, along with trepidation he might fail to please her. But he'd dreamed of touching her for so long the joy outweighed the fear. "Come over anytime. I'll have the house clean and will stock the fridge with Slayer blood."

"That's very thoughtful. Perhaps have some wine too. That will make us both less nervous." She bit her lip, making her look adorable.

"Why would you be nervous?"

Her expression fell slightly, and he caressed her cheek.

"Raina?"

"Because I am making love to someone besides my bonded. It will be the first time."

Dragos mulled her words, telling himself not to let them sour the moment.

"I don't say this to hurt you or to make you doubt yourself," she said, tenderly cupping his jaw. "It's only to let you know this is a big step for me too. I would only take it with someone I know to be a good man. Someone who is brave and has shown such kindness to me and my boys. I trust you, Dragos, and that means so much to me. Do you understand?"

"Yes," he whispered, pressing a tender kiss to her lips as ecstasy welled in his chest. Her trust was such a precious gift, and he would do everything in his power to be worthy of it. "I'm so honored you trust me, Raina."

Her lips formed a poignant smile before she drew back. "Now that you've thoroughly riled me up, I need to right myself before I put my boys to bed." Patting her hair, she bit her lip as she tilted her head. "How do I look? Ravished or acceptable?"

Chuckling, he stroked her soft curls, helping to comb them in place. "You look perfectly acceptable."

"Thank you," she said with a nod. Standing, she extended her hand. "And thank you for being so wonderful with Galen this morning. He enjoyed his time with you."

"Both your boys are lovely," he said, following her to the door, wishing he didn't have to go. "I am happy to help you with them anytime."

"That's very sweet." She opened the door and leaned her temple against it as he stepped outside. "Have a good night, Dragos."

He longed to reach for her—to pull her tight and never let go. Instead, he gave a salute and said, "Good night, Raina."

Pivoting, he walked over the soft grass as the door clicked behind him. Touching his lips, he realized they were slightly swollen, causing him to smile. Tonight, Dragos had experienced his first kiss, and it was...*glorious*. Most likely because it was with the woman who consumed his every thought. In a week, she would appear at his door, and he would finally make love to his beautiful Raina. Trepidation welled within, and he reminded himself to remain calm. Open. Vulnerable. She had been the one to suggest they make love, so he would do his best to please her.

Stepping inside his cottage, he closed the door and trailed to the couch. Lowering to the plush cushions, he acknowledged the perma-grin that now sat affixed to his lips. It would most likely remain firmly in place until next Saturday, when Dragos would finally lose his virginity to his gorgeous Raina.

Chapter 6

Dragos all but skipped through the week, counting down each day until Saturday arrived. He cleaned his cottage, making sure it was spotless, and placed fresh sheets upon his queen-size bed. Raina had informed him that Galen and Ekon were heading to their friend's home around 10:00 a.m., and nerves flitted in his stomach as he waited for her knock upon the door.

Grabbing two wineglasses from the rack, he polished them until he thought his fingers might bleed. But it was a mundane task and offered him something to do until she arrived. Three firm raps echoed from the door, and he froze, cloth in hand, as her voice chimed.

"Uh, hello? I hope you're not having second thoughts."

Furiously shaking his head to regain some sense, he set the glass on the counter and trailed to the door. Pulling it open, he smiled, overcome by her beauty. Her deep blue eyes shone in the bright morning sun, and her lips were covered with sparkling gloss. Long brown curls hung below her shoulders, covered in a light purple sweater atop khakis and sandals.

"Well," she said, lifting her hands and making a slow turn. "Do I pass muster?"

Unable to exist for one moment longer without kissing her, he snaked his arm around her waist and drew her body against his. "You're stunning." Lowering his head, he cemented his lips to hers, pushing them open so he could thrust his tongue inside. She emitted a tiny yelp before slinging her arms around his neck and holding on for dear life.

Their mouths and tongues roved over each other until he broke the kiss and rested his forehead against hers.

"Sorry if I was staring," he murmured, nudging her nose with his. "You just look so pretty, Raina." Her smile lit a torch in a darkened corner of his heart he didn't even know existed.

"Thank you. You're pretty handsome yourself."

Dragos had tossed on some comfortable pants and a T-shirt, hoping she didn't mind if he kept it casual. His feet were bare, and he nudged her sandal with his toe. "Take these off and make yourself at home. I figured we could have some rosé before we…"

"Bone each other's brains out?" she asked, arching a brow. "I'd love some rosé."

Chuckling, he drew back and held her hand as she toed off her sandals. Closing the door, he locked it and led her to the kitchen. He poured two glasses of the rosé he'd recently opened and lifted his glass to hers.

"To you."

"To *us*," she corrected, grinning as she clinked her glass with his. He urged her toward the couch, where they sat and caught up on their week as they drank the wine. Twenty minutes later, he eyed her wineglass before glancing at his own.

"Do you want another glass?" he asked, noticing she only had a small portion left.

"No," she said, setting the glass on the table and rising. Extending her hand, she wiggled her fingers. "I'm nervous as hell. I think I just want to get on with it so we can get over the hump of being nervous. Sorry if that's not very romantic." Her lips formed a shy smile. "Are you okay with that?"

Dragos's throat closed with desire as he tried to swallow. "Yes," he whispered.

"Then lead me to your room, Dragos."

He set his glass on the table and took her hand, allowing her to pull him to his feet. Arousal swam in her gorgeous eyes, and he was overwhelmed with the knowledge he was finally going to touch a woman—touch *Raina*, the woman he coveted above all others. Tugging her hand, he led her to the bedroom.

Once they were beside the bed, he faced her, feeling clumsy and inept as he wondered what to do first.

"I'd like to give you pleasure first," she said, lifting her hand and caressing his arm in a soothing motion. "If you're open to that. It will take the edge off and improve your...um..."

"Stamina?" he droned, arching a brow.

"Yes," she said, biting her lip. "Sometimes men...*release* before they wish to during their first time. If you get the first release out of the way, you can relax."

"I can't imagine relaxing when I'm anywhere near you and a bed at the same time," he teased. "But I'll follow your lead."

"Good. Now, be a good neighbor and take off my shirt." She lifted her arms high, and he gripped the hem before dragging it off her body and tossing it to the floor. She wore a white bra that cupped the mounds of her breasts, and he sucked in a breath at the sight of her supple flesh.

Her fingers trailed to the button of her pants, and she unfastened them and pushed them to the floor. Stepping out, she was left in cute pink panties and bra. Slowly turning to face the wall, she lifted her hair and spoke over her shoulder.

"Unclasp my bra."

Dragos lifted shaking fingers to the clasp of her bra, frustrated when he couldn't figure out how to unlatch it.

"They're hooks," she said, her voice calm and laced with a hint of desire. "Slide them out."

Recognition blazed in his mind, and he slid open the clasps before throwing the garment to the floor.

"Now, take off my underwear."

Inhaling a shaky breath, he slid his fingers under the hem of her panties, thrilled when she hissed in response. Hooking over the elastic, he glided them down her body, and she stepped out of the soft material. Rising, he swept her hair over one shoulder and lowered his lips to the shoulder he'd bared. Placing soft kisses against her skin as his front pressed into her back, he tenderly cupped her ass and squeezed, loving her soft groan.

"Oh, this is going to be fun," she murmured, pushing into his hand. "I'm already dripping for you." Tilting her head to rest on his shoulder, she gazed into his eyes. "Touch me between my legs so you can feel."

Violent trembles shook his body as he hesitated.

"Touch me, Dragos," she whispered, wriggling against him. "It's a requirement of making love, you know?"

Smiling at her teasing, he glided his fingers from her ass across her hipbone, eventually landing on the springy hairs that covered her mound. Delving below the coarse hairs, he slid his fingers between her wet folds.

"See?" she rasped, eyes glazed as she stared up at him. "Sopping wet...for you, Dragos."

"I want to make you come," he whispered, running his fingers up and down her slit.

"You first," she said, rotating and clutching the fabric of his shirt in her hands. "It will take some time to bring me to the peak, and you will need instruction. I want to make you come first." She tugged his shirt off before reaching for the snap of his pants.

Dragos helped her and all but ripped them from his body before shucking his boxer briefs.

"Oh my," she said, her voice sultry as she regarded his stiff cock proudly jutting from his body, ready to claim her. "Someone is excited."

"I've never been so fucking excited," he growled, grasping her hand and pulling her toward the bed.

Her resulting smile set him on fire, and his knees almost buckled when she crawled atop the comforter, positioning herself on her hands and knees as she faced him. "Come here," she commanded, hooking her finger.

Blood pounded so furiously through his body he wondered how his heart didn't beat out of his chest. Slowly approaching the bed, he groaned as she took him in her hand. She gently began jerking his sensitive flesh, and he closed his eyes, overwhelmed by the sensation.

"Come closer," she whispered, causing his eyes to snap open. "Let me kiss you here."

"Are you sure?"

Her fangs flashed as she nodded. "I'm going to make you come in my mouth. Don't hold back, okay?"

Threading his fingers through her thick hair, he gently squeezed. "I want to make you feel good, Raina. I want to focus on your pleasure."

"Oh, don't worry," she said, lust blazing in her eyes. "I'll enjoy this as much as you." Her tongue darted out to bathe her lips, and his eyes crossed with arousal. "Fuck my mouth, Dragos." She opened those wet, glistening lips, and he lost the ability to do anything but follow her directive.

Pressing the blunt head of his engorged cock to her lips, he gazed into her eyes as she closed around him. A deep groan exited his throat as she began slowly moving back and forth, lathering his sensitive skin with her tongue. She took him deeper, purring in approval when he gripped her hair harder and began jutting his hips back and forth.

"Oh, *goddess...*" he groaned, sliding his taut flesh between her lips, careful not to slide against her sharp fangs. "Sweetheart, look at you." Moving his hand under her chin, he held her tight as he fucked her mouth in long, deep strokes. "This can't be real. Oh...*fuck!*"

Her moan vibrated against his shaft, increasing the pleasure, and he closed his eyes in ecstasy. Her fingers toyed with his balls before cupping the sacks and gently squeezing, all but sending him over the edge. Lifting his lids, he spoke in hushed words.

"I'm already going to come. Oh, god, this is so embarrassing."

She grinned around his cock, saliva dripping from her full lips as she assured him with her gaze. Fisting her hair, he began to furiously pump his dick into her wet mouth, ready to collapse when the blunt head jutted against the back of her throat. Tossing back his head, he screamed her name and began to come, shooting thick, sticky jets of release deep inside her mouth.

Raina mewled around his cock, sucking him dry as she balanced upon the bed. Succumbing to the orgasm, Dragos saw stars explode beneath his eyelids as his body jerked and quaked. Eventually, his strong pulses turned to tiny jerks, and he emptied the last of his release into her mouth. Huffing out a breath, he lifted heavy lids to gaze down at her.

Raina released him, grinning as she tenderly ran her palm over his hip and thigh. Placing a firm smack to his ass, she laughed at his resulting growl.

"See what I mean about taking the edge off?" she asked, arching a brow.

"Holy shit," he murmured, balancing on wobbly legs. "I need to sit down."

Her warm chuckle surrounded him as she took his hand and tugged him to the bed. He collapsed on the soft comforter, thrilled when she wrapped her body around him and snuggled into his side. Resting her elbow on his chest, she placed her chin atop her fist and gazed down at him. "Your first blow job. Well done. You taste salty." She shot him a smoldering glare before running her finger over her lips.

"Can't...talk..." he managed before lifting his finger to twine with hers. He drew them across her full lips as they gazed into each other's eyes. "How can I possibly make you feel that good? I have no idea what I'm doing. Yikes."

"You're going to be just fine," she assured him, running her nails through the spiky hairs on his chest. "I'll let you recover for a few minutes, and then we're going to help you find my clit."

He grinned and squeezed her hand. "I won't stop until I find it. And I will do anything to make you feel good, Raina. I swear."

"Oh, my dear Dragos," she said in an arousal-laden voice, "I'm counting on it."

Destroyed, Dragos struggled to catch his breath as he replenished his energy, determined to please his stunning Vampyre.

Chapter 7

Dragos eventually recovered and urged Raina to lay upon the pillow. She slid her hands under her hair, fanning it over the white pillowcase as her naked lover gazed at her. It had been so long since a man eyed her with lust, and it brought her great pleasure to know how much her sensitive Deamon desired her.

If someone had asked her a year ago if she would be making love to a virgin Deamon, she would've laughed them into the next compound. But Dragos was different...kind...handsome...thoughtful. When he first moved in beside her, she'd worried he might inspire terrible memories of the war. Instead, his presence was a blessing, and she thanked the goddess for her good fortune.

"What are you smiling at?" he asked in a low, sexy tone that curled her toes. He maneuvered his strong frame over hers, aligning their bodies as she slid her arms around his neck.

"I'm just so glad we met," she said, lifting her lips to his. "You've changed my perspective on Deamons."

The corner of his lips curved, although the smile didn't meet his eyes. "Not all Deamons are good, but the ones who wish to reform have good hearts. At least, I think we do."

"You do," she said, placing her palm over his chest, feeling the organ beating strongly beneath. "I have no doubt."

His dark eyes searched hers before he lowered to capture her lips in a blazing kiss. Raina returned his embrace, anticipation coursing through her at the idea of teaching him exactly how to touch her...how to *love* her. Dragos broke the kiss and roved his lips over her jaw...and neck...and gently over the valley between her breasts. Resting on his forearm, he cupped her breast with his free hand, his gaze inquisitive and a bit hesitant.

"My nipples are sensitive, much like your cock is," she said, running her fingers through his thick hair. "The more you touch and kiss them, the tighter they will become."

"And this feels good?"

"Yes," she whispered. "It feels very good."

He licked his lips, sending a burst of arousal to her core, and his eyes darted over her nipple. Pressing the pad of his thumb to the edge of her darkened areola, he swept it across the tiny nub.

"More," she demanded softly.

His eyes darted to hers, and he gave her a poignant smile. "I'm telling myself to go slow."

"You're doing fine. Take it between your fingers and squeeze."

He followed her directive, pinching her nipple between his thumb and forefinger. Raina groaned, feeling her body tighten. Spurred on by her reaction, Dragos lowered his head and ran his tongue over her nipple.

"Oh, yessss..." she cried. "Again. Don't stop."

Dragos opened his mouth and encircled her breast with his lips. Tugging her into his mouth, he sucked hard and deep, causing desire to burn every cell of her skin. The soft, greedy moans that emanated from his throat as he sucked her were sexy as hell, and she wrapped her leg around the back of his thigh, pulling him closer. He licked and nibbled, appearing pleased with himself when he drew back to observe his handiwork.

"It's so tight," he said, running his finger over her turgid nipple.

"Damn straight." She gently pushed his head toward her other breast. "Now do this one."

Her eager lover dove into the act as if she were his last meal. Taken by his innocent enthusiasm, she pulled him close, pushing the taut nub against his tongue as he ravished it. Eventually, he drew back and began to trail kisses over her stomach and toward her core. On his way, he delved his tongue into her navel, causing her to shiver as she taunted him.

"You're a fast learner, Dragos."

"You are easy to love, Raina," he whispered against her skin.

The romantic words spurred something deep within—something that welled from emotion rather than lust. Unable to deal with the feelings, she pushed them aside to concentrate on her avid lover's actions.

Balancing between her legs, Dragos placed his palms on her inner thighs and pushed them open. His eyes grew wide as he gazed upon her center, and she chuckled.

"First, you assess me at the door, and now in my most private place. Do you approve?"

"I'm sorry," he whispered, licking his lips as he reached for her folds. "I've never seen a woman…like this… It's…strange…and *wet*."

Tossing her head back on the pillow, she laughed. "Yes, the wetness surges when I'm aroused to help ease your cock inside."

Lifting his gaze to hers, he placed his fingers on her folds. "I want to make you come before I fuck you with my cock."

"Then let's teach you how." Running a hand over his hair, she slid it down to cup his chin. "First, you'll need to wet your fingers to make them slick. You can do this by sliding them inside me."

Heavy breaths exited his lungs as he glided his fingers to her opening. Staring deep into her eyes, he urged a finger into her tight warmth. "Like this?"

"Yes," she rasped. "You'll need to wet two fingers. Go on. You won't hurt me. It feels good."

Dragos placed the pads of his index and middle fingers at her slick core, eyes glued to her pussy as he tenderly pushed them inside. "Good?" he asked, brows lifting under a slight sheen of sweat. She would've chuckled at his determined concentration but didn't want to make him feel uncomfortable.

"So good," she grunted, pushing against his fingers.

He fucked her, strong and deep, and she reveled in the sensation.

"Okay, now you're going to rub them against my clitoris."

His eyes locked onto hers, filled with doubt and what looked like a slight twinge of fear.

"No judgment, Dragos. Openness and communication, remember?"

He nodded, and she reached down to pull open her folds. "It's located here," she rasped, running her finger under the hood of her mound until she found the taut nub. "You'll feel it."

Following her lead, he slid his wet fingers up her slit, replacing her fingers with his own. Recognition lit in his eyes as he felt the firm bundle of nerves.

"Oh, goddess...that's it," she moaned. "You found it. Now, you need to stimulate it in even concentric circles with firm pressure."

Giving a slight nod, he began to swirl his fingers around her bud, causing Raina to close her eyes in ecstasy. His fingers twirled and circled her clit, sparking tiny fires of arousal all over her skin.

"I want to kiss you here too," he almost growled.

"Okay," she groaned, nodding against the pillow. "It might take some time for you to perfect it, but give it a shot."

He buried his face between her thighs, licking her slit with frenzied strokes before settling against her tight nub. His tongue flicked and stimulated as his fingers dropped to her core to gather more of her honey.

"You taste so fucking good," he growled into her drenched folds. "I've never tasted anything so sweet."

Raina barked a laugh as her body drowned in pleasure. "'Sweet' might be a stretch, but I'll take it. Oh, god, that feels good, but I think I need your fingers again."

His nimble fingers replaced his mouth, swirling and circling her clit as she felt the orgasm looming. Thrusting her fingers in his hair, she pressed into his ministrations, reaching for the peak.

"*Dragos...*" she cried, writhing on the bed. "Oh, *goddess*... I'm coming..."

His ragged breaths echoed off the walls as his fingers continued the frenzied pace against her nub. Fireworks exploded in every corner of her brain as she fell off the cliff headlong into a blinding orgasm. Shudders wracked her frame as she lost herself in the first climax from something other than her own hand in so very long. Taken by the moment and her handsome lover, she clutched the comforter as her back arched, clinging to every moment of bliss.

Emitting a loud groan, she melted against the bed, barely able to remember her own name. Joyful laughter erupted from her throat, and she felt Dragos slide over her burning body. He rested his weight on his forearms before sliding his fingers into her hair where it lay strewn across the pillow.

Lifting her lids, she gazed into his eyes, filled with delight at her obvious pleasure.

"I never knew you could be more beautiful," he whispered, his eyes wide as he grinned. "Look at you..." He ran his finger over her flushed cheek, and she felt his hard cock against her thigh.

"Make love to me," she whispered.

"Now?"

Breathing a laugh, she nodded. "Now."

His eyes searched hers as he aligned the head of his hard shaft with her drenched opening. "Raina..."

Wrapping her leg around his back, she pulled him close. "Fuck me, Dragos."

He surged inside, causing her to gasp as her back arched upon the bed.

"Fuck!" he cried, eyes closed in ecstasy as her tight walls surrounded him. "It was too much. I'm sorry. I—"

"Don't stop," she commanded, lifting her hips to his. "Fuck me hard."

He stilled for one silent moment before withdrawing and thrusting deep into her core. Raina cried his name, clutching onto his hair as he began to hammer her ravaged body.

"Is this what you want?" he grunted, his flesh slapping hers as he pushed himself into her tight channel, again and again. "Do you like taking my cock, Raina?"

"Oh, goddess, he's a dirty talker," she cried, overcome with laughter and desire at once. "Keep going. It's so sexy."

"Take me inside your tight, sweet body, Raina," he growled, capturing her lips in a torrid kiss as he pressed inside her. "Goddess, I must be in the Passage. Nothing can feel this good."

She slid her hands over his back, digging her nails into his shoulder blades as he groaned with desire. The pace of his hips increased until she thought he might fuck her straight through the headboard. Overcome with joy, she held on tight as he surged so deep she felt full and weightless, both at once.

"I'm going to come. Should I pull out?"

"IUD," she cried, knowing the chances of them conceiving a child were small since they were different species with non-royal blood, but the possibility was still there. They couldn't transmit disease due to her self-healing body, and she thanked the goddess she'd gotten the IUD after Ekon was born. "Come inside me."

Lifting his head, he gazed into her eyes as he slid his turgid cock between her wet folds. Palming her face, he held her riveted so she couldn't even think of looking away.

"Raina...I have to tell you... You have to know..."

"*Shh...*" she said, covering his lips with her fingers. Losing one's virginity was profound, and she didn't want him confusing love with lust. Although he was a wonderful man and a surprisingly proficient lover with some gentle instruction, those words were better left unsaid. She had only ever said them to her bonded and didn't want to hurt Dragos by not saying them back. "Keep fucking me. There's a spot you can hit with the head of your cock deep inside—"

He surged deep, and she gasped. "Yes. Right there. *Oh, goddess....*"

Clenching his jaw, Dragos undulated his hips at a frenzied pace, pushing her to the edge of another orgasm. Closing her eyes, she dug her nails into his back and allowed herself to plunge into the abyss. Her body bucked as her inner walls began to spasm, and Dragos screamed her name as he began to come. The tight walls of her core milked him, drawing his release from his shaft as it throbbed inside her quaking body. They vibrated in tandem, each overcome with pleasure as they trembled and shuddered atop the bed.

Releasing one last ragged groan, Dragos collapsed over her body and buried his face in her neck. "Help," he murmured into her sweaty skin, the timbre of his deep voice causing her skin to tingle.

Chuckling, she wrapped her legs around him and held tight, sifting her fingers through his hair as he hummed in approval. Their heavy breaths and satisfied moans permeated the room as their sweaty bodies cooled upon the sheets.

"Well, my dear neighbor," she finally said when she could muster the energy to speak. "You are no longer a virgin."

Dragos released a long sigh as he lay against her sated body. "That was... I have no words."

"It was lovely. You are a magnificent lover, Dragos." She placed a soft kiss on his forehead. "I am honored to be your first."

Lifting his head, he ran a finger over her jaw as he contemplated. "I won't ply you with words of love you do not wish to hear." The sadness in his voice made her heart weep, and she ached to soothe him.

"Dragos—"

"It's fine, Raina," he said, placing a kiss on her lips. "I understand. But I want you to know how special this was for me. Thank you."

"It was special for me too," she said, feeling her throat close as tears welled in her eyes. "You are a good man, Dragos."

"As long as you think that, I am happy." His lips curved into a tender smile. "Can I hold you like this for a while? I like being inside you when we're all sticky and sweaty."

"Yes," she said, drawing his head to her chest. He nuzzled into her as she stroked his hair, and Raina marveled at the emotion welling deep within. She'd never expected to feel it with Dragos. Lust? Sure. Desire? Most definitely. Emotion? She hadn't even considered it. But lying there with her sated Deamon in her arms, the tentacles of emotion wrapped around every limb and crevice of her satiated body.

A sudden fear laced her veins as she acknowledged the feelings. Where had they come from? Were they true? How could she feel them for someone other than her bonded?

Dragos softly snored against her neck as she lay awake pondering answers that never came. Eventually, she gave up the maddening quest and relaxed in her lover's arms, allowing herself to enjoy the poignant moment.

Chapter 8

Raina returned home that afternoon a half hour before her boys arrived. They were playing at a friend's home two neighborhoods away, and she wanted to shower before they walked home. As she stood under the spray washing away the remnants of her tryst, Raina acknowledged the murky emotion that sat deep within. She was shaken by her reaction to making love with Dragos and wondered what that meant for their future interactions. She certainly wanted to make love to him again but worried her heart would begin to crave more. Was it possible for her to develop feelings for a Deamon?

If it was Dragos, then...yes...

Raina stepped from the shower and dried herself as she admitted the truth: she didn't see Dragos as a Deamon or soldier who'd fought against her bonded in the war. She just saw *him*—a man who was kind to her and who had saved Galen. Sighing, she ran the towel over her damp skin, unsure how to move forward. Should she take some time before she saw him again to let the feelings dissipate?

The quiet bathroom held no answers, so she dressed and prepared some Slayer blood for dinner. Ekon and Galen bounded through the front door and drank their dinner as she caught up on their day.

That night, as she lay in bed long after the boys were asleep, Raina struggled to sleep. Never had she imagined one lazy afternoon lovemaking session would cause her to question things she'd been so sure of only hours ago.

Frustrated, she punched the pillow and closed her eyes, determined to push away the swirling questions.

Several days after their passionate lovemaking, Dragos had the nagging feeling Raina was avoiding him. He'd stopped by her home several times, offering to help with some of the obvious work she needed in her yard. Each time, she gave him a kind but brief smile and assured him she would take care of it. Then she would make an excuse that her boys needed her and gently close the door in his face.

On Saturday morning, Dragos noticed Galen and Ekon trail out of the house, disappearing across the hill after running across the yard. Understanding Raina was alone in the home, he debated approaching her. As he stood at the sink washing the omelet pan from that morning's breakfast, he pondered if she regretted being with him.

Or perhaps she was angry you tried to tell her you love her...

Sighing, Dragos turned off the faucet and began to dry the pan with the nearby cloth. He hadn't meant to bring feelings into their lovemaking. Of course, he understood she still loved her husband and could probably never feel affection for a Deamon. But he'd been so taken by her graciousness—and overwhelmed from his first sexual experience—that he'd nearly blurted out the words. Although he didn't fully utter them, she must know. Dragos had no experience with love, nor did he profess to understand it, but there was one thing he knew to be true: he loved Raina with every fiber of his being.

It might not make sense, and others might think him insane for loving a woman who didn't return the sentiment. A woman who was in love with someone else and could never be his. But Dragos figured love was often unexplainable and he wouldn't waste time denying something that was inarguably true.

He loved so much about the enigmatic, stunning Vampyre who lived next door. Loved how caring and protective she was with her sons. Loved her blue-flecked irises and the way she threw back her head to release her melodic laughter. The way she teased him when she saw him in the yard, reminding him he could laugh a little while he performed his chores. And when they made love...he was enamored by how gentle yet instructive she'd been. How she'd opened her body to his untrained soul and let him in...so deep he wanted to burrow inside her and never let go.

Furiously shaking his head, Dragos set the pan in the drying rack and rested his hands on the edge of the sink, wondering what the hell to do. Now that he'd tasted her, he wanted so much more. If he could only have her body, it would have to be enough. Living with that part of her would be better than having nothing at all. Realizing he had to tell her this, he rushed to his room and threw on a shirt before sliding on his sneakers.

He breezed out his front door, closing it behind him and noting his palm was sweaty against the knob. Nerves sizzled in every cell of his body as he crossed the lawn to her home. Lifting a hand, he knocked, swallowing thickly as anxiety closed his throat.

She pulled open the door, and her full lips curved into a knowing smile. "You must've noticed my two heathens head to their friend's house."

"I did," he said, returning her smile. "I'd like to come in and talk to you...if you have a moment."

She rested her temple on the door as she pondered. "You only want to talk?"

Dragos expelled a rush of air and shook his head. "No," he whispered.

"What else should we do besides talk?"

Stepping forward, he cupped her face, tilting it to his. "Whatever you want, Raina."

Something flashed in her eyes, and it gave him pause.

"If you don't want to make love—"

Her fist flew to his shirt, grabbing the fabric and tugging him inside. Dragos breathed an excited laugh as he slammed the door behind him and then snaked his arms around her waist. Cupping her ass, he lifted her as her legs wrapped around his waist. He swooped in for a torrid kiss, sucking her tongue into his mouth as he gasped, "Bedroom?"

"That way." She pointed toward an open door, and he bounded through, tossing her onto the half-made bed as she snickered. "I was going to make it after the boys left. Ekon spilled his breakfast everywhere, and it took forever to clean."

"I don't care," Dragos rasped, pressing his lips to hers as he lay atop her lithe body. "Goddess, Raina, I missed you." He swirled his tongue around the depths of her mouth, thrilled to taste her once again. She squeezed her legs, drawing him closer as he surged his rapidly swelling cock into her mound.

They tore at each other's clothes, ripping them away until they were both naked upon the soft bed. Dragos encircled her ankles and dragged her toward the edge of the bed. Staring into her eyes, he placed one of her ankles on each shoulder.

"Sweetheart," he murmured, aligning his cock with her opening. "I need you—"

"Yes," she interjected, furiously nodding against the bed. "Please—"

Dragos thrust inside, groaning at the pleasure of returning to her tight, wet core. Grasping her ankles atop his shoulders, he undulated his hips, sliding his sensitive shaft through her slick folds.

"Rub my clit while you find the spot inside with your cock," she commanded.

Dying to please her, he placed the pad of his thumb on her taut nub and began to circle.

"Lick your thumb!" she cried. "Need...wet..."

Taken by her obvious arousal and flushed cheeks, he followed her direction and placed his slickened thumb over her clit. Concentrating with all his might, he began to circle the nerve-filled bud as he hammered deep inside her. Watching her with half-lidded eyes, he gritted his teeth as his balls began to tighten.

"I wish I could last longer with you," he gritted, overcome by the feeling of her wet folds against his cock. "I want you to think I'm a good lover..."

A laugh bounded from her throat, and she clenched the covers in tight fists. "You're...oh, *goddess*, you're definitely good. I love having you inside me."

The words spurred his hips to move faster as he slid back and forth through her taut channel. Their guttural moans mingled as he saw her eyes close. She parted her lips, still swollen from his ardent kisses, and cried his name.

"I'm here, Raina," he gritted, feeling his knees buckle as he pounded into her with all his might. "Goddess, I think my cock was made for you."

Joyful laughter sprang from the bed seconds before her back arched and she fell into the orgasm. Drowning in lust, Dragos watched his woman as she exploded beneath him, proud he could give her such pleasure even if she could never accept his love. Nerves exploded at the base of his spine, and he joined her in the climax, his body bucking into her as he jetted his release into her gorgeous body.

Her blissful purrs were melodious as he emptied everything inside her. Unable to stand on wobbly legs, he collapsed over her, careful not to crush her. Their sweaty skin pressed together as they both heaved air into their lungs. Eventually, their heaves turned to soft pants, and Dragos rested his head in his palm as his elbow dug into the bed.

"Hey," he said softly, running a finger over her reddened cheek.

"Hey." Her eyes glowed with sated desire as she gave him a sultry smile.

"I really did come here to talk."

Her warm chuckle surrounded him as she winked. "You told me your cock was made for me. I think that says it all."

The corner of his lips curved at her teasing. "It says quite a bit, I guess. I feel so much more, but that's a good start."

Her lips thinned, and Dragos inwardly kicked himself for bringing up his feelings...again. "Shit. I told myself I wouldn't profess things you didn't want to hear. That's what I wanted to talk to you about."

Her chest rose as she inhaled a deep breath. "Okay, let's talk."

"Here? We could get dressed first."

She lifted a shoulder. "We could, but this is where we're going to be most honest, isn't it? We're literally bared to each other."

Breathing a laugh, he glanced down at their naked, cooling bodies. "True."

"Dragos," she said, cupping his jaw and tilting his face to claim his gaze. "It is normal to experience feelings of affection for the first person you have sex with."

His eyebrows drew together as he allowed the words to settle. "I'm sure it is, but that isn't what's happening here, Raina."

"We barely know each other—"

"Not true," he said with a firm shake of his head.

"Oh, so you know me that well?"

"Yes."

"Fine. Prove it."

Grinning, he brushed a curl off her forehead. "You like to sit in a chair in your back yard on nights you've had a hard day. It's usually after the sun goes down and I figure the boys are in bed. You gaze at the moon, and sometimes you cry, and I long to hold you and tell you everything is going to be okay."

Tears glistened in her eyes as she listened.

"I imagine you're missing your husband and railing at the unfairness of the world."

"Something like that," she said, arching a brow.

"But you always get up after a few minutes, straighten your shoulders, and head inside. It's a testament to your strength and perseverance."

Her lips pursed as she contemplated. "Should I worry that you watch me in my moments of solace?"

"No more than I should worry that you watch me from the grass where our properties meet. Don't deny it, Raina. I've seen you many times."

She huffed a laugh. "I won't deny it. I was curious."

"Your life revolves around your sons. Getting them to school, ensuring they have Slayer blood, making sure they learn right from wrong. It's extremely important to you that they become good men like their father."

She nodded against the bed, her brown curls rustling over the sheets.

"You do all the chores yourself, even the ones you assign the boys, because you don't think they're thorough enough. You're the CEO of this house and an excellent mother. You love them with your entire heart and feel terribly guilty you let someone touch you besides your husband."

Her expression turned morose as she inhaled a shaky breath. "My *bonded*. And yes, if you must know, it is hard for me. These...*times* we've had together, I enjoy them, but...it is strange."

She sifted her fingers through his hair. "I hope that doesn't hurt you. I don't want to hurt you, Dragos."

"I know." They softly caressed each other as they gazed into each other's eyes—hers filled with doubt, and his brimming with emotion. "I don't need you to love me back, Raina. Having you as my lover is enough."

Her nostrils flared, and he could tell she was struggling to hold back tears. "That isn't fair to you."

"I gave up needing fairness long ago. I want to be your lover and your friend. I want you to lean on me when you or your boys need something."

"I just learned how to do everything myself. Where were you four years ago?"

"I'm here now, Raina," he said, placing a peck on her lips. "Let me be your friend. Let me love you and be with you in the ways I can."

"I can't ask you to do that—"

"You're not asking," he said, covering her lips with his fingers. "I'm offering."

She drew in a large breath as she pondered. After several soul-wrenching seconds, she finally whispered, "Okay."

Dragos broke into a huge smile. "Now, see? Was that so hard?"

"It's never hard with you," she said, caressing his face. "Why is that?"

"Maybe we just fit, sweetheart. Now that we've decided we're friends and lovers, I'd like to tackle the huge pile of brush you have outside while you make the bed and do the multitude of things you need to inside the house. And then I'd like to make love to you again."

Laughing, she rubbed her calf against his. "I mean, would any woman say no to that from someone as handsome and proficient at yardwork as you?"

Throwing back his head, he barked a laugh. "Never." Withdrawing from her luscious body, he rose and extended his hand. "Come on. Chores then lovemaking. What a day. I can't wait."

Raina grabbed his hand, and he tugged her to her feet, pleased with the conversation. It set a foundation for them to be friends and lovers, and he could sense her relief. Thankful she was happy, he set about to accomplish the tasks of the day.

Chapter 9

Dragos and Raina fell into an easy pattern, and Raina struggled to reconcile her affection for her new lover with the strange concept of having a man around who wasn't her bonded. Dragos was extremely helpful with a multitude of tasks, and the boys quickly grew to revere him. He was gentle and kind with them, and she'd never seen them so eager to learn.

On his days off, Dragos would invite Ekon and Galen to his shed and ask them to help with the projects he was tinkering with. Over the span of a few weeks, they helped him build some shelves they could place above their beds to store books and a new coffee table for Raina's living room. Several weeks after they first made love, Dragos and the boys carried the finished mahogany table into the home, placing it in front of Raina's couch as they beamed.

"I applied the stain myself, Mom," Galen said, puffing out his chest.

"I helped too!" Ekon chimed.

"You both did a wonderful job," she said, running her fingers over the smooth wood. "I'm sure Dragos helped too." She winked at him where he stood behind the boys, arms crossed over his chest as he grinned.

"Maybe a little, but the boys did the majority of the work. I'm proud of you both." He slid a hand over each of their shoulders, and Raina's eyes welled as they gazed at him with pride.

"Can you stay over tonight, Dragos?" Ekon asked. "We can have a sleepover and camp in the back yard."

"Oh, I'm sure Dragos has other plans for his weekend," Raina said, shaking her head.

"I would be open to camping, but your mom has to join us," Dragos said, a challenge in his eyes as he arched a brow.

"Sleep outside in a tent as opposed to my comfy bed?" she asked, amusement in her tone. "My back will love it."

Dragos chuckled at her acerbic tone. "Come on, Raina. It will be fun. We can make s'mores. I know Vampyres don't eat a ton of food, but I discovered s'mores a few years back, and they're amazing."

"I want s'mores," Ekon said, raising his hand.

"Me too!"

"Well," Dragos said, his lips forming a knowing, sexy grin, "what do you say, Raina?"

"Fine, I'll hang out with you all and eat s'mores. But I'm sleeping in my bed afterward," she said, lifting a finger. "You all can sleep in the tent. I'm sure the three of you can tell lots of scary ghost stories before you fall asleep."

"I have some good ones," Galen said with an excited nod.

With that settled, Dragos led the boys to the back yard, where he taught them how to trim the hedges lining the back edge of the property. Raina gazed at them from the window above the kitchen sink as she washed a Slayer bloodstain from one of Ekon's shirts. Dragos instructed each of her sons as they held the shearers, and an image of Soran's face popped into her mind. Raina realized her bonded would be thrilled their children had found someone strong and kind to guide them as they grew into young men.

"I wish you could meet him," Raina softly whispered, closing her eyes as Soran's image gently smiled in return. "He is such a good man, Soran."

I know...

Raina's lids flew open as the words flitted through her brain, spoken in her bonded mate's deep voice. Was it possible he sensed her affection for Dragos from his place in the Passage? Did he begrudge her feelings, which she couldn't seem to control, especially the more Dragos became entrenched in their lives?

The silence held no answers, and she sighed. "Soran gave his blessing, Raina. It's okay to move on." But saying it and doing it were two different things, and she wasn't quite sure she was ready to fully admit her feelings. That would require her to ponder things such as bonding and creating a home with someone new. Those thoughts were too real—too *raw*—so she pushed them away, telling herself she had time.

That evening, once the sun had set behind the far-off mountains, Raina trailed outside to sit with her boys beside the small bonfire Dragos had built. She spread blankets around the burning pile and made s'mores for the first time. Dragos was jovial as he instructed them on how to spear the marshmallow with the pointed sticks he'd fashioned before placing the warm puff between the chocolate and graham crackers. Ekon and Galen giggled with delight as they ate the sweet treats. Raina had never cared much for food, but she found the s'mores delightful. After taking a huge bite, she grinned when her boys devolved into gleeful laughter.

"And what are you two laughing at?"

"You have chocolate all over your chin!" Galen exclaimed, pointing as he snickered.

"Do I?" She wiped her chin, searching for the sticky substance.

"You're missing it," Dragos said, amusement and mischief in his eyes. "Want me to help?"

She nodded, and he swiped his finger under her bottom lip, wiping the chocolate. Lifting it to his mouth, he sucked it as desire flared in his eyes, magnified by the flames of the fire.

"I think he likes Mom!" Ekon whispered loudly to Galen.

Dragos lifted his brows, silently asking her if he should confirm their suspicions.

"Mom likes him," she said softly, her voice reverent as she plunged toward the irrevocable decision of informing her children about her growing feelings for their neighbor. "I hope that's okay."

"Fine with me," Galen said, shrugging. "Dragos is really cool."

"Me too," Ekon said with a nod. "If you like Mom and want to stay over more, that would be awesome because you could play with us more."

Dragos's full lips curved into a poignant smile as he grasped her hand. "I like hanging out with you guys too," he said, squeezing. Raina clutched back, understanding they'd crossed a small but important line. Her boys now knew of her feelings for Dragos, and their acceptance warmed her heart.

After the s'mores were finished, Dragos put out the fire while Raina prepared the large tent. Three sleeping bags rested inside, and the boys crawled into them as Dragos wiped his hands.

"I just need to hit the restroom before I crawl in with you," he said. "Be back in a few."

"Good night, boys," Raina called.

"Night, Mom," they chimed in unison.

She clutched Dragos's hand as they trailed to the house, dragging him inside and pressing his back to the wall once they'd entered her kitchen.

"Whoa," he said, excitement lacing his features. "I like this forceful side of you—"

She pressed her lips to his, cutting off the words as she encircled his neck and thrust her tongue in his mouth. His deep groan shot to every nerve ending in her core, and arousal gushed between her thighs.

Plunging his fingers in her hair, he drew back and panted as he stared at her with lust-glazed eyes. "You're really going to kiss me like that when I'm relegated to sleeping in a tiny tent with the boys?"

Tossing back her head, she gave a sultry laugh. "Yes. Now, kiss me like you mean it before I kick you out."

He captured her lips in a torrid kiss, swirling his tongue over hers as she melted in his arms. Lost in how easy everything was with him, from his genial relationship with her boys to their unflappable chemistry, Raina inwardly admitted something profound: she could fall in love with Dragos. Judging by the way things had evolved over the past few weeks, she could imagine it so clearly. The notion was strange but not as terrifying as she'd anticipated. Instead, it was just...*there*...lingering in her mind as her handsome Deamon set her lips on fire with his stunning kisses.

Finally, he pulled back and swiped a curl from her forehead. "I like your good-night kisses, Raina."

Breathing a laugh, she rose to her tiptoes and pecked his lips. "I like yours too. Take care of my boys tonight."

"I'll always take care of them, sweetheart."

Her lips formed a gentle smile as he disengaged and headed for the bathroom. When he returned, he pressed a soft kiss to her lips and wished her sweet dreams. His broad shoulders advanced under the moonlight as he traipsed across the yard and entered the tent. Flashlights shone inside until they eventually dimmed.

Unable to squelch her glowing smile, Raina headed to her room to prep for bed.

Chapter 10

Time was a slow-moving constant in the immortal world, and as the days wore on, Dragos willingly pledged his heart to Raina. Although he understood she could never love him back, the flashes of affection and reverence in her eyes when they made love, or when he spent time teaching something to her boys, were priceless. He'd never expected to have any part of her and was thrilled she'd let him into the close-knit circle she'd created with her children.

Sometimes, she would gaze at him with longing, and he felt she was contemplating...*more*. Envisioning allowing herself to love him, if only a little. But eventually, she would retreat behind her protective shield, and Dragos didn't begrudge her for that. Losing her bonded mate must have been devastating, and he understood her desire to protect her heart.

One morning, Dragos heard a knock on his door, and his eyes narrowed as he sat on the couch sanding the small wooden sword he'd fashioned for the boys. They enjoyed sparring in Raina's back yard, and the handle on one of their toy weapons had broken, so he'd offered to create a replacement. Setting the sword on the table, he strode toward the door. Raina had taken the boys to town to buy new shoes, so he knew it wasn't her on the other side. Swinging it open, he smiled down at Miko.

"Hey, Dragos," she said, beaming as her short blond hair spiked above her pointed ears. "Long time, no see."

"Miko," he said, dragging her into a firm hug. She was a Deamon Crimeous had kept in his harem and was also liberated when Evie killed her evil father. "It's so nice to see you." Drawing back, he cupped her shoulders. "What are you doing here?"

"First of all, I wanted to bring back your book." She thrust the hardback toward him. "When Lila taught us to read, you let me borrow this one, and I never returned it."

"Thanks," he said, grasping the book. "Don't you live on the other side of the compound? You came a long way to return a book."

"Um, yeah. So, I have another favor to ask you."

"Come in," he said, stepping back and gesturing with his head. "It's not big, but it's clean. Want some coffee?"

"Sure."

He urged her to sit on the couch while he made a full pot. Once he'd poured them both a cup, he sat across from her.

"Okay, shoot. What to you need?"

"So, this is going to sound weird...but I remember you mentioning you're handy at building things."

"I am," he said with a nod.

"I'm working as a housekeeper in one of the Vampyre aristocrat's mansions and knocked over one of their tall tables where they keep their fancy vases. Not only did I break the vase, but the corner of the table cracked, and they had to throw it out. They were really nice about it, but I feel terrible. I thought I could commission you to make a new table for them."

"That's nice of you," he said, sipping his coffee.

"I told them to take the money to purchase a new table out of my pay, but they refused. I figured I could at least buy them a new one."

"Well, you've come to the right place." Leaning over, he set down his cup and picked up the pad and pen on the coffee table. "I can make one in a snap. Why don't you tell me what you want, and I'll sketch it out?"

She began to describe the table, and Dragos drew it as her smile grew wider. Eventually, they agreed on a design, and she tapped the pad.

"This is perfect. Thank you. How much will it cost?"

"No fee for a friend," he said, shaking his head.

"Oh, please. I wouldn't feel right not paying you."

"I wouldn't dream of it. It should take me a few days. Why don't I start on it, and you can come back to check on it at the halfway point and before I apply the finish?"

"Oh, that would be lovely. Thank you, Dragos."

They caught up on life and their transition into the immortal world before she glanced at her watch.

"Okay, I have to head to work. My shift starts in an hour."

Dragos led her to the door and grinned as she stood on the front stoop.

"I don't know how to repay your kindness." Lifting to her toes, she gave him a firm hug.

"It's nothing, Miko. I love building things in my shed. I'll make it sturdy and presentable for you."

"I have no doubt." With a wave, she headed across the yard and toward the open meadow that led back to the main part of the compound. Since Raina was gone, Dragos decided he would begin working on his new project. Grabbing the pad from the table, he trailed to his shed and got to work.

Raina stood at her living room window absently chewing her lip as she watched Dragos walk beside the woman who'd shown up at his house three times over the past week. The first time was when Raina realized she'd forgotten her wallet on the way to town to buy the boys new shoes. When they returned home to grab it, Raina had passed the pretty Deamon as she walked through the meadow leading to town. She hadn't thought much about it until the woman showed up several days later. Dragos had given her a passionate hug on his doorstep before ushering her inside. And now she was back, smiling up at Raina's lover as they trailed to the shed.

Who was she? What purpose did she have at Dragos's home? The week had been busy, and Raina had barely had time to speak to him. Was it possible he'd made a new friend and didn't tell her? After all, she was the one who kept the line between them officially drawn. Dragos had been honest about his feelings for her, and she'd brushed them away, too scared to acknowledge or dissect them.

"Damn it, Raina," she whispered, her tone angry as she rubbed her forehead. "He is a kind, handsome man. What did you think would happen?"

Frustrated, she buzzed around the living room, tidying up in a flurry as she waited to watch the woman leave through her front window. Finally, after the sun had set behind the horizon, Dragos exited the shed, the woman at his side. He threw back his head, laughing at something she said, and Raina felt a swell of jealousy deep within. She had no right to feel the swirling emotion, but it curled in her gut, sticky and corrosive. After the woman waved and began walking toward town, Raina called to Galen.

"Yes, Mom?" he asked, jogging into the room.

"I need to go speak to Dragos. Can you stay here with your brother and be the man of the house?"

He nodded. "I'm almost eleven, Mom. I can do it."

"Good boy." Leaning down, she kissed his forehead. "I'm only going to stay a few minutes. See you soon."

With her boys safe inside, she closed and locked the door behind her. Her feet were hard on the grass as she stomped toward Dragos's cottage, telling herself to calm down. When she arrived, she lifted her hand to knock, and he swung the door open, his lips forming a sexy smile that made her knees buckle.

"I saw you marching over here. You look like you're heading off to war. Should I be worried?"

Raina's throat bobbed as she swallowed, jealousy almost squeezing her airway shut. "If you would rather spend time with another woman, the least you could do is tell me."

His eyebrows lifted as he assessed her. "What are you talking about?"

"The pretty blond Deamon," she said, gesturing toward the meadow where the woman had recently retreated. "Don't deny it."

The corner of his lips curved as he crossed his arms and leaned on the doorframe. "Your eyes are on fire right now, Raina. They're so pretty. Even jealousy looks gorgeous on you."

Sighing, she crossed her arms over her chest. His eyes darted to the swell of her breasts above the neckline of her V-neck sweater, sending a rush of heat through her entire body.

"I won't deny I'm jealous. Do I need to worry someone else has caught your eye?"

His dark eyes roved over her face as he contemplated. "I don't think that's possible. I only want you, Raina."

Her nostrils flared as she struggled to rein in the swirling emotion. "If you ever wish to end this, I hope you will be honest with me. I don't think..." She closed her eyes, hating the tears that welled under her lids. "I don't think I can share you, Dragos." Lifting her lids, she stared into his eyes, the dark irises brimming with equal parts desire and frustration.

"Raina," he murmured, the low tone of his voice surrounding her like a warm blanket. Reaching for her, he gently palmed her cheeks, tilting her head so she was forced to gaze into his eyes. "I love you. With all that I am and to the depths of my soul. I love your boys and want nothing more than to marry you and be a true partner to you for eternity." Angling his head, he inched closer, his gaze searing into her. "But you have been clear you don't want the same thing, so we are stuck in the limbo of being...neighbors with benefits? Is that a fitting title?" His lips formed a tender smile as her heart melted.

"I don't know what I want anymore," she whispered, shaking her head against his warm hands. "How can I do this again knowing it might not last? Knowing I might lose you too? How do I take vows to love two men for eternity? It's daunting."

His dark eyes simmered with understanding, showcasing his empathy and compassion. Stepping back, he exhaled a deep breath and ran a hand through his hair.

"I will never begrudge you for loving your bonded, Raina. I only wish you would find the strength to love me too. You are one of the strongest people I know, and there is space in here for both of us if you would allow yourself to find it." He tapped a finger on her chest, directly over her heart. "Perhaps you should take some time to think about what you truly want. I will be here when you figure it out."

"Dragos," she rasped, tears burning her eyes as her chin wobbled.

"It's okay, Raina," he said, backing inside and clutching the door. "Good night." The door clicked softly as he shut himself in.

After angrily swiping away the twin tears that rolled down her cheeks, Raina returned home. Once the boys were in bed, she lay in the large bed wishing she weren't alone. Wishing Dragos's strong arms were surrounding her as she drifted to sleep. Staring at the ceiling, she placed her hand over her heart, comforted by the rhythmic beating as she pondered.

"Soran," she whispered, nostrils flaring as she prepared herself to finally accept her feelings. "I love him. By the goddess, I love him. And if I don't admit that to myself, and to him, I might lose him."

Seconds ticked by, and she closed her eyes, clutching onto the emotion. She expected to see Soran's face appear, but instead, it was Dragos's handsome face that materialized in her vision. Feeling her lips curve, she envisioned all the times he'd made her laugh, the time he'd saved her son, and the time they'd enjoyed s'mores before he camped with her boys. He fit into their family so seamlessly, and she realized something quite profound: she was ready to bond again. Ready to promise herself to another man for eternity. A joyful cry exited her lips as she finally embraced her love for Dragos.

Accepting the newfound feelings brought a sense of peace, and she felt as if a weight had been lifted from her shoulders. If she chose to build a life with Dragos, she would have stability and companionship and love. It was something she desperately wanted to feel again and finally accepted she deserved. Yes, Raina deserved to build a life with the man she loved.

Releasing a huge breath, she smiled at the darkened ceiling and prepared herself to approach Dragos. In the morning, she would go to him and apologize for the spurt of jealousy. And then she would finally tell him she loved him and pray to the goddess she wasn't too late.

Chapter 11

Dragos spent a sleepless night tossing and turning as he recalled the discussion with Raina. He was compassionate toward her struggle with moving on from her husband, but he wasn't quite sure where that left them. Eventually, he gave up on sleep and got out of bed, sitting at the table to have some oatmeal as the sun rose. A knock sounded on his door, followed by Raina's melodious voice.

"Dragos? It's your annoying neighbor with the absurd jealous streak. I hope you'll let me in."

Grinning, he rose from the table and trailed to the door. Pulling it open, he felt his heart slam in his chest as it always did when she smiled at him with those full lips.

"Good morning."

"Hey," he said, taken by the glow of her deep blue eyes in the morning sun. "You look pretty."

Her eyes glistened as her smile deepened. "Good. Perhaps that will encourage you to let me say what I've come to say."

"Of course." Giving a nod, he stepped out onto the stoop.

She slid her palm over his and laced their fingers, tugging him toward the grassy spot where their properties met. Turning, she stood on her side while he stood on his.

"I don't like how this is divided," she said, pointing toward the grass. "I don't want a barrier between us, Dragos. Not between our properties, and not between us as lovers and partners."

His lips curved as blood pounded through his body at her words. "Me neither."

Inhaling deeply, she gazed toward the horizon before facing him once again. "You and Soran are very different men," she said, and he gave a resigned nod.

"I know. I accept you'll always love him, Raina. It makes perfect sense, and I don't begrudge you for it."

"Wait," she interjected, holding up a finger. "I wasn't finished."

"Okay," he said, his lips twitching at her stern tone, which she often used with her boys.

"I am very lucky to have found two men who decided to love me even if I can be a *bit* difficult." She arched a brow.

Dragos chuckled. "A bit?"

Amusement sparkled in her eyes before she continued. "You are different men who both represent something very special to me. Soran was my past, and I loved him with my entire heart." Stepping forward, she placed her palms on his chest. "But my love for him has no bearing on my love for you, Dragos. I feel it, strong and true, deep in my soul." She placed her hand over her heart before returning it to lay against his chest. "I have no idea what I did to find love with another man who will surely be my future…if he will have me, that is."

Gliding an arm around her waist, Dragos drew her close. "He will definitely have you," he growled.

Laughter bounded from her throat as she nodded. "I love you, Dragos. You are everything I could ever want, and I would be honored to be your bonded mate and have you as the father to my children. Please say you'll bond with me." Rising to her toes, she softly kissed his lips. "I just needed a bit more time to realize I can't live without you. Thank you for being patient with me."

"Raina," he whispered, wondering how his heart was still beating since it had shattered in his chest from her reverent words. "I would be honored to build a future with you. To hopefully have more children if we're able to, and to be a father for your sons. I don't wish to take Soran's place. I want to learn about him and help keep the memories alive for you and your boys."

"That's so sweet," she said as tears streamed down her cheeks. "You would've liked each other and been fast friends. I want to tell you about him too because he was an important part of my life, and so are you. I want to tell you everything, Dragos. That will make us true partners, and we deserve that."

"We do." He pressed a soft kiss on her lips. "I want to be your friend, your lover, and your bonded mate. And I appreciate the proposal, but I aim to propose to you, Raina. I just need to plan it now that I'm pretty sure you'll say yes."

Laughing, she nodded. "I'll say yes. Plan it soon because you're moving in with me. Tonight."

"Is that so?" Lowering, he cupped her ass and lifted her.

Raina couldn't control her grin as she wrapped her legs around his waist. "Yes, soldier, it certainly is."

"Well, then, let's get to it."

Holding her tight, Dragos turned and carried her home...toward the house where they would raise their sons and build their eternity together. Once inside, he hugged the boys when they ran toward him, promising to spend the day playing in the yard with them. His beautiful Vampyre took his hand and squeezed, and Dragos reveled in the moment, realizing he finally understood the true meaning of the word "love."

Epilogue

Dragos stood beside Galen and Ekon at the altar he'd built. It sat in Raina's back yard—*their* back yard now—and he grinned at the boys as they fiddled with their neckties. "You both look like young men," he said, squeezing their shoulders. "We'll be done soon, and then we can play in the treehouse."

"I hate this thing," Galen said, tugging at the tie.

"I know, son. Just a few more minutes."

Raina exited the house and strode toward them, gorgeous in her flowing white dress. Her brown curls were pulled into a fancy updo, and Dragos felt his eyes bulge. By the goddess, he would get to gaze upon her beauty every day for eternity. Get to hear her laugh and console her when she cried... It was the greatest honor he'd ever known.

Raina approached, winking at her boys before facing him. Lila cleared her throat and addressed the small crowd. When Dragos had informed her he was getting married, she'd offered to perform the ceremony. It was completely unexpected for a revered royal aristocrat to marry commoners, but Lila was so gracious, and he had accepted. Her bonded mate Latimus sat in the small crowd of attendees with their sons Jack and Symon and daughter Adelyn. Miko waved at Dragos from her seat, and he gave her a nod.

"I'm ready if you are," Lila said, eyebrows arching as she held the bonding ceremony guide in her hands.

"Ready," Dragos and Raina said in unison. He took her hands, remembering the first time she'd touched him in the kind act of soothing the salve on his arms. Overcome with love for her, he said his vows before she said hers.

"I now pronounce you bonded mates for eternity," Lila said, beaming. "You may kiss your bride, Dragos."

Dragos kissed her so sweetly before leaning in and whispering, "Just a peck for now, but I'm going to kiss you everywhere tonight, Raina. Can't wait."

Drawing back, she swatted his chest. "Behave," she chided.

He flashed her a grin before lifting their joined hands as everyone cheered. Afterward, they danced upon the soft grass to the music Raina had prepared for the reception playlist.

Eventually, the celebration wore down, and everyone began to head home.

"I think Miko loves your cabin," Raina said as they folded the last of the chairs under the darkened sky after the boys were asleep. "You were so nice to sell it to her for the price you did."

"Well, I didn't need it anymore since I moved in here. Now that we're bonded, I can get started on building several more rooms. It will be nice if we have another child."

She trailed toward him and slid her arms around his neck. "Do you think we can conceive? Separate species have a much harder time if they don't have royal blood. And I'm pretty sure our blood is the farthest thing from royal."

"I have no idea," he said, placing a sweet kiss on the tip of her nose. "But I want to try as much as we can." He waggled his brows as she laughed.

"Oh, my dear bonded mate, I'm counting on it." Lifting to her toes, she pressed her lips to his. "I love you."

Gliding his hands to her ass, he gently squeezed. "And I love you. Now, let's get you out of this dress. We have a baby to make."

Tossing her head back, she released a joyful laugh, and Dragos reveled in the sound. Determined to make her laugh for eternity, he led her inside and made love to his wife, the woman he cherished with his entire soul.

Before you go...

Thank you so much for reading this sweet, steamy novella. If you want to read more in the Etherya's Earth series, you can find all of Rebecca's books at RebeccaHefner.com.

∞

Please consider leaving a review on your retailer's site, Goodreads and/or BookBub. Your friendly neighborhood author thanks you from the bottom of her heart!

Two Souls United

Etherya's Earth, Book 5.5

By

Rebecca Hefner

This book is a work of fiction. Names, characters, places and incidents are the product of the author's imagination and are used fictitiously. Any resemblance to actual events, locales or persons, living or dead, is coincidental.

Copyright © 2021 by Rebecca Hefner. All rights reserved, including the right to reproduce, distribute or transmit in any form or by any means.

Cover Design: Anthony O'Brien, BookCoverDesign.store
Editor and Proofreader: Bryony Leah, www.bryonyleah.com

Contents

Title Page
Copyright
Dedication
Mapy of Etherya's Earth
A Note from the Author
Chapter 1
Chapter 2
Chapter 3
Chapter 4
Chapter 5
Chapter 6
Chapter 7
Chapter 8
Chapter 9
Chapter 10
Chapter 11
Chapter 12
Epilogue
Before You Go
Also by Rebecca Hefner
Acknowledgments
About the Author

For Sam and Glarys, two supportive characters who deserve their happy ending...

A Note from the Author

Hello, lovely readers. I'm thrilled to bring you **Sam and Glarys's** love story and add to the Etherya's Earth world. I originally wrote this novella for an anthology that never came to fruition, which worked out rather well since this story is perfect for a release date near Valentine's Day.

If you're new to the Etherya's Earth series, please note that this novella falls between Books 5 and 6 in the series and, therefore, *there are a ton of spoilers*. If you'd like to read Book 1 first to get an idea of Etherya's world, make sure you check out **The End of Hatred**. If you're fine with spoilers, then read on, my friends.

I really enjoy writing books with more mature characters and was so excited to see Sam and Glarys get their happy ending after centuries without a soulmate. Here's wishing you happiness too, and I hope you enjoy their sweet, steamy story!

Chapter 1

Sam, son of Raythor, sat in the uncomfortable chair waiting for Lila to walk down the aisle. The sun was high in the clear blue sky, and he closed his eyes, inhaling the fragrant air. Vampyres had only regained the ability to walk in the sun weeks ago. For a thousand years, they'd been cursed by the goddess Etherya to live in darkness, a punishment for their role in the War of the Species with the Slayers. Now that the war had ended and Vampyre King Sathan and Slayer Queen Miranda were married, the goddess had finally rescinded the curse. So thankful to feel the warmth on his skin, Sam basked in the glorious rays.

"Isn't it magnificent?" a melodic voice asked beside him.

Lifting his lids, he smiled at Glarys. The house manager for the sprawling Vampyre royal estate at Astaria was a lovely woman, and he was happy he'd found a seat next to her at the wedding. He'd met her a few times when he'd come to eat dinner at the estate, and the food she prepared was heavenly. Although Vampyres relied on Slayer blood for sustenance, Sam had always enjoyed food and had never tasted anything like Glarys's succulent dishes.

"Amazing," he said, smiling. "I'd almost given up hope."

"For some reason, I never did. Somehow, I knew our people would find a way to end the war. After that, I was sure Etherya would let us walk in the sun again."

"I admire your optimism."

Light blue eyes sparkled as she grinned up at him. "I've always been pretty optimistic. It seems like a waste to be otherwise, right?"

Giving a nod, he said, "It sure does. Life should be lived to the fullest and all that jazz."

"Exactly." The tips of her fangs rested upon her bottom lip as she beamed up at him, and Sam felt a tiny jolt as his heartbeat quickened. Realization swept over him as he envisioned her scraping the tiny points over the vein at his neck...and then piercing the skin as she drank from him.

Processing his attraction to the kindhearted adopted family member of the Vampyre royals, Sam let the sentiment settle in. He certainly didn't expect to feel desire for her, but his body's reaction was undeniable.

Lila chose that moment to walk down the aisle, saving Sam from further analysis. As the ceremony progressed, the stub of his arm tingled as if it wanted to reach for her.

Sam had lost his arm in the Awakening but still felt the limb's presence on occasion. Nolan, the physician at Astaria, called it "phantom arm" and informed Sam he would most likely feel the sensation indefinitely. It was a stark reminder that he'd never quite be whole.

Glancing down at Glarys, he wondered if the sight of the missing limb bothered her. She simply grinned up at him, giving him a wink as Latimus and Lila exchanged their vows, and his throat tightened. She was so pretty, her cheekbones slightly reddened from the sun, and Sam reveled in the moment.

For the first time in so very long, Sam was attracted to a woman. Embracing the feeling, he settled into the chair to watch the ceremony.

Glarys flitted around the ballroom of the huge castle at Astaria making sure glasses were full and empty plates were removed. Doting on people was one of her favorite pastimes, and she was masterful at it. Perhaps that was why she excelled at running the large royal estate. Sathan's father, King Markdor, had hired her centuries ago, before her husband died, and she'd become part of the family. Since she and Victor never had children, her window had closed, leaving her with a soft spot in her heart for the royal Vampyre siblings, whom she loved as her own.

Glarys had gone through her immortal change at sixty-five years old, locking her into a body that was less agile and more withered than most. There was no rhyme or reason as to when a person went through their immortal change, but many Vampyres experienced it in their twenties or thirties.

Sighing, Glarys caught a glimpse of her reflection in the kitchen window as she washed the dishes, inwardly remarking that she looked like an old lady. Her short hair was white as snow, and stubborn little laugh lines extended from her eyes. At least her irises were blue, and the wrinkles weren't that noticeable. She had long, black lashes surrounding her ice-blue eyes and hoped that made her somewhat passable. Telling herself to release the ridiculous musings and get back to work, she finished washing the dishes and set everything in the rack to dry.

Turning, her gaze fell upon Sam, and she gasped. He held up his hand, palm out, looking contrite.

"Sorry, Glarys, I didn't mean to scare you. Jack sent me back here to see if there's any orange juice. He said you squeeze it fresh, and I think he might be addicted to it."

Wiping her hands on the towel before throwing it on the counter, she trailed to the refrigerator and pulled out the pitcher. "I made some just for him. Somehow, I knew he'd ask for it. Want to grab a cup out of the cabinet?"

"Sure." He turned, opening the cabinet and searching inside.

Glarys took the opportunity to steal a glance at his broad back and delicious butt in his dress pants. His tapered waist was accentuated by the black belt he wore, and she breathed a tiny sigh, wishing she could unbuckle it and discover what was inside. Of course, the probability of that happening was slim to none, so she waited, smiling when he approached her with the glass.

She poured a generous portion for his nephew, Jack. Lila and Latimus's adopted son was hands-down the cutest kid on the planet with his freckled face and mop of red hair. Studying Sam, she realized his features mimicked his nephew's. Reddish-blond hair sat above firm features and lightly freckled skin. Deep brown eyes seemed to pool like melted chocolate as he grinned.

"That's real nice of you to make this for Jack. I know he appreciates it."

"Of course," she said, waving her hand and turning to put the drink back in the fridge. "He's stolen my heart, the little munchkin. I'd do just about anything to see that crooked smile of his."

Turning back, she saw Sam's gaze lift and wondered if he'd been staring at her backside. Glarys always carried an additional ten pounds she never had the energy to shed despite wanting to. Maintaining an estate as large as Astaria was exhausting, and she usually fell into bed each night already half-asleep.

"You look pretty in your dress," he said, eyes roaming over her blue frock as she damn near shivered. Telling herself he was just being kind, she gave a slight curtsy.

"Thank you, sir," she teased. "You look wonderful too. I wouldn't be surprised if one of the aristocratic ladies snatched you up for a dance."

His features scrunched. "I've never really had much use for aristocrats. Find them kind of haughty. Except for Lila. She's a damn saint. And Latimus is pretty great too."

"Lila has always been such a sweet girl. I'm so happy she and Latimus finally decided to act on their feelings. It's so beautiful. Isn't true love amazing?"

"It is." His eyebrows drew together. "Lila told me you were married before."

"Yes," she said, trailing her fingers over the counter. "Victor was a lovely man. He was a winemaker and supplied the king with several barrels at the Awakening. Sadly, he was slain, as so many others were."

"That's how I lost my arm," Sam said, lifting the stub. "I was a young soldier and tried like hell to fight back. It got sliced clean off with a poison-tipped blade that rendered my self-healing abilities useless."

"I'm so sorry," she said, taking a step toward him. "Does it still hurt?"

"Nah," he said, shaking his head. "It hasn't hurt in a long time. Still tingles sometimes just to remind me it was once there, I guess."

Chuckling, she bit her lip. "Well, nothing like a good reminder."

Kind eyes studied her. "Do you miss your husband?"

A small sigh escaped her lips. "Every damn day. I miss being in love. Having someone to love me back. Sadly, I don't think I'll ever experience that again. He was a wonderful man."

"I'm real sorry, Glarys."

She smiled, realizing she found his colloquial way of talking quite endearing. Many who frequented the castle were quite formal, and Sam's easygoing natural charm was refreshing.

"Thank you."

Gesturing with the glass, he said, "Well, I'll stop bothering you so you can get back to work. Lila said to tell you to stop working but also said it wouldn't do any good. I think she wants you to have some fun."

"Working is fun for me," Glarys said with a shrug. "It gives me purpose."

"I hear that." He took a step toward the door and then pivoted back. "I really enjoy talking to you, Glarys. Maybe we can find a time to talk again. I mean, if you want to."

She almost swallowed her tongue, overcome with excited surprise. Was it possible that Sam was attracted to her? If so, what the heck should she do? She hadn't been romantically involved with anyone since Victor, and the thought was terrifying for some reason. Choking on the fear, she said, "Of course. Bring Jack over anytime. I know he loves pasta. The three of us could eat together and chat."

His brown eyes roved over her. "Me and Jack. Yeah. Okay, sounds good." Disappointment laced his tone, and she wanted to kick herself. "See you later." Lifting the glass in a salute, he exited the kitchen.

Falling against the counter, Glarys lifted her eyes to the ceiling and rubbed her forehead. "Way to go, Glarys. Now he thinks you're not interested. Good grief." Realizing she'd ruined her first foray into romance in centuries, she blew a breath between puffed cheeks. Chalking it up to a lesson learned, she resumed working, hoping it would clear her head of the images of Sam's broad shoulders and sexy smile.

Chapter 2

Glarys continued to see Sam over the years, mostly when he joined the royal family for dinners. For immortals, time was a slow-moving constant, and the years bled together with stable regularity. After their conversation in the kitchen at Lila's bonding ceremony, Glarys held out hope Sam might ask to spend some time with her again.

Vowing she wouldn't blow it if he did, she eventually realized he wasn't going to make the move. Unsure whether she'd inadvertently portrayed disinterest or perhaps misconstrued his sentiments, she carried on, immersed in her busy life. After all, she adored the royal siblings and their children, and taking care of them brought her immense joy.

But eventually, they all began to create families of their own. Sathan started to divide his time between Astaria and Uteria, leaving the house devoid of his kingly duties. Latimus moved to Lynia, and Arderin married and moved to the human world. And then, her sweet Heden fell for a human. Overcome with joy that he'd found his soulmate, his announcement he was moving to the human world all but broke Glarys's heart. On the day before his relocation, he found her in the kitchen.

"How am I going to live without you, Glarys?" he asked, eyes sparkling as he smiled down at her. "You're the love of my life."

"Oh, stop it," she said, swatting him with the dish towel. "You and your brothers always tease me. Sofia is a wonderful cook and she'll treat you just fine. I'm so glad you found her, sweet boy."

Heden took her hand, squeezing as he spoke reverent words. "You're so special, Glarys. I never knew my mother, but I thank Etherya every day that you were here to raise us. You deserve to be cherished, and I want so badly for you to be happy."

"I'm happy, son," she said, palming his cheek. "Don't you worry about me."

"I do worry," he said, pulling her into an embrace. "I love you, Glarys."

"I love you too," she whispered, the words true to the core of her soul. "Go make some babies for me to dote on, okay?"

Chuckling, he pulled back. "I'm going to try like hell. I mean, trying's the best part."

She playfully whacked him with the towel again, understanding how much she would miss his gentle jibing. When he drove off in the four-wheeler the next day, he all but took a piece of her heart with him.

Glarys still enjoyed overseeing the large compound, although it was now bereft of the vibrant life it once held. Each day, the duties brought her less joy until she realized she was lonely. It was a strange feeling—and one she hadn't experienced in many centuries. Determined to push through, she began searching for ways to be more involved with the family now that they were scattered across the kingdom. Jack loved pasta, so Glarys began to make a huge vat for him once a month, which she brought to Lynia. It gave her an excuse to have dinner with Jack, Lila, and Latimus as well as Sam, who would come every so often.

Glarys had almost convinced herself she'd eradicated her tiny wisps of desire for the man, but deep inside, she knew that to be a lie. Each time he showed for dinner, her heartbeat would accelerate, and she would feel a burst of pure joy inside her chest. Silly, but it existed all the same. Reminding herself a harmless crush was nothing to be embarrassed about, she carried on, hoping the man didn't notice the flush of her cheeks when he trained that gorgeous brown gaze on her. No—he seemed completely unfazed by her, confirming she'd all but imagined any hint of mutual attraction all those years ago at the bonding ceremony.

One night, a few months after Heden moved to the human world, Glarys joined them for dinner at Latimus and Lila's house at Lynia. The meal was filled with wine and wonderful conversation as well as their three adorable children: Jack, Adelyn, and Symon. Moments like this spurred such gratefulness in Glarys's heart, reminding her how lucky she was to be a part of their family. During these dinners, the loneliness seemed so far away, and she reveled in their comradery.

"We're so happy you're staying with us now that Milakos has decided to move to Takelia and join the council," Latimus said. "You're welcome to stay as long as you need, Sam."

"Thank you," Sam said as he spooned out some pasta sauce. "Council members get their own security detail funded by the compound, as you know, so he no longer needs me as private security. I'm going to take a few weeks off since the job was pretty intense, and then I'll find something new. I'll be out of your hair in no time," he said, winking at Lila.

Lila wrinkled her nose. "I wish you'd just move in with us, but I know you crave your independence, so I won't badger you."

"If you need help finding another post, let me know," Latimus said. "I know a plethora of stuffy aristocrats who don't know the first thing about protecting themselves and would hire you in a second."

"Daddy hates aristocrats," Adelyn said, staring up at Sam. "He says they're titled."

"That's *entitled*, sweetie, and most of them are," Latimus said, shrugging.

"Daddy doesn't hate anyone, does he?" Lila corrected, shooting a look at her husband. "We don't believe in hate in this house."

"That's right," Latimus said, although his tone was less than thrilled. "I agree with Momma so she'll keep kissing me. I've learned that's the best way to make that happen."

Lila scrunched her features. "Very funny. But let's remember to be kind, okay, guys?"

They all murmured their agreement while Glarys enjoyed the interplay.

"Well, thanks, Latimus," Sam said, his full lips curving into a smile. "I'll let you know when I'm ready."

The dinner progressed until the hour grew late, and Glarys prepared to head home. As she reached for her light jacket hanging by the door, a strong arm entered her line of view and grabbed the coat instead. Turning, she smiled up at Sam.

"Thought I could help you with your jacket," he said, his expression kind. "But it's probably not that helpful since I only have one arm."

"It's lovely," she said, threading her arm through the jacket as he shimmied it over her skin. Rotating, she slid the other arm in and tugged it tight across her abdomen. "Perfect. What a gentleman you are."

"Happy to oblige," he said, giving her a mock salute. "It was real nice to see you tonight, Glarys. Hope you make it home safely."

Before she could speak, Latimus appeared. "Ready for me to drive you to the train?"

"Yes," she said, shooting Sam one last smile. "Have a good night."

He gave a nod, and she pivoted to walk down the front porch steps with Latimus. As he drove the four-wheeler to the Lynia train station, Glarys couldn't shake the image of Sam's handsome face and muscled arm.

"How are you doing at Astaria, Glarys?" Latimus asked. "You know you can come live with us anytime."

"Thank you, dear," she said, exiting the vehicle. Although the offer had been issued repeatedly, she didn't want to be a burden on the young family. "Someone has to take care of that big ol' house, especially since you've all left me."

He pulled her into an embrace, kissing her white hair. "I worry about you, Glarys."

"I'm fine, boy," she said, drawing back and waving a dismissive hand. "But you're very sweet. Now, let me get on home. I don't want to miss the train. Talk to you in a few days." Keeping her voice light, she waggled her fingers as she trailed down the stairs.

As the train chugged along, she sat in the almost empty car figuring most people were home with their families since it was late. At least it was quiet and she could possibly catch a catnap before they pulled into Astaria's station. Closing her eyes, she rested her head on the seat.

Suddenly, the train ground to a halt, and her lids snapped open. Yells and cries of war sounded from outside the train car, and terror seized Glarys's veins. Standing, she pulled the handgun from her bag. Latimus had given it to her decades ago and trained her on how to use it, but she was no expert. Still, she would wield the weapon valiantly against any enemy who tried to harm her.

She might not have the most exciting life, but it was a life she damn well wanted to keep living.

The Deamons stormed the train, Glarys realizing they must've been sent by Bakari. The outcast royal sibling had built a Deamon army, spawned from the prisoners he'd freed at Takelia, and they were now a new foe for the Vampyres and Slayers.

Two male passengers began to fight the beady-eyed creatures, and Glarys lifted the gun, firing at one and catching him in the abdomen. Pride surged through her as he fell to the ground. More fighting ensued, and she thought she saw the immortal troops out of the corner of her eye. Thankful that Latimus's soldiers were well-trained and had responded so quickly, she whirled around when something grabbed her neck. As she stared into one of the Deamon's eyes, he whacked his forehead against hers.

The last thing she saw before she succumbed to unconsciousness was the malicious curl of his lips, cruel and menacing.

Chapter 3

Sam tapped his foot against the floor, hand covering his mouth as he anxiously waited in Latimus and Lila's living room. He'd been about to turn in when Latimus's cell rang. The massive soldier had informed them that the trains were being attacked by Bakari's Deamon forces.

Fear for Glarys had immediately surged in Sam's heart. He'd offered to go with Latimus to help the troops, but the commander had asked him to stay and keep an eye on Lila and the kids. Now, the kids were upstairs sleeping, and he and Lila waited, worried and pensive.

The front door swung open, and Latimus walked in, gently leading Glarys, who looked unstable on her feet. Sam and Lila rushed over, and she shooed them away.

"Please don't make a fuss," she said as Sam noticed the shiner beginning to form under her eye and the huge knot on her forehead. "I wasn't hurt at all. Latimus really should've let me go home."

"No way, Glarys," Latimus said, taking her jacket and hanging it up as she massaged her head. "You were hit pretty hard, and I'm not sending you home alone. Sathan's at Uteria, and the castle only has the barebone staff. You're staying here, and I'm putting my foot down."

"Oh, fine. I don't have the energy to argue anyway. I'm just shaken. That was a lot of energy for this old lady."

"She can have my guest room," Sam said, stepping forward and offering out his arm. "Please, Glarys, I insist. I'll lead you there."

"Okay."

Gritting his teeth at the purple bruise forming on her head, he vowed to strangle every Deamon who had touched her. Gently taking her hand, he led her into the room and turned down the bed while she removed her shoes. Lila entered behind them, and they both ushered her into bed.

"Nolan says we need to check on you every few hours, so we might wake you up," Lila said, tenderly wiping the white hair from Glarys's temple. "I promise we'll take care of you."

"I don't need anything, dear," she said, shaking her head on the pillow. "Please don't go out of your way." Her lids blinked slowly a few times before fluttering closed. "I'll be fine tomorrow," she murmured as she drifted off.

Lila lifted her fist to her mouth, and Sam saw the tears forming. "Come on, sweetie," he said, taking her hand. "She's out of danger now. We need to let her rest."

Lila clasped his hand, and he led her back to the living room, where Latimus was speaking to Slayer Commander Kenden. Shutting off his phone, he ran a hand over his slick black hair.

"Those bastards attacked three train lines tonight. Bakari is growing bolder. Ken and I will begin implementing updated posts and training tomorrow."

"Thank the goddess Glarys is okay," Lila said, hand over her heart as she sat beside Sam. "Lattie, we have to assign a bodyguard to her. I know Bakari can't infiltrate the goddess's protective wall at Astaria, but I'm terrified for her safety."

"I asked her again tonight to live with us, but she won't budge. She's pretty stubborn and independent, which is one of the things we all love most about her. I mean, we can't force her to move here."

"I can do it." The words left Sam's mouth before he even realized he'd uttered them.

"What's that, Sam?" Lila asked.

"Assign me as Glarys's bodyguard. I'm free now that my private security post for Milakos has ended. I'll guard Glarys."

Latimus and Lila exchanged a look. Arching his brows as he considered, Latimus said, "It's not a bad idea. I could pay you out of the military funds since she's technically a member of the royal family. I don't think I'd get any pushback at all from Sathan or Miranda."

"I don't care about money," Sam said, waving his hand. "I'd just really like to keep her safe. If she's determined to keep living at Astaria, I'll guard her."

"I think it's a lovely idea," Lila said, grasping his hand. "And of course Latimus will arrange for you to be paid. I would feel so much better knowing you're around to keep her safe, Sam."

"Me too," Latimus said with a nod. "Do you mind relocating to Astaria for a while? I don't know how long the post will be, but it could be years before we defeat Bakari. Are you up for that?"

"Yes. I was planning on moving to wherever my new post eventually took me. I can move to Astaria just as easily."

"Since you'll be guarding Glarys, you'll have to live at the castle. There are a lot of unoccupied rooms there, mine and Heden's being the most recently vacated. You can have your pick."

Sam's breathing quickened as he comprehended what he'd just signed up for. But he'd been in private security for years now and was extremely capable. With his missing arm, he could no longer fight in the military, but his skill set came in quite handy as a bodyguard. And he'd get to spend a plethora of time with Glarys. Although she'd made it quite clear she wasn't interested in him romantically, she was still an amazing woman whom he liked very much. His clumsy attempts to spend one-on-one time with her had been met with suggestions of involving others, which he understood was a nice way of brushing him off.

He couldn't say he blamed her. Although she was a paid servant of the royal family, she was a white-collar worker, one who'd been educated along with the aristocrats she served. Sam could barely read and write since he'd always been more interested in becoming a soldier than studying. His lack of formal education, compounded by the fact he was missing an arm, probably wasn't all that attractive to Glarys, who was surrounded by royalty at every turn. Still, he had an affinity toward her and would strive to protect her.

"It would be an honor to keep her safe. Do you think she'll be resistant to having a bodyguard?"

Latimus exchanged a look with Lila. "Maybe. She's a tough one. But Lila and I will insist upon it, don't you worry about that."

"Good. I'll sleep on the couch tonight. Y'all go ahead and go on to bed. We can tell her tomorrow."

Standing, Lila took his face between her hands. "You're too good, Sam." She softly kissed his lips. "Thank you."

"Of course."

Lila and Latimus trailed up the stairs, leaving Sam in the darkened living room to process what he'd committed to.

Lila watched her bonded mate remove his shirt as she brushed her hair. Every so often, her eyes would drift to his magnificent chest, reflected in the mirror, and her body hummed with desire. By the goddess, he was glorious. Biting her lip, she wondered if he was in the mood for sexy times since he was most likely exhausted from his efforts with the troops earlier.

He removed his pants and underwear, standing tall and naked as he slowly approached her. Finding her gaze in the mirror, his ice-blue eyes locked onto hers.

"Are you staring at me, little temptress?"

"Yes," she whispered, baring her neck so he could place butterfly kisses over the pulsing vein.

"Good wives would let their tired husbands sleep after such a long day."

Setting down the brush, she arched a brow. "You know I'm only good in public. In here, anything goes."

"Which is why this bedroom is my favorite place in the whole damn world," he said, waggling his eyebrows as she chuckled. "Sam's offer was interesting," he murmured against her skin.

Nodding, she tried to concentrate on the conversation—difficult, since her mate was doing something amazing with his tongue against her skin. "I can't believe I didn't see it. He's smitten with her."

"I've noticed for several years now," Latimus said, sliding his arm around her waist and drawing her still-clothed body into his.

"You have? Why didn't you tell me? I would've tried to matchmake for sure."

"Once you've secretly longed for someone yourself, it becomes easy to see it in another man."

Emotion filled her lavender irises as she clutched his hand above her abdomen. "I wish I had known. So much time wasted where we could've loved each other."

His fangs nipped her earlobe, causing her to shiver. "We won't let them make our mistakes. Hopefully, their newfound proximity will lead to something more. And it will keep her safe, which is paramount."

Sighing, she tilted her face to his. "When did you become so romantic?"

"When you turned me into a lovesick sap." Pressing his erection into her lower back, his fingers found the button of her jeans, releasing it before sliding the zipper down. Gliding his fingers over her mound, he found her slick warmth. "Now, be a good girl and bend over the dresser, honey."

Her fangs squished her lip as she grinned. "Someone's bossy."

"Do you want me, sweetheart? Because I'm desperate for you. Let me take you while you give me that sexy smile in the mirror. Come on, honey."

Reaching behind her back, she gripped his straining shaft. "Oh, my, you do feel ready."

"You little temptress. Bend over."

Shimmying out of her jeans and thong, she pulled her shirt over her head and tossed it to the floor. The last coherent memory she had was spreading her palms wide over the dresser before her bonded's skillful loving erased every other musing in her aroused mind.

Chapter 4

Glarys's lids fluttered open, and she immediately reached for her pounding forehead. "Ouch."

"You've got a really bad bump, Glarys," Lila said, sitting on the bed, concern lacing her tone. "It's probably going to hurt for a few days even with your self-healing body."

"Well, I guess it could've been worse, so I can live with a headache." Struggling to sit up, she realized she was still wearing yesterday's dress. "Oh, my. I've got to get home and shower. Miranda's having some of Tordor's friends over for a sleepover tonight, and I've got to prepare the mansion."

"Miranda's staying at Uteria tonight, and Jana is going to host there," Lila said, referencing Glarys's counterpart at the Slayer castle. "You just need to focus on resting and healing."

Feeling off-balance, she struggled to stand as her legs threatened to turn to jelly. "Whoa, there," Sam said, rushing to her side. "Lean on me."

"Thank you," she said, wondering why he was in her room. For the love of the goddess, she must look hideous. "I'm fine. Just a little woozy."

"Sam will get you home and make sure you're all set, Glarys. He's volunteered to be your bodyguard for however long this conflict with Bakari lasts."

Glarys's heart slammed in her chest. "Oh, that's not necessary."

"It's already done," he said, giving her a sheepish grin. "Latimus processed the paperwork and everything. I'm trained in private security and promise you'll be safe."

Feeling her knees buckle, she sat back on the bed. Of course the man she had a terrible crush on would sign up to guard her when she was in her weakest state and probably looked like a damn invalid. Annoyed, she tried again to dissent.

"I'm a grown woman and am perfectly capable of taking care of myself."

"It's non-negotiable, Glarys," Latimus said, arms crossed over his thick chest as he stood in the doorway. "You've never shied away from giving me much-needed stern lectures, so don't think I won't reciprocate. Sam is now your assigned bodyguard, and he's vowed to protect you. I care more about your safety than you being mad at me. Sorry." He shrugged and grinned.

"All this fuss for little ol' me... I just think it's silly."

"I'm honored to ensure your safety, Glarys," Sam said in his silken baritone, causing parts deep in her body that she hadn't felt for ages to flare to life. "This doesn't have to be a big thing. I'm pretty low-key and promise I won't restrict you."

Inhaling deeply, she contemplated the three people who stared at her with such concern. "Oh, fine. If you want to waste your time watching a boring old lady cook and clean, that's your life. I'm ready to get home, so, if we're going, let's go."

Sam beamed at her, offering his arm so she could balance. They ambled out the door, Sam hopping behind the wheel of a four-wheeler after she was situated in the passenger seat.

"Tell the kids I'll come see them when I'm healed. I don't want them to see all these bruises on my face."

"Will do." Lila gave her a firm embrace before they began the trek toward Astaria.

"You don't have to do this, Sam," Glarys said, noticing his gorgeous profile as he drove. "I'm sure there's some other security job you would enjoy more."

"Good try, but you're stuck with me," he said, flashing her a grin. "We're going to get you better, and I'm moving to Astaria as your bodyguard. I'll do my best not to drive you nuts."

Settling in, she realized that was the least of her worries. No—Glarys was more consumed with the idea her attraction to him would continue to grow until she did something embarrassing, such as beg him to kiss her. Determined to keep her desire in check, she accepted her fate.

∞

Two days after the attack, Glarys pushed the flesh around her shiner with the pads of her fingers. It was still a bit swollen and looked absolutely terrible—like a dark half-moon under her eye—but that meant it was healing. Two more days, and she hoped her self-healing body would eliminate it.

Since she'd gone through her change late in life, her self-healing properties worked a bit slower than those of a Vampyre locked in a younger body. The abilities were still appreciated, though, since Slayers didn't possess such powers. Like humans, they could be killed instantly, even though they were immortal, and Glarys was thankful her body would eventually return to its regular state.

Craving normalcy, she headed downstairs to begin her daily chores. As she was wiping down the marble island countertop in the expansive kitchen, Sam sauntered in, looking absolutely delicious in jeans and a black T-shirt. His shoulders were broad above his trim waist, and she'd bet anything a six-pack adorned his taut abdomen.

"Good morning," she said, hoping he couldn't see the vein pulsing at her neck. "Would you like some coffee?"

"Sure would," he said, lowering onto one of the stools at the counter. "You've already figured out what makes me tick, Glarys. Good coffee and nice conversation. You're a master at both."

"Why, thank you," she said, pouring him a cup with cream and one sugar since that was what he'd taken yesterday morning. Placing it in front of him, she rested her hands on the countertop. "Well, I need to go to town today. I guess you're going to accompany me?"

"Sure am," he said, eyes sparkling as he sipped the coffee. "Are you still secretly pissed you have to put up with me?"

"Of course not," she said, playfully swatting him with her dish towel. "I just think guarding me must be an incredibly dull use of your time. At least Latimus is paying you. Otherwise, I'd feel terrible."

He took another sip as he studied her. "Actually, I really like spending time with you, Glarys. I was pretty sure you'd figured that out by now."

Heat flooded her cheeks, and she tried to keep herself from covering them to hide her blush. "Oh, well, that's nice of you to say. Most young people I know enjoy hanging out with other people their age."

Setting down his cup, he pondered her. "I don't want to overstep here, but why do you keep calling yourself old?"

"Oh, I..." Feeling like an idiot, her gaze fell to the counter as she absently wiped it with the cloth. "Well, it's obvious I went through my change later in life. I've already had a marriage and lived so many decades before being frozen in my immortality."

He squinted. "When did you go through your change? Sixty?"

She breathed a laugh. "Sixty-five, you charmer. But thank you."

"I went through at forty-three. So I'd lived a few decades myself."

Her eyes roved over his muscled arm and chiseled face. He was extraordinarily handsome and didn't appear a day over forty. "Well, you look young compared to me."

"But we're both over one thousand years old in the scheme of things. So even though you were born a few centuries before me, we've certainly caught up to each other now."

"Yes, but I'll always look like this," she said, pointing at her slightly wrinkled face and white hair. "I could dye it but just never really cared enough to do it."

"I like your hair," he said, eyes narrowing as he studied her. "It looks real soft."

"Oh," she said, patting her curls as she tried not to faint at the reverent compliment. "Well, thank you. It's easy to maintain, so I just leave it."

Finishing the last of the coffee, he gave a nod and stood. "Well, I'll let you finish what you need here, and then we can head to the main square at ten a.m.?"

"Sure thing. That sounds perfect. I'll meet you outside the back door."

He flashed a grin before pivoting to leave. Only a moment later, he called her name from the doorway.

"Yes?" She noticed the whites of his knuckles on the frame as he seemed to hesitate.

"I'm happy you'll always look like you do now. I think you're real pretty." With a tilt of his head, he said, "See you at ten."

When he'd disappeared through the door, Glarys placed her hand over the space where her neck met her chest, wondering what the hell had just happened. Her new bodyguard, whom she was all but lusting over, had complimented her. Was it out of kindness or a mutual attraction? Glarys had no idea since she hadn't been involved with anyone romantically since Victor, but suddenly, she was aching to find out.

Chapter 5

Glarys had a lovely time at the market with Sam, noting how attentive he was. As they strolled through the farmers market, he urged her to lead and ensured he walked between her and the street. As the empty bags she'd brought became heavy, he offered to carry them, stacking them on his arm.

"I can carry the bags, Sam," she said, smiling up at him under the blue sky. "You're my bodyguard, not my servant. I don't want to take advantage of you."

"A gentleman never lets a lady carry her own bags," he said, lifting them as his sinewed muscles strained underneath. Flashes of him working that arm and his long, broad fingers around her nether regions caused her to clear her throat. "Please, let me help you. I remember you telling me that working made you happy. Well, doing my part to help makes me feel the same way."

"Okay," she said, wondering if she'd ever met someone so kind. "I only need a few more items, and we'll head home."

Once back at the castle, she threw herself into baking cupcakes for Symon's upcoming birthday party. After that, she decided she needed to clean the gym since the kids would want to play there if it rained. Donning her yoga pants and an old T-shirt—her most comfortable housecleaning attire—she headed to the gym and gasped when she entered.

Sam was punching the bag with his arm in sure strokes. Shirtless, beads of sweat ran down his magnificent chest and abdomen to the waistband of his black athletic shorts. His feet were bare, showcasing the springy brown hair on his legs. Overcome with desire, all she could do was stare.

"Hey," he said, straightening. "I'm almost finished. Did you come to work out?"

"Oh, no, although I probably should." Glancing down at her stomach, Glarys prayed her love handles weren't too pronounced. "I just came to clean. I can come back."

"It's fine," he said, grabbing the water canister on the bench and taking several gulps. The line of his throat was glossy with sweat, his Adam's apple bobbing as he swallowed. God, but she wanted to bite him there. Just close her eyes, stick her fangs in his neck, and lose herself in his taste.

Realizing she was staring like an idiot, she ran her hand over her hair. "I'll come back. Take all the time you need." Pivoting, she told herself not to run from the room.

His warm hand slid over her shoulder before she could exit. "I don't want to mess up your routine, Glarys. I'm the visitor here. Please, I'd feel terrible if you rearranged your schedule for me. I know you keep a tight ship in this place."

"I do," she said, grinning up at him.

"Okay then. I'm going to shower. See you tomorrow for the trip to Takelia, right?"

She nodded. "We can leave any time after nine a.m. I told Evie I'd be there by ten to prepare the lunch she's having with the council and the donors."

"Perfect." His eyes roved over her face. "Latimus told me Heden left an awesome collection of movies behind in the theater room. I'm going to find one to watch tonight. You're welcome to join me if you're not too tired. Hope to see you there." With one last curve of his full lips, he exited the gym.

Glarys stood frozen for several seconds, allowing her pulse to return to some semblance of normalcy. Sam had now told her she was pretty and asked her to spend time with him. She'd convinced herself he was just being nice—that he wouldn't desire someone who looked more mature—but she'd misread people before. Chewing her lip with her fangs, she contemplated and decided she would indeed watch a movie with him tonight. It would allow her to study him and hopefully figure out if he desired her even half as much as she did him.

∾

Sam's heart slammed in his chest when Glarys tentatively rounded the corner into the theater room later that evening. Throwing the blanket aside on the brown leather couch, he rose to meet her.

"Hey," he said, extending his hand and leading her to the couch. "Have a seat here."

She slid into the corner, those apple-ripe cheeks glowing red, and he almost blushed too. Wanting to make her feel comfortable, he sat on the opposite corner and lifted the remote.

"I just started Star Wars. It said Episode IV, but it's actually the first one released. Have you seen it?"

"No," she said, reaching for the blanket located on the shelf of the nearby table. "But Heden was always quoting it. Something about Han Solo and how he was pretty badass. I'm excited to finally see it." Covering herself with the blanket, she settled in.

Pressing play, Sam relaxed back, overcome with her presence and her smell. Her scent reminded him of the pretty purple flowers Latimus had planted for Lila in front of her cottage at Lynia all those years ago. Wispy and full of spring, he reveled in it as they watched the movie.

Always aware of her out of the corner of his eye, he noticed her relax as the movie progressed, shifting her legs onto the couch and eventually stretching them so they almost touched his thigh. Her feet peeked out from the blanket, and blood surged to his shaft at the sight of her red toenails. He'd never really been a toe guy, but hers were absolutely adorable.

During an exciting scene in which Darth Vader was battling Obi-Wan Kenobi, they both jumped at a particularly thrilling exchange, and her feet surged into his leg.

"Oh, sorry!" she said, drawing back her legs. "This is so good!"

Smiling, he surrounded both of her feet with his hand. "It sure is. Heden was right about these movies being fantastic." Scooching toward her, he pulled her feet atop his thigh. Settling back into the couch, he began to massage them as they watched the climax of the movie.

"You don't have to do that," she said, grinning at him as the side of her head rested on the back of the couch. "I didn't mean to kick you."

He dug his thumb into her arch, arousal flaming deep within as her eyes lit with pleasure. "You were on your feet all day and survived a Deamon attack less than a week ago. I think you deserve a good foot massage."

Her breathy sigh surrounded him like a warm blanket. By the goddess, he wanted nothing more than to feel her breath against the shell of his ear...and against his neck as she drank from him...and around his cock before she slid those pink lips over the straining, sensitive skin...

"Well, if you insist, I'm not going to argue."

"I think that's a first from you," he said with a wink. "Relax, honey. I've got you."

When the movie was finished, Sam muted the TV and set the remote aside. Sliding his hand back around her feet, he softly stroked them.

"Your skin is so smooth," he murmured.

Her features scrunched. "If you like my feet, you should feel my neck. I moisturize the hell out of it in hopes of keeping the wrinkles away. I know my body's supposedly locked in time, but I'm not taking any chances."

Gaze locked with hers, his breath began to quicken. Slowly, he placed her feet on the couch and glided toward her. Encircling her arm with his fingers, he tugged her toward him.

"Slide over me," he whispered.

Her blue eyes were wide as the vein in her neck pulsed. "Why?"

"Come on," he said, gently tugging her. "Slide your leg over mine."

White fangs squished the flesh of her lip as she contemplated. Tentatively, she glided her jean-clad leg over his thigh until she straddled him, her hands gripping his shoulders tight, revealing her nervousness.

"You've got me in a death grip there, honey."

"Sorry," she whispered, relaxing her fingers. "I haven't done this in a long time."

Lifting his hand, he placed his palm over the juncture where her neck met her chest. Slowly caressing her, he trailed his hand over her skin, loving how it reddened in its wake.

"You're right," he murmured.

"Hmm?"

"Your skin here is really soft." He continued to stroke her, content to let her relax into the ministrations.

"Sam," she breathed.

"Yes, sweetheart?"

"I think I want you to kiss me."

His lips curved into what must've been the sappiest grin of all time. "Yeah?"

She swallowed thickly before nodding. "I think I remember how to do it."

Chuckling, he cupped her neck, gently urging her closer. "What if I don't know how to do it?"

"You're so handsome," she said, tightening her arms around his neck. "I bet you've kissed all sorts of women."

"Honestly," he said, inching closer to her lips, "I think I've damn near forgotten any woman exists except you, Glarys." Reveling in her quick inhale, he brushed his lips against hers. "In fact, you're all I think about."

"I am?"

Nuzzling her nose, he nodded. "Every damn second of every damn day." Extending his tongue, he swiped it over her lips.

"Oh, god," she moaned, wriggling over his cock and sending jolts of pleasure through his body.

Pressing his lips to hers, he consumed them, unable to hold back any longer.

∞

Glarys settled into a man's body for the first time in so very long. Parts she'd thought to be long dormant flared to life as his magnificent lips moved over hers. The hard jut of his cock against her core through their clothes spurred a rush of moisture between her thighs. Craving contact she'd been so long denied, she shimmied over his straining shaft, reveling in his resulting groan.

"I can smell your arousal," he whispered into her mouth, breaths mingling as he stroked her tongue with his.

"I haven't felt arousal in so long. I wasn't sure if my lady parts still worked."

Chuckling, he kissed her, pulling her bottom lip between his own before changing the angle and plunging his tongue inside. Glarys melted, encircling his neck as she pressed her breasts against his broad chest. Her nipples tingled along with her slick core, which throbbed as she wriggled atop his strong body.

"Man," he whispered, breaking the kiss and resting his forehead upon hers. "You taste so good, honey."

Smiling, she ran her thumb over his lip. "I wasn't sure you wanted me back. I convinced myself you were just being nice."

"Nice?" Arching an eyebrow, he jutted his erection into her mound. "Does that feel nice, sweetheart?"

"Actually, it rather does."

Throwing back his head, he laughed, baring his neck to her. Overcome with desire, she began to trail kisses over his vein.

"I want to drink from you. Goddess, I can't believe I just said that, but it's true."

Threading his fingers through her hair, he gently tugged her head away. "I want that too. So much, Glarys."

Her fangs toyed with her lip. "But you have reservations?"

Sighing, he nodded. "You're really special, and I don't want to cross a line here. First, I need to know if you're okay dating your bodyguard."

"As long as you don't have a problem with it, I don't."

"I feel a calling to protect you," he said, causing something to swell in her chest, "so I'm extremely honored to have this assignment. But I want to speak to Latimus before we take this any further." Her expression must've fallen because he cupped her cheek. "I want to do this right, honey. Bodyguards have fallen for their wards before. I saw it happen all the time at Valeria, and it's not unacceptable in Vampyre culture. But Latimus is paying me to protect you, and I want to make sure he understands my intentions toward you."

She arched a brow, trying to appear sexy. "And what are your intentions?"

Expelling a ragged breath, he slid his thumb over her lip, his gaze focused on her mouth. "To have those sexy fangs plunged into every part of my neck while I'm deep inside your gorgeous body."

Moisture gushed between her legs at the amorous words spoken in his deep baritone. "You want to make love to me?"

"Oh, hell yes. More than I've wanted anything in centuries, honey. I can't believe you haven't realized I'm smitten with you. Why do you think I volunteered so fast to guard you?"

"Because you're altruistic and kind," she said, placing a peck on his lips.

"Eh, maybe." He slid his hand down her body, gliding it over her ass. "Or maybe I had ulterior motives."

"Probably both." Winking, she stroked the thick hair at his temple. "Latimus will be leading a training at Takelia tomorrow...you know, if you want to talk to him while we're there."

"I'll do that."

They stroked each other for a while before Sam said softly, "Let me carry you to bed."

"Oh, I can walk," she said, waving a dismissive hand.

"I know, but this will be more fun." He waggled his eyebrows. "I wish I had both arms so I could whisk you upstairs and hold you tight, but I can still manage with one. Clench my neck tight."

Following his directive, she gave a little squeal when he lifted her, carrying her as if she were weightless while her legs encircled his waist. "I hope I'm not too heavy. I swear, I'm going to lose the extra ten pounds I'm carrying one day."

"You're perfect, honey."

The words shot thrills of pleasure to every cell in her body.

Once he'd carried her up the stairs, Sam laid her down, and Glarys's head fell to the pillow. Sitting by her side, he traced the healing shiner under her eye.

"It's almost gone."

"Yes. Does it look terrible?"

"No, but I'm really pissed they hurt you."

"I'm fine. I'm a tough old broad."

Melted brown eyes washed over her face. "I can't wait to hold you again," he whispered.

"Tomorrow," she whispered back.

"Tomorrow. But for now…" Lowering, he placed a slow, reverent kiss on her lips. Lifting from the bed, he gave her a salute. "Night, Glarys."

"Night."

Once he'd closed the door behind him, she rolled over and all but screamed into the pillow like a teenager with her first crush. Still overcome with arousal from his ardent kisses, it was hours before she eventually fell asleep.

Chapter 6

When the sun rose, Glarys put on one of her most flattering dresses and even applied a little makeup. She rarely wore the stuff but wanted to look pretty for Sam. When he strolled into the kitchen with that lazy swagger, her heart slammed in her chest. He looked delicious in jeans, a brown T-shirt, and boots. A gun was holstered on his waist by his leather belt. Physically restraining from licking her lips in anticipation, she prepared a cup of coffee and set it in front of him.

Mahogany eyes sparkled as he drank it, sitting still while she buzzed around the kitchen. When everything was prepared, she plopped her hands on her hips.

"Well, I had most of the food delivered to Takelia, and all my supplies are packed. You ready?"

"Ready," he said, standing and grabbing the two bags from the counter.

"Should I even try to carry those?"

"Nope." The sexy curve of his lips all but made her gush in her panties. By the goddess, he was handsome. "A gentleman never lets a lady carry her own bags. Let's go."

They sat together on the train to Takelia, her skin warm beneath her dress as it brushed against his side.

"I think green is your color. That dress looks fantastic on you, Glarys."

"Oh, this ol' thing? I just threw it on this morning," she teased, realizing he'd probably already guessed she spent extra time primping.

"Well, you look pretty as always. I like the stuff on your face," he said, circling his hand in front of his face.

"It's called makeup, and thank you very much. I might have put on extra for you."

She thought he uttered a small growl. "You don't need it, but I sure do like the thought of you thinking of me in your bedroom."

"Oh, you flirt," she said, swatting his chest.

He placed a peck on her head, and she settled into his side, loving their interplay. When they arrived at Takelia, Evie and Lila met them at the station.

"You're a godsend, Glarys," Evie said, hugging her. "These donors are so freaking demanding, but I need their money, and half of them refused to come unless I had those damn crab cakes and bacon-wrapped melons you prepared last time. You're a victim of your own success. Thanks for making the trip."

"I'm happy to do it, and it warms my heart that both the Slayer and Vampyre aristocrats enjoy my cooking."

"Hello, Sam," Evie said, arching her scarlet eyebrow. "My, oh, my...there are just all sorts of lascivious thoughts circling about today. Have you been a naughty bodyguard?"

Sam chuckled, remembering Evie was quite powerful and possessed the ability to read others' thoughts. "Now, Evie, you know I'm too much of a stickler for protocol to cross the line too far...even if Glarys looks like a million dollars in her pretty green dress."

"Oh, will you both stop?" Glarys held her palms to her flaming cheeks. "This is all sorts of embarrassing."

"Come on," Lila said, sliding her arm around Glarys's shoulders and leading her toward the castle. "Those two are just having fun, but you do look really stunning today, Glarys. The shiner's all but gone."

"Thank you, sweetie. That's nice of you to say to this old lady."

"I don't think Sam sees you that way." Lila chucked her golden eyebrows.

Walking up the stairs, they entered the mansion and began to trail to the kitchen.

"We'll see. He's going to speak to Latimus while we're here. Wants to ask permission to date me while he's guarding me. It sounds silly when I say it out loud, but I appreciate the sentiment."

"Oh, that's wonderful." Pulling her close, Lila whispered, "I knew it. You two are perfect for each other."

"Are you ladies talking about me?" Sam asked, smiling as he filtered in and placed the bags on the counter.

"Less talking and more working," Glarys said, picking up the cloth on the countertop and using it to shoo them all away. "I need to get to work, and you all need to give me space. Now, go on, so I can fix this spread for Evie."

"You're a saint." Evie placed a kiss on her forehead before breezing from the room. "Call me if you need anything."

"I'll take you to Latimus," Lila said to Sam.

Nodding, he walked over and squeezed Glarys's upper arm. "Let me know if you need any help."

Inwardly sighing at his thoughtfulness, she nodded. "Good luck. I feel like we're teenagers asking permission to go to prom."

His deep chuckle enveloped her. "Feels like it." With a nod, he left the room with Lila.

Opening the fridge to assess the supplies she'd requested, Glarys got down to business.

∞

Sam found Latimus atop a small hill, leading the soldiers in drills. Placing his fingers between his lips, the commander gave a loud whistle and yelled, "Take five, soldiers!"

"Didn't mean to interrupt you," Sam said.

"They needed a break anyway. How are things at Astaria? Is Glarys feeling okay?"

"She's fine," Sam said, sliding his hand into his back pocket. "But I want to talk to you about something."

Latimus's eyebrow lifted. "About the fact you've been pining for her for years?"

Huffing a laugh, he nodded. "Yep. That would be it."

"Did you finally make a move? Lila and I were thrilled when you offered to guard her."

"I made a move," he said, looking out across the meadow. "Haven't been with a woman in a long time. It took a while to convince myself I was still whole after losing this." Lifting the stub of his arm, he felt his lips thin. "Still have to convince myself some days, but it's gotten easier over the centuries. Glarys is so sweet and pretty and probably a hell of a lot smarter than me, but she seems to like me anyway."

"That's fantastic, Sam," Latimus said, patting his shoulder with friendly affection. "I know she's been lonely since she lost Victor, and we all worry about her being alone in the mansion. She's like a mother to all of us. I wish you both happiness."

"I don't want to overstep my bounds. If you think this crosses an ethical line, dating her while I'm employed as her private security detail, I'll resign."

"Hell, I can name so many of my former soldiers who married their wards. It's bound to happen in a society wracked with war for as long as ours was. Although the Vampyre kingdom is stuffy and traditional in a lot of ways, romance between a bodyguard and their ward has always been perfectly fine. Expected, even." Latimus grinned. "Lila and I were hoping this would happen when you volunteered to guard her, although we didn't expect it so quickly. Way to go, man. I could've taken some pointers from you when I was desperately in love with Lila for all those centuries."

Chuckling, Sam shrugged. "I've been smitten with her since your bonding ceremony, but every time I asked her out, she always suggested I bring Jack along."

"That's Glarys. She most likely convinced herself you were just being nice."

"She did, and I misread it as her not being interested in spending one-on-one time with me. I've never been all that great at reading women."

"Who is?" Latimus murmured. "Apologies go a long way. And flowers. I've learned a lot. Maybe I can teach you something now."

Breathing a laugh, Sam patted his upper arm. "I'll take any advice you have. I haven't taken a woman on a date in so long, I don't even remember the last time. What the hell do I do?"

Staring at the blue sky, eyes narrowed, Latimus contemplated. "Glarys is always doting on other people. I wonder how long it's been since she was doted upon. I'd say, take that angle. Find something that focuses on making her feel really special. And then there's wine. Lila loves wine, and she gets so adorably tipsy when I bring home a fancy bottle. Maybe it will work for you too."

"Duly noted," he said, giving a salute. "I can't wait to make her feel special. I've rarely met another person who's so thoughtful. The pasta and the freshly squeezed orange juice for Jack—that's just the beginning. She'd probably break her own back just to see any of your children smile. Hell, to see any of us smile."

"That she would. She's one in a million."

"Well, I appreciate you being on board with me taking the next step while I guard her." Sam extended his hand. "If you ever change your mind, let me know."

Shaking, Latimus grinned. "Make her happy, Sam. That's all I care about."

"Me too, Latimus. I swear."

When the training resumed and Sam returned to the kitchen, Glarys's sky-blue irises lit with joy.

"Oh, here," she said, urging him to sit at the kitchen island and placing a plate of steaming-hot appetizers in front of him. "I prepared this for you. I need a taste tester."

It was a good excuse, but Sam understood she'd made the plate for him as a gesture of affection. Taking a bite of the little puffy thing, he closed his eyes in ecstasy as he chewed.

"My god, woman. This is amazing. What is it?"

"Baked brie and spinach puff pastry." She was enchanting as she reveled in his obvious enjoyment. "I'm so glad you like it." Waiting for him to swallow, she asked, "How did it go with Latimus? Is he on board with us, um, you know…?"

"He's on board," Sam replied with a wink.

Her cheeks flushed, sending every drop of blood in his veins to his shaft. Goddess, she was so stunning.

"So should we go on a date?"

"I'm kind of traditional, here, Glarys, so if it's all right with you, I'd like to surprise you. Give me a few days so I can plan a proper date for us. Is that okay?"

"Yes," she said, eyes twinkling as she spoke in a gravelly voice. "That's very okay."

She got back to work, her gorgeous backside accentuated by her green dress, and Sam finished the succulent food, wondering when in the hell he'd become the luckiest man on the damn planet.

Chapter 7

The fundraiser at Takelia went well, as did Symon's birthday party the following day, and by the end of the week, Glarys was exhausted. She made sure to get a good night's sleep on Friday since Sam had informed her to be prepared to spend the entire day with him on Saturday. Excitement sparkled in his eyes as he told her to expect several surprises. It all seemed a bit silly to Glarys, who never wished for anyone to go out of their way for her, but she told herself to relax and enjoy being courted by a thoughtful, handsome suitor.

Sam had told her to dress casually Saturday morning but to pack a bag with nicer clothes and toiletries for later in the evening.

"Oh, is this an overnight thing?" she'd asked as she wiped the kitchen countertop Friday afternoon.

"Not unless you want it to be," he'd replied slyly. "You'll want to shower and refresh after our morning activities, and you'll have access to do so."

She'd given him a curious glare, wondering what in the heck she was in store for.

On Saturday morning, she stood in the kitchen dressed in yoga pants and a T-shirt, bag slung over her shoulder. Sam trailed in, black sweatpants clinging to his muscled legs, and she licked her lips in anticipation. Would she get to run her hands over the springy hairs beneath the fabric later?

"Ready?" he asked, fangs glowing as he grinned.

With a nod, they were on their way.

Sam drove them to a property on the outskirts of Astaria that looked rather fancy. As they parked, Glarys read the sign out front: **Astaria Day Spa and Resort**.

"A spa?" she asked, eyes wide. "I've never been to one."

"Didn't think you had since you spend all your time pampering everyone else. Today's about you, sweetie. Come on."

She took his extended hand, feeling a bit trepidatious. "I can't spend all day getting mollycoddled. This is too much—"

"Let me spoil you, honey," he said, squeezing her hand. "Please don't fight me on this. If you relax, you might just enjoy it," he said with a wink.

They entered the large front doors, and a butler awaited them with two glasses of champagne.

"Samwise, Son of Raythor," the butler said, handing him the glass before bowing to Glarys, "and Glarys, Daughter of Davel. So lovely to meet you both. I'm Artor and will be your host today."

"Oh, thank you," Glarys said, taking the glass and sipping. "This is lovely."

They followed Artor to a sitting room with plush couches, and a woman appeared dressed in fancy scrubs.

"Hello, Glarys. I'm Sana, your masseuse and facialist. I'm going to whisk you away with me while Sam takes care of some business."

"Business?" Glarys asked, arching a brow at Sam.

"No questions," he said, leaning down to kiss her on the forehead. "Have fun with Sana. I'll see you at the salt bath later."

Salt bath? Curious excitement flowed through her veins as she reveled in the touch of his firm lips. Sam followed Artor from the room, and she stood to address Sana.

"I don't know what I'm doing here."

"Looks like you're getting wooed," Sana said, her tone wistful. "How romantic. This way, please." Gesturing with her arm to the door, she stared expectantly at Glarys.

"Well, I guess I am," she muttered, following the nice lady through.

Three hours later, Glarys felt like a wet noodle. After the first massage of her life, Sana had given her a facial, which she thought might just be heaven on Earth. After showering in the expansive locker room shower to rid her body of the oil, she donned the bathing suit Sana had supplied and headed toward the spa area.

There were several rooms with private whirlpools and salt baths, and Sana led her to one, her eyes twinkling.

"Have fun," the kind lady said before swinging open the door.

She noticed Sam standing by the salt pool, green smoothie in hand, clad only in swim shorts. The muscles of his abdomen formed a firm six-pack under springy brown hair, and saliva pooled in her throat. Approaching him, she asked, "Is that for me?"

"Yep," he said, handing her the smoothie. "That's lunch. I have a surprise for dinner later. But for now, I'm going to hang in the pool with you—if you're okay with that."

Nodding, she slipped her hand in his, and he led her into the salt pool. She caught him up on her amazing morning, unable to believe he was treating her to such splendor. Eventually, they moved to the steaming whirlpool, Sam scooching beside her and placing his arm over her shoulders as the jets pounded their upper backs.

"Goddess, this feels heavenly," she said, eyes closed as her head rested on his arm. "How am I going to go back to regular life? You've ruined me."

Chuckling, he rested his head against hers. "I figure you deserve pampering more than anyone, Glarys. You're so damn thoughtful."

"I think you might have surpassed me," she said, snuggling into his side, not even caring that her love handle was brushing against his perfect abdomen. Who had the energy to care when they felt so fantastic?

"Oh, there's more to come—just wait."

Lifting her lids, she smiled up at him. "Thank you. Just in case I forget to say it later."

"You're welcome." His wet fingers combed through the hair at her temple. "I mean, I should be thanking you. All that soft, wet skin against me. You're absolutely gorgeous, Glarys."

Tears pricked her eyes as emotion overcame her. "Sam," she whispered.

"Don't cry, honey," he said, concern filtering over his strong features.

"They're happy tears. You've made me so happy today."

His lips curved as her heart thrummed. "Good." Placing a poignant kiss on her lips, he asked, "Are you ready for the next part of our day?"

"I'm not sure I can take any more, but why not?"

He led her from the spa room, and Sana met them outside. She directed Glarys to shower again before taking her to the styling room. A professional stylist blew out her hair while a makeup artist applied some cosmetics, although Glarys told her to keep it natural. Glancing at her watch, she realized it was almost dinnertime.

Artor met her outside the locker room and led her through the spa to an outdoor patio. A table was set for two overlooking the meadow, two candles burning atop the white tablecloth.

"My lady," Sam said, appearing and offering her his arm. After she was seated, he sat across from her, looking rather nervous.

"What are you up to?"

"So while you were getting pampered today, I spent hours preparing tonight's meal. I'm an okay cook but have always wanted to get better. I hired the chef to teach me and prepped and cooked everything we're having tonight. I felt like someone should cook for you for once."

"How thoughtful," she said, overcome by the gesture.

"Don't say that yet. Let's see how it tastes, and then we'll assess."

Chuckling, she sampled the white wine the server poured, noting it was excellent, and settled in for the first course.

She and Sam made easy conversation, getting to know each other better as she savored the food. The arugula salad with walnuts and gorgonzola was fantastic, but the main course was excellent.

"Glazed salmon with gnocchi and steamed vegetables," the chef said, setting the plates in front of them. "Your husband here worked really hard to plan the menu and prepare the dishes with me, ma'am."

"I love salmon," she said, winking at Sam in reference to the chef calling him her "husband."

"Lila told me." Red splotches appeared on his cheeks, causing her body to enflame with heat. "And she said you like cannoli too. Those are next."

"Oh, my. I'm going to gain a hundred pounds. Thank you, Chef," she said to the man before he politely nodded and walked away. Gazing at Sam, she said in a gravelly voice, "And thank you, Sam. I don't know what to say."

"Less talk, more eat," he teased, lifting his fork. "Dig in."

Several glasses of wine and a full belly later, she placed her hands over her abdomen and sat back, expelling a huge breath. "That's it. I'm never eating again. Vampyres aren't supposed to like food anyway, but that was absolutely amazing."

"I'm so glad you enjoyed it." Twirling the wine in his glass, Sam's gaze was hooded. "I hope you've had a good day, honey."

"So good," she said, overwhelmed with gratitude. "You might have shot yourself in the foot. Not sure how you're going to top this for our next date."

Chuckling, he sipped his wine. "I'll find something up my sleeve."

He drove them home, Glarys content and sated as she sat beside him. When they entered the darkened castle, he began trailing to the kitchen, but she grabbed his wrist and tugged him toward the large staircase.

Brown irises studied her as he hesitated. "I didn't do all this to make you feel obligated to me, Glarys. I'm okay just watching a movie and holding you...and maybe kissing you a few hundred times." He grinned, giving a playful shrug. "I'm not sure what pace you prefer, but any pace is fine with me as long as you look at me with those pretty eyes."

Closing the distance between them, she palmed his cheeks. "There hasn't really been any pace since my husband died. I was so sure I'd never be held by someone again. Time is precious, and I don't want to squander it. If you want me, I'd really like to make love to you, Sam. Does that make me a hussy?" She giggled.

Sliding his arm around her waist, he aligned their bodies, nuzzling her nose with his. "If it does, I'm here for it. Are you sure, honey?"

Nodding, she bit her lip, loving the desire that flared in his eyes. "I'm sure."

"Put your arms around my neck," he all but growled.

Complying, she held tight as he slid his arm under her knees and lifted her.

"Remember, I'm carrying extra weight from that amazing dinner. Don't strain yourself."

Charging up the stairs with her against his body, he said, "Well, let's burn those calories off, sweetheart."

Sighing, she figured making love to Sam would probably be the best form of exercise ever invented. Heart pounding in anticipation, she placed fervent kisses on his neck as he crossed the threshold to her room, closing the door behind him.

Sam placed Glarys atop the bed, marveling at her snow-white hair and smiling face as she stared back at him. Whatever the stylists had done made her look stunning. He couldn't decide whether he liked her more like this—all gussied up—or makeup-free and half-naked in the plain swimsuit she wore at the spa. Thrilled he didn't have to choose, he lowered above her, balancing on his arm before settling most of the weight on his hip. Sprawling over her, he devoured her mouth, loving the little shrieks of pleasure she mewled down his throat.

He wanted to rip her clothes off and plunge into her quaking body, but he told himself to go slow. Only having one arm precluded him from being able to ravish her as extensively as he wanted, but he'd focus every ounce of energy from his good arm to make her scream. Palming his pecs, she gently pressed, urging him to break the kiss.

"I love kissing you," she said, breathless. "But I need to feel you against me. Let me take this dress off."

Sitting up, he pulled her to stand, leaning back on his arm as she unclasped the two front buttons and slid the dress over her head, tossing it over the nearby chair. Clad in her white bra and panties, Sam gazed at her beauty. Thick, succulent thighs led to full calves and those adorable toes. Her waist curved with hollows he craved to explore with his tongue. Full breasts heaved as she stared down at him.

"I wish I could unclasp your bra, but I can't," he said, lifting his one hand, slightly discomfited. "Can you do it?"

Gaze cemented to his, she reached behind and unfastened the bra, tossing it to lie with the dress. "Do you want me to take my underwear off too?"

"Come here," he said, crooking his finger at her. "I can definitely manage that."

She stepped forward, and he hooked his fingers inside the cotton material, dragging it down until she stepped out of it. Hurling it toward the chair, he grinned at her soft chuckle.

"Are you eager, Sam?"

"So fucking eager," he murmured, gliding his arm around her waist and drawing her toward him. Resting his forehead beneath her breasts, he inhaled her lavender scent as she whispered his name. Placing a soft kiss on her stomach, he smelled her resulting gush of arousal as the skin quivered beneath his lips. Vampyres had heightened senses for arousal, and hers was intoxicating.

Standing, he reached behind and grabbed a fistful of his shirt, pulling it over his head. His belt and pants were next. After centuries of learning to function with one hand, he knew how to remove them, but she placed her hand over his, stilling him.

"Let me."

Nodding, he proceeded to watch her unbuckle his belt and slide it off before slowly unfastening his pants. Kicking off his shoes, he shimmied everything to the ground, including his boxer briefs, and kicked them away.

Naked, he gazed at her as she stared at his engorged cock.

Encircling it with her fingers, she lightly squeezed as he gritted his teeth, determined to let her explore at her own pace.

"My god, it's been so long since I've touched one of these…" Biting her lip, she looked up at him and ran her thumb over the mushroom-shaped head, spreading the tiny wet droplet over the aching skin. "I hope I don't disappoint you."

"Honey, you've already made every dream I've ever had come true. Look at that pretty hand around my cock." Jutting into her palm, he growled. "Goddess, I want you so much."

Wrinkling her nose, she asked, "Are hands pretty? I've never thought of them that way."

Done with conversation, he slid his arm around her waist and tugged her to bed, gently urging her to lie across the comforter. "Yours are," he said, crawling over her. "Just like every other part of you." Lowering his lips to hers, he plunged his tongue inside her mouth, desperate to taste her again.

As he kissed her, he trailed his hand over her breast, running his thumb over her nipple and tweaking it with his fingers. She moaned beneath him, her body writhing against him, and he ached with gratitude that she would let him love her this way. Trailing kisses over her neck toward her breast, he sucked the nipple between his lips, lathering her with his saliva, wanting to mark her with his scent. Thin fingers thrust into his hair, the tugging sensation driving him insane with lust.

Once her nipple was puckered and tight, he kissed his way to the other, lavishing it with the same attention until it stood pointed and ready. Sliding his hand to the juncture of her thighs, he cupped her mound, the prickly hairs scratching his palm.

"I want to kiss you here," he said, flexing his hand, "but I think I might explode if I don't get inside you, honey."

"You can kiss me there next time," she said, tugging his hair so he rose above her. "And I might just kiss you down there too."

He groaned, moving his body into position as the erotic thought of her mouth around his stiff cock blazed in his mind.

"Do you want me to use a condom?"

Although Vampyres couldn't transmit disease through intercourse due to their self-healing bodies, there was still the chance of pregnancy.

Her expression grew somber. "No. I went through my change after menopause, so I can't get pregnant anymore."

Hating that he'd brought up something that seemed to make her sad, he cupped her face. "I'm sorry."

"Don't be," she said, covering his lips with her fingers. "Please, Sam. I need you. Make love to me."

Balancing on the stub of his arm and his side, he glided his hand between her silky legs and pushed her thigh open. Probing, he found her swollen folds with the head of his shaft, nudging until he was seated at her wet opening. Gaze cemented to hers, he began to push inside.

"Oh, yes," she cried, lips wet from his previous kisses, looking like a goddess beneath him. "I feel you *everywhere*."

"Glarys," he gritted, pushing inside her, inch by inch. "You feel so good, sweetheart. All slick and hot. Damn, honey." Settling over her, he lifted her leg across his back before placing his palm on the comforter beside her head. Resting his weight on his good arm, he began to undulate his hips, hissing tight breaths as her silken channel squeezed his sensitive skin.

She wrapped her arms around him, pulling him close, as her leg pushed against his ass. Urged on by her excited mewls, he plunged into her, over and over, understanding this must be what one experienced in the Passage. Pure, unadulterated bliss. Merging his lips with hers, he kissed her thoroughly and deeply as he loved her, striving to reach a place inside that drove her wild.

Frustrated he only had one hand, he wondered if he should stimulate the little nub hidden in her folds as he loved her, knowing some women needed that extra stimulation to reach orgasm. Oh, how he'd love to balance above her and hammer into her while circling the tiny bud, but his injury made that impossible.

Shifting his hips, he changed the angle, hoping to rub against the sensitive spot with the base of his shaft while he plunged deep inside. It must've worked because she gasped, lids flying open as her mouth fell agape.

"Yes! Like that. Oh, Sam, please don't stop. That's perfect."

"Like this?" he asked, increasing the pace of his hips, struggling to breathe but desperate to make her come.

"Mm-hmm..." Her short hair fanned over the mattress as she nodded, those sexy fangs squishing the flesh of her bottom lip. "Just like that. Oh, god..."

As focused as he'd ever been, he gyrated into her, feeling his balls constrict as her body tightened. Her taut channel gripped his cock as she began to come, head thrown back as she cried his name. He pumped into her, his lungs spasming, desperate for air, before he closed his eyes and released the orgasm. Milky jets spurted from his jolting shaft, coating her deepest place as he claimed her. Collapsing atop her trembling body, they gulped air into their heaving chests until she began to giggle.

"*Ohmygod*," she breathed, the words jumbled together as she ran her fingernails over his sweaty back, causing his body to lurch against her with pleasure. "Sam...that was...oh, my..."

"Nothing has ever felt so good," he murmured into her neck, limp and sated. "I think your gorgeous body was made for me, honey."

"I'm so happy you think I'm pretty," she said, emotion in her voice.

Lifting his head, he stroked the tear that escaped her eye. "Sweetheart?"

"I just haven't felt pretty in so long. I felt old and unwanted and convinced myself that was okay because I had the kids around. But you would look at me and tell me such nice things." She stroked his jaw, her gaze reverent. "It means so much, Sam. I'm incredibly lucky to be with you. You could have any woman you set your sights on."

"I don't want any woman but you," he said, the statement true on every level. "I think you're magnificent. And you don't seem to mind that I'm not quite whole." His gaze trailed to his stub before returning to her.

"You're whole in every way." Lifting her head, she placed a poignant kiss on the stub of his arm, causing a pang in his solar plexus. It was an acceptance of something he'd been ashamed of for centuries before finally learning to bear it, and he felt his own eyes well with moisture.

"Thank you," he whispered, lowering to kiss her. "I wish I had two hands to touch you twice as often, but I'll do my best with the one I've got."

"Your best is amazing. I feel like I could sleep for twenty years after the pampering and fantastic sex. You made my decade, for sure."

Chuckling, he planted one last kiss on her lips before pushing away and sliding from her body. Striding to the bathroom, he grabbed a cloth and returned, wiping away his release while her cheeks glowed red. After tossing it on the bathroom counter, Sam found Glarys turning back the covers. Rubbing the back of his neck, he wondered if he should ask to sleep with her. He'd love nothing more than to cuddle but didn't want to impose.

"Well?" she said, extending her arms as she sat with her back against the pillows. Her breasts called to him, still flushed and full as she stared at him expectantly. "You're not going to love me and leave me, are you?"

Laughing, he inched closer. "I don't want you to feel obligated to sleep with me. I know some people like their privacy."

Her lips formed a frown. "I mean, I'd really like you to hold me, but if that's not your thing, that's okay. I like snuggling. Always have."

Feeling himself beam, he crawled into bed and pulled her to his side, loving how she wiggled against him. "I like snuggling too. Especially with you."

"Good night," she said, yawning as she rested her cheek on his chest. "Feel free to wake me up in a few hours and do that to me again, okay?"

Breathing a laugh, he stroked her hair as she relaxed against him. "Count on it, honey. Now that I've loved you once, I don't think I'll be able to stop."

"Thank the goddess," she mumbled into his skin.

Closing his eyes, he sent a prayer of thanks to Etherya. Wrapped in his woman's luscious scent, he succumbed to slumber.

Chapter 8

They fell into a cozy pattern, and Sam reveled in how comfortable he was around Glarys. He'd always been somewhat of a loner, preferring solitude and quiet, but spending time with her was amazing. He would accompany her as she buzzed about the kingdom spearheading parties for wealthy aristocrats and the royal children. Although the functions were quite different, she poured just as much energy into the children's fetes as she did the stuffy royal soirees. For someone who insisted she was past her prime, the woman had a plethora of infectious energy.

Sam had never craved companionship but now understood how magnificent a relationship could be if one found the right person. As the months wore on and their relationship flourished, Sam became increasingly convinced Glarys was the one.

One night, as they sat on the couch watching The Hunger Games, he lifted the remote and paused the movie.

"Do you need more popcorn?" she asked, peering over at the empty bowl.

"No," he said, turning to face her and taking her hand in his. "I'd like to talk to you about something and can't decide on the right time, so I figure it's best to just blurt it out."

"Okay," she said, eyes growing wide. "What is it?"

Swallowing thickly, he rubbed her hand with his thumb. "I really enjoy spending time with you, Glarys."

Those plush pink lips curved into a smile. "I love spending time with you too. Even when you snore against my neck when we're sleeping."

Chuckling, he shook his head. "Never kept anyone around long enough to tell me whether I snore or not. I sure am sorry it's so loud."

"You know I'm only teasing," she said, swatting his chest. "I love having you close to me, so it's a small price to pay."

Feeling his eyes dart between hers, he tamped down his nervousness. "Are you open to bonding with someone again?"

Her shoulders straightened as surprise washed over her features.

"Because I sure would like to ask you to bond with me. I'll do it right and make it all formal, but I figured it's best to ask you first and make sure you'll say yes."

Exhaling a slow breath, she palmed his cheek. "Sam," she said, her voice raspy. "That's so lovely for you to say…"

"But?"

"Well…" Her fangs toyed with her lip as she contemplated. "I can't have children of my own anymore and feel like it would be selfish to tie you to me. Don't you want children one day? What if you wake up centuries from now and realize you're bound to someone who can't give you what you need?"

Eyes narrowed, he stared at the ceiling as he pondered. "I've never had a hankerin' for kids like some people do. When Jack lived with me after my sister passed, I didn't mind raising him but didn't feel like I was giving him everything he needed. That's why I asked Lila to adopt him. That woman was born to be a mother."

Chuckling, Glarys nodded. "She certainly was."

"I've always functioned pretty well on my own and never really craved kids or a family. Until you. Now, I see myself wanting to bond with you and build a future together. If we decide we want kids down the road, we could always adopt. I mean, what are your thoughts on kids?"

"I've always been so consumed with the royal children, and now their children, they've filled any void I might've had from not having my own kids. As long as they're around, I don't think I'll want to have children down the road. If that changes, I'd be open to adoption. Still, I want you to think this through, Sam. I don't want to deny you anything."

"Deny me?" he asked, incredulous. "Goddess, Glarys, you're gorgeous and caring and so much smarter than me. Hell, I bet you've read every book in this room," he said, gesturing to the bookshelves overflowing with human and Vampyre manuscripts. "I can barely read the books Symon and Adelyn bring home from school when we visit Lila and Latimus. Sometimes, I speak and wonder if I conjured the words right and hope you're not internally laughing at me."

She pursed her lips, laughter in her ice-blue eyes.

"What?"

"It's conjugate, not conjure, and I'm only laughing because you're so adorable right now."

"See?" he asked, playfully rolling his eyes. "I don't even know the difference."

"If you think for one second I give a fig about that, you still don't know me." Sliding her arms around his neck, she rubbed her nose against his. "I couldn't care less if you can't read a damn word. You're a skillful soldier who does everything in his power to ensure my safety. When I think about all the places and functions I drag you to—and you've never complained, not once. Talk about patient and kind... You're wonderful, Sam, and I'm so enamored with the way you speak. It's quite endearing and makes my knees week every damn time."

"Yeah?" he asked, brushing her lips with his.

Nodding, she tugged him closer. "I *really* like it when you whisper in my ear while we're making love."

Overcome with desire for her, he joined his lips to hers as he pressed her back into the couch. Loving her resulting giggle, he proceeded to speak a multitude of words in her ear—some dirty, and some unintelligible—as he made love to her.

Once they were sated and struggling to catch their breath as they lay entwined on the couch, she playfully nipped his jaw.

"Well, in case you haven't figured it out, if you're okay bonding with someone who can't have kids, I'll say yes, Sam."

Thrilled to his core, he hugged her close. "Okay, let me think of something real special, honey. You deserve that."

"All I want is you," she mumbled against his skin.

Replete and happy, he closed his eyes and relaxed into her sweat-soaked body as they recovered.

Chapter 9

Sam set about planning the perfect proposal for Glarys as he continued to protect her. Using a large chunk of the cash he had saved from his previous private security job, he visited the jeweler in the main square and bought her an expensive ring. It was a diamond surrounded by tiny sapphires that matched her eyes. Hoping like hell she'd think it was as pretty as he did, he handed over the cash once the jeweler had boxed it up.

"Congratulations on your upcoming nuptials, sir," he said with a smile. "I wish you all the best."

"Thanks," he said, holding the box high as he shrugged. "I've just got to get her to say yes."

"Well, that ring is one of our finest. I'm sure she'll appreciate it."

"Hope so," Sam said, giving him a friendly salute before heading back to the castle.

Glarys was flitting around the kitchen as always, and he hid the ring in the dresser in Heden's old room, content she wouldn't find it. He planned to take her on a romantic picnic by the river next week and would propose to her there.

Already nervous, he entered the kitchen, his heart skipping a beat as her eyes twinkled with ever-present fondness for him. They hadn't said the "L" word yet, but he certainly was in love with her, deep in his bones and to the tip of his toes. Hopefully, once he proposed and professed his love, she'd reciprocate in kind.

"There's my handsome bodyguard," she said, wrapping an arm around his neck and placing a wet kiss on his cheek. "Did you get everything you needed in town?" Mischief sparkled in her eyes as he realized she was onto him.

"Yup," he said, running his hand through his hair. "Got the same haircut I always get."

"It looks sexy." She waggled her eyebrows. "Is that all you got in town? A haircut?"

"Yes, ma'am."

"Mm-hmm…" Eyes narrowing, she playfully swatted him before backing away. "The meal is almost done for family dinner tonight, and everyone should be here soon. Want to set the table?"

"Sure." Making himself useful, he helped his woman, inwardly chuckling at how perceptive she was. Life with her would always keep him on his toes, and damn if that didn't make him a hundred shades of excited.

Consumed with thoughts of their upcoming centuries together, he set the table in the exact way she'd shown him, feeling proud of himself when she complimented him. Hell, he might even become fancy with a little help from her. Leaning down, he drew her into a breathless kiss where they stood by the set table.

"Oh, my," she said, bringing her fingers to her lips. "What was that for?"

"For teaching me new things. It's one of the things I love most about you, honey."

Her resulting smile all but melted his heart. "Thank you. I love learning from you too."

"What have you learned from me?" he asked softly.

Cupping his face, she whispered, "How to love again."

Overcome with feeling for her, he pulled her close and held her in a passionate embrace until the pitter-patter of tiny feet interrupted them, and they eventually sat down for dinner.

A few days later, Glarys was running late, which was unusual for her structured schedule. Placing her supplies and baked goods in the bags upon the counter, she dropped a container and uttered a curse.

"Hey," Sam said, swooping in and picking it up as she struggled to temper her frustration. "You okay, honey?"

"I'm never late, but I forgot Miranda asked me to make deviled eggs. They're her favorite. Thank the goddess I had some extra boiled eggs in the fridge, but it set me behind this morning."

"That's okay. I can drive us in the four-wheeler so we don't have to rush to the train."

Feeling her shoulders relax, she inhaled a few deep breaths. "Are you sure?"

"Of course. It's a nice day, and I could use some sun. Take your time—we'll head out whenever you're ready. I'm going to go to the barracks and grab a knife to stick in my boot, just in case."

Worry washed over Glarys. "Latimus told me about the attack last week outside Uteria. Will we be safe?"

"I won't let anything happen to you, honey. It's always good to have a backup in case your firearm gets knocked away." His hand curved over her shoulder. "Let me put that salary Latimus is paying me to use, okay? I've got you."

The words rang true as she'd never felt safer with anyone than she did with Sam. "Okay, let me get everything together." She shooed him away as she resumed packing everything. "I'll be ready in five minutes."

Once he was armed with his glock and a knife in his boot and the four-wheeler had been loaded, they headed through the meadow and eventually through Etherya's protective wall. As they drove along the open fields to Uteria, Glarys was overcome with love for her strong, thoughtful Vampyre. She knew he was close to proposing, and she was ready to profess those three magic words to him. Once they returned to Astaria that evening, she would hold him tight as he moved inside her deepest place and whisper the words while she stared into those deep brown eyes. Shivering in anticipation, she could barely contain her grin.

Suddenly, a shrill yell sounded to her right, audible above the engine of the four-wheeler, and she realized they were being attacked. Deamons seemed to appear from every angle as they charged the car, causing Sam to bring it to a grinding halt.

"Stay in the car," he ordered before exiting the vehicle. Pulling the gun from his holster, he shot a Deamon directly in the eyes before another grabbed Sam's arm, whirling him around and then landing a solid punch on his face.

Sam grunted and shot the creature in the abdomen, spinning to kick another in his side. As that Deamon fell to the ground, he shot two more approaching from the rear between the eyes. Pivoting around to where the last Deamon lay gasping for breath on the ground, Sam aimed his gun and released the bullet into the monster's brain.

Chest heaving from the exertion of fighting five Deamons, Sam held up his hand. "Stay there, honey. Let me assess."

Glarys admired his prowess as he inspected the area around the car. Never had she seen someone fight off five assailants so effectively. Marveling at his skill, she truly understood what a magnificent warrior he was. Grateful for his fervent protection, she waited.

"I think they're all dead," he said, still clutching the gun, as his gaze roved over the slain bodies.

Suddenly, a Vampyre appeared in front of the four-wheeler, materializing from thin air, and Glarys gasped. As he came into sight, she noticed his resemblance to Latimus and understood this was Bakari, the lost Vampyre royal sibling, and their newest foe.

Sam lifted the gun, aiming it at the man's chest.

Bakari gave a sinister chuckle, shaking his head as Sam stood firm. "You know my self-healing abilities are vast considering I have the pure blood of the Vampyre king and queen flowing through my veins, Samwise. It's pointless to shoot me."

Surreptitiously reaching into her purse, Glarys dialed Latimus, leaving the line open so he would hopefully hear the conversation. Clicking the volume button so his voice wouldn't boom, she heard him answer and closed her eyes in relief.

"Your girlfriend just called my brother, Sam, and I'd really like to punish her for that, so you're going to need to get out of my way. I can kill you, or you can step aside. Your choice."

"Glarys and I don't want no trouble," Sam said, legs spread wide as he stood immobile. "We have no part in the vengeance you seek."

"I'm not sure that's true. Glarys was there when I was born, yet she never noticed I was mercilessly whisked away by the traitorous soothsayers to a world that wasn't mine."

"I'm so sorry for what happened to you, son," Glarys said, shaking her head as she trembled in the seat. "I had no idea what occurred all those centuries ago. If I did, I would've done my best to help you."

"Lies," Bakari gritted through his teeth. "You all lie and have damned me to be an outcast from the realm in which I should thrive. In return, I will decimate each one of you and rule in perpetuity, showcasing my true heritage. My siblings' affinity toward you makes you an excellent target, Glarys."

Glarys felt such overwhelming sympathy for him. Yes, it was a strange sentiment being that he was threatening their lives, but she felt it all the same. Wishing she could travel centuries into the past and rewrite his tragic history, she waited, hoping Latimus had figured out by now that they were under attack.

Lifting a sword from his back, Bakari held it high. "It's poison-tipped, Sam. Don't make me cut off your other arm. Somehow, I think that would be worse than dying for you."

Neither budged until Bakari began to step forward.

"Out of my way, peasant."

Sam charged, lunging out of the way when Bakari sliced the sword through the air. Rotating, he swiped Bakari's legs with one of his own, causing the massive Vampyre to lose his balance and fall to the ground. Scrambling, Sam stood and whirled, appearing to contemplate the best place to lodge a bullet in Bakari's self-healing body. If Sam hit the right spot, he could temporarily maim him and hopefully restrain him while they waited for backup.

As Sam faced his foe, Glarys marveled at how quickly Bakari jumped to his feet. His muscular arms held the sword high as Sam pulled the trigger, releasing the bullet at the same time the hulking Vampyre sliced the blade through his arm.

Glarys screamed, noting the blood that began to spurt from the wound as Sam's severed arm lay on the ground.

Bakari rushed her, and she closed her eyes, praying to Etherya for a quick death. Suddenly, Bakari gasped and gripped his neck. Blood pumped through his fingers, and he pivoted.

"One more move, and I'll use the eight-shooter instead of the gun, asshole," Latimus said from behind. "I don't want to kill my own brother, but you're making it really hard, Bakari."

"Let this be a lesson that I will come after everyone you love," Bakari spat, "even this old hag. Until we meet again, *brother*." Closing his eyes, he dematerialized.

"Are you okay?" Latimus asked, rushing toward her.

"Yes," she said, climbing from the vehicle and rushing to Sam, who now sat on the grass staring at his bleeding arm where it rested several feet away.

"Evie transported me here and should be back any minute with Nolan."

Nodding, Glarys crouched beside Sam. "Hold on, sweetheart," she said, pulling her scarf from her purse and holding it to his wound.

"I'm sorry I didn't protect you better," he said, appearing utterly defeated.

"You were amazing." She placed a kiss on his lips and cupped his jaw. "Thank you, Sam."

Nolan appeared with Evie and rushed to Sam's side. "The blade was poisoned?" he asked.

"Yes," Sam said.

"Okay. Glarys, please wrap the limb in that scarf."

She rushed to follow his directive, attempting to be careful. Taking the limb, Evie hugged Sam close.

"Hold on," Evie said, closing her eyes. "Sadie's waiting for us at the infirmary. Let's go." With a whoosh, she and Sam disappeared.

"Will you and Sadie be able to reattach the arm?" Glarys asked softly.

"I don't know," Nolan said. "It depends on the amount of damage."

"Oh, my," Glarys said, tears forming in her eyes. "He was already frustrated that he'd lost one arm. I hope you can repair the other."

"If we can't, we can certainly work to make a functioning prosthetic. There have been many advancements in the human world with prosthetics, and losing multiple limbs isn't nearly the challenge it used to be."

"I hope not," Glarys said, knowing the loss would be emotionally devastating to Sam. Determined to help him through it, she lifted her chin. "I need to be by his side. Can one of you call Evie to transport me?"

"I'm on it, Glarys," Evie said, appearing beside her. "Come on, put your arms around my neck."

Listening to the Slayer-Deamon, she followed her command and closed her eyes as the woman transported her to the infirmary at Uteria.

Chapter 10

Sam awoke feeling groggy. He licked the roof of his mouth. It tasted awful, and his throat was so dry the air scratched his windpipe. Struggling to clear his throat, he glanced down at his left arm, the stub slightly protruding. Gazing to his right arm, he saw the white bindings, so pristine as they covered his now-severed limb.

Resting his head back on the pillow, he wanted to weep for everything he'd lost but realized tears wouldn't ease the pain. Nothing could. He was now as useless as a shot of whiskey in a dry town.

Overwhelmed with emotion, he struggled to regulate his breathing as he felt a presence beside him.

"You're awake," Glarys's sweet voice said, nearing his ear as she plopped down in the chair beside the bed. "Thank the goddess. How are you feeling?"

Swallowing, he gazed into those gorgeous eyes, understanding it would be one of the last times. No way in hell would he let her waste her future on an armless man with no means to protect her. Feeling utterly defeated, he turned his head and focused on the ceiling, unable to bear the pity in her ice-blue irises.

"I'm fine," he said tersely.

She was silent a moment before reaching to cup his jaw. "Sam—"

"No," he said, shaking her hand away. "I don't want you to see me like this, Glarys."

"Like what?" she asked, anger infusing her tone. "Like the man who valiantly protected me and ensured my safety?"

Clenching his lids, he tried to will her away. "I'm not doing this now, while I'm lying here like an invalid."

"Sam…"

"Please, Glarys. If you care for me at all, you'll give me some space." He could see her chin quivering out of the corner of his eye and hated himself for hurting her, but he just couldn't handle being near her, surrounded by her scent and ethereal beauty. They reminded him of things he'd never deserve now that he'd truly lost everything.

Thankfully, they were saved from the awkward moment by Nolan, who entered the room with a kind smile under his short chestnut brown hair.

"Good morning, Sam. Glad to see you're awake. I'd like to update you on your prognosis and options moving forward. Glarys is certainly welcome to stay if you'd like."

"Actually, I'd rather talk alone, doc," Sam said, agony wracking his frame at the look of pain that shot across Glarys's face.

"Well, then," she said, standing and holding her hand over her heart as if to hold it together while it broke in her chest, "I'll leave you to it. I'll come back to check on Sam later." All but fleeing from the room, she left her lavender scent behind, flooding his nostrils.

"Sam," Nolan said, sliding into Glarys's chair. "I understand this is a huge shock, but losing a limb isn't the tragedy it used to be. Humans have made so many advancements recently. I've studied them closely and am ready to help fit you with a prosthesis."

"So it's gone for good?"

Nolan gave a slow nod. "Yes. I tried to reattach the arm but was unable to render it effective. After several hours of surgery, Sadie and I couldn't see a way to save it. The limb was severed above the elbow. I'm so very sorry, Sam."

"Well, that gives me a few more inches on that side than this one, I guess," he said, gesturing with his head toward his left stub.

"Both of your arms are eligible for a new type of prosthetic called a Modular Prosthetic Limb or MPL. It's capable of interpreting and converting signals from the body's nervous system and channeling them into motion."

Sam contemplated, thinking it all sounded a bit too futuristic and plastic for his taste. "Can I feel through the fake arms?"

"The fingers are equipped with over one hundred sensors that detect sensations such as force, contact, and temperature. It's not perfect, but it does allow for tactile feedback. I postulate it will restore ninety percent of your arm function."

"But I'd always look like a damn robot," he said, frustrated. "And how would I ever hold or touch someone again?" he asked, thinking of Glarys. "It all seems phooey to me."

"Well, you don't have to make any decisions now. You've been through a hell of an ordeal, Sam. Let's get that wound healed and back to one hundred percent, and then we can discuss options."

"Thanks, doc. I appreciate you trying so hard to save it."

"You're welcome." Standing, Nolan contemplated him. "Glarys has been here since the second you arrived, Sam. It's obvious she's deeply in love with you. I hope you let her support you through this."

"She's in love with someone strong who strived to protect her, not the man I am now."

"You're still strong, Sam," Nolan said, sliding a hand over his shoulder. "This injury hasn't changed one bit of your inner fortitude or kindness. Sadie is an expert in human psychology and PTSD, and I hope you'll sit down to talk with her. She's available anytime you're ready. All of us want to support you through this."

"Thanks." Feeling exhausted, Sam observed Nolan leave the room and tried like hell not to focus on the fact he wished Bakari had killed him in the meadow instead of rendering him inept and hopeless.

Chapter 11

Glarys threw herself into her work, cleaning every inch of the mansion as if her life depended on it. Perhaps it did, since her heart had devolved into a heap of broken mush. After she left Sam a week ago, he'd refused to see her when she returned to the infirmary. Sadie, the kind physician and Nolan's wife, had hugged her as she burst into tears.

"It's a devastating loss, Glarys," she'd said, rubbing her back in a soothing gesture. "He's got to come to terms with it in his own way. You'll know when he's ready to see you."

"What if he's never ready?" she asked, sniffling into the wadded tissue she pulled from her purse. "Doesn't he understand I don't give a fig about his arm?"

"He's as stubborn as you are. Give him some time. I promise, it will work out."

Glarys had left the kind doctor and returned home, wondering how her life had devolved to this level of extreme despair. She missed Sam so desperately that she would cry into her pillow each night, craving his gentle snores and loving caresses. Perhaps that was why he was pushing her away: he felt his inability to touch her would preclude her from loving him back. Nothing could be further from the truth. Glarys longed to wrap her arms around him and show him they could still maintain their fervent and passionate connection. If only he understood how much she craved his presence; how vehemently she missed his sweet kisses.

A few days after the attack, Sadie informed her Sam had moved into one of the vacant cabins at the edge of Uteria. She and Nolan checked on him daily, making sure he was stocked with Slayer blood and ensuring he drank it. Although he was stubborn, he was reluctantly imbibing enough to stay alive.

Glarys debated the best way to approach him since he was still adamant he didn't want to see her. The sentiment stung. She ached to comfort him and help him heal—not just from the wound, but from the emotional scars it had invoked.

A week after his injury, as she cleaned Heden's room, furiously wiping down every speck of the vacant chamber, the anger that had been welling burned inside her gut. Opening the dresser drawer to dust inside, she gasped when she saw the black bag. Pulling it open, she clutched the felt box inside. With shaking fingers, she opened it to reveal a magnificent ring.

Tears flooded her eyes as she realized Sam had hidden it so she wouldn't find it before he proposed.

Closing the box, she tightened her fist around it, squeezing for dear life. Unwilling to let him push her away any longer, she rushed to her chamber to shower and then called Latimus.

"Hey, Glarys," his deep voice answered. "You okay?"

"I need you to pick me up and drive me to the cabin Sam's staying in at Uteria. You know I wouldn't ask you to interrupt your day if it wasn't important, but I need to speak with him, and I'm done letting him push me away."

She could almost feel his smile through the phone. "I'll be there in twenty-five minutes."

Over an hour later, she felt a crack in her resolve as they pulled up to the remote cabin on the outskirts of Uteria. Steeling herself, she exited the vehicle and straightened her shoulders, silently staring at the wooden shack.

"You can do this, Glarys," Latimus said from behind the wheel. "I'll be at the barracks behind the castle if you need me. Call anytime. Good luck." With a salute, he drove away.

Inhaling a deep breath, she climbed the creaky stairs and knocked on the door. Answered by nothing but resounding silence, she began to pound until she heard, "For the goddess's sake, come in before you beat the door down!"

Pushing it open, she headed inside, noting the dimness of the small cabin. Sam sat on the bed with his back against the headboard, long legs stretched in front of him, bare feet crossed at the ankles. He only wore sweatpants, that gorgeous abdomen making her mouth water. God, but she'd missed the sight of his smooth skin.

Planting her fists on her hips, she tapped her foot. "Well? You don't remember how to return a phone call?"

Sighing, he pressed his head against the headboard. "In case you haven't noticed, I can't really work a phone these days."

With a *harrumph*, she closed the cabin door and proceeded to open the curtains, causing beams of sunlight to blanket the room.

"Hey!" he said, squinting. "I wanted those closed."

"Well, too bad," she said, suddenly furious he'd all but given up. Where was the strong, steady soldier she fell in love with? "I'm pretty disappointed in you, Sam, and mad as hell that you're pushing me away."

"What do you want me to say, Glarys?" His tone was devoid of emotion, sending a jolt of fear down her spine. "It's over for me."

"Oh, holy hell." Stomping over to him, she gripped his shoulder and tugged. "Stand up."

He glared at her. "What are you doing, woman—?"

"I know you still have perfectly functioning legs, so I want you to stand the hell up, Sam. Come on."

Grumbling, he wriggled off the bed and stood. He was disheveled and unshaven as he stared down at her. Even in this state, he was so achingly handsome.

"Sweetheart," she whispered, sliding her hand to cup his jaw. She moved slowly, understanding he was raw and wracked with pain. Caressing his cheek with her thumb, she willed the tears in her eyes to abate. "Do you realize you're breaking my heart?"

A ragged breath exited his lungs as he shook his head. "It's what's best for you, Glarys. You'll see that one day. I'm choosing to end this so you can be with someone whole."

"Hogwash," she said, wrinkling her nose. "I have no desire to be with anyone but you. And I'll remind you that I get to choose whom I love, so you can stop making choices for me right now."

"Do you really want to sign up for this?" Flailing his stubbed arms, he appeared incensed. "A life with a man who can never touch you? Never hold you? I'm helpless, Glarys. A damn invalid. I'm doing you a favor, whether you realize it or not."

Furious, she stomped her foot. "First of all, you can touch me just fine."

"No, I can't—"

"Yes, you can." Standing on her toes, she kissed him, reveling in his quick intake of breath. "See? You just touched me with those magnificent lips. You'll have to use those more. I think I'll like that just fine."

Brown irises darted between hers. "I won't become a burden to you."

Rolling her eyes, she pulled the papers from her purse. "Nolan gave me these," she said, shaking them. "Did you even look at the research he did on the prosthetic limbs? They're absolutely amazing, Sam. They have the capability to do everything a functioning arm can do."

"And you'll be stuck with a man who looks like a damn cyborg."

"Like Luke Skywalker," she said, feeling herself grin. "I thought his mechanical arm was quite fancy. You'll be like the last Jedi. Like *my* Jedi. I'd be honored to be at your side while you sport something like that."

Lowering his gaze, he studied the floor, looking so forlorn that she set her purse down and slid her palms over his pecs. Closing her eyes, she shivered as the tiny hairs scratched her skin.

"Goddess, Sam," she whispered, "I feel like I haven't touched you in so long." Lifting her lids, her gaze bore into his. "I love you, you daft man. Whether you have a hundred arms or zero. Don't you understand?"

Lowering his forehead to hers, he shook his head. "Glarys, if I truly loved you, wouldn't I let you go? I feel like it's so selfish to tie you to someone who's broken."

"You're not broken. Please don't say that. You're the man who regenerated my heart. I never thought I'd ever feel love or desire again. You've given me the world, Sam. I just need you to love me enough to stay."

"I love you more than I ever thought possible," he whispered, brushing a kiss across her lips. "I'm just terrified you'll be sacrificing so much to be with me."

"Love requires sacrifice, sweetheart." Sliding her arms around his neck, she drew him close. "Will times be hard? Sure. Can we get through them together? I believe we can. The question is, do *you* believe we can?"

He was quiet for a moment. "I believe in you."

Feeling her lips curve, she drew him closer. "That's enough for now. Let's start there. We'll forge this new path together. I don't care if it's hard. I just care that you're by my side."

He studied her in silence as his shoulders slowly released their tension. "Okay," he whispered, pushing his body into hers. "I wish I could hold you."

"I've got you," she said, squeezing her arms around his neck as their bodies molded together. "And you're doing just fine, Sam. Now, do me a favor and kiss me, will you?"

Cementing her lips to his, she threaded her fingers through his hair and succumbed to his skillful tongue. Feeling her knees buckle, she held on for dear life, so thrilled to be in his presence.

Once she'd been thoroughly kissed and blood was pounding through her veins, she drew back and bent to search her purse. Finding the box, she lifted it.

"I found this in Heden's drawer."

"I wanted to give it to you by the river. I had it all planned out. It was going to be perfect."

"Life gets in the way of perfect sometimes," she said, setting the box on his bedside table. "I'll leave it there, and you can figure out another time to give it to me. How does that sound?"

His lips curved. "It sounds pretty good." Stepping toward her, he leaned down and nuzzled her temple with his nose. "Everything inside me is reaching for you right now, honey. I wish you could feel it."

"I do," she whispered, sliding her arms around his waist. "I feel it, Sam. Now, kiss me again and tell me you love me."

Chuckling, he placed a poignant kiss on her lips. "I love you so much, Glarys. To the bottom of my soul. I hope I'm worth the struggle. I promise I'll try."

"The struggle makes the good times better—I've learned that over the centuries. We'll do this together, Sam. All the way."

Pressing his lips to hers, he drew her to him, sucking her tongue into his mouth and bathing her with his taste.

"Oh, yes," she murmured, feeling the slickness at her core. "We're going to do just fine, Sam."

Breathing a laugh, he nodded and kissed her into oblivion.

Chapter 12

One Month Later

Glarys watched her lover as he tested the prosthetic arms with Nolan. After some urging, Sam had agreed to try the contraptions and quickly became enthralled by them. With the human technology Nolan had employed, the circle placed on the stubs of his arms picked up nerve signals from the muscles beneath. From there, he could dictate the arms to perform several functions: grabbing, pinching, wiggling—nothing was off-limits. More exciting than the new abilities was the look on his handsome face as he realized his true capabilities.

"Okay, Sam, reach down and pick up the apple and place it next to the orange," Nolan said, gesturing to the fruit on the counter.

Sam followed the instructions, grinning the entire time. "I think I've got the hang of it, doc."

"I think you do," Nolan said, grinning. "And how about the sensations from the fingertips? Can you feel the skin of the apple?"

"Sure can. I'd like to try it on something else."

"Go for it."

Sauntering toward Glarys, he lifted the arm and brushed the prosthetic fingers over her collarbone.

"Oh, that feels nice," she said, beaming up at him.

"I can feel the softness of your skin," he murmured. "It's amazing."

"See? There's always a way, sweetheart. And you look pretty sexy with those Jedi arms."

Waggling his eyebrows, he cupped her shoulder. "We can test them out later tonight with some adult activities, if you'd like?"

"Shh..." Swatting his chest, Glarys felt her cheeks burning. "Nolan can hear you."

"Can't hear a thing," Nolan teased as he typed notes into Sam's electronic medical record on the laptop atop the counter.

"Will I be able to shoot a gun, doc?"

"Yes," Nolan said, turning and leaning back against the counter. "You'll need to practice to retrain the muscles, but you should eventually be able to aim and shoot just as effectively as before."

"Thank the goddess. I want to keep protecting my very pretty ward."

Glarys winked at him, delighted by the compliment.

"How about my knees? Can I still kneel?"

"Why would your knees be affected?" Glarys asked, feeling her eyebrows draw together.

Reaching into his pocket, he withdrew a felt box and lowered to one knee. Tears welled in Glarys's eyes as he opened it, fangs exposed as he smiled up at her.

"Just making sure because I want to do this right."

Glarys lifted a shaking hand over her lips.

"Glarys, Daughter of Davel, I never even thought I could love someone as deeply as I love you. You shattered every notion that existed about companionship and devotion. I'd be real honored if you'd agree to bond with me so I can spend eternity thanking you for everything you've given me. What do you say?"

"Yes!" she cried, clutching his face as tears streamed down her cheeks. "I love you so much, Sam."

The prosthetic fingers were deft as he slipped the ring on her finger and stood to kiss her. "Thank you, honey. You've made me so happy."

Nolan and Sadie clapped behind them, and Glarys realized she must've stepped in to observe the proposal. Embracing Sam, she smiled at the kind doctors over his shoulder. Filled with anticipation of the future they would create together, she embraced her magnificent Vampyre, overcome with joy. Not so long ago, she'd felt an aching loneliness deep inside. Now, she'd found the other half of her soul.

Sending a silent, thankful prayer to Etherya, she swayed in Sam's arms, excited to spend the centuries ahead by his side—her magnificent, soulful bonded mate.

Epilogue

Glarys was exhausted by the time the last guest left Astaria after the reception. The bonding ceremony was lovely. She and Sam had exchanged vows under the white altar covered with flowers by the River Thayne. The reception overflowed with a multitude of food and wine, accompanied by Heden's DJ skills as he stood in the booth at the head of the room and pumped out the tunes. Now, she and Sam had retired to her room—their room now—and she sucked in a breath as she removed her heels.

"You okay?" he asked, rubbing her arm.

Nodding, she sat on the bed and began to massage her feet. "Those shoes were so pretty, but they squished the heck out of my feet. I'm happy to be rid of them."

"Here," he said, sitting beside her and pulling her feet to rest atop his thighs. "Let me do this, honey." The agile fingers of his prosthetics moved as he sent her to heaven with his ministrations.

"Oh, my," she sighed, closing her eyes and leaning back against the pillows. "That's wonderful, Sam."

He massaged her for a while before she took note of the growing desire in his hooded gaze. Feeling her body begin to hum with arousal, she crooked her finger at him.

"Why don't you move a bit higher?"

Chuckling, he grasped her hand and pulled her to stand. Leisurely, they removed their clothes, letting the anticipation intensify. When they were naked, she removed each of his prosthetics, gently setting them on the dresser before returning to his side.

He slid over the sheets, resting his back against the headboard, and reached for her. He was so achingly beautiful, the stubs of his arms completely healed as he held them open. Gliding over him, she rubbed her slick center over his engorged cock, loving his desirous hiss.

"You're drenching me, sweetheart," he murmured.

"What can I say? Looking at you naked gets my body humming."

Chuckling, he squirmed below her. "Me too. Come on, honey. Ride me. I'm dying for you."

Reaching between them, she gripped his cock, rubbing the sensitive head over her opening before slowly taking him inside her quivering body. Ragged breaths filled the room as she began to move over his smooth skin. Whispering her name, he undulated his hips, pushing so deep inside her he stimulated the sensitive spot that held a thousand tiny nerve endings. Cupping his shoulder, she slid her free hand to her clit, circling her fingers over the swollen nub as desire flamed in his eyes.

"Yes, honey," he said, a muscle clenching in his jaw. "You look so pretty when you play with yourself like that. Goddess, you feel so good."

"I love you," she whispered, leaning forward to cement her lips to his.

Their bodies moved in tandem as she trailed kisses over his cheek before heading lower. Extending her tongue to lick his neck, she coated him with her saliva to shield him from the pain. Placing her fangs against his vein, she plunged them into his skin, groaning when his cock surged inside her. He uttered muted curses against her skin as he repeated her ministrations with his tongue upon her neck. She felt the scrape of his fangs against her wet skin a second before he pierced her, moaning in pleasure as her blood invaded his mouth.

They were joined in every possible way, his shaft claiming her as they imbibed each other's essence. Threading her fingers through his thick hair, she rode him in a blissful dream that was somehow now reality. The movement of their hips increased until she felt her orgasm on the horizon. Purring against his neck, she gave in to the pleasure, feeling her body snap as he hammered into her. Lost to pleasure, she held on for dear life as jets of his release coated her core. Breaking contact with his neck, she buried her face against his skin and rode the magnificent wave.

Slowly, they came back to Earth, licking each other's wounds to aid the self-healing properties. Slick and sweaty, they held each other for what seemed like hours until she felt his release slip between them.

"Be right back," she murmured, gently pecking his cheek. Sliding off his lap, she trailed to the bathroom, returning with a wet cloth to clean them both.

Tossing the cloth in the hamper a moment later, she joined him in bed, pulling the covers over their cooling bodies as she rested her cheek on his chest. Gently, Sam caressed her upper back with the stub of his right arm, which extended to where his elbow once began. Closing her eyes, Glarys reveled in the tender strokes, so proud he'd conquered his fears and doubts. As sleep began to sink its claws into her consciousness, she mumbled against his chest.

"I'm so honored to be your bonded mate, Sam."

He sighed beneath her, the action filled with reverence. "Glarys, you have no idea how happy you've made me. I was so sure it was over for me, but you saved me from myself. I wish I could repay you. Since I can't, I'll just love you in every way I know how and with every cell in my body. I swear, I'm going to do everything in my power to put you first."

"You already do," she said, overcome with emotion at his tender words. "You're perfect, sweetheart. One day, you'll realize that. For now, I'll just hold the sentiment deep in my heart."

Firm lips placed worshipful kisses on her forehead as her eyes drifted shut. Enveloped in her bonded's loving embrace, Glarys yielded to the darkness, firm in the knowledge Sam would be there when she eventually returned to the light.

Before You Go

Well, dear readers, I hope you enjoyed Glarys and Sam's love story! If you enjoyed meeting Lila and Latimus in this book, their story is told in Book 2 of the series, **The Elusive Sun**. And you can continue on to read Book 6, **The Cryptic Prophecy**, now! Thanks so much for spending some time in Etherya's Earth with me!

Garridan's Mate

Etherya's Earth, Book 6.5

By

REBECCA HEFNER

This book is a work of fiction. Names, characters, places and incidents are the product of the author's imagination and are used fictitiously. Any resemblance to actual events, locales or persons, living or dead, is coincidental.

Copyright © 2021 by Rebecca Hefner. All rights reserved, including the right to reproduce, distribute or transmit in any form or by any means.

Cover Design: Anthony O'Brien, BookCoverDesign.store
Proofreader: Bryony Leah, www.bryonyleah.com

Contents

Table of Contents
Title Page and   Copyright
Dedication
Map of Etherya's Earth
Chapter 1
Chapter 2
Chapter 3
Chapter 4
Chapter 5
Chapter 6
Chapter 7
Chapter 8
Chapter 9
Chapter 10
Chapter 11
Chapter 12
Chapter 13
Chapter 14
Before You Go
Also by Rebecca Hefner
About the Author

To my fellow Hearts Unleashed anthology authors. It was an honor to hit the USA Today bestseller list with you!

Chapter One

Garridan, son of Astaroth, stood atop the grassy hill observing the field below. Thick arms crossed over his chest as his eyes narrowed. Several soldiers in the vast immortal army were competing to become squadron leaders in the final battle against Bakari. The long-lost Vampyre royal sibling had a massive army of his own and was intent on defeating them so he could rule in perpetuity. Garridan was determined to prevent that at all costs.

"How's the competition going?" a deep baritone asked.

"Excellent, Commander," Garridan said with a nod. "Radomir and Cian have won the majority of the physical contests as expected, with Siora close behind. The three of them excelled at the obstacle courses, the written leadership exam, and the hand-to-hand fights, although Cian did get a nasty black eye that took two hours to heal even with his self-healing abilities."

"You can call me Latimus, you know?" the commander said, arching a brow under his black hair, slicked back into a tiny tail secured by a leather strap. "We've fought together since the Awakening. Although we're both technically aristocrats, you know I hate the formal shit."

Garridan smiled into his friend's ice-blue eyes. "You're the son of King Markdor and Queen Calla and second in line to the throne. I think you're a tad more aristocratic than me, but I see your point."

"Tordor is second in line to the throne," Latimus said with a firm nod. "Thank the goddess my brother did his kingly duty and sired an heir."

"Do you think they will have another? Tordor is no longer a child. Perhaps they both long for more children."

"Perhaps." Latimus's eyebrows drew together as he stared across the sparring field. "Miranda's pregnancy was extremely difficult since Tordor was the first ever Vampyre-Slayer hybrid. She almost died in childbirth, and Sathan is hesitant to put her in danger. But"—he held up a finger—"Miranda wears the pants, so if she says she wants another child, Sathan will have her knocked up before the next sunrise."

"Said by a man desperately in love with his own bonded."

Latimus's lips twitched. "Indeed. I don't even try to deny it anymore. Lila has me in the palm of her hand. I just do what I'm told and try to be the best bonded mate and father so she'll let me keep kissing her. So far, it's working."

Chuckling, Garridan patted Latimus on the shoulder. "Our great and powerful commander, reduced to the whim of a pretty Vampyre aristocrat."

"One with a generous soul and selfless spirit," he said wistfully. "I'll never deserve her, but that's never seemed to bother her. I'm one lucky bastard." Facing Garridan, he asked, "And what of you? I heard rumors you were contemplating asking Celine to bond with you."

Garridan grimaced. "Did you happen to hear that from Father? He's been hounding me to settle down for centuries. Aristocrats rarely become soldiers, but I always felt a calling to fight, even when I was young. Since I'm second-born and my brother performs our formal duties, Father let me train. I think your position as commander was helpful in that decision."

"I'm thankful he allowed you to join the army. You're one of my most cunning and loyal soldiers."

"And I'm pretty good at combat, I think?" he joked, rubbing his chin.

Latimus breathed a laugh. "You are. We've fought so many skirmishes side by side. Thank the goddess the War of the Species ended and we vanquished Crimeous. Once Bakari is defeated, we will hopefully secure peace for the immortal world. Do you wish to wait to settle down until our conflict with him is over?"

Garridan kicked the ground with the toe of his black boot and shook his head. "I'm not in love with Celine," he said softly. "She is a wonderful female and should bond with someone who can love her in all the ways she deserves."

Latimus's brows lifted. "I see. Does this mean you're in love with someone else?"

Pursing his lips, Garridan gazed over the broad field, his eyes landing on the woman who consumed his every thought. She was sparring with Cian, expertly wielding her sword as the much larger male attempted to fight her off. White fangs glinted in the sun as she sliced and swung the weapon through the air, the metal clanking each time it connected with her opponent's sword.

Garridan had no rhyme or reason for his uncontrollable desire for her. By all accounts, they were opposites in every way. He, the second-born of wealthy Vampyre aristocrats from the sprawling compound of Valeria. She, a feisty lowborn female from a farming village on the outskirts of the laborer compound, Lynia. Her firm, curvy body and broad shoulders were perfect for carrying the bales of corn her father harvested from the fields that surrounded her small family home. She'd told him of it once, when they'd had a small moment of reprieve—and when she'd somehow forgotten, if only for a short time, that she detested him.

"Ah," Latimus said, slowly nodding. "I see."

"It is nothing," Garridan said, straightening his spine. "Siora is just another soldier to me."

Silence stretched between them before Latimus cupped his shoulder. "My friend, you are a terrible liar."

He scoffed and elicited a sigh. "Siora seems to think I'm a misogynistic snob who doesn't believe women deserve a place in our army."

"That's not even close to true," Latimus said, bristling. "You were one of the first to support allowing females to join the combat troops. Where did she obtain that notion?"

"She is a talented soldier, and I push her. She finished a clear and resounding third place in all the physical trials we've held over the past week and finished first on the written exam. There is no doubt she will secure one of the squadron leader positions."

"Our first female squadron leader," Latimus said, reverence in his tone. "My mother would be proud."

"Yes. Siora thinks I single her out because she is a woman, but that isn't true. She has the potential to become a multi-squadron lieutenant one day, and I push her because I want her to excel. But she's exceedingly stubborn and often antagonistic, which I see as her greatest drawback."

"Perhaps she is antagonistic because she desires you as well."

"I never said I desire her," Garridan muttered.

Latimus gave him a droll look. "You didn't have to."

Sighing, Garridan rubbed his hand over his face. "Desire has no place in our army or the conflict with Bakari. I will train her and help her succeed, and then she will become squadron leader. That is my main focus. I'm tired of being consumed by war and wish for our people to live in peace."

"As do I, my friend. Hopefully, it will happen in the upcoming battle. I'm going to join the troops in their sparring session. Want to join me?"

"I'll stay here and continue observing. I'll record my notes this evening before heading home. We should be able to announce the new battalion leaders next week."

"Fantastic," Latimus said, fangs flashing as he gave a salute and began trudging down the hill.

"Don't let Cian kick your ass again!" Garridan teased, chuckling when Latimus lifted his fist and extended his middle finger as he trailed toward the troops.

Glancing at Siora again, he noticed she had knocked the weapon from her sparring partner's hand and now held the tip of her sword against his neck, waiting for him to call mercy. Damn, she was fierce. Tamping down his admiration, he reminded himself he needed to focus on observing *all* the soldiers, not just the one who always drew his gaze with her masterful skill, gorgeous body, and piercing ice-blue gaze.

Siora gritted her teeth, thrusting her sword into her opponent's chest before he grunted and backed away.

"Damn it, Siora," Cian said, holding his hand to his chest. "That fucking hurt."

"You're wearing protective gear," she said, scowling. "You struck me just as hard in the side, and I didn't even wince."

"Maybe you're tougher than me," he said, still rubbing his chest as he grinned, "or maybe you don't have the ability to hit like a girl."

"Hit like a girl, my ass," she muttered, tossing her sword to the ground before picking up the container to chug some much-needed water. Wiping her mouth with the back of her arm, she sighed. "I've never hit like a girl."

"Truer words."

Latimus approached, calling all the troops together and informing them they would spar another hour before heading home. Siora glanced at the sun, noting it was still looming above the horizon, and was pleased she'd have time to help her father at the farm before darkness settled in.

"You're doing very well, Siora," Latimus murmured, and she turned to stare into his sky-blue eyes. "I have no doubt you will become a battalion leader before the final battle with Bakari. After we win, you can have your choice of assignments, whether it be field-based or tailored toward security. I still plan to maintain an army, although it hopefully won't need to be as formidable since we will finally be at peace."

"I love combat," she said, lifting a shoulder. "There's something cathartic about kicking someone's ass."

Chuckling, he gave a nod. "That there is. Keep excelling, and you could become head of security at one of the compounds. That should keep you busy."

"Lynia is my home, so that's where I'd like to be stationed regardless of which position I attain. I'll do my best to earn it."

"I have no doubt." Lifting his brows, he asked, "Want to spar with this old man?" He pointed his thumbs at his chest. "I'm feeling the need to expend some energy."

Siora couldn't contain her smile. A request from the powerful commander to spar with him in front of the troops was an honor and would help cement her status as a competent soldier. The army had only recently allowed women to join the combat troops, and she felt an intense obligation to prove the decision was warranted.

"I'm not going to go easy on you," she said, arching a brow.

"I'd be disappointed if you did." Striding toward the weaponry rack, Latimus selected a sword. Soldiers milled around, gathering to watch the impending showdown.

Lifting her sword, Siora crouched and pointed it straight at his chest. "Ready when you are."

He settled into position before charging, and she felt the magnificent surge of adrenaline she always felt when an impending challenge occurred. Then, she swung her sword through the air, thrilled when the metal clanked against the commander's, and got down to the task of kicking his ass.

Chapter Two

Siora arrived home that evening as the sun lingered over the far-off mountains, a bright, orange orb in the graying sky. Tossing her bag on the porch, she headed behind their small two-bedroom house to the fields lined with corn. Her father was hunched over, picking the husks and depositing them in his basket.

"Hey, Dad," she said, her tone soft so she wouldn't startle him. "Want me to help? I can grab a basket from the shed."

"Hi, sweetie," he said, rising and extending his hands. Grasping them, she placed a kiss on his forehead. "I'm almost finished, but thank you. The harvest has been good this year. Thank the goddess for the growing population of hungry Slayers and Deamons on our tiny compound. I've been selling out at my booth every weekend. The reconciliation of the species has been fantastic for business."

"Better than all the centuries harvesting corn for the Slayers imprisoned at Astaria, that's for sure. Maybe we'll make enough to actually build the annex onto the house this year."

"I think we might," he said, light blue eyes the mirror image of hers sparkling in the rays of the lowering sun. "Your mother would be proud."

"I'd like to think so," she said, sifting the toe of her boot through the tilled dirt. "I still remember her singing to me all those years ago, before she was slain in the Awakening."

"Goddess, but she had a beautiful voice," he said wistfully, briefly closing his eyes. "You were the light of our lives. Our little Siora."

"And then I became your big Siora," she teased, lifting her arms. "I think I'm a head taller than you, Dad."

"You have the constitution of a warrior. I have no idea where it came from, although your mother's brother was a fine soldier, Etherya bless his soul." He laid his hand over his heart. "I miss both of them terribly."

Siora's eyes darted between his. "Would you consider bonding again? If I continue to excel in the army, it's possible I'll have to move closer to the main castle at Lynia's town square if I get promoted. I don't want you to be alone."

"It's only a forty-minute walk into town," he said, waving his hand, "and I know my daughter will come to visit me."

"I will, and I can also teach you to drive a four-wheeler."

"None of that," he said, shaking his head. "I'm not interested in the human technology you soldiers toy around with. I have two working legs, and they can carry me into town just fine."

Chuckling, Siora tilted her head. "You know, I'm pretty sure I get my stubborn streak from you. It runs pretty deep."

"Then I am proud," he said, lowering to pick up the basket full of corn. "It is a noble quality no matter how badly your mother used to tease me for it. One must stand by their convictions."

Siora reached over and tugged the basket from his hands, settling it on her hip as he emitted a huff.

"I can carry it, dear."

"Let your daughter help you. You've worked all day."

They trailed toward the home, Siora placing the basket in the shed before locking it.

"I'll get to shucking them in the morning," he said. "Let's have dinner. I've got some Slayer blood ready, and Ophelia dropped off some nice wine she picked up in town."

Grinning at the mention of their neighbor, who Siora suspected had a crush on her dad, she cupped his shoulder. "She's a nice woman, Dad."

"She is," he said, climbing the wooden steps to enter their home. "I wasn't sure when Queen Miranda and King Sathan decreed reformed Deamons could live on our compounds, but she is lovely."

"You could take a day off and escort her into town for one of the street fairs."

"Stop trying to matchmake, girl," he said, shooing her with his hand. "I'm too old for that nonsense."

"You're never too old—"

"Enough," he interrupted. "We should be discussing finding a mate for *you*."

Rolling her eyes, she huffed. "Thanks, but I'm all set. I told you, I like being single."

Curiosity entered his gaze. "Don't you want someone to come home to after your long days of training to protect our world? Don't you want to give your father some grandbabies?"

"Oh, brother," she muttered. "We've officially entered the uncomfortable portion of the evening. Come on—let's table this and have dinner and wine. That should take your mind off grilling me."

They trailed inside, her father dismissing the subject for now, but Siora knew it would rear its head again. Reminding herself that he loved her and wanted what he thought was best, she let the conversation go.

Siora had never longed for a partner or to have kids. Was she against it? Not really. But being a plain, stocky girl who'd grown into a brawny, intimidating woman didn't really appeal to men in her experience. She wasn't biddable or coy or whatever the hell Vampyre males wanted in their mates. Although the immortal world had evolved somewhat from its stuffy, traditional history, it still remained quite staid in her opinion. Now she was a warrior in the army and that only decreased her chances of finding a mate.

In her experience, Vampyre males wanted soft, wispy women who would giggle and bat their eyelashes as they flirted. Siora had never flirted in her damn life and had no reason to start now. She could never fake being someone she wasn't. It just wasn't in her DNA.

She liked being tough and was pretty sure she would one day become the highest-ranking female officer in the immortal army if she kept up her grueling training. No one knew she woke up at 4:00 a.m. every day and trained an extra two hours before reporting to duty. She was determined to be as formidable as any man on the field—*more* formidable if she had her way—no matter the energy she had to expend.

There was honor in that, and it satisfied her more than any man ever could.

Even General Garridan...

Gritting her teeth at the words as they silently flitted through her brain, she squeezed her lids shut, trying to rid her mind of the image of his strikingly handsome face. Deep amber eyes stared back at her, refusing to vanish no matter how hard she tried. His fangs glistened atop his full lower lip in her vision, above strong shoulders and a chiseled chest. The aristocrat towered over her, which had always been disconcerting. Very few men made her feel small, but the infuriating general certainly did. If he wanted to envelop her in his thick arms and tug her head back to claim her lips, he could overpower her in a second...

"Dear?" her father asked, perplexed as he held up two goblets. "Ready for dinner?"

"Yes," she uttered, frustrated she was daydreaming *yet again* about the asinine general's kiss. The visions had become more frequent lately, especially since he sparred shirtless around the troops. How was her brain supposed to function when he bared that magnificent chest at every opportunity?

"Bastard."

"Who is?" her father asked.

Damn, she'd said it out loud. Sighing, she shook her head and sat at the small table, grasping the goblet of Slayer blood and lifting it high. "No one. To another great harvest. Congrats, Dad. It's going to be a good year."

Clinking his glass with hers, his eyes sparkled. "It certainly is."

Settling in to the lovely meal with her favorite person on the planet, Siora tried to push thoughts of Garridan from her mind while inwardly admitting the task was futile.

∞

Garridan scowled behind the wheel of the utility vehicle as he approached his home at Valeria. It sat beside his parents' austere mansion but wasn't as large. They'd given him the plot of land centuries ago, hoping he would build a home, settle down with a bonded mate, and have children. Well, one out of three wasn't bad, he guessed.

His father sat on the porch, his face an impassive mask as always. Turning off the four-wheeler, Garridan stepped from the vehicle and approached.

"Hello, Father. I expected you to already be at dinner with Mother and Sebastian."

"Sebastian was held up at the governor's mansion and won't make dinner tonight. It afforded me the opportunity to speak to you."

Lowering into the chair opposite his father, Garridan eyed him warily. "If you're looking to argue, I'm exhausted and would rather wait until I have the energy."

Astaroth's eyes narrowed. "Don't be antagonistic. This will only take a moment, but it's important."

"Okay."

"Would you like to go inside?"

"It's a nice evening," Garridan said, relaxing in the chair. In truth, he cherished his space and didn't want his father's toxic energy inside his home. "Let's chat here."

"Very well." Lacing his fingers, he rested his hands in his lap. "There is a fundraiser in two weeks as the king and queen are looking to raise money for the army. It will be held in the main ballroom at Valeria's governor's mansion."

"Good," Garridan said with a nod. "The new TECs are expensive, and it will be nice for the aristocrats to contribute to the cause."

"As opposed to you, who contributes with brawn and sweat. I am still frustrated you donated your entire trust to the immortal army. I can't fathom how you exist on a soldier's salary."

"This land you gave me was all I needed," he said, gesturing with his hand. "I have a home and a job I love. Wars are expensive, and we must win them if you want to keep living your lavish lifestyle."

"Don't mock me. You are still the beneficiary of much privilege as my son."

"I know," he said, softening his tone. "I appreciate what you and mother have done for me. I'm sorry you don't understand my choices. We've been doing quite well at agreeing to disagree, haven't we?"

His father's lips twitched. "We have, but I fear that might soon change."

Garridan's eyebrows lifted. "Because?"

Silence stretched between them before he spoke. "Because I have promised Handor you will accompany Celine to the fundraiser as her escort."

Grimacing, he shook his head. "No. It's possible I won't even be available that evening. The training sessions are becoming more intense as we near the final battle with Bakari."

"Son," Astaroth said, leaning forward, "when the battle is over and the immortals win by the grace of Etherya, you will have no place as a soldier. It will be time to resume your aristocratic duties. Time to find a mate and settle down. Celine would be a fine choice."

"Celine is a lovely woman, but she is not my mate," he said with finality. "And I will still remain in the army in some capacity. I love it too much to leave."

"Ridiculous," he spat, sitting back and huffing in frustration. "You have a duty!"

"Duty is what we make of it, Father." Running a hand through his thick, dark hair, he sighed. "I won't let you push me into a life I don't want. I'm sorry."

Rising, his father's thin body vibrated with anger. "You know nothing of duty," he said, jabbing a finger in his face. "Nothing of what it means to uphold your aristocratic obligation with honor!"

"Don't yell at me," Garridan said, rising to his full height, several inches above his father. "I don't want to argue. Focus on Sebastian if you must. Perhaps you can 'save' one of your sons from ruin," he said sardonically, making quotation marks with his fingers.

"Sebastian is another story, and I won't let you change the subject. At least he sits on the council and fulfills his aristocratic obligation. You both need to bond with an honorable female, but he does not shirk his duty."

"You have some nerve to say I shirk duty when I've fought by Commander Latimus's side for centuries. Go home to mother. I'm done with this conversation." Dismissing him, he began to walk toward the front door.

His father grabbed his arm, causing him to whirl around, and anger simmered in his gut.

"I will donate the funds to Queen Miranda for her to purchase a thousand additional TECs for the final battle *if*"—he lifted a finger—"you escort Celine to the fundraiser in two weeks' time.

If not, you can explain to the queen why I have withdrawn my donation."

"That's absurd. Defeating Bakari will help solidify your safety as well. You're drowning in money and will barely miss the donation."

"I've made my decision," he said, slicing a hand through the air. With a final nod, he began trudging down the stairs. "I would like an answer tomorrow so I can confirm to Celine's father you will accompany her. Good night, son. I won't tell your mother of your disparagement of our heritage. It would break her heart."

Garridan watched him stalk away with slitted eyes, furious at being manipulated with the one thing he loved most: protecting his people. Wondering for the millionth time how he was related to someone so cold and unyielding, Garridan muttered to himself as he unlocked the door and stepped inside.

After a warm shower and much contemplation, he sat down to enjoy his dinner of Slayer blood and wine. Furious, he admitted he would accompany Celine to the fundraiser because his men needed all the extra weapons they could get.

"Your *soldiers* need all the weapons they can get," he murmured in a self-deprecating tone, acknowledging Siora would shoot him a hate-filled glare if he called the troops "men." He'd done it a few times in front of her—out of habit and certainly unconsciously—and she'd raked him over the coals for it each time.

Feeling the corner of his lips curve, he acknowledged how much he cherished her furious scolding. Hell, he actually longed for it. She would stare up at him with those gorgeous eyes, spittle flying between her fangs as she laid into him. Sometimes, she would even shove him or punch his arm before he gave her a look of warning, reminding her he was her superior. Her glorious features would form a scowl under her short cap of black hair, and she'd grunt before walking away, muttering to herself what an ass he was.

Would she grunt like that if he returned her touch? If he drew her toward him and fashioned those full red lips into some action other than scolding him? Perhaps kissing him with fervor, as he longed to do to her, or placing the plump flesh over other parts of his body...

Glancing down, Garridan grimaced at the erection now tenting his sweatpants. All it took was one thought of Siora's gorgeous lips, and he was hard as a damn rock. Deciding he needed a release, he slid his hand beneath the waistband, gripping his turgid cock as he groaned.

"Siora," he whispered, sliding his hand back and forth over the sensitive flesh, imagining it was her hand...her lips...her *tongue*...

And then, he closed his eyes, allowing himself to fully succumb to the vivid dream he wished was reality.

Chapter Three

The next day, Siora sparred with one of the new recruits from Naria as Garridan and Latimus observed. The new soldier, Kristoff, was skilled and quick as a damn jackrabbit. Every time she tried to gain the upper hand, he anticipated her strike. Frustrated, she gave a grunt and thrust her weapon. He knocked it to the ground and promptly held his blade to her neck, causing her to curse.

"You're dropping your hip, Siora," Garridan's deep voice boomed from several feet away. "It's a tell, and that's how Kristoff keeps gaining the advantage."

"I'm doing nothing of the sort," she gritted, knocking Kristoff's weapon away with her arm. "Get that thing away from me. You won this skirmish. I concede." The words tasted like gravel on her tongue, but she figured they were the fastest way to get everyone's attention off her and back to something else so she could lick her wounds.

"You'll need to remedy your weaknesses if you want to become a battalion leader," Garridan said. "Not to mention, it will come in handy against Bakari's Deamon soldiers."

"Thanks, Captian Obvious," she said, rolling her eyes before giving him a scowl. "I've been training in my father's fields for centuries, waiting for the time you cavemen would let women into the army. I think I've got this."

"Take five," Latimus commanded to Kristoff and the other nearby soldiers, although his gaze was firm on Siora's. "We'll resume after you all grab some water across the field." The soldiers dispersed while Siora held firm, understanding the commander was displeased with her.

"I'm sorry," she said, lowering her gaze and kicking the ground. "I got frustrated."

"I understand," Latimus said, approaching her. Garridan followed close behind, and she felt the annoying sting of tears behind her eyelids. The last thing she wanted was for the handsome soldier she claimed to detest to see her vulnerable.

Straightening her spine, she cleared her throat. "It won't happen again."

"You are a natural leader, Siora," Latimus said, compassion and firmness in his tone. "But you cannot disrespect General Garridan. He is your commanding officer and has earned the respect that entails."

Feeling like a scolded child, she nodded. "I'm sorry, General Garridan."

Garridan shot Latimus a look before those deep amber eyes locked onto hers. "You almost sound contrite. Good job, Siora."

Her chin jutted forward. "Don't placate me! You've observed the soldiers sparring for two hours on this field, and I'm the only one you've critiqued!"

"Siora—" Latimus said.

"It's okay," Garridan interjected, showing his palm. "She's right." Facing her, he tilted his head. "I called you out because I see the most potential in you, Siora. You are already an excellent soldier, but there is another level you can attain. I push you because I believe in you."

Feeling her eyebrow arch, she placed her hands on her hips. "Or because I'm a woman, and you think I'm not capable."

A wounded expression crossed his features before it vanished, and guilt welled in her chest. Damn it. Now, she felt like a jerk.

"I know I've slipped up since females joined the army, and I'm working on that, Siora. I've been a soldier for centuries in a male-dominated army. It would be nice if you could cut me some slack."

Wanting to be done with the annoying and uncomfortable conversation, she gave a nod. "Fine. I'll work on not dropping my hip. I have to work ten times as hard to excel, and even with that effort,

I make mistakes I'm not even aware of. It's infuriating. I apologize for taking it out on you."

His eyes darted over her face. "I could help you...if you'd like. No obligation or pressure. We already work long hours as it is."

"What do you mean?" she asked, eyes narrowing.

He shrugged. "I can have some sparring sessions with you early in the morning, or after our daily training, where we work on ensuring you don't drop the hip. I think I can help since I've observed you in several sparring sessions."

"That's an excellent idea," Latimus said. "I want you to be our first female battalion leader, Siora. You've worked hard for it, and you deserve it. Plus, it will make my feminist sister-in-law and her hardheaded sister happy," he said, referencing Queen Miranda and Governor Evie. "Any opportunity to improve your skills only helps get you to that position faster."

Swallowing thickly, Siora contemplated. She couldn't tell them she already got up early to perform extra training each morning. It was something she didn't want anyone to know, lest they perceive her needing the extra conditioning as a weakness. Still, she saw the merit in Garridan's offer.

"I can only do evenings," she said, her voice gruff although she didn't know why. It certainly had nothing to do with the fact she was about to sign up for private sparring sessions with the hottest Vampyre she'd ever met. Nope. Not at all.

"Evenings are fine," he said with a nod. "We can use the indoor facilities at Lynia's training center."

It rarely rained in the immortal world. Many credited their revered goddess Etherya, who they believed blessed them with warm, sun-kissed days. However, each compound in the immortal world had an indoor training center for the days it did rain, designed by Kenden, the brave and cunning Slayer commander, and built by laborers from Naria, Lynia, and Restia.

"Okay," she said, nodding. "I appreciate the offer. Should we start this evening?"

"I have a commitment this evening, but tomorrow evening works. We can pick up some Slayer blood along the way and ingest it before we begin our training."

Curiosity threatened to choke her as she wondered what his plans were this evening. Did they involve Celine? She'd heard various rumors Garridan would bond with the aristocrat after the final battle with Bakari. Siora had observed Celine a few times, mostly when she'd been tasked with delivering various firearms and weapons to the soldiers who guarded Valeria's large castle. Celine frequented the castle since she was good friends with the governor's daughter, and Siora admitted the woman was exceedingly gorgeous.

She had long, flaxen hair that flitted in the breeze, and she seemed to walk as if she was in slow motion. Her frame was willowy and always covered with the flowing, regal gowns many aristocratic women still insisted on wearing even though their kingdom had become more modernized over the past decades. Glancing down at her own tactical gear—black cargo pants, a T-shirt, and dirt-stained boots—Siora admitted she and Celine were polar opposites.

The woman was a tiny wisp of a thing, whereas Siora was thick and brawny. There wasn't a feminine curve on her, nor was there an undefined muscle. She was sinewy and strong, and she damn well liked it that way. Garridan might covet a porcelain beauty like Celine, and that was just fine, because it added yet another reason to the ten thousand others tallied in her head as to why she needed to squelch her unwanted attraction to the general.

"Siora?"

"Tomorrow's fine," she said, lifting her chin. "Thank you, General Garridan. Hopefully, I can learn quickly, and we'll only need a few sessions."

Something unreadable flitted across his face before he spoke. "I'll do my best. It's a pretty bad tell."

Biting the inside of her cheek, she resisted the urge to tell him to stuff it before catching Latimus's almost inaudible chuckle.

"I think he's joking with you, Siora."

"I am," Garridan said, smiling. By the goddess, the gesture transformed his features into something so sexy her damn knees felt weak. When had she become one of the simpering women she professed to hate? Good. Fucking. Grief.

"Maybe we'll even become friends as we spar," he continued, arching a brow.

"I don't need any more friends," she said, although the statement rang false. In truth, her friends were comprised of the other soldiers, especially Jack, Latimus's son, and his friend Brecken, both of whom she held great affection for. Other than that, her best friend in the world was her father. Which was pretty fucking lame. Sighing, she shook her head. "But I'm sure it will make me detest you less. That's a good start."

Amusement entered his amber gaze along with a slight twinge of mirth, and she damn near fainted. What were women supposed to do when the man they'd had a multitude of unwanted lust-filled dreams about looked them straight in the eye like that? Clenching her thighs together, she commanded her body to stay calm. Vampyres had a heightened sense for arousal, and if she grew slick from his searing gaze, he would certainly smell it.

"I look forward to the opportunity to make you like me, if only a little." He held his thumb and forefinger an inch apart. "On that note, I'm going to grab some water before we resume." Pivoting, he sauntered toward the soldiers who stood by the far-off replenishment station, his broad shoulders beckoning to her.

"He believes in you, Siora," Latimus said, palming her shoulder. "Someone of his rank doesn't have to dedicate one-on-one time to training a cadet."

"I know, and I'm grateful," she said, feeling her throat bob. "I'll make an effort to do better with him. I have a rather large chip on my shoulder, in case you didn't notice. You all kept us out of the army for a long fucking time, Commander."

"We did," he said, grimacing. "Believe me, Miranda and Evie have raked me over the coals extensively for that oversight. Having you and the other fifty women in this first batch of recruits has only made us better. I look forward to the day when our army is comprised equally of men and women."

"Me too. Thank you for believing in me. I won't let you down."

"I know you won't. Now, I know you're a super soldier compared to the rest of us, but I need some water. Come drink some with me so I don't feel bad."

With a grin, she fell into step beside him, pushing away her reservations about training with Garridan. She would plow through them like she always plowed through tough situations, and it would ultimately make her a better soldier. Focusing on the positives, she replenished her electrolytes, ready to embark on the next round of training.

Chapter Four

Garridan found Celine that evening in the fragrant gardens surrounding the massive governor's castle at Valeria. He'd quickly headed home and showered after finishing with the troops and felt it imperative to speak to her regarding the upcoming fundraiser. She was friends with Governor Camron's daughter, Hilara, and could often be found at the mansion.

"General Garridan," Celine said, rising from the stone bench beside a row of green bushes. "How lovely to see you."

"Hello, Celine," he said with a courteous nod. "And hello, Hilara. You both look like you're enjoying the nice weather before the sun sets."

"We are," Hilara said, rising, "but it's almost time for dinner. You'll call me later, Celine?"

"Yes," she said as her straight blond hair flitted in the breeze. "Have a good evening."

"May I escort you home?" Garridan asked, offering his arm as Hilara waved before heading back toward the mansion.

"You may, sir." Her tone was teasing as she placed her arm in his, and they began to stroll past the soldiers who lined the path, ensuring the safety of the governor's family. "I assume you want to speak about the fundraiser."

"Yes," he said, hoping the conversation didn't become uncomfortable. He'd always liked Celine, and although it wasn't a love match, he didn't want to hurt her feelings. "Our fathers are intent on matchmaking. Although we come from traditional families, I rather thought they would see the benefit of us choosing our own bonded mates."

Blue eyes sparkled as she grinned. "So you do not desire to sweep me off my feet? My heart is broken." She placed a hand over her chest.

"I hope you're joking," he said as they trailed onto the sidewalk lining the two blocks that led to her family's large home. "If not, I might be the cad my father accuses me of being."

Chuckling, she shook her head. "You are wonderful, Garridan, truly. But..."

"Yes?"

"I...well, this is hard to say out loud." Clearing her throat, she said, "I fear I love another. Or, at least, I *think* I do."

Curiosity coursed through him. Celine usually wore a polite expression that showed nothing of her feelings—a manifestation of her strict aristocratic upbringing. He'd never seen one hint of desire or longing on her pretty features.

Unable to squelch the curiosity, he asked, "Anyone I know?"

White fangs squished her lip as she gazed up at him, contemplating. "Hilara is the only other one who knows. I don't want to tell anyone else, lest it start an untoward rumor. Regardless, he does not return my affection, so it matters naught."

"I find that hard to believe, Celine," he murmured. "You are one of the most beautiful women in our kingdom and would make a wonderful bonded mate."

"To everyone but you," she chided, amusement in her eyes.

"I would not make you happy. I'm a brute who enjoys war and combat. You'd do better with someone more refined like Sebastian."

She tensed for a brief moment, and realization slammed through him.

"By the goddess, is it Sebastian you have feelings for?"

She quickly shook her head. "Of course not. He's a proclaimed bachelor, and I have it on good authority he asked Mila to accompany him to the fundraiser."

Smiling, Garridan inwardly acknowledged his brother's cleverness. They'd known Mila since they were children as her family's estate bordered their own. The three of them were close, which meant Garridan and Sebastian knew secrets Mila kept close to her heart—the most closely guarded one being that she preferred women to men.

In their provincial kingdom, Mila had guarded the secret for centuries, enjoying her independence and remaining solo. Now that Queen Miranda and Governer Evie of Takelia had modernized the kingdom, Garridan hoped Mila would one day feel comfortable enough to find a female mate who would make her happy. In the meantime, she and Sebastian had a nice ruse going. They often accompanied each other to functions, ensuring both sets of parents wouldn't meddle or try to match them with an unwanted suitor.

Of course, Garridan would never divulge this information to Celine. It was Mila's to tell, whenever she was ready. But he could at least ease Celine's doubt as to his brother's intentions.

"I assure you, Sebastian is not interested in Mila romantically. They are friends and nothing more."

They halted in front of the black metal gate that arched above the walkway to her home, and she studied him. "How do you know?"

"I just know," he said, dropping his arm to his side once she slid hers away. "Sebastian has no desire to bond right now, which I understand, but when he does, I hope you will not be shy."

Wrinkling her nose, she said, "A proper Vampyre female aristocrat is taught to be soft-spoken and demure."

"Which is rubbish," he muttered. "Our queen does not believe that, and neither should you."

She glanced toward the mansion. "I don't want to embarrass my parents."

"Perhaps asserting yourself could land you a bonded mate they would be proud of. It might be something to think about."

"Perhaps." Lifting to her toes, she gave him a quick peck on the cheek. "Thank you for walking me home. I look forward to accompanying you to the fundraiser."

"As do I. Thank you for understanding. I didn't want to make things awkward."

"Of course not," she said, waving her hand. "I'm not an idiot. I know you don't desire me." Narrowing her eyes, she contemplated. "I think you need someone strong who will challenge you and keep you on your toes. Whoever she is will be very lucky." Lowering into a slight curtsy, she rose and pushed open the gate. "Good night, General Garridan."

"Good night, Celine."

Garridan strode back to the four-wheeler at Valeria, contemplating their conversation. For some reason, he liked the idea of Sebastian courting Celine. His brother would fight it, of course, since he much preferred focusing on his council duties and remaining unattached. But he'd also been drifting like that for years. Hell, they both had in their own ways. Was it time for them to possibly contemplate settling down?

Siora's face appeared in his mind, dirt-stricken and fierce, and he sighed as he slid into the vehicle. Frustrated her image appeared every time he envisioned a bonded mate, he pushed the four-wheeler into gear and drove home, determined to let go of something that could never be. After all, one certainly didn't bond with the person who detested them more than anyone else on the planet. He'd do well to remember that.

Chapter Five

After a grueling day of training, Siora grabbed her pack and slung it over her shoulders, aware of the butterflies that flitted inside her belly. She was nervous as hell to train with Garridan but was determined he would never know. Approaching him where he stood by the four-wheeler, she observed him wave goodbye to Cian before he turned and trotted away.

"Ready?" she asked, unable to control the gravelly rasp in her voice.

"Ready," he said with a nod. "I'll drive us to town to grab some Slayer blood on the way to the training center."

"Cool." She slid into the passenger seat, awareness coursing through her as he folded his large body behind the wheel.

The engine roared to life, and he maneuvered the vehicle to the proper gear. Glancing at his tanned arm, Siora noticed the muscles, strained and sinewy, and licked her suddenly dry lips. Damn it. When did *arms* become sexy? She really needed to get a grip.

He drove to town, where they purchased two portable containers of Slayer blood from the market before proceeding to the training center. They spoke rarely, about their fellow soldiers mostly, but the energy between them wasn't uncomfortable. Instead, she found their moments of silence felt quite...*natural*, which she hadn't expected.

"What's that smirk for?" he asked, his deep baritone lined with amusement.

"I just…" Waving her hand, she searched for the words. "I thought being stuck in a four-wheeler with you would suck, but it's not so bad."

"Why, Siora," he said, resting his hand over his heart, "you have such a way with words."

She punched his arm, causing him to chuckle as he rubbed away the sting. "Ouch. Wait until we start sparring at least."

She'd never seen him like this, more relaxed than when they were training, and it melted something inside she didn't know was frozen. Deciding to roll with the sentiment, she softly uttered, "Thank you."

He glanced over, thick hair ruffling in the wind of the open-topped vehicle, but remained silent.

"For training me," she explained as if he were daft. "You didn't have to. I know I've been a huge bitch to you, and I'm…well, I'm sorry."

Full lips curved into a genuine smile, causing her heart to slam inside her chest. *Keep it chill, Siora*, she inwardly chided. Being friendly was one thing, but she could *not* let her arousal take over. He would smell it in an instant, and she would be mortified, especially since he was all but betrothed to Celine.

"I appreciate the apology, and I'll reciprocate with one." Amber eyes shone in the newly risen moonlight as they approached the training center. "I've fallen into bad habits and needed someone to break me of them. I'm very glad you came along, Siora. Maybe you can rid me of my caveman habits once and for all. Or is it cave*person*?" Parking the vehicle, he rubbed his chin as he stared at the sky.

"*Ha ha*," she chided, knowing he was making fun of her. "You haven't called the troops 'men' in a while, so I'll let that one go." Jumping out, she slung her bag over her shoulder and fell into step beside him.

Once they were inside, he illuminated the training room, and they walked to the corner where the floor was lined with blue mats.

"I figured we can spar here," he said, pointing to the mats. "They're soft enough that if you throw me on my ass, I'll survive."

"Good, because I'm planning on kicking your ass."

His resulting grin was so sexy she squeezed her thighs together, willing her arousal to stay at bay. "Can't wait."

Setting her bag on the nearby bench, she pulled out the Slayer decanter, drinking before replacing the top. "I'd like to change into yoga clothes if that works," she said, glancing down at her tactical wear. "Better for sparring inside."

"I brought a change of clothes too. Let's change and get to work."

After changing in their respective locker rooms, Siora exited to find him stretching atop the center mat. He was barefoot beneath black sweatpants and a tight black muscle shirt. Although her eyes were dying to glance at the juncture between his thighs—which she *may* have noticed held a significant bulge for the scant moment she assessed him—she aimed her gaze at his stunning eyes and straightened her spine.

"Okay, let's work on this damn dropped hip I can't seem to shake."

Approaching, she stood before him, noticing his eyes dart to the swell of her breasts, pushed high by the sports bra she wore beneath her loose tank top. Suddenly, she felt small in her bare feet beneath her capri yoga pants as he towered above her. The tactical gear she wore on the field added an extra layer that had now been shed. Feeling vulnerable, she glanced toward the weaponry rack that lined the wall, needing a break from his solid gaze.

"Should we grab a sword or sparring stick?"

"Let's give it a go without the weapons first. We'll pretend we have them so your body can move naturally, and I can point out the tell." Crouching, he held up his hands, fisted as if he were holding a sword. "Ready?"

With a nod, she crouched as well, and they got to work. They began a series of sessions where he attacked different parts of her body—shoulder, side, thigh, and so on—so she could analyze where she was dropping her hip. With each new set of motions, she began to understand her weaknesses. Garridan pointed out that she favored her right side, which made sense because she was right-hand dominant. It was something she'd tirelessly worked on in her early-morning sessions during her conditioning. She'd spend countless hours wielding weapons with her left hand to train it to be proficient, but there was only so much one could do when the body was set in its ways.

"No," Garridan said, stepping back and holding up his hands about an hour into their session.

Panting, Siora fisted her hands on her hips and huffed. "I was balancing on my left foot."

"You weren't," he said, shaking his head. "You leaned back on your right foot for leverage before shifting your weight. That's a tell. You have to learn to summon strength without anchoring on your right leg."

Frustrated, she sauntered over to the bench and grasped the water container, angrily chugging before slamming it down. "Damn it. I didn't even feel myself do it."

"That's why we're here," he said, shrugging. "You'll shake the habit with enough practice. Come on. Again." He beckoned to her with his fingers.

Annoyed he was summoning her, she stomped toward him and set her feet. Lifting her hands, she mimicked thrusting a sword, and he charged forward. Attempting to sideswipe his thigh, she shifted her balance, and he landed a soft blow to her back, right above her kidney.

"Fuck!" she yelled, stepping back and rubbing her forehead. "I did it again."

"Come on," he said, encircling her wrist and drawing her back. "Keep going. You're thinking too much."

Annoyance pervaded her veins as they began to spar again, and she reminded herself not to take it out on Garridan. Although his persistence grated on her nerves, he was attempting to help. Her knee-jerk reaction had always been to lash out at him, but *she* was the source of her anger. Hating that she couldn't control her tell, exasperation bubbled within.

"No, Siora!" he said, his tone gruffer than before. "You dropped the hip when I lunged at your side."

"Don't yell at me!" she screamed, unable to control the irritation at her continued failure. "I'm trying—"

"Trying doesn't work in battle," he interrupted, further inflaming her rage. "One false move, and you're dead."

"Why do you care?" she asked, lunging forward to resume their sparring.

Grunting, he blocked her blow and grabbed her wrist, whirling her around so her back slammed into his front. Emitting an "*oomph,*" he slid his arm around her waist, holding her in place so she didn't strike him.

The silken skin of his lips brushed the shell of her ear as he muttered, "Low blow, Siora. You know I wasn't ready—"

She elbowed him in the side, knocking the air from his lungs before trying to spin out of his grasp. Of course, she was no match for his strength and centuries of combined skill. Growling, he swiped her legs, causing her to yelp before she fell to the mat. He tumbled behind, his large body landing atop hers as he cushioned the fall with his arms.

"You son of a bitch," she uttered through clenched teeth, struggling beneath him. Somehow, she managed to turn flat on her back and jutted her fist through the air, determined to knock the fangs straight from his perfect face.

"Damn it!" he gritted before grabbing her wrists and lifting them above her head. Pinning them to the mat, he held them there as he loomed over her, panting and breathless.

Siora struggled, her body wriggling under his, causing him to settle more firmly between her thighs. And then, she felt him against her leg. His hard, throbbing shaft pulsed into the tender flesh through her thin yoga pants, and his grip on her wrists tightened.

Lust blazed in his deep amber gaze before he closed his lids, his body stilling as he seemed to struggle to regain control. His erection pulsed against her skin, beckoning to her body even if her mind wanted no part of it. Knowing she was seconds away from gushing in her damn yoga pants, she emitted a soft whimper.

Those gorgeous eyes slid open and assessed her, the orbs weary but simmering with arousal. Confusion coursed through her as her eyes darted between his. Why was he aroused? Surely not because he was attracted to her. She wasn't beautiful like Celine. Hell, she was light-years from beautiful. Was it just a visceral reaction to a close female body? Of course, that had to be it—right?

"Sorry," he whispered, tongue darting out to bathe his full lips, and she wondered how in the hell she'd somehow entered the most erotic moment of her life. Goddess, but she wanted that tongue on hers, licking and stroking before he trailed it down the smooth skin of her neck and moved lower to lather her nipple...

"You're...aroused," she said, realizing how lame the blatant observation must sound.

A muscle clenched in his jaw as he gritted his teeth. "Yes," he said, contrition in his tone. "I'm sorry. I just need a second. *Fuck...*"

"Why...?" Struggling to find the words, she studied his flushed cheeks and mussed hair. "I'm not... I don't understand."

"You're not what?"

She worked her jaw, trying to find the words. "I'm not...pretty...or womanly...or whatever Celine is."

Breathing a laugh, he shook his head. "You are certainly not what Celine is."

Stiffening, she tried to pull her hands free. "Let me up—"

"Wait," he said, clenching her wrists above her head with one hand as he slowly lowered the other. "That came out wrong." Gently cupping her face, he inched closer. "You aren't what anyone else is, Siora. Don't you know that?" His throat bobbed as he searched her gaze. "You're so much more than anyone I've ever met."

Tears stung her eyes as emotion welled within. "No, I'm not—"

He placed the pad of his thumb over her lips, stopping the words as her body hummed below him. "You *are*," he said, running his thumb across her now quivering lips.

Heat began to curl in every crevice of her body, and she knew hiding her arousal was about two seconds away from being a lost cause. Throwing caution to the wind, she asked softly, "You want me?"

With a harsh laugh, he pushed his erection against her thigh. "I think the answer to that question is obvious." Sliding his hand behind her head, he threaded his fingers through her short hair, gently tugging and urging her closer. The slightly possessive act made something roar inside, and the dam broke free, sending a surge of arousal to her core. Slickness flooded the walls of her deepest place, and his body tensed above her. "The real question is, do *you* want *me*?"

Blood pounded in every cell, preventing her from answering.

"Holy shit," he breathed, closing his eyes and inhaling deeply. Lifting his lids, he stared into her soul. "Goddammit, Siora. Your arousal smells so fucking good."

Shallow breaths mingled with his as her body opened beneath him, inch by slow inch as he settled further between her thighs.

"Yes," she whispered, realizing her body had already accepted the inevitable even if her brain hadn't quite caught up. "I want you."

His fingers tightened in her hair before tugging once again, causing her to purr in anticipation. "If I kiss you, I won't be able to stop there. Do you understand, Siora?"

Nodding, she arched her hips, causing him to hiss.

"You little vixen," he murmured, lowering his head. Touching his lips to hers, he gently brushed them back and forth, driving her wild. "Do you want me to touch you, Siora? Tell me what you want."

"*Oh, goddess...*" she moaned, undulating beneath him.

"The goddess isn't here, sweetheart," he murmured against her lips, "just you and me. Tell me. I don't want any lingering doubt that we both want this."

"Let go of my wrists," she commanded softly, and he released his grip. Gliding her hands around his neck, she slid them into his thick brown hair. "Garridan, shut the hell up and fuck me."

His resulting smile would've melted her panties if she'd been wearing any underneath her yoga pants. Instead, she grinned back before he slid his lips over hers and consumed her as if she were his last breath.

Chapter Six

Garridan had no idea when he'd become the luckiest son of a bitch on the planet, but he sure as hell wasn't going to squander the moment. Pushing Siora's lips wide with his own, he plunged his tongue inside, tasting her for the first time. She tasted like rain and honey, damp but sweet, and he was overcome by her essence. Her words were direct, which drove him wild, but there was a vulnerability in her embrace, and he longed to earn her trust. Her words about Celine had all but broken his heart, and he would do everything in his power to show her how gorgeous and sexy she was.

Sliding his tongue over hers, he drank her moans, sipping them as he felt her pounding heartbeat beneath his own. Longing to touch her, he broke the kiss, chuckling when she emitted a frustrated whimper.

"Take this off," he murmured, tugging the tank top from her body and tossing it aside. Her pert breasts jutted from the tight sports bra, and his shaft pulsed in response to the trembling globes.

"They're small," she said, glancing down at her breasts, although they looked fine as hell to him. "The bra makes them bigger, I think, because they're all scrunched up in there."

Laughing, he lowered and kissed one of the swells, causing her to toss her head back on the mat and thrust her fingers in his hair. "Yessss..." she hissed.

"Is it one of your favorites?" he asked.

"The bra? Not really."

"Good." Gripping the top of the garment with both hands, he ripped it in half. Her pert breasts sprang free, all but popping in his face, and he felt his release pulsing in his shaft. Goddess, he could come just from staring at her sweet, succulent breasts.

With a grunt, he tore the bra from her body and focused on the mounds. Cupping them in his hands, he squeezed, forcing her nipples high. The tight little buds were several shades darker than her pale skin, and he yearned to suck them.

"Garridan," she moaned, spurring joy inside his desire-ravaged frame.

"You sound so sexy when you say my name," he rasped, licking his lips before blowing on one of her turgid nipples. "Say it again."

She complied, sending him to heaven as he lowered his mouth to her breast. He trailed soft kisses around her nipple before nudging it with his nose.

"Look at me."

Those stunning blue eyes lasered into his before he extended his tongue to lick the sensitive bud. Her body bucked, jutting into his erection as he groaned. Gazing into those gorgeous eyes, he closed his mouth around her nipple and began to suck.

"Oh...yesss..." she purred, fingers clenching his hair as she watched him devour her. "That feels so good...oh...god..."

"Mmm..." he murmured, knowing the taste of her nipple against his tongue was one of the finest delicacies he would ever savor. He sucked her deep, tugging the sensitive nub, before flicking his tongue against it as she squirmed. Determined to please her, he kissed a path to her other breast and repeated the ministrations, overcome by her tiny mewls.

"Get inside me," she groaned, tugging at his pants while her other hand fisted in his hair. "I need you."

The words sent shivers of pleasure through his frame, and he lifted, yanking off his shirt and pants before dragging off the rest of her clothes.

"I want to make you come first, but I don't know if I can wait—"

"Goddammit, fuck me!" she gritted, frustrated amusement in her tone.

Settling between her thighs, he slid his hand behind her knee and lifted her leg high. "Do you want it hard?"

"Yes!"

Positioning himself, he rubbed the head of his shaft through her slick folds. It felt amazing, and he longed to surge inside her. "Should I grab a condom?"

Vampyres couldn't transmit disease through sex due to their self-healing abilities, but they could still get pregnant.

She shook her head, her short hair fanning across the mat. "Sadie gave me an IUD years ago. I'm set."

Aligning his shaft with her opening, he drew back his hips, ready to claim her. She stared back at him, eyes glazed with lust, and he suddenly understood he needed to slow down. Garridan had fantasized about fucking Siora for months, and he craved her reaction. Pushing her leg high, he began to ease inside.

"Faster," she demanded, and he shook his head as her tight folds enveloped him.

"I need to watch you take me, sweetheart," he murmured, sliding deeper before withdrawing and pushing into her wetness. "You look so pretty."

Confusion entered her gaze as he glided inside, and he was desperate to reassure her. "You have no idea how gorgeous you are. I'm in heaven right now, don't you understand?" Thrusting his hips, he buried himself to the hilt, clenching his teeth as she surrounded his sensitive flesh. "Fuck, you're tight, honey."

"It's been a while."

"Not anymore." Drawing back, he withdrew until only the tip remained inside her sweet body. Steeling himself, he surged inside, the pleasure almost unbearable as her taut channel swallowed him whole. "You're mine now."

"I'm not anyone's—"

Leaning on his forearms, he thrust his fingers in her hair and captured her lips as he began to undulate his hips. Consuming her in a passionate kiss, he began to fuck her in long, hard strokes that set his body on fire.

"Mine," he growled into her mouth, thrilled when she wrapped her leg around his waist, opening her sweet pussy to his invasion.

"Oh, *god*," she groaned, head tossed back on the mat as she accepted his deep pounding.

Garridan hammered inside, his cock covered with her essence, as she shuddered beneath. The slickness was everywhere, drenching his aching skin, and he pressed his cheek against hers, needing the connection.

"Can you come like this?"

Shaking her head, she speared her short nails into his back, the pleasure-pain driving him mad. "I need my clit rubbed. It's fine...still feels good...don't stop..."

No way in hell was he going to get off without ensuring she did too. Lifting his hand, he licked his fingers before sliding them between their bodies. Pushing her folds apart, he searched for her sensitive bud as he continued to fuck her. Lifting his head, he assessed her reaction, elated when she gasped.

"Right there," she cried, and he began circling the taut nub of her clit. "*Ohmygod*...keep doing that, and I'll fucking explode."

"Yes," he rasped, his hips now working at a frenzied pace along with his fingers. "Come all over my cock, honey. I want to be covered in your scent. Do you hear me?"

Whimpering, she clenched her arms tighter around his neck, cheeks flushed below her hooded eyes. "*Garridan*..."

Labored breaths exited his lungs as he hammered inside her warmth while beads of sweat formed along his heated skin. They dripped from his chest onto her breasts, coating her as he claimed her, and he felt the primal urge to drink from her. Drinking from another Vampyre was sacred in their culture, and it was usually only done between bonded mates. Still, the longing persisted, and he felt something well deep within. Never had he yearned to drink from a woman during sex, but with Siora...by the goddess, he *craved* it. He ached to feel her blood rush against his tongue as her pussy drenched his cock.

"I'm going to come!" she cried, lips falling open as her mouth formed an "O." "Oh...yes...fuck!"

Her body bowed beneath him, drawing him deeper inside her body as he lunged forward. Lifting his hand from her clit, he slid both palms under her shoulders, anchoring her as he continued to ram inside. Pleasure sparked at the base of his spine as his balls tightened, and he pressed his face into her nape. Clutching her close, he felt the spasms of her orgasm choke his cock in a thousand tiny deaths. Giving into the pleasure, he let go, allowing her tight folds to jerk his release from his cock.

Pressing against her, he moaned her name into the wet skin of her neck as he came. Thick, sticky jets of release shot into her viselike channel, coating her core as the thrill of claiming her deepest place overwhelmed him. Eliciting shouts of bliss, he purged every last drop inside her, wishing he could imprint himself upon her. Her body fit against his as if they were made for each other, and he inwardly laughed at the romantic thoughts. If Siora knew his sappy inner musings, she'd most likely jibe him for it for centuries.

Quakes and shudders wracked his frame until he settled into her, resting his weight on his side so he didn't crush her. Sprawled half-atop her luscious body, he sank into her as she sighed below.

They were tangled together, sweaty and sated, and he nuzzled her as his fingers sifted through her soft, short hair. He knew she wore it that way so she wouldn't have to mess with it during training. It showcased her prominent cheekbones and stunning eyes, which was probably why he caught himself staring at her more often than he should. How could she think Celine was more beautiful? By the goddess, he loved Siora's pretty face and strong features. And her body? It was smooth and powerful, with slight curves in all the right places. To him, she represented true beauty, someone who fought for their people while remaining true to herself. In his eyes, there was nothing more noble.

"You're quiet," she said, running her nails over his back as he shivered. "You're never quiet. Shouldn't you be scolding me? Do you have the urge to point out any tells in my lovemaking?"

Chuckling, he kissed her neck before resting his head on his fist as his elbow dug into the mat. "No complaints here. You were perfect."

Her fangs rested atop her bottom lip as she smiled, making her look adorable—so much softer than she appeared on the field. By the goddess, he wanted to see her like this every day, relaxed and sexy and *open*.

"I did *not* expect that to happen during our training session. I'd apologize, but I think you actually made the first move."

"Why would you apologize for having fantastic sex?" Tracking his finger across her jaw, he regarded her. "Let's do it again next training session."

Joy entered her gaze before she squelched it. "Garridan," she said softly.

"Don't," he whispered, leaning down to kiss her. "Don't take us to the place where we have some serious discussion about whether this was a mistake or not."

"It was."

"Fine," he said, playfully rolling his eyes, "so what if it was? Did you enjoy it?"

"Um, yes," she said, her expression one of mock exasperation.

"Me too. So let's do it again. We have a huge battle before us, and it can't hurt to enjoy ourselves while we work off some steam. I think it will take several more sessions for you to fully let go of your tell. We'll practice each night, and then we'll have sex afterward. It only seems fair." He waggled his eyebrows.

Laughing, she shook her head. "I'm not sure I see the logic, but, hey, you're right about our impending battle. If we're going to die, I'd like to have some magnificent sex before I bite the bullet."

"Exactly." Winking, he smoothed his palm over her shoulder. "No labels, and no serious conversations. We can do all that after the battle, if we both survive."

Her eyes narrowed as she studied him. "I thought you were going to ask Celine to bond with you. The rumor is public knowledge at this point."

Sighing, he shook his head. "My father wants me to marry an aristocrat even though I've told him I have no desire to do so. Celine is a lovely woman, but I don't want an aristocratic life. I enjoy the army and protecting our people."

"That's what I want too. I love being a soldier. It's about time you Neanderthals let us join you."

Feeling his lips curve, his eyes roved her flushed features. "You've taught me a lot. I thought I was so progressive, but I guess you can't see what you've never experienced."

"When I first joined, I couldn't understand why you were so hard on me. I wanted so badly to do well, and I felt like you singled me out."

"I saw your potential from the first day," he murmured, running the backs of his fingers over her cheek. "I knew if I pushed you, you would get better. You might've decided you hate me, but you'd get better."

Her fangs toyed with her lip, causing his shaft to jerk inside her. "I pretty much detested you," she teased. "I was too stubborn to see you were trying to help. And you kept calling us 'men,' which really pissed me off."

"I'm a creature of habit," he said, lifting his shoulder. "I've done better lately, right?"

Nodding, she ran her leg over his hairy one. "You have. I'll try to turn my disdain to something more palatable. Keep fucking me like that, and I'm sure it will happen."

"Mission accepted," he murmured, giving her a peck on the lips. Sighing, he brushed a tuft of hair from her forehead. "I guess we should call it a night."

"Yeah. I want to hang with my dad for a bit before he goes to sleep. We usually have dinner together, but he sees the benefit of my training sessions with you."

"I'd like to meet him one day."

Those stunning eyes widened. "That's definitely moving into 'serious' territory. My dad is my rock. I don't bring home random dudes to meet him."

The challenge swelled in Garridan's chest, and he felt the consuming urge to meet it. One day, he would earn Siora's trust and meet her father. It was a lofty goal for someone as private and guarded as she, and he vowed to make it happen. For now, he gave her a soft smile and arched an eyebrow.

"I'm pretty sure it's insubordination to call your commanding officer a 'random dude,' but I'll let it slide."

Their chuckles filled the room before he helped her to her feet. Once dressed, he drove her home. When they approached the tiny house, he offered to walk her inside, but she declined.

"We're not formal out here on the farm, Garridan," she said, exiting the vehicle and closing the door. "I don't need the red carpet. Thanks for the training, and for...well...thanks."

"You're welcome," he said softly, giving her an informal salute. "See you in the morning."

"See you in the morning." With a wave, she turned to walk up the wooden steps, and he put the car into gear to head home, not giving a damn he wore a perma-grin the entire way.

Chapter Seven

Siora threw herself into training, reminding herself that although it was exhausting, she would have plenty of time to rest after they defeated Bakari. For now, she focused on conditioning her body and mind to excel. She still got up early each day for her solo conditioning, spent several hours on the field, and ended each day with her sessions with Garridan. Most nights, she fell into bed after kissing her father on his bearded cheek and apologizing for not spending more time with him. He would gaze at her with his gentle eyes and tell her how proud he was, which made all the hard work worth it.

Each day on the field, Siora did her best to ensure no one suspected her relationship with Garridan had turned sexual. He treated her the same, still calling her out slightly more than the other soldiers and maintaining it was because he saw her potential. She did her best not to slip into her old pattern of bristling at his coaching, although she sometimes failed. It was on those evenings, after she lost her cool and became frustrated with him on the training field, they ended up having the hottest sex. So, she guessed it wasn't a total failure since it led to such an enjoyable outcome.

"What are you thinking about?" Garridan murmured in her ear, coming to stand behind her as she sipped water on the outer edge of the training field. "You have a shit-eating grin on your face."

Gazing up at him, she almost melted at the desire simmering in his eyes. "I was remembering last night when you punished me for losing my cool on the field yesterday."

His nostrils flared as he emitted an almost imperceptible growl. "I loved bending you over and taking you from behind." His gaze trailed to her breasts, hidden beneath her loose tank top and sports bra. "But taking you from the front is also very enjoyable."

Breathing a laugh, she glanced around the field. "Careful, General. People might begin to suspect something. We can't have that."

He was silent, causing her to stare up at him. He wore an unreadable expression, and it caused nervous butterflies to flit in her stomach.

"Garridan?"

"Right. Don't want anyone to know about our undefined, clandestine affair. Got it."

Latimus summoned them from across the field, and she set her container on the table.

"I think Latimus wants me on the obstacle course."

"I'm working with Cian's group on deploying the new TECs today," he said with a nod. "See you after training. I stocked some Slayer blood in the fridge at the training center, so we can have that before we spar tonight."

"Okay," she said, swallowing thickly as she wondered if she'd somehow upset him. "See you later."

As she jogged to the obstacle course and began the grueling exercise, she couldn't stop her mind from wondering about Garridan's reaction. They'd only been having sex for a few days. It was a casual fling to work off some steam...wasn't it? It wasn't as if they had any sort of a future together once the conflict with Bakari was over. Garridan would most likely assume a high-ranking role in their army while Siora hopefully became head of security at Lynia. Garridan's role would span the entire kingdom, so he'd most likely be stationed at one of the more prominent compounds, while Siora had no desire to live anywhere but Lynia. Her father lived there, and she would always choose to live nearby so he wouldn't be alone.

Although Garridan claimed to have no desire to bond with an aristocrat, it was very unlikely he would consider bonding with her. The scandal of a high-ranking Valerian aristocrat of Garridan's prominence bonding with the daughter of a Lynian farmer would send shock waves through Valerian society. Although the kingdom had evolved from the strictest adherences to tradition since Miranda became queen, there were limits to the progressiveness. Hell, Garridan's parents would most likely disown him if they knew he'd even touched a poor farmer's daughter from Lynia.

Still, knowing all that, Siora wouldn't lie to herself. As she maneuvered her body across the obstacle course, daydreams flashed through her mind. Ones of her and Garridan working together to secure the kingdom by day and heading home together at night. To a shared home where her father was waiting and tiny Vampyres with Garridan's amber eyes and thick brown hair ran to them with open arms. In her vision, she embraced the tots before settling in for dinner and eventual sleep. Then, once the house was quiet, he would hold her as they recounted stories from their day before making passionate love and falling asleep wrapped in each other's arms.

"What the fucking hell?" she muttered to herself, grunting as she scaled the rock wall that lined the obstacle course. "Ditch the daydreams, Cinderella."

"You talking to yourself, Siora?" Radomir chided as he climbed beside her. "Keep it up so I can kick your ass."

"In your dreams, buddy," was her confident reply before she high-tailed it over the summit and scaled down the opposite side. Once on the ground, she disengaged from the rope and wiped the dirt from her hands.

"Damn, you're fast," Radomir said, landing beside her and unclasping the hook that held his rope. "It's a good reminder not to jibe you. Just makes you more likely to beat me." He tapped his temple before pivoting and heading toward the cooler that held fresh canisters of water.

"Get your fucking mind out of la-la land, Siora," she scolded, kicking the dirt with the toe of her boot. Fantasizing about any sort of future with Garridan was futile and an extreme waste of time. They were just fucking, and when their one-on-one sessions were over, their trysts would end too. The thought flooded her with a thousand tiny prickles of sadness, but she lifted her chin, determined to push them away.

And when in the hell had she started visualizing having children? For the goddess's sake, she'd never dreamed of having kids with anyone. She wasn't opposed, necessarily. It just didn't seem like something one did when their primary goal was to excel as a soldier. If she chose that path, she would need a partner who understood her desire to balance her military career *and* motherhood, which was extremely hard to find in a society where women had only recently obtained the ability to join the army.

But Garridan would understand...

The words floated through her brain before she could stop them, and she waved her hand, somehow attempting to shoo them away although it was pointless. They lingered deep within, forcing Siora to acknowledge they were true. Garridan was perhaps one of the only men on the planet who would support her military aspirations and wish for her to succeed. He was invested in ensuring it happened, and there was a nobility in that, which made the complex emotions she experienced around him even more confusing.

"Great job, Siora," Latimus said, approaching. "You were the fastest on all the obstacle course challenges today. I'm excited to announce it to the entire regime later."

Pride swelled within that her early-morning conditioning exercises were paying off. "Thank you, Commander. I want to do well so I can lead a battalion when we face Bakari."

"I've been thinking about that," he said, tilting his head. "You and Garridan have been getting along in your one-on-one sessions, right?"

If he only knew. "Yep," she said, feeling like a dolt at the overly cheerful tone of her voice. *Keep it cool, Siora. Good grief.* "I've learned so much from him. He's extremely skilled at one-on-one combat."

"Good. I've been thinking about the battle, and I want you two to team up and lead three battalions. He will be commanding officer, but you'll be second-in-command. If all goes well, it's a natural step toward your progression in the army. Afterward, if we win—"

"*When* we win," she said, lifting a finger.

"When we win," he said with a grin, "I'll speak to Commander Kenden and nominate you for head of security at Lynia. After co-leading a successful mission with Garridan, it should be a no-brainer."

Elation bloomed in her chest, and she couldn't contain her smile. "That would be amazing. I'll lead the troops with everything I have and will work with General Garridan to ensure we remain as safe as possible while kicking Bakari's ass."

"Excellent. In the meantime, keep it up on the obstacle courses and in the training sessions. Cian and Radomir still have the edge on you in sparring history. Hopefully, you'll close the gap as you learn to hide your tells."

"I will." Straightening, she puffed out her chest. "I'm determined to even the score, believe me."

Chuckling, he cupped her shoulder. "I have no doubt you will. Speaking of, it's time for the afternoon group sparring sessions. You ready?"

Vowing to kick Cian and Radomir's asses no matter how much energy it took, she gave a firm nod. "Ready."

Turning, they headed toward the open meadow, excitement coursing through Siora's veins as she digested the commander's praise.

Chapter Eight

That evening, about an hour into their session, Garridan held up a hand as his full lips formed a smile. "By the goddess, I think we've done it," he said, his words slightly breathless from their exertion.

"Done what?" she asked, straightening from her crouch.

"Fixed your tell. You haven't dropped your hip once today. Well done."

Elation coursed through her. "Sweet. I was hoping I was getting better. It took about a week. Not bad." She patted herself on the back.

Chuckling, he stepped closer and placed his palm over the juncture between her neck and shoulder. "I'm proud of you. I hope that doesn't sound placating or pompous. In the past, I'd probably be afraid to tell you I was proud of you because you'd tell me to shove it."

She gave a playful eye roll. "I wasn't *that* bad."

"Okay," he mocked, scrunching his features.

"It's just different when *you're* different," she said, shrugging. "When you're a woman, and a man in a superior position says he's proud, it indicates surprise. You know, like he had no expectation you could do it in the first place."

His eyes narrowed as he pondered. "I guess that makes sense. It's tough for someone who's never experienced misogyny to put themselves in the shoes of someone who has. But I'm trying, Siora."

"I know," she said softly, sliding her hands over his lower abdomen. He'd ditched his shirt a while ago, and his skin trembled beneath her palms. "You're doing an excellent job, General." Hooking her fingers over the elastic of his sweatpants, she began to ease them down his legs.

"I guess we're done with training," he muttered as she lowered to her knees, dragging his pants to his ankles before urging him to step out and tossing them against the wall. His impressive cock sprung toward her face, already hard and turgid as the veins swelled beneath the sensitive skin.

"Oh, we're done with *training*," she said, arching a brow as she gripped his shaft, "but there will still be *lots* of physical exertion."

"Holy fuck," he breathed, threading his fingers through her short hair and gently clenching. "You have no idea how hot you are kneeling in front of me like that."

"Like this?" she asked, pursing her lips and rapidly blinking. "Or like this?" Lowering her hand, she gripped the hem of her sports bra and tugged it off, tossing it to lie atop his sweatpants. Her breasts sprang free above the yoga pants she still wore, and she felt a moment of self-consciousness. After all, she was stocky and muscular, and her breasts weren't anything to write home about. But Garridan seemed enthralled by them, always spending time on each of her sensitive nipples when they made love, so she figured it wouldn't hurt to bare herself.

"Like that," he growled, inching closer and tilting her head with the fingers entwined in her hair. "Cup them while you suck me."

Grinning, she palmed the small globes in her hands and widened her stance so she could balance more firmly on her knees. Pushing her breasts high, she tilted her head further and opened her mouth.

"You sexy little vixen," he murmured, placing the underside of his cock on her waiting tongue. "Goddess, you're so gorgeous."

"Mmm..." was her sensual response as she closed her mouth around him.

He released a ragged groan as he began to slowly jut back and forth. Staring into his amber eyes, Siora pinched her nipples as she sucked him, sending pleasure through her frame as he loomed above her.

"Yesss..." he hissed, sliding the smooth skin of his shaft across her tongue and lips. "Play with those sexy nipples while I fuck that smart mouth."

Her eyes narrowed, and he breathed a strained laugh.

"Don't give me that look, Siora. You have the smartest mouth I've ever fucking heard. And the sexiest...and the fucking sweetest...oh, god..."

Figuring she'd let him off the hook since she enjoyed the spicy compliments, she began to move her head, maneuvering it around his cock as he shoved it inside her willing mouth. Saliva coated the taut skin, making it glisten as he fucked her lips in the quiet room.

"Yeah, honey," he said, his fingers so tight in her hair they sent twinges of pain through her scalp, although they were pleasurable. They were reminiscent of a good workout, where her muscles were tired and sore but endorphins still coursed through her body. Holy shit. Watching Garridan pound her mouth while he gritted his teeth in ecstasy *definitely* sent endorphins through her rapidly heating body.

"Can I move your head?" he asked, making her heart swell. Although she chided him for being an unwitting misogynist, he was a stickler for consent, and damn, if that wasn't sexy as hell. "I don't want to hurt you."

Popping his cock from her mouth, she flashed him a sultry grin. "I'm not some weak aristocrat, Garridan. Pull my hair and fuck my mouth. Use me however you want and come down my fucking throat. Do you hear me?"

A deep growl rumbled in his chest as he yanked her hair. "Goddammit, that's sexy. Say it again."

The corner of her lip curved before she extended her tongue, running it over her top lip and then the bottom one, slow and deliberate. "Garridan? Fuck my mouth. *Hard.*"

Groaning, he complied, sliding his cock between her lips as she closed around him. Gripping her short tresses, he began to fuck her in earnest, plunging toward the back of her throat as she reminded herself to relax. Opening to him, she felt so full when he began to push deep, pulling back so she could suck in breaths between the firm thrusts.

"Do you like swallowing my cock, sweetheart?" he rasped, eyes locked with hers as he possessed every crevice of her mouth. "God, you're driving me wild. Every part of you feels so good."

She purred around his sensitive flesh, wondering when making him feel pleasure became so important to her. Damn, but she craved to hear his deep moans and growls as he loved her. His caresses were always so passionate—and surprisingly tender—and she longed for these nights with him. What would happen now that she'd improved? Would he stop making love to her?

Gliding her hands up his thighs, the tiny hairs prickled her palms as she slid them to his buttocks. Clasping the firm flesh, she helped drive his hips toward her mouth, showing him how much she desired him...hoping he understood she wasn't ready to stop their passionate trysts.

"Fuck!" he gritted, slamming his cock in her mouth. "I'm going to come... Suck me dry, honey...oh...*god*..."

Warm pulses of release began shooting down her throat, and she moaned, closing her eyes as he emptied himself inside her wet mouth. Shouts of pure ecstasy escaped his lungs as his large body pulsed beneath her hands. Spearing her nails in his buttocks, she grinned when he shouted her name.

"You fucking vixen," he groaned, jerking as his body shook from the orgasm. "Damn it, that feels good."

She pushed deeper, knowing he enjoyed the slight pleasure-pain as much as she did, and he shuddered before tugging her hair.

"Enough," he murmured, and she relaxed her hands. "Sheathe your claws, woman."

Smiling, she sucked his sated cock, loving the feel of him relaxing against her tongue. Eliciting a deep sigh, he gazed down at her while he stroked her jaw.

"*Siora*..." he whispered, the word reverent upon his lips.

Releasing him from her mouth, she smoothed her hands over his thighs. "You look like you're about to collapse."

His lips formed a sexy, sated smile before he lowered to the mat, drawing her into his arms before collapsing on his back. Siora shimmied into his side and rested her chin on her fist as her elbow pushed into the mat.

"I like making you feel good," she said, trailing her finger over his cheek.

Encircling her wrist, he lifted her hand to his lips and kissed her palm. "Sweetheart, if you only knew. I swear, I'm going to make you feel good too. I just need to catch my breath."

She made a *tsk, tsk, tsk* sound. "That's unacceptable, General. You need to be in tip-top shape for our upcoming battle."

Laughing, he arched a brow. "Is that supposed to be an impression of me telling you to perform better on the field?"

Closing an eye, she glanced at the ceiling. "Maaaaaaybe."

"Okay, I'm a tyrant. I get it," he teased.

"You're not, but it was fun to hate you just a little."

His lips formed an adorable pout, sending her heart into overdrive. "You don't still hate me, do you?"

"Debatable," was her cheeky reply.

Breathing a laugh, he shook his head against the mat. "No way. You couldn't destroy me like you just did if you detested me. No one is *that* good of an actress."

She mimicked flicking her hair over her shoulder. "Maybe I missed my calling."

"Okay, Meryl Streep. Let's leave the acting to the humans."

Grinning, she relaxed into him as they softly stroked each other. Finally, he broke the silence, a slight hesitancy in his tone.

"It's up to you if you still want to spar in the evenings. You've corrected the tell with your hip, but I'm happy to keep training you. I think it's helping to improve your overall performance on the field."

Contemplating, she traced a finger over the scratchy hairs on his chest. "Are you saying that because you want to keep fucking me?"

Sliding his fingers under her chin, he gently lifted it to claim her gaze. "Yes. I don't want to lie to you. I love the time we spend together training *and* fucking. I don't think there's anything wrong with that."

"It would hurt my career if anyone finds out," she said, fangs toying with her lower lip as she searched for the words. "We have to keep it secret until it ends."

An unreadable reaction flickered in his eyes. "If that's what you want."

Feeling her eyes dart between his, she asked, "Isn't that what you want? Once the conflict with Bakari is over, there will be no need for me to train this vigorously for combat."

"We'll both still be in the army, Siora. I'll still see you unless you're dead set on avoiding me."

She wrinkled her nose. "I know. But you'll be back at Valeria and will resume your life there. I'll hopefully become head of security at Lynia, but I'll still just be Luthor's daughter from a meager farm on a rural compound."

"That's not how I see you," he said, running the backs of his fingers over her cheek.

"How do you see me?" she asked before she could stop the words from tumbling out of her mouth. Goddess, she sounded desperate and realized with each vibrant pound of her heart how important his answer was to her.

"As a beautiful, fierce warrior. One who will partner with me to protect our people in the battle against Bakari."

Her lips twitched. "I guess Latimus told you."

Nodding, he cupped her jaw. "I'm proud to have you as my first-in-command at the final battle. I can think of no one I'd rather have by my side."

Tears burned her eyes, making her feel vulnerable, and she willed them away. Sentiment and feelings had no place between them. They were teammates who gave each other pleasure, and she would do well to remember that before she did something completely stupid like fall in love with him.

"Well, I'll do my best to make sure you don't get bludgeoned," she teased, attempting to lighten the heavy mood. "And then, we'll both go on to build our lives on Valeria and Lynia. It will be nice to be free from war for once."

Deep brown eyes skated over her face as he studied her. "If that's what you want," he repeated, running his thumb over her lip.

Lifting a shoulder, she grinned. "I think it's just how it is. In the meantime, I'd like to continue training with you at night. I've learned a lot and definitely see an improvement. I mean, if you have time. I don't want to drain you."

"I'll always have time for you," he murmured, the tender words squeezing every ounce of breath from her lungs. "You know that, right, sweetheart?"

Swallowing thickly, she commanded her heart to slow the fuck down. "Thank you."

"In the meantime, there's something I need to take care of."

Lifting her brows, she shot him a questioning look.

He lurched, encircling her with his arms and flipping them over as she yelped. Looming over her, he smiled. "You took my cock like a champ, honey. Now, I need to suck you dry. You ready?" Waggling his brows, he began to trail wet kisses down her neck, between the valley of her breasts, and over the quivering skin of her abdomen. Pressing his hands to her inner thighs, he gently spread them apart.

"Are they your favorite?" he asked, running his hands over the soft fabric of her yoga capris.

"My yoga pants? Not really."

"Good." Gripping the hem, he ripped the pants in half, destroying the garment before tossing it aside.

"I really like this whole 'ripping my clothes' thing you've got going on," she said, smiling down at him as she made quotation marks with her fingers. "Not great for my workout attire, but *really* sexy, General."

His lips curved into a sexy grin as he palmed her thighs and pushed them wide. "If I have it my way, I'll rip every damn piece of clothing you own." Blowing on her drenched core, his eyes swam with amused desire. "Now, be a good little vixen and let me taste you, honey."

He dove into her pussy, causing her back to arch as she thrust her fingers in his thick hair. And then, she closed her eyes and let him return the very pleasurable favor.

Chapter Nine

A week later, Garridan stood in front of the mirror straightening the bow tie that went with his tuxedo. He hadn't dressed up in ages and could barely remember how to tie the damn thing. Deciding it looked fine, he gave a sigh and leaned down to grab his tuxedo jacket. Sliding it on, he assessed his reflection.

He looked like the aristocrat his father had always wanted him to be, and something about that rankled the hell out of him. If he weren't escorting Celine, he would've just worn a suit and called it a day. But tongues wagged throughout aristocratic circles at Valeria, and he didn't want to hurt her reputation. She was still looking for a bonded mate, and he wanted to look his best to support her.

Once he was fully dressed, he headed out, locking the door behind him and trailing down the front porch stairs. Glancing at his parents' mansion, he noted the windows were dark and assumed they were already at Valeria's main castle.

His shoes clacked against the pavement as he took the fifteen-minute walk to Celine's home. It was a nice evening, and he figured it was best spent in the fresh air rather than driving a four-wheeler. In truth, he would've much rather spent it with Siora, training her before they fell into one of their earth-shattering lovemaking sessions. But the army needed his father's donation, and he would escort Celine to ensure it happened.

It was the first night he hadn't spent with Siora since they began their sessions almost two weeks ago. Although it was a short time, it somehow felt like an eternity. Not in a bad way, he thought, grinning. Goddess, no. In the best way, like the fairy tales that spoke of the eternity of peace and goodness that existed in Etherya's realm before the War of the Species.

Like the kind of eternity you wanted to continue...long as you both shall live...

The inner thoughts were serious and ones Garridan had never had about another. Sure, he'd courted women off and on over the centuries, but none had even come close to taking up residency in his brain like Siora. At this point, her face was emblazoned in his mind, and he'd even begun to dream of her at night.

"You're getting sentimental in your old age, soldier," he muttered, inwardly chuckling at his sappiness.

But the truth was, he had lived for ten centuries, blazing a path as a competent soldier and advisor to Commander Latimus. When the War of the Species ended two decades ago, they had a brief moment of peace in which Garridan considered settling down...before Bakari appeared and upended that notion. Now, if they vanquished Bakari, he would finally have an opening to consider settling down and having children.

He'd always thought of having kids one day, but it seemed a faraway dream—one he would consider when he met someone compatible enough to understand his desire to protect the kingdom would always rank highly as he built his family. Siora sometimes uttered her belief he would bond with an aristocrat one day, but Garridan didn't see that making him happy. Aristocratic women wanted patrician bonded mates who held prominent positions in their kingdom, not soldiers who worked tirelessly and didn't give a damn about rank or privilege.

If he were honest, he could see himself settling down with Siora. She was a bit rough around the edges, but damn, that was one of the things he admired most about her. She was honest and straightforward, and it was so refreshing after being raised in a stuffy society where people only spoke their minds in dark corners behind others' backs.

And there was one other thing: Siora was achingly beautiful and hands-down the best lover he'd ever had. If he could stare at her stunning face and hold her until the world turned to dust, it wouldn't be long enough. She sometimes spoke of how she wasn't pretty and her body wasn't womanly, and he longed to reassure her. To him, she was the essence of beauty. Much more so than someone like Celine, who seemed more like a porcelain doll than the real, visceral woman Siora was.

Unfortunately, Siora had made it quite clear she didn't see a future between them. He couldn't tell if it was because she didn't want to settle down, didn't want to share a future with him, or truly just saw their trysts as a fun outlet to let off steam. Every time he had the urge to tell her he would consider trying to make their arrangement more serious, she shut him down. Not in a mean way. No—it was more...resigned, if anything. As if she simply couldn't contemplate them having anything more than the scant moments they stole after their training.

It frustrated Garridan, but he didn't want to push her, knowing her well enough to understand that would make her close up even more. She responded to his stern urgings on the field, but on a personal level, she didn't receive them the same way. Since he longed for her to be open with him, he usually conceded, allowing her to steer the direction of their conversations...allowing her to assert they didn't have a place in each other's lives.

"Well, hello. Is this my handsome date?"

Celine's wispy voice dragged him from the depressing thought as he trailed down the sidewalk to her house.

"It is indeed," he said, offering his arm. She wore the long, red gown of a Vampyre aristocrat and looked stunning as she slid her arm into his.

"I hope I don't fall. I'm wearing new heels, and I already want to burn them."

Laughing, he escorted her down the walkway and onto the sidewalk so they could stroll to the castle. "You look lovely, Celine. Are you trying to impress anyone in particular?"

Red splotches appeared on her cheeks as she grinned. "I fear you know my secret, so let's just get it out in the open. I'm hoping Sebastian asks me to dance even though he's bringing Mila."

"Since we're being honest, why don't I help? I can be your wingman."

"And dupe your own brother?" She arched a straw-colored brow. "How scandalous."

"Valeria could use a good scandal. We haven't had one in a while. And I think it's time my brother stopped focusing so much on his council seat and actually spent time outside of his duties. You two would make a nice couple, Celine."

"He doesn't even know I exist," she murmured, clutching his arm. "And I'm not...well, I'm not... Oh, this is so embarrassing..."

"You're not experienced?" Garridan asked in a supportive tone. "There's nothing wrong with that. I have it on good authority my brother hasn't been with anyone in a long time. Let's knock his socks off tonight. I'll dance with you, and we'll try to get him to notice you in that gorgeous dress. If he can stop talking to Governor Camron about the upcoming infrastructure project for more than two seconds, I think he'll fall under your spell."

"You have much more confidence than I, General, but I will try."

Giving her a reassuring nod, he led her to the castle, ready to endure what was sure to be a boring but necessary evening.

Chapter Ten

Siora buckled her strappy flat sandal and straightened, brushing her hands over the smooth fabric that covered her thighs. Donning her favorite pair of silver earrings, she headed into the living room where her father sat by the fireplace.

"You look lovely, dear," Luthor said, eyes sparkling from the nearby embers. "You even did something to your hair."

"I sort of, um, spiked it with gel," she said, circling her hand over her head. "I don't know, I figured it would go with the theme. I refuse to wear a dress because I detest them, but I bought this jumpsuit from one of the Lynian street vendors a few years ago, and I don't hate it."

"It's perfect for you and still very formal." Standing, he approached and kissed her on the cheek. "It is an honor for you to attend the fundraiser as Commander Latimus's special guest. I couldn't be prouder."

"I can't believe he asked me," she said, still in shock from when Latimus approached her earlier that afternoon. "He wants to introduce me to Queen Miranda and Governor Evie. Says we're three of a kind. I mean, I'm going to meet the queen. Holy shit." She lifted her hands, eyes wide as she shook her head.

"And you deserve it. It was nice of Latimus to let you borrow the four-wheeler."

"It's the fastest way to get to Valeria." Trailing over to the table by the front door, she began packing a small purse. "The compounds have been relatively safe from attacks lately, but I'll have this baby on me." Lifting her Glock, she ensured the safety was on and stuck it in her bag. "Can't be too prepared."

"Or too careful," he said, walking her to the door. "I'll be asleep when you get home, but I can't wait to hear about it tomorrow night when we have dinner."

"Thanks, Dad. Lock both deadbolts behind me, okay?"

"Stop worrying about your old man," he said, shooing her out the door. "I've survived this long, haven't I?"

Chuckling, she gave him one last peck and trailed to the four-wheeler. Once inside, she was thankful for the gob of gel she put in her hair. She usually didn't bother since she kept it short, but it would maintain the style so she looked presentable to all the fancy people who would be at the fundraiser. Of course, that included Garridan, which made her heart tumble in all sorts of directions.

He'd informed her he was attending tonight and had promised to resume their training the following evening. Would he be surprised when she showed up? Latimus's invitation was last-minute, and she didn't think Garridan knew she was attending. Would he ask her to dance, or would he rather keep up the pretense of them just being comrades? Perhaps he wouldn't want to dance with a poor farmer's daughter in front of the plethora of aristocrats who would be in attendance.

He often spoke of how he'd left the aristocratic life behind, but that was easy to say when you weren't surrounded by a roomful of peers. Narrowing her eyes, she contemplated as she drove through the grassy fields that separated Lynia and Valeria. Regardless, she wished to keep their relationship secret as well, and there was really no point in pondering things that were pointless.

Forty-five minutes later, she pulled up to Valeria's main gate. After stating her name, which Latimus had put on the list, the guards ushered her inside, and she drove toward the governor's castle that sat in the middle of the compound. The mansion was brightly lit, and she could hear music wafting from the ballroom inside. Parking her vehicle, she slung her purse over her shoulder and headed inside.

Nerves tingled within as she grabbed one of the champagne flutes from a server who passed by with a tray. Taking a large gulp, she reminded herself that she was the guest of Commander

Latimus, the esteemed brother of King Sathan. Siora had always possessed an inner self-confidence, and she clutched onto it as she searched the room.

"Siora!" Latimus called, grinning as he trailed toward her. He looked handsome in a tuxedo with his slicked back hair and ice-blue eyes. A stunning blond woman accompanied him, and Siora knew it was his bonded mate, Lila.

"You must be Siora," she said with a tilt of her head. "I'm so honored to meet you. Latimus and Jack speak so highly of you."

"Thank you..." She trailed off, not knowing how to address the woman who was a respected diplomat in their kingdom.

"Just Lila is fine," she said, grinning. "Although I was born a stuffy aristocrat, my bonded mate is trying to break me of my formality. I think he's done a pretty good job so far."

"You still made me wear this monkey suit," Latimus muttered, sticking his finger in between his collar and neck and tugging. "I hate these things."

"You look very handsome," she said, tone stern as she smoothed his jacket. "If your son and Garridan can tolerate the tuxedo, you can too."

"Jack wore a tuxedo to make you happy, and so did I. You'll owe me later," he murmured, giving her a sultry look.

Lila's cheeks turned seven shades of red as she swatted his arm. "Latimus! We're in public. Please excuse my bonded's rudeness."

He scrunched his features at her as Siora held back a chuckle.

"Anyway, I'm so thrilled to meet the first woman battalion leader. How exciting. I can't wield a weapon to save my life."

"She just wields my balls instead—"

"Hush," Lila scolded, glancing around the room. "Camron will have a fit."

"Governor Camron can suck it, but I'll let it go," he said when she opened her mouth to argue. "Let me call over Miranda and Evie," Latimus said, turning and waving to them. They trailed over as Siora's heart leaped into her throat.

"We finally meet the magnificent Siora," Queen Miranda said, grinning from ear to ear beneath her olive green eyes and black, shoulder-length hair. "I'm honored."

"It is me who is honored to meet you, Queen Miranda," she said, dropping into a curtsy she hoped didn't look idiotic. "And you as well, Governor Evie. Thank you so much for having me."

The half-sisters gave each other a look before grimacing.

"Good lord, Siora, please don't bow to me. I hate all this formal crap. Why didn't you tell her I hate the formal crap?" Miranda asked Latimus, slapping him on the arm.

"Hey!" he said, swatting away her hand. "My wife has already landed a blow there, Miranda. Ease up."

"I tried like hell to get this caveman to let women into the army for years," Evie said, pointing to Latimus with her thumb. Her green eyes mirrored Miranda's, although she had fire-red hair atop her stunning face. "Thank you for proving me right."

"About what?" Siora asked, eyebrows lifting.

"That we're just as capable as men. More so, if you ask me. Welcome to the kick-ass females club, honey. Dear ol' sis and I saved you a seat," she said, jerking her head toward Miranda. "It's a super-fun club, and we're glad to have you."

Miranda and Evie were both fierce warriors who'd fought in battles decades ago, before women could formally join the army. They were legends in Siora's mind, and Evie's words spurred intense pride deep within.

"Thank you, Governor Evie and Queen Miranda. I'm so honored to fight in our army and protect our people."

"Just Miranda is fine," she said with a nod. "Thank you for coming tonight, by the way. I'd like to introduce you to some of the aristocrats if you don't mind. There are some rich widows I think support females in the army even if they're silent about it. I think you'll help me garner some extra donations. These wars are expensive, and we need the aristocrats' money to fund them. Believe me, we all pretty much detest the formality, but it's a necessary evil."

"Parade me to whomever you like," Siora said, smiling as she lifted her arms. "I'm happy to help the cause."

"Good. Let me grab some booze before we start the rounds," Miranda said, giving a playful grimace. "Need to dull the senses before I start to schmooze aristocrats."

"Me too," Evie said. "Nice to meet you, Siora."

After they left in search of a drink, Lila asked Latimus to dance, causing the commander to give an annoyed eye roll. Still, he led his bonded mate onto the floor, showcasing how much he loved her even though Siora could tell he'd rather be stabbed by a thousand Deamons than dance.

Sipping her champagne, Siora studied the room, refusing to admit she was searching for Garridan. Finally, she saw his broad shoulders where he stood across the large ballroom next to a willowy, golden-haired woman. *Celine*. Bristling, Siora watched as he slid his arm around Celine's shoulders, tugging her to his side. Smiling down at her, he whispered something in her ear before she tilted her head back and laughed.

The pale line of her throat glistened in the light of the chandelier beneath her perfect fangs, and Siora felt tears sting her eyes. Goddess, she was so pretty. Draped in her formal gown with long, flowing fabric, she looked like a statue of a beautiful goddess. Glancing down at her black jumpsuit and flat sandals, Siora realized how stupid she must look. She would never be in the same league as Celine when it came to appearance.

A small kernel of anger began to well in her gut, growing to a ball of full-on fury as she observed them together. He'd had ample time to tell her he was escorting Celine to the fundraiser. Hell, he'd been *inside* her every night for two fucking weeks. But he hadn't thought to mention it. He hadn't even thought to ask her if *she* might want to accompany him.

"Why would he?" Siora muttered to herself. "What aristocrat would ask a farmer's daughter to a fundraiser? Stop being ridiculous, Siora."

It was irrefutable proof she was right about their circumstances. Two people as different as she and Garridan would never be able to forge a life together. She would never fit into his world of wealth and privilege, and he certainly wouldn't be happy as the bonded mate of a female warrior on a rural compound.

And still...even though she knew it was futile, Siora longed for it anyway. Goddammit, she'd begun to yearn for things that were all but impossible.

Annoyed at herself and angry at him for not telling her he was bringing Celine, she clenched the glass. Reminding herself not to shatter the damn thing, she chugged the rest of the contents and set it on one of the trays that lined the wall.

Why in the hell hadn't he told her? She wouldn't have been upset he was bringing a date—that was standard at these events—but the fact he omitted the information, especially since they'd been spending so much time together, pissed her off. And, honestly, it just fucking hurt. After all the times they'd been intimate...and he'd stared deep into her eyes as he claimed her...didn't that matter enough for him to tell her he was choosing to bring someone else to a public event?

"You told him you didn't want anything serious, Siora. No labels. He's just following your directive."

As she stood in the corner murmuring to herself like a dolt, she realized she wished he hadn't listened to her. That he'd tossed her insistence aside and reassured her they could make it work somehow. *Stupid fucking daydreams.* She was really getting aggravated at the asinine musings that became more imprinted in her mind every damn day. Sighing, she straightened as Miranda approached from the corner of the room.

"Okay, I'm pleasantly buzzed and ready to dazzle some old rich dudes," Miranda said, eyes slightly glazed. "You with me? We're in this together now."

Brushing away her doubts, Siora nodded, ready to help her queen. She would deal with Garridan another time, when her heart didn't feel like a jumbled mess of scattered glass inside her chest.

Chapter Eleven

Garridan spotted Siora out of the corner of his eye, surprised she was at the event. Wondering why, he approached Latimus as he exited the dance floor with Lila.

"You invited Siora?"

"It was last-minute," Latimus said, nodding. "Miranda thought she could help raise some money as one of our preeminent female soldiers. And I think she just wanted to meet her."

"Right," Garridan said, rubbing the back of his neck. "Makes sense."

Latimus's eyes narrowed. "Should I have...told you? I know you've become friendly during the training, but I also didn't think it was a big deal."

"I..." He worked his jaw, realizing he should've told Siora he was escorting Celine. "No, it's fine."

"Look, Garridan," he said, placing his hand on his shoulder, "I don't want to get involved in your personal business. All I care about is that you two will be able to lead the battalions against Bakari. Is this going to jeopardize that somehow?"

"You know me better than that, Latimus," he said as annoyance flared. "I just wish I'd known, but it's no big deal."

"Sorry, brother. I didn't mean to make things awkward."

"It's fine. By the way, nice job on the dance floor."

Grimacing, Latimus ran a hand over his face. "If I didn't love my bonded so much, I'd never set foot near a dance floor. The things we do for our women. She's turned me into a fucking sap."

"It looks good on you, man. May we all be so lucky to find our one true mate."

"Truer words." Craning his neck, he gave a short nod. "Speaking of, she's summoning me. Let me know if you need me to smooth anything out with Siora."

Garridan nodded before Latimus walked away, and he glanced toward Siora. Miranda was leading her around the room, introducing her to various aristocrats as she reaffirmed they needed donations to fight the war against Bakari. He was viscerally aware of Siora, as he always was, and knew she felt his gaze. The muscle in her jaw clenched several times, and he understood she was pissed, which in turn spurred frustrated anger in his own gut.

He would've loved nothing more than to escort Siora as his date for all to see, but she'd been very clear their relationship was casual and she wished for it to remain secret. Compound that with the fact his father had bribed him into escorting Celine, and he was left with his current clusterfuck. Garridan hadn't mentioned he was bringing Celine because he didn't think it mattered. Damn it. Now, it looked as if he were hiding something, which wasn't true.

Sighing, he resumed his place at Celine's side, vowing to keep his promise to be her wingman. There would be time to deal with the situation with Siora later. For now, he had a vested interest in seeing his brother find happiness, and the more time he spent with Celine, he felt they would make a fantastic match. His brother was a self-proclaimed bachelor who spent way too much time on his aristocratic duties. Garridan knew life was short and wished for his brother to find a companion, someone who made him laugh and held him when he needed affection.

Someone who made him feel what Siora inspired every time Garridan was in her presence. By the goddess, he loved spending time with her and had no idea what he would do when their one-on-one sessions ended. Thinking about it generated a feeling of intense melancholy, so he just let it simmer as he rejoined Celine.

The fundraiser dragged long into the night, Siora avoiding him the entire time. She barely made eye contact with him for the few minutes they spoke when Miranda introduced her to Celine and Sebastian. And finally, when he was ready to walk Celine home,

Garridan searched the entire ballroom for Siora, realizing she'd already left without saying goodbye.

✧

Siora sat on Garridan's darkened porch, thankful for the plushy outdoor chairs that lined the expansive structure. She guessed the home to be five or six bedrooms minimum. Not as large as his parents' mansion, which bordered his property, but still sizable. Aristocrats flaunted their wealth, and Astaroth had his family's crest emblazoned atop the large black gate that surrounded his property, which meant Garridan's home was easy to find.

She'd debated confronting him tonight. After all, she was angry, and that never led to a productive discussion. But she felt it was best to tell him she wished to end their sexual relationship. After tonight, there would be no more one-on-one training. They would fight together in the final battle, and she would build her life at Lynia. A life without the handsome soldier who'd become the focus of her every damn thought.

He walked into her line of view, his broad shoulders visible in the moonlight as he strode on the sidewalk. Unlocking the gate, he stepped through and closed it behind him. He didn't acknowledge her as his shoes clacked on the pavement of the walkway that led to the porch, but she knew he was aware of her presence.

Finally, he stopped before the porch steps and lifted his eyes to hers. "Hello, Siora."

"Hello," she said, lifting her brow. "Wasn't sure you'd be home tonight, but I figured I'd wait for a while before I went back to Lynia."

A muscle ticked in his jaw before he spoke. "Why'd you think I wouldn't be home?"

"I wasn't sure if you were fucking Celine," she said with a shrug. "Aristocratic women are taught to guard their virginity, but you never know. It always seemed like an antiquated rule to me."

His nostrils flared as anger clouded his expression. "Not to be a dick, but it's none of your business whether I'm fucking Celine or not."

Scoffing, she stood and ran her fingers through her hair. "Well, you've certainly made that clear—"

"No!" he interrupted, ascending the first step and jabbing his finger at her. "You do *not* get to pin this on me."

"Pin what on you?"

"The fact I escorted Celine to the fundraiser tonight. Not that you deserve an explanation, but my father blackmailed me into taking her. Otherwise, he was going to withdraw his donation for the new TECs."

Pursing her lips, she contemplated the words, wondering if they were true. "Well, you didn't seem like you were suffering, so I'm sure it wasn't a chore."

"There are things you don't know, Siora," he said, climbing another step. "Things I haven't told you because you insisted you wanted to keep this casual."

"Of course I want to keep it casual," she said, crossing her arms. "We have nothing but sex between us, and a romantic relationship would never work. Especially with our circumstances."

Cresting the last step, he towered over her as he gazed into her eyes. "Circumstances are what you make of them. I think it's time we started truly communicating, Siora." Glancing toward his father's home, he scowled. "My father will be home any minute, and I don't want him involved in this."

"Embarrassed he might see you with a poor farmer's daughter?" she asked, tapping her foot.

His eyes narrowed into angry slits. "You're really pissing me off right now. You came here looking for a fight, so let's have one. I think we should have it in private, in a language we'll both understand."

It sounded like a challenge, and she was intrigued. "Meaning?"

Stepping forward, he unlocked the door and gestured inside. "Come on."

She contemplated for several seconds before acknowledging his words held merit. In truth, she *was* looking for a fight and would rather have it without prying eyes so she could figure out why he didn't tell her about escorting Celine. Giving him a glare, she stepped inside before he closed the door.

Locking it, he began walking down the darkened hallway. "Follow me."

She complied, realizing she trusted him although she was mad as hell.

He led her through the home until they arrived at a back room. He flipped the switch, flooding the room with light, and she noticed the workout room filled with tons of weights, exercise machines, and a large black mat in the corner.

"You want a fight, so we'll have a fight," he said, stepping into the room and kicking off his dress shoes and socks. He tugged at his bow tie, pulling it off before he removed his jacket. After ditching the cummerbund, he began unbuttoning his shirt.

"Whoa," she said, stepping forward and holding up her hands. "What are you doing?"

"I'm getting ready to spar with you," he said, shrugging his shirt off his shoulders and tossing it aside. "At least combat is a language you understand." Trailing to the black mat, he stood in the middle and beckoned to her. "Come on. Let's fight, sweetheart. Tell me everything you came here to say. I can take it."

"I can't fight in this jumpsuit," she said, glancing down at the material. "It's the only nice piece of clothing I have."

"Then take it off," he said, arching an eyebrow. "It will certainly give you an advantage since I can barely think when you bare your skin to me, Siora."

"You want me to fight naked?" she almost shrieked. "Garridan—"

"If you don't think you can do it, I'll take your concession."

Bastard. As if she'd ever concede in *any* battle. "Are you fucking serious?"

His lips twitched. "Take off your clothes and fight me, Siora."

Huffing, she unclasped the button behind her neck, and the twin tufts of fabric that had been covering her breasts fell to her waist. Lust blazed in Garridan's eyes as she shimmied out of the jumpsuit and kicked her sandals aside. She left her panties on and trailed over to where he'd thrown his shirt, shrugging it on and cinching a few of the buttons. It fell to her knees, and she padded over to stand before him on the mat.

"This is ridiculous—"

His hand jabbed at her face, and she maneuvered away, her body instinctively knowing what to do after all her training. Gritting her teeth, she punched back, frustrated when he blocked her jab, and she turned to land a kick in his side.

Garridan muttered an *"oomph"* when she landed the kick before scuttling past her and grabbing her arm. Twisting it behind her back, he sandwiched it between them as his front pressed against her back.

"For the last time," he breathed in her ear, "I'm not fucking Celine. I don't *want* Celine. There's only one woman I want."

Grunting, she twisted out of his grasp and kneed him in the stomach before he doubled over. Grasping his thick hair, she jerked his head to stare into his eyes. "You were all over her tonight."

Quick as lightning, he jolted away, rotating to slide his arms around her waist and lift her before slamming her onto the ground. He was careful, as he always was when they sparred, but it knocked the breath from her lungs.

"I think she'd be a good match for my brother. We came up with a stupid plan to make him see her in a more flattering light. Like I said, there are things you don't know, Siora."

Placing her hands flat beside her head, she kicked her feet high and used the momentum to jump into a wide-legged stance. "You should've told me you were going with her."

"Yes," he said, crouching and lifting his hands to protect his face from any future blows. "I'm sorry I didn't tell you. I didn't think you wanted to know personal details about my life. I don't know what the rules are here."

"There are no rules," she said, although the words didn't ring true. "We're just fucking."

Amber eyes darted between hers before he whispered, *"Liar."*

"Don't call me names," she gritted as confusing emotions welled within. "And it's time to end this, Garridan. No more training, and no more fucking. It's over."

His features softened as he gazed at her. "Is that what you really want?"

"It doesn't matter what I want!" she yelled. "*This* can never happen." She gestured back and forth between them.

"Why?" he asked, slowly approaching her, palms held high as he assessed her. "You've made up some story in your head that isn't true, Siora."

"Of course it's true," she said, mortified when a single tear slipped down her cheek. Swiping it away, she held out her hand. "Don't come any closer."

"I'm beginning to think you say things you don't mean, sweetheart," he said, continuing to slowly approach her. "I think you're dying for me to touch you."

Her chin trembled as she shook her head. "No, I'm not."

The corner of his lips curved, the smile both sexy and filled with compassion. "Man, you're a really bad liar."

Eliciting a ragged cry, she lurched forward, aiming a punch at his jaw while attempting to swipe his leg. He anticipated the move, grabbing her wrist before swiping her legs instead and sending them both crashing to the floor. Tangled together, they struggled as he held her down with his large body, half-sprawled over hers.

"Damn it," he grunted, struggling to catch her wrists, one in each hand. Lifting them above her head, he held them there as they panted. Warm breaths mingled as their gazes remained locked, both too stubborn to look away.

"Let me go," she said, hating the sound of her voice, so weak. So much like the simpering woman she never wished to be.

His throat bobbed before he slowly shook his head. "I can't," he whispered, staring into her with such raw affection she felt her body melt beneath him. "Haven't you realized I can't let you go?"

"You don't want someone like me," she whispered, shaking her head upon the mat. "I don't fit in your world. We don't fit."

Settling into the juncture of her thighs, he pressed his straining erection into her core, causing her to moan. "I think we fit just fine, Siora. In all the ways that count. You're the sexiest woman I've ever seen, and I love that you fight as well as you fuck. What else do we need?"

"I never wanted a mate," she warbled, his face slightly blurred by the wetness in her eyes. "I don't know how to do this. I'm..." She stopped before admitting she was scared. The words made her feel too vulnerable as he stared at her with such longing.

"I know," he whispered, lowering to nudge her nose with his. "I am too. I never wanted a mate either, but sometimes, life doesn't go as planned."

"It will never work," she whispered, pleading for him to understand they had no future.

Forming a slow grin, he shook his head. "Thank the goddess I've always been an optimist, because you've definitely got the gloom and doom part down."

A breathy laugh escaped her throat. "I just don't want to set us up for failure. There are so many reasons—"

"Siora?" he interrupted, releasing one of her wrists and covering her lips with his fingers. "Will you do me a favor?"

Feeling her eyes dart between his, she nodded.

"Shut the fuck up and kiss me."

Lowering his head, he consumed her lips, drawing her against him as she surged her tongue inside his mouth. He groaned, low and raw, into the back of her throat, causing her arousal to rush between her thighs. Craving him more than her next breath, she tugged at his pants as he viciously kissed her, pulling them off his legs before he ripped her panties off. With his lips still cemented to hers, he plunged into her body, causing her hips to buck as his shaft claimed every inch of her wet, throbbing core.

"Yesss..." he hissed, furiously pumping his thick, pulsing cock into her taut channel as she sucked his tongue for dear life. He speared it into her mouth, mimicking the frenzied juts of his shaft, and her eyes rolled back in her head as she gave into the delicious pounding.

"Just like that," he rasped, gripping her thigh and wrapping it around his waist. "I love it when you relax like that when I'm deep inside you, sweetheart. Do you know how good it feels to have you open up like this when I fuck you?"

She wanted to tell him it was terrifying. That opening herself up to anyone was terribly disconcerting for the strong woman she'd always had to be. One who blazed her own path and never needed anyone. Never needed a partner. Of course, it was impossible to tell him that when her body had all but disintegrated into a pile of inflamed arousal as he consumed her with his words and his touch.

"I'm not stupid enough to let you go, Siora." Clenching his fingers in her short hair, he tugged, forcing her eyes to fly open. "It's not happening, so stop making excuses for why it won't work. Do you hear me?"

Her mouth fell open as he hammered inside her trembling body, and she struggled to answer. The overwhelming sensations were just too damn much.

Sliding his hand between their bodies, he ran his fingers through her slick essence, which now coated her folds and inner thighs, lubricating them before finding her clit. Stimulating the engorged nub with his fingers, he pressed his forehead to hers as they reached for the peak.

"Oh, *god*, I'm going to come," she wailed, his fingers maddening on the nerve-filled bud of her clit. "I can't take it."

"You can take it," he murmured, lips vibrating against hers as their faces pressed together. "Open that pretty pussy and come all over my cock, Siora. *Now*."

Tossing her head back, she succumbed to the pleasure, feeling her body snap as he continued to piston deep within. He was everywhere—inside her body…inside her brain…inside her *heart*. Something bloomed in the deep confines of her chest, and she understood that as her body was shooting over the precipice of pleasure, her heart was undeniably falling into the abyss for the magnificent Vampyre who was loving her so vehemently. Crying his name, she clutched her arms around his neck and buried her face in the juncture between his nape and shoulder.

The vein that ran from his neck to his heart pulsed against her cheek, and she longed to plunge her fangs into the tender flesh; to drink from him as bonded mates often drank from each other when they shared bouts of pleasure.

"One day, sweetheart," he rasped, reading her thoughts as if she'd sent them to him in fucking bold text. "One day, we'll drink from each other while we do this."

The words were serious, causing her to thrust her nails into his upper back. The action elicited a ragged moan from him before he snapped, freezing for a millisecond before plummeting into his own orgasm. Bucking above her, he shot his release into her body, spraying her with his essence so it mingled with her own. Every part of their bodies connected as she lay below him trying to make sense of the earth-shattering experience. Small, visceral grunts escaped his throat as he lunged into her…once…twice…and one last time before he elicited a soft, sexy wail. Gathering her against his body, he slid his arms under her back and held her close, pressing his face into her neck.

They lay there, sated and replete, silent as their labored breaths echoed against the walls. Eventually, their bodies cooled, and Siora melded into the mat, her eyelids heavy as the cadence of his breathing began to slow. Expelling a long breath, she closed her eyes, promising herself she'd only sleep for a moment.

An indiscernible amount of time later, she awoke to feel Garridan lifting her into his arms before trailing to the doorway of the gym. Flicking off the light, he carried her to his bedroom, sliding her between the sheets before crawling in behind. Drawing her close, he spooned her, resting his face against the back of her neck before falling into slumber.

She lay there terrified to clutch onto the happiness that wanted to envelop every cell of her frame. It was too overwhelming, and she panicked as his deep breaths warmed the sensitive skin of her neck.

After he lay still for several minutes, she quietly eased from his embrace and donned her clothes in the gym. Heading out the front door, she ensured the lock on the knob was secure and scurried back to the four-wheeler parked at the castle. Jumbled thoughts rushed through her brain during the short, brisk walk before she hopped into the vehicle and drove back to Lynia as fast as the damn thing would take her.

Chapter Twelve

Garridan awoke as the first light of dawn glowed outside his bedroom window. Rolling onto his back, he placed his hands under his head and stared at the ceiling. Siora had run away, and that was...well, he realized it was a natural progression in their complex relationship. It meant she was scared, and if he'd learned anything in his long life, it was that the greatest joy always resided on the other side of fear, *if* one was willing to take the leap.

Chewing on his inner lip, he contemplated the best path to take with Siora. After last night, there was no doubt he wanted to pursue her. Yes, the time for total honesty had arrived. Garridan had lived for ten centuries and never even come close to feeling about someone the way he felt about Siora. She was fierce and stubborn and so achingly beautiful. He didn't know if she wanted to build a family and understood they'd need to make their way to having that very serious discussion, but there were other things he needed to tackle first.

To begin with, he wanted to court her. Garridan saw the importance of spending time with her outside the army so she could get comfortable with him—and with the idea they were meant to be together. She swore they didn't belong in each other's world, but he saw that excuse for what it truly was: Siora wasn't sure he would choose her. Somewhere along the way, she'd decided an aristocrat didn't belong with a farmer's daughter, and the story had become her reality. Smiling, Garridan realized he couldn't wait to relieve her of that notion. The great thing about immortals? Well, they had a lot of time, and he was a very patient man. He would take time to court her as she deserved to be courted, until his stubborn mate rewrote the tragic story.

"You sound as sappy as Latimus, old man," he chided, running his hands over his face. "But damn, if she isn't your mate, then no one is."

The belief was embedded deep within, and he knew with a little time, Siora would see the light as well. In the meantime, he would let her pull back as she seemed determined to do. He'd give her some space and take the gamble she would eventually realize she wanted to build something with him too. Hopefully, she would recognize they were perfect for each other and overcome her fear. He'd waited centuries to find his mate. Waiting a few weeks longer surely wouldn't kill him, although he certainly would miss her soft, silken skin and passionate kisses...and the way she moaned his name when he was deep inside her sweet body.

Feeling himself harden, he emitted a groan before lowering his hand to his shaft to ease his burgeoning erection, anticipating the next time Siora's firm grip would replace his own.

The next few days were chaotic for Siora as the final battle drew near. The timeline was established, and they would fight Bakari in a matter of days. As if that wasn't enough to process, Garridan had reverted to treating her like one of the soldiers, which rankled her. Yes, she'd bolted after their passionate night together, but she didn't expect him to act as if it didn't matter. The morning after, when she'd shown up on the battlefield, his expression was polite and detached, which worried her more than any flares of anger she'd ever observed.

"I'm sorry I left without saying goodbye," she said as the morning sun shined on the training field. "I needed to get home and change before training today."

"It's fine," he responded, his deep baritone sending shivers across her skin. "We need to focus on training since the final battle is near. I think you're right about ending our one-on-one sessions. You fixed the tell, and your combat skills have improved."

Kicking the grass with her boot, she nodded, understanding this meant they would end their sexual trysts too. "Okay. Thanks for...everything." Goddess, she sounded so lame.

"You're welcome." His eyes looked like melted amber in the glinting sunlight, and she almost wanted to weep for what she was throwing away. Reminding herself he was never hers to begin with, she braced herself and threw all her energy into training.

Throughout the training sessions, she and Garridan worked together to ensure their three battalions would be ready. During the battle, they would flank the north side of the forest along the field as Commander Kenden's troops flanked the south side. Bakari would certainly have Deamon troops hidden in the thick forests, and they would do their best to prevent casualties. Although Vampyres had self-healing abilities, they were still vulnerable to poison-tipped weapons that prevented self-healing. Siora was determined to ensure they didn't lose one Vampyre or Slayer soldier and took that vow very seriously.

The afternoon before the battle, Siora approached Garridan as he slung his backpack over his shoulder. "Can I talk to you for a minute before you head back to Valeria?"

"Sure."

They walked toward the edge of the field, and Siora noted most of the soldiers had already headed home. It was imperative they rest before they gathered early the next morning.

"Our battalions look good, and they're following our orders implicitly. I was a bit worried some of the male soldiers wouldn't accept a female as first officer, but it hasn't been an issue."

"Because you're a natural leader, Siora," he said, cupping her shoulder. "And you've excelled at every challenge. We're extremely prepared, and I fully expect our troops to shine."

She'd missed his touch, and his broad hand upon her shoulder caused her heart to pound. "And if we win, we'll be free of war. Hopefully." She lifted her hand, crossing her fingers.

Smiling, he nodded. "I hope so."

"I..." Glancing around, she told herself not to blurt out something embarrassing, such as how much she missed him. "Training with you was a fantastic experience. I really appreciate you taking the time to teach me."

"Sure." His eyes traveled over her face before he tilted his head. "Well, I'll see you in the morning. We'll meet here two hours before sunrise and load the troops into the utility vehicles before heading to the battlefield." Pivoting, he began to trail away.

"Wait," she called, grabbing his arm.

He turned, gazing at her, although his expression was unreadable.

"We said so many things the last night together, but we...we also *didn't* say a lot. I just... Fuck, I'm terrible at this." She released her grip and crossed her arms over her chest. "I expected you to be pissed I left that morning."

Shaking his head, he lifted a shoulder. "We're past that, Siora."

Feeling her eyebrows draw together, she studied him. "Past what?"

"Past our petty arguments and base emotions. There's so much more beneath the surface. The question is, are we too afraid to dig deep and find it?"

Inhaling a deep breath, she pondered. "I don't know how to answer that."

Grinning, he gave a slight nod. "Let me know when you figure it out." With a small salute, he turned and meandered across the field. She still had the urge to call him back, but what could she say? *Leave your aristocratic life behind to bond with me?* The words sounded ridiculous as they clanked in her mind.

Lowering to the grass, she ran her hand over the soft blades as she contemplated. She'd always been so confident in her abilities as a soldier, and her determination and drive were unparalleled. But in her personal life? She'd never seen herself as anything outstanding. She'd always assumed she was a normal person destined to have one goal: to excel as a female in the army. But what if she allowed her confidence in her physical skills to extend to her personal life? To believe she deserved to marry an aristocratic man, love him with all her heart, and have him love her in return?

The sentiment seemed foreign to her, and she wrinkled her nose. When did she decide she wasn't good enough? It was so counterintuitive to her strength and inner fortitude. Lifting her face to the setting sun, she closed her eyes, allowing realization to wash over her.

"You've sold yourself short your whole life, Siora," she whispered. "You deserve success in your career and in *every* aspect of your life."

Smiling, she expelled a heavy breath, releasing her fears and doubts across the expansive field. Of course, they would continue to rear their head, but she had to embrace the belief she was worthy in *all* segments of her existence. Believing in herself as a warrior had always come naturally. Believing in herself as a person fully deserving of love and happiness was harder, but she was determined to release her fears.

Garridan's face flashed through her mind, increasing the longing she felt for him. Finally, she was ready to admit the truth: she cared for him and wanted to try to build something together. Hell, she was likely falling in love with him, which would be a first. It was daunting and a bit terrifying, but it also felt...*liberating*, as if she was emancipating those old, toxic beliefs and clutching onto something with so many exciting possibilities.

Would he accept her acknowledgment and want to court her? She had no idea, but judging by his words their last night together, he experienced some intense feelings for her too. Armed with that knowledge, Siora set her plan into motion. She would focus on the battle and ensure they prevailed. Once they defeated Bakari, she would approach Garridan and be completely honest about her feelings.

Excited for the future, she rose and wiped off the dirt before grabbing her bag and heading home. Siora had a battle to win, and she was ready to kick some ass.

Chapter Thirteen

The morning of the battle arrived, and Siora awoke with a fresh, vibrant energy. Embracing her feelings for Garridan had set something free deep inside, and she was ready to fight like hell so she could focus on the future.

Two hours before dawn, the Vampyre immortal battalions gathered. Latimus gave a rousing speech before they loaded into the armored vehicles and drove to the battlefield.

The combat would take place in an open field south of the Slayer compound, Restia. It was where the wall of ether stood that separated the human world from the immoral realm and therefore kept their people secret from humans. Etherya's world had existed this way for countless centuries, and the humans remained oblivious to their existence.

When they arrived at the battlefield, they prepared their battalions, and Siora and Garridan faced Latimus.

"May the goddess be with you," Latimus said, lifting his hand in a salute.

"May the goddess be with you, brother," Garridan said, saluting in return as Siora did the same.

Latimus and Garridan clenched each other's forearms, indicating their strong bond.

"We've fought so many battles together over the centuries," Garridan said. "Hopefully, this is the last one for a while."

"With Siora as your first-in-command, I have no doubt."

"Thank you, Commander Latimus," she said as nervous energy coursed through her body. "We'll stomp out every Deamon in the northern flank."

With one last nod, he returned to his own battalion while Siora and Garridan began to lead the troops. As they marched, Siora grinned at the strong, handsome general, acknowledging how happy she was to have him by her side.

"What's that smile for?" he murmured as the soldiers marched behind.

"I'll tell you afterward. Don't die, okay? I've got some really important shit I need to tell you."

His lips curved into that sexy smile she'd come to covet. "Can't wait."

They directed the troops across the north flank of the forest, preparing them for the imminent conflict. Bakari appeared, his throng of Deamon warriors close behind, and Siora double-checked the TECs lined on her weaponry belt. They were special weapons that would obliterate the immortal Deamons instantly, and she was ready to use every last one if needed.

Several loud cries sounded from the battlefield, and Siora drew her rifle around her shoulder, ready to defend her kingdom.

Multitudes of Deamon soldiers began to rush in from both sides—half from the main battlefield, and half from the nearby forest. She and Garridan commanded their soldiers to commence combat, and they were thrust into physical battle. Gritting her teeth, she got to work.

For long minutes, she attacked the barrage of soldiers, using her semi-automatic rifle as well as the TECs to eliminate them one by one. Garridan fought off to her side, and she caught glimpses of him from the corner of her eye, besting the Deamons as he'd done for centuries. An enemy soldier approached, knocking her rifle from her hand and sending it flying behind her back. Grasping one of the TECs, she deployed it, disintegrating the creature, but another one closed in behind. Realizing the TEC was out of deployments, she tossed it to the ground and reached for another.

The Deamon knocked her hand away, and she lunged forward, landing a punch in his throat, causing him to clutch it and gasp for breath. Reaching for her rifle, she tried to swing it around but felt a tug from behind. Another Deamon had grabbed the strap, and he pulled it from her body before turning it on her.

"Time to meet the goddess, Vampyre!" he spat, placing his finger over the trigger.

Instinctively reacting, she launched a laser-focused kick into his abdomen before he doubled over and dropped the rifle to the ground. Approaching, she began to fight the creature in one-on-one combat as he tried to fight back. Pride welled inside as she realized she was kicking his ass rather expertly, and a portion of her enhanced combat skill could be attributed to Garridan's training. Planting her weight on one leg—*without* dropping her hip—she launched into a jump kick and knocked the bastard to the ground. Grabbing a TEC from her belt, she plunged it into the Deamon's forehead and blew him to bits.

"Nice job not dropping your hip!" Garridan yelled from several feet away before he turned to fight an oncoming Deamon.

"Damn straight!"

They fought for what seemed like hours, although it was most likely minutes in the grand scheme of things. The immortal army was making slow, steady work of defeating the Deamons, and she remained focused as she fought.

A bright light exploded on the field, almost blinding her. Siora heard a gruff shout and saw Garridan clutching his lower neck before plunging a TEC into a Deamon's forehead and instantly killing him.

"Garridan!" she shouted, running toward him as she blinked away the brightness. Approaching his side, she saw him fall to the ground and crouched beside him.

"The bastard stabbed me with a poison-tipped sword, but I think I pulled it out quickly enough that my body will heal."

Examining the wound, she touched her fingers to it, softly pressing. "Yes, you just need some blood flow to the area. It's a surface wound. Thank the goddess."

Suddenly, her hand froze against his chest, and she struggled to move. Garridan froze too, and Siora gazed around the battlefield, realizing everything had come to a sudden halt.

"Callie has frozen everyone with her powers," came a voice over the walkie-talkie, and Siora recognized it as Nolan's, the kind Slayer physician who was stationed in the infirmary tent. "We're far away enough from the battlefield that it's not affecting our movements. Stay tuned for updates."

"I can't move anything below my neck," Siora said, willing her body to move. "I need to massage the area around your wound to increase blood flow. That will help counteract the poison. Shit!"

"It's okay," Garridan said, slightly rasping. "This most likely has something to do with the prophecy. I'm not dead yet."

"Don't joke about that," she said, emotion welling in her throat. "I mean it, Garridan. I have a lot of stuff to say to you, and I can't do it if you're dead."

Labored breaths exited his lungs as his fangs flashed in a smile. "I have a lot to say to you too. I was waiting for you to realize you can't live without me."

Breathing a laugh, she ached to hold him. "So, you were intentionally avoiding me."

"You needed space to figure things out. I understand you, Siora. You'll get that one day."

Their conversation was interrupted by several more bright flashes from the battlefield. All at once, every Deamon soldier who stood frozen on the battlefield disintegrated, each of them turning to dust and scattering over the field as if they'd never existed. A loud boom echoed across the field before Siora regained her ability to move.

Leaning over Garridan, she examined the wound that sat at the juncture of his neck and shoulder. "Here," she said, massaging it with her fingers. "We need to urge your blood to circulate around it so it expels the poison and you can heal." She maneuvered her fingers for a minute before he sat up and pushed the skin with his fingers.

"I think I'm good. That was a close one, but thankfully, Deamons have terrible aim."

Overcome with joy, she nodded. "They pretty much sucked. Did we win? What the hell happened?"

Lifting the small walkie-talkie from his belt, Garridan radioed Latimus. "Commander, the Deamons we were fighting seem to have disappeared. Am I imagining things?"

Latimus's voice crackled over the device. "Callie fulfilled the prophecy and defeated Bakari. In the meantime, she also somehow managed to destroy every soldier in his Deamon army and obliterate the ether."

Garridan's eyes grew wide as he looked at Siora. "So...we no longer have a barrier that shields us from the humans?"

"Looks that way. I'll know more when we debrief. In the meantime, I want to gather all our troops on the field and assess the damage and casualties, especially from our Slayer soldiers. After that, we'll address them and send them home for a nice long break."

"Ten-four, commander. Siora and I will round everyone up and meet you at the center of the battlefield."

Placing the device back on his belt, he dug his hand into the ground to anchor himself to stand. Siora rose, extending her hand and helping him up.

"Thanks," he said, affection glowing in his deep brown eyes.

Giving a nod, she squeezed his hand before turning to face the soldiers. There would be time for them to say what needed to be said, but first, they had a job to do. Placing her fingers between her lips, she gave a loud whistle and circled her hand in the air.

"All battalions, assemble for roll call."

The troops began to gather in front of her so they could assess the formation before marching back to the main field.

Looking up at Garridan, she asked, "Do you want to do roll call?"

"No, ma'am. It's all you, Battalion Leader Siora. Go for it."

Grinning from ear to ear, she turned to face her battalions and commence her duties as a full-fledged officer in the immortal army.

Chapter Fourteen

After addressing the troops, Latimus informed them they would have a few weeks off to spend with their families and rest. Now that Bakari had been vanquished, his threat was diminished, but the destruction of the ether created a new set of challenges. Humans were wily creatures, armed with nuclear weapons and almost limitless technology, so the army would need to be refashioned into a force that could defend the immortals from an attack. Although Queen Miranda and King Sathan were working on a plan to approach the humans, only time would tell if they were friend or foe.

Siora headed back to the compound of Takelia in the armored vehicles and divested her weapons and combat gear before preparing to head home. Garridan approached her, a glint in his eye as he gave her that sexy grin.

"Heading home to the farm?"

"Yep," she said, placing her hands in her pockets. She desperately wanted to have some alone time with him but knew they were both exhausted.

"You know," he said, rubbing his chin, "after I go home and take a massive nap, I'd really like to head over to Lynia and see you. And maybe meet your dad."

Biting her lip to contain her grin, she shrugged. "I only introduce him to people who are really important to me."

Lifting his brows, his grin deepened. "Is that so?"

Nodding, she felt herself beaming like a lovesick dolt. As her heart pounded in her chest, she said softly, "You could come over for dinner. We're having Slayer blood and corn chowder. Dad loves food, even though we don't need it, and it's pretty much a staple at this point. Oh, and there will be wine too."

Affection swam in his eyes. "I'd love to come over for dinner."

"Sweet." Kicking the ground with the toe of her boot, she glanced around. "Don't tell anyone yet, okay? I want to talk to you first and figure out how we're going to do this. I don't want the soldiers thinking I got ahead from sleeping with my commanding officer."

"No one in their right mind would think that, but I understand." Glancing at his watch, he said, "I'll come over at six if that works."

"Perfect. See you then."

He gave her an almost imperceptible wink, visible only to her, that set her heart aflutter. Flashing one last grin, she hopped into a four-wheeler and drove home, anticipating her father's reaction when she informed him they were having company from a very handsome, eligible Vampyre. Knowing he'd be thrilled, she gave a tiny squeal—which was completely out of character for her, but so was falling in love, so she figured she'd just go with it.

As the wind whipped her hair, Siora took a moment to thank the goddess for their victory and for Garridan, the man who, somehow, had tunneled his way into her heart.

Garridan awoke from his nap rested and filled with anticipation about meeting Siora's father. It was a big step for them, and he understood how meaningful it was for her. Donning his black pants, polo shirt, and loafers, he marveled at how nice it felt to dress in something besides tactical gear for once. Locking the door behind him, he hopped into his four-wheeler and drove to Lynia.

The farm sat on the outskirts of the rural compound, and Garridan noticed the rows of corn that lined the field behind the small home. Now that Slayers and reformed Deamons lived on all the compounds, growing food was a lucrative business for Vampyres, who only needed Slayer blood for sustenance. Although Vampyres ate food for taste and pleasure, they didn't need it like other immortals.

Garridan climbed the front porch steps and lifted his hand to knock, but the door was swung open by a smiling Siora.

"You're right on time."

She looked beautiful in her casual attire, and her hair was fuller, causing him to wonder if she'd put something in it to style it.

"You look pretty."

Red splotches appeared on her cheeks, and she gestured him inside. "Thanks. We're almost ready. It's not as big as your house, but it does the job."

Garridan observed the dining room table lined with wine, corn, and goblets of Slayer blood before a man approached him, arms outstretched.

"General Garridan," he said, pulling him into a firm embrace. "It's so nice to meet you. I've heard wonderful things. Thank you for taking the time to train my Siora, and thank you for defending our people."

"You're welcome," he said, drawing back. "Siora is a talented soldier, and I'm glad Bakari's threat is quelled so we can hopefully enjoy some peace."

"Dad, you're smothering him," Siora said, tugging his arm. "Come on—let's eat. I'm starving."

They had a lovely dinner, filled with laughter and embarrassing stories from Siora's childhood that had her playfully rolling her eyes on more than one occasion. Garridan found Luthor a jovial man, and he was honored to be included in their small family gathering.

After dinner, Luthor retired to his room, and Garridan and Siora headed outside to sit on the couch that lined the far side of the porch. When he slid his arm around her shoulders, she nestled into his side, and he kissed her temple as they stared across the rapidly dimming horizon.

"Dad really likes you," she said, snuggling into him. "I can tell."

"I'm glad to hear it since I plan to see him quite often."

Pulling back, she tilted her head as her eyes glowed in the light of the newly risen moon. "You do?"

"Yes," he said, running the backs of his fingers along her jaw. "If that's all right with you."

Swallowing, she licked her lips, the gesture sending shards of desire through his veins. "There's so much to figure out if we really do this. I'm woman enough to admit I'm scared, but I also don't want to lose you. So I guess we need to figure some shit out."

Chuckling, he nodded. "For starters, I was thinking I might sell my house at Valeria. I have nothing tethering me there, and I can live on Lynia as easily as I can live there."

"But you haven't gotten your assignment yet," she said, eyebrows drawing together. "Latimus will certainly assign you to a high-ranking position. You'll most likely have to visit the military centers on each compound. Lynia is a distant compound and living here will require a ton of travel."

"Yes, but *you're* at Lynia, and I assume you want to remain close to your father. Plus, I'm sure Latimus will assign you as head of security for the compound."

Her eyes darted between his. "It's not fair of me to ask you to sell your home and move here."

"You're not asking. I'm offering of my own free will. I have no ties to Valeria since I'm not close with my parents, and I can continue to see Sebastian when I visit."

"Will you be happy on a rural compound? It's probably boring here compared to Valeria."

"If I'm with you, I'm pretty sure I'll be happy." Running his thumb over her cheek, his tone was reverent. "I want to court you, Siora, and when we're ready, I want to bond with you and build a future. If you want to have kids, we can work our way up to that too."

Her fangs toyed with her lip as she grinned. "I can see myself having kids down the road if I'm with the right person. It wasn't ever a pressing desire because I was so fixated on becoming a soldier, but it would be nice to build a family. And my dad would be thrilled to have some grandbabies. He would definitely offer to help so we could still build our military careers, which is pretty freaking awesome."

"I think we can build something amazing if we try, Siora. I've never wished for a bonded mate, but you burst into my life, and I fell for you before I even knew what was happening."

"I'm so honored you want to court me," she whispered, cupping his jaw. "You could have anyone, Garridan."

"I only want you, sweetheart. Don't you know that by now?" Pressing his lips to hers, he gave her a tender kiss before drawing back.

"Will your parents be upset you're settling with a commoner?"

"Probably," he said, arching an eyebrow. "But I just don't give a damn. It's my life, and I aim to live it exactly as I please."

"That's pretty badass for an aristocrat," she teased. "Who knew you guys had the ability to be tough?"

Lowering his hand, he tickled her side as she laughed before burying his face in her neck. Inhaling her fragrant scent, his body hardened as she shimmied into him.

"I want to drink from you," he whispered, nuzzling her neck. "Goddess, you smell so good."

Sliding her fingers into his hair, she gently tugged him closer. "Then drink from me."

Lifting his head, he gazed into her eyes. "That's a huge step, sweetheart. If I drink from you, I won't be able to let you go."

Clenching her fingers in his hair, she gave him a sultry smile as his cock jerked inside his pants. "I'm counting on it, General."

Emitting a low growl, he pressed his face to her nape, extending his tongue to lick the pulsing vein. His saliva would help prepare her sensitive skin for his invasion as well as numb the pain. Her body trembled beneath his as his tongue rasped over her skin, and he moaned before placing the tips of his fangs over her vein. Supporting her neck with his hand while the other one closed around her waist, he inhaled a sharp breath and pierced her sweet skin.

Her responding mewl sent shivers of lust through his frame as thick rivulets of blood coated his mouth. Drawing her between his lips, he drank her essence, imbibing everything that was his beautiful Siora. She whimpered beneath him, clutching his hair and shoulder as her fingernails dug into his scalp. Wracked with pleasure, he swallowed her sweet spirit until he felt himself begin to lose control. The scent of her arousal surrounded them, and if he wasn't careful, he'd rip her clothes off and fuck her right there on her father's front porch. Understanding that wasn't an option, he released her vein, resting his forehead against her as he licked the wound closed.

"Oh, god, I almost came," she whispered, the words ragged as she expelled heavy breaths. "I can't wait for you to do that when you fuck me."

"I can't wait either," he growled, placing a kiss on the spot, which was rapidly healing thanks to his saliva and her self-healing abilities. "And you're going to drink from me too."

"I'm so excited to taste the pure blood of a fancy aristocrat. Don't tell your father—he'll be scandalized."

Chuckling, he rested his lips against the shell of her ear. "Even more reason to spread the news far and wide."

Her laughter surrounded them as they cuddled together on the couch. As her fingers sifted through his hair, she whispered his name.

"Hmm?"

"I think...I think I'm in love with you."

Drawing back, he gazed into her stunning eyes. "That's good, because I think I'm in love with you too."

Her grin was adorable as she caressed his face.

"And if our kids grow up to have horrible tells when they fight, I'm blaming it on you."

"Hey!" she said, swatting him. "My tells were perfectly legitimate. I kicked your ass a time or two, didn't I?"

Chuckling, he drew her into a tender kiss. "You sure did. If we have kids, they're going to be tough as hell."

Wrapping her arms around his neck, her lips formed a beaming smile. "They'll be the best warriors in the kingdom. Can't fucking wait."

Consumed by her, Garridan trailed kisses over her face and neck before walking her inside and finishing the wine. Filled with the knowledge this would be the first night of so many spent together, he settled into his future with his magnificent Siora, the warrior who had stolen his heart and his perfect immortal mate.

Before You Go

Thanks so much for reading this fun, heartfelt, steamy story! I love when kick-ass women like Siora find their HEA. Hope you enjoyed it too! Thanks so much for spending some time in Etherya's Earth with me!

Have you read my **Prevent the Past** trilogy? It follows a brilliant scientist who must solve time travel and the handsome, mysterious soldier who offers his protection. **Let's just say LOTS of sparks fly!** Happy reading.

Sebastian's Fate

Etherya's Earth, Book 7.5

By

Rebecca Hefner

Contents

Title Page and Copyright
Dedication
Map of Etherya's Earth
Chapter 1
Chapter 2
Chapter 3
Chapter 4
Chapter 5
Chapter 6
Chapter 7
Chapter 8
Chapter 9
Chapter 10
Chapter 11
Chapter 12
Chapter 13
Chapter 14
Chapter 15
Before You Go
About the Author

This book is a work of fiction. Names, characters, places and incidents are the product of the author's imagination and are used fictitiously. Any resemblance to actual events, locales or persons, living or dead, is coincidental.

Copyright © 2023 by Rebecca Hefner. All rights reserved, including the right to reproduce, distribute or transmit in any form or by any means.

Cover Design: Anthony O'Brien, BookCoverDesign.store
Proofreading and Editing: Bryony Leah, www.bryonyleah.com

For Julie Burns and all the readers who asked for Celine and Sebastian's story after reading **Garridan's Mate.** I never expected so many people to want their story, and I'm thrilled to bring it to you. Thanks to all of you who love Etherya's Earth as much as I do!

Chapter 1

Sebastian, son of Astaroth, sat at his desk in the governor's mansion at Valeria angrily shuffling papers. Muttering as he found the document he needed, he shoved the rest away so he could concentrate. Narrowing his eyes, he read the decree from Queen Miranda and King Sathan:

To the Esteemed Governors and council members of the immortal realm:
In honor of the destruction of the ether and the imminent immersion with humans, it is imperative we learn the basics of their most popular traditions. As Prince Tordor and Princess Esme continue to slowly integrate the species, we feel it is important to become educated on their common practices.

One of the most important human holidays is Christmas, so this year we have chosen Valeria to hold a Christmas celebration for the realm. Any immortal is welcome to join and learn about the holiday, and Prince Heden's wife, Sofia, will be in attendance to help.

Although many revere Etherya in our realm and we encourage her worship, we see the benefit of learning about our new neighbors on the Earth. Etherya has given King Sathan her blessing to hold the Christmas festivities, and we hope you find them educational and enjoyable.

As always, we are your humble rulers and encourage anyone to contact us with questions.

Sincerely.

Queen Miranda and King Sathan

Swiping a hand over his face, Sebastian swore and reached for a blank piece of paper. He began to scrawl notes, reminding himself there was still much to do before next week's Christmas celebration.

The festivity would last several days, culminating in a lavish banquet to be held on the final night. A huge team had already been dispatched to cover Valeria's main square with Christmas-themed decorations, and he'd noticed the tinsel-wrapped streetlamps and poinsettia plants lining the street on his walk to the governor's mansion earlier that morning.

Sebastian only lived a few blocks from the mansion—a renovated castle that had resided in the center of the Valerian compound for centuries. Governor Camron lived there with his family, but it also held the council offices. It was close to Sebastian's home, so he usually walked to work. As the head of the Valerian council, he took his job seriously and was always early. He'd worked hard to become the youngest council leader in Vampyre history and was determined to prove his worth.

Even if he had to plan a four-day celebration for a human holiday he knew nothing about.

Gritting his teeth, he scowled when his friend Mila breezed into the room.

"Well, don't you look like you've been run over by a four-wheeler?" she chided, plopping into one of the leather chairs that faced his desk. Reaching over to the bowl that held fresh apples, she snagged one and bit off a huge chunk.

"Nice to see you too," he droned, "and please, help yourself."

"Thanks." Gesturing to his desk with the hand that held the apple, she squinted. "Still drowning in administrative crap for the Christmas celebration? Why don't you have Camron help you?"

"Camron is busy with the governor's duties, and as head of the council, it's a good way to show the older members I'm deserving of the title they all secretly crave."

"Still trying to prove you're the best," she said, taking another bite, her jaw working as she chewed. "Do you think one day you might actually believe it? You're the only one who still needs convincing. Everybody else respects you, Sebastian. Maybe it's time you took a *tiny* break and had some fun." She held her thumb and forefinger an inch apart. "Look at Garridan. He's head over heels for Siora, and I've never seen him happier. Maybe getting laid would take that scowl off your face too."

Shooting her a glare, Sebastian waited several seconds for effect before speaking. "I have no desire to get laid or spend time with any woman at the moment. I'm drowning in work here." He waved his hand over the multitude of paperwork. "On that note, I need your help."

"Oh no," she said, sitting up and tossing her apple in the nearby trash can. "I'm not going as your date to the gala. We've used each other as fake dates for long enough, and I'm ready to play the field a little."

Lifting his brows, he grinned. "No way. Mila, the staunch, independent woman, finally wants to find a mate?"

"*Mate* might be a stretch," she said, scrunching her features, "but the kingdom has evolved far enough that I can at least try." Her lips curved. "Queen Miranda, Governor Evie, and Princess Arderin have ushered in a new era for this realm, and I can finally hold my head high like the lesbian Vampyre I am and date who I want."

"Wow," he said, sitting back and rubbing his chin. "I'm proud to hear you say that, Mila. I've always respected who you are and hated you had to hide your true nature."

"You and Garridan have always accepted me even if the other stuffy aristocrats don't. I'm thankful for you both."

"But not enough to be my fake date to the Christmas gala."

Chuckling, she shook her head. "I can't keep being your fallback, Sebastian. I need to get out there, and you do too. It's time you found something else to focus on besides work."

"I like my work," he said, forming a small pout.

"And you're an excellent council leader, but you deserve companionship, and yes, I think you deserve some really good sex too."

Pursing his lips, he considered her words. "It *has* been a long time, but I don't even know where to start. You know I detest the aristocratic women Father wants me to date. They're all so vapid and boring."

"Well, I hate to break it to you, but you're an aristocrat too, so maybe *you're* boring."

Glancing at the mound of work on his desk, he breathed a laugh. "I want to argue with you, but you might be right. Regardless, I have no desire to date. If you won't go as my fake date, the least you can do is help me find someone else. You do run a matchmaking agency after all."

Mila had opened the matchmaking agency a year ago with tremendous success. Many Vampyres, Slayers, and reformed Deamons had found love through her services. Pride swelled in his chest that his friend had triumphed doing something she enjoyed.

"Yes, but all my clients *want* to fall in love. I can't set them up with someone who doesn't want a relationship."

"The Christmas gala is a masked formal affair. I won't even have to see the woman's face, for the goddess's sake, and she won't have to see mine. It can be a hands-off business transaction that will only last a few hours. If you can find an amenable client, tell her I'll purchase drinks for her all night and leave a gift certificate for five thousand lira in her name at the boutique in the main square." He pointed out the window to the sprawling street that led to the main square. "That should do it."

"You want to pay one of my clients to be your date?" Mila asked incredulously. "Come on, Sebastian. You're a good-looking guy with that mop of thick brown hair and those chocolate-brown eyes. Plus, I bet most women would think your fangs were cute if you ever smiled."

"I smile," he said, discounting the statement as he frowned.

"Rarely," was her sardonic response. "But seriously, if you put in a little effort, I'm sure you can find a date."

"I don't want the hassle," he said, shaking his head. "Please do this for me, Mila."

Rising, she placed her fist on her hip. "You're a pain in my ass, you know that?"

Chuckling, he stood and walked around the desk to gently grip her upper arms. "Just think about it, okay? Look through your client list and see if there's someone amenable. I'm sure there's a woman who needs some new fancy dresses. There always are on this stuffy compound."

Squinting one eye, she studied him. "Fine. I'll look through my list, but I don't think I'm going to find any—"

"Perfect," he said, turning and urging her toward the door. "I'm sure if you look hard enough you'll find the right woman." Gesturing across the threshold, he gave a slight bow. "I have faith in you, Mila. Now, let me get back to work. I have way too much to do and barely any time left to do it."

"One day, I'm going to find a mate for you out of sheer spite," she said, cocking a brow. "The work is always going to be there, Sebastian. You need to live a little—"

"Bye for now!" he interjected, waving and closing the door in her face.

"Hope you get a thousand papercuts!" she teased through the door.

Laughing, he strode back to the desk ready to finish the last of the planning so he could begin the final phase of ensuring everything was perfect. Hoping like hell Mila would take his request seriously, he didn't give any more thought to finding a date. No—Mila would come through for him, allowing him to mark that chore off his list.

Chapter 2

Celine, daughter of Handor, stood atop the ladder in her sprawling back yard, reaching for the juicy peach that was just out of reach. Her father had instructed their landscapers to plant a row of peach trees several years ago, and she loved the succulent fruit. Although Vampyres only needed Slayer blood for sustenance, they still ate food for pleasure.

Grunting, she reached further, gasping with excitement when she clutched the fruit. Tugging it from the branch, she wobbled on the ladder before slowly climbing down. Thrilled with her successful conquest, she sat on the soft grass and brushed the skin of the fruit with her hands. Satisfied, she took a bite and slowly chewed, savoring the taste.

"Look at you out here picking fruit like a laborer," Mila called as she approached. "Handor would have a fit."

"We all know I'm his favorite since I'm the only girl," was her cheeky reply as she took another bite. Swallowing, she grinned when Mila sat beside her. "Three brothers, but I'm the baby girl. What can I say?"

Chuckling, Mila rested her forearms on her bent knees. "Everyone underestimates you, Celine. It's a damn tragedy. They all think you're just some vapid aristocrat with a pretty face, but you're always plotting under all that beauty." She circled her hand over her face. "It's not fair to the rest of us normal-looking immortals."

Sighing, Celine leaned back, resting on her palm as she gazed over the rolling hills. "What does it matter anyway? No one seems to notice me in this stupid kingdom, and I might as well be an old spinster at this point."

"I think most men are intimidated by your wealth and looks—"

"I'm not wealthy," she said, lifting a finger. "My father is."

"True, but you're his responsibility until you find a mate and bond. So, technically, you're wealthy too."

"I guess." Sliding her hand over the soft grass, she frowned. "It also doesn't help that I'm determined to catch the eye of someone who doesn't even know I exist."

"Ah, Sebastian," Mila said, stretching out her legs and crossing one over the other. "He's determined not to notice *any* woman, believe me. I just had the most annoying conversation with him."

Celine's ears perked at the mention of the man she was slightly obsessed with—and who barely ever acknowledged her. "Do tell," she said, trying not to sound *too* interested.

"You know we always take each other as dates to the stupid galas we hate, but I want to attend the Christmas gala solo. There are a few ladies I have my eye on, and I don't want to squander the opportunity to secure some one-on-one time with them. Being by Sebastian's side isn't going to cut it."

"Oh," Celine said, trying to tamp down her excitement that he needed a date. Was there some way she could maneuver herself into the position? "That's lovely, Mila. I want you to find love."

"I want you to find love too, but you insist on pining for a man who isn't interested in anything but his council position."

"I've tried to get him to notice me so many times," Celine said wistfully, glancing down at the functional clothes she'd worn to pick fruit. "I never wear anything like this when I know he's going to be near. I always put my best foot forward, make sure my gown and makeup are perfect, and he still doesn't have a clue I'm alive."

"He's an idiot, Celine," Mila said, shrugging. "Most men are."

"Garridan even tried to help me. He thinks I'd be a good match for his brother. Remember when he took me to the fundraiser? We tried to make Sebastian jealous, but he only stayed for an hour and then went downstairs to his office to work."

"He's married to his job and too stubborn to open himself up to meeting a mate. It's no way to live, but you can't help someone who doesn't want to change."

Celine's eyebrows drew together. "Why was your conversation with him annoying?"

"Because he wants me to set him up with one of my clients for the Christmas gala."

"Oh…" Swallowing thickly, Celine tried to tamp down the jealousy that immediately swelled at the thought of him taking someone else. "What did you say?"

"No, of course," Mila said, bristling. "My clients want a relationship, and he doesn't. It wouldn't be fair to them."

"I wish my father would let me sign up for your matchmaking service. He says it's beneath my station."

"My dear," Mila said, leaning closer, "your father is a stick in the mud."

Tossing back her head, she laughed. "I guess he is. He's consumed with tradition and proper etiquette, but he tries. Still, I might wither away if I don't employ *some* new tactics to find a mate." Lifting her gaze to Mila's, Celine slowly cocked her eyebrow.

"Oh, no," Mila said, showing her palms. "I'm not falling for that. I can't set you up with Sebastian. You remember what he said to me, right?"

Her lips formed a pout as she nodded. "He told you he wasn't interested in me and thinks I would've been a better match for Garridan." Glancing over, she said, "Which isn't true. Obviously, Siora is Garridan's perfect mate."

"Sebastian is a proud man, Celine. Rumors were rampant about your possible betrothal to Garridan, so he'll never see you as a viable option. He doesn't want to be seen as the man who ended up with a woman his brother didn't choose. It's completely ridiculous, but he's hardheaded."

"Men," Celine huffed, cocking her arm before tossing the peach far into the meadow. "Screw him and his stupid pride. If he'd just be open, I could show him I'm not the bumbling idiot he thinks I am."

"I want you to be happy, Celine, but he might not be worthy of you. Perhaps there's someone better-suited for you out there. You'll never know unless you release this infatuation with a man who doesn't want you back." Covering her hand, she squeezed. "I'm not trying to be harsh, but I want the best for you."

Inhaling the fragrant air, Celine stared toward the horizon, wishing with all her might she could be open to someone else. It would be infinitely easier to focus on someone who actually *liked* her and didn't see her as a boring, empty-headed aristocrat.

Unfortunately, she was rather consumed with Sebastian. His broad shoulders, thick hair, and deep brown eyes should've appeared quite normal, but to her, they were gorgeous. His features were austere and aristocratic, and she often daydreamed about lying in his arms and trailing her finger down his nose. It may seem silly to others, but she craved that intimacy with a mate...with *him*.

Many across the kingdom saw Sebastian as rigid and unyielding, consumed with his council position. They'd never seen him as she had, when no one was watching. Celine loved to walk through the manicured neighborhoods of Valeria and often strolled by Sebastian's home. He still lived in his parents' house, as most aristocrats did until they bonded and had families, and she would observe him doing chores in the back yard as she strolled by.

Many aristocratic men would hire others to perform the duties, but she'd overheard Sebastian tell Garridan once that doing the menial tasks allowed him to release some steam and maintain his physique. Garridan had mumbled something about him needing to get laid, which had promptly caused her cheeks to flush and she'd rushed away, ashamed she was eavesdropping.

During her walks, Celine had observed him tackling many tasks. There were the times when he would chop wood, his skin glistening in the sun as rivulets of sweat ran down his chest between the spiky dark hairs. How would it feel to lick away the wetness? To drag her tongue over his copper-colored nipple as she gazed into his fathomless eyes?

"Earth to Celine," Mila interrupted, snapping her fingers. "Where did you go?"

"Just daydreaming," was her wistful reply as she curled her knees into her chest. "Did you know Sebastian chops wood for his parents' fireplace even though they have staff who could do it instead?"

Shooting her a derisive look, Mila droned, "Yeah, he's a saint."

"Oh, stop," Celine said, swatting her arm. "He also helped the little girl who lives next to them train all three of her puppies. He would get up early each morning and help Chandra before he went to work."

"That's nice to know, creepy stalker," Mila teased, leaning back on her palms. "Tell me more."

Ignoring her dismissive tone, Celine continued. "He also offered to hold Lila's literacy group sessions in his back yard when the governor's mansion was being renovated and the meeting rooms weren't available. Not only did he provide the space, but he helped teach the citizens to read."

"He's a council member. Maybe it was just to get in Lila's good graces. She *is* bonded to the king's brother after all."

"Goddess, you're cynical." Celine wrinkled her nose. "I think he's a genuine person who excels at his council job so he can prove to the world he's worthy. Being the oldest son carries great pressure. Xandor speaks about it often," she said, referencing her eldest brother.

"I actually said something similar to him earlier," Mila agreed, rubbing the back of her neck. "Maybe he is all gooey inside and just needs something to shake up his regimented demeanor so he'll stop working so much."

"You want to know the sweetest thing?" Celine asked, leaning forward as if imparting words of great importance.

Mila's eyebrows lifted as she nodded.

"One day when he was chopping wood, there were these two chipmunks who kept circling the stump. Instead of shooing them away, he picked up one of the leaves that had fallen from the nearby tree and fashioned it into a bowl. He poured some water from his canister into the leaf so they'd have fresh water to drink. Isn't that thoughtful?"

Glancing toward the sky, Mila rolled her eyes. "Goddess, please help my friend before she swoons to death."

"Oh, forget it," Celine said, stomping her foot in the grass. "I'm sorry I told you. I just think it's sweet."

Mila considered her for a moment before speaking. "Wow, you've got it bad for him. I wish things were different for you, Celine. I really do."

Turning to face her, Celine gently gripped her forearm. "Then let me go as his date to the Christmas gala."

Confusion entered her eyes. "I can't. He'll never agree to have you as his date. You may think he's Prince Charming, but he's made up his mind about you, Celine."

"Then don't tell him it's me."

Mila's mouth fell open, and she worked her jaw as she appeared baffled. "Um, that would be great, but you two have known each other forever. Not quite sure how—"

"I have a plan," Celine said with a confident nod. "You'll tell Sebastian that one of your clients agreed to be his 'business' date." She made quotation marks with her fingers.

"But it will be you?"

"Yes," Celine said, excitement blooming in her chest. "It's a masked gala, so I'll wear a mask the entire time, and also a wig." Pointing to her long blond hair, she lifted a shoulder. "I've always thought I'd look pretty good with black hair. This is a perfect time to try."

"You'd look great in a paper bag, Celine," Mila muttered, features scrunching as she considered her plan. "I think you're the most beautiful woman on the compound. But even if you wear a wig and a mask he'll see your eyes."

"Oh, eighty percent of Vampyres in the kingdom have ice-blue eyes. Since they're not rare, I'll be fine."

Tilting her head, Mila studied her. "Your eyes are still unique, Celine. Everyone's are. Windows into the soul and that whole thing."

With a harumph, Celine crossed her arms. "It's not like Sebastian has ever even looked me in the eye, so that's a moot point. He won't suspect a thing, trust me. He thinks I'm some timid wallflower content to drink tea and die of boredom each day."

Amusement, along with a faint glint of respect, lit Mila's eyes. "Damn, this plan is kind of badass. I admit I didn't expect it from you."

"Look, I know what people think of me, and I can only live the life I've known. Yes, I'm an aristocrat and I do my best to make my parents proud, but deep inside, I long to be so much more. This will allow me to explore being someone else for a night. It's so exciting!"

"And if he falls for it?" Mila asked, cupping Celine's shoulder. "What will you do then? What if he wants to kiss you? Or more?"

Wrinkling her nose, Celine pondered. "Well, I would certainly kiss him back. Goddess knows I've dreamed of it about a million times."

"And your virginity? What if he wants to go further?"

"Ah, yes, my aristocratic virginity that I must hold intact until I bond." Sighing, she plucked the grass as she spoke. "It's so stupid. I wish I were more experienced so I could please him..."

"Celine, giving your virginity to someone is a huge deal. Hell, I'm still a virgin too. You can't do that while you pretend to be someone else. It's not you."

Staring at the ground, Celine contemplated the words. "Maybe I could or maybe not. I won't know until I'm in the heat of the moment, I guess."

They sat for a moment considering all the outcomes—both successful and disastrous—before Mila finally spoke.

"It's crazy, Celine. The whole hair-brained scheme." Her lips curved into a mischievous grin. "But honestly, Sebastian could use some excitement in his life, and you could too." Gnawing her lip, she mulled over the details. "I can't believe I'm going to say this, but..." she waggled her eyebrows. "I think we should do it."

"Yeah?" Celine asked, trying not to give in to the urge to break into cartwheels on the open field.

"Yes," she said, facing her and crossing her legs. "I'll tell Sebastian I found a client named..."

"Anya," Celine said, eyes widening with eagerness. "I've always thought that name was so sexy. *Kiss me, Anya...*" she said in a deep voice, mimicking Sebastian's.

"Oh, brother," Mila said, rolling her eyes. "Okay, *Anya*, I'll set you up with Sebastian. But if he figures it out, I'm going to tell him it was your idea."

"Thank you, thank you, thank you!" Celine said, throwing her arms around her friend and hugging for dear life. "This is amazing. I'm finally going on a date with Sebastian!"

"No," Mila said, drawing back, "*Anya* is."

"Oh, whatever," she said, waving a dismissive hand. "I'll know it's me and that will be amazing."

"Celine," Mila said, taking her hands and squeezing affectionately. "This might not change anything. It might just be one night and you'll return to your regular lives afterward. I don't want you to be disappointed."

"I know," she said, nodding. "But maybe it will help me build my confidence at least. If he shows any sign of attraction to me, perhaps I can begin to believe *someone* will want to bond with me, even if it isn't him."

"You deserve to hold every confidence, Celine. You're beautiful, smart, and very strong-willed although your father hides you in a gilded cage. As I said, I think the men of this kingdom are idiots who are either too intimidated or too stupid to see your true brilliance. You're so much more than Handor's daughter."

"Thank you." Celine shook Mila's hands, gripping them by the wrists as they held each other. Mila had been her friend for many years, and she was grateful to have her in her sometimes sheltered life. "You deserve the same, Mila. I hope you find love one day."

"From your lips to the goddess's ears," Mila said, pointing to the sky. "I'll call Sebastian later today and give him the good news." Arching a brow, she muttered, "At least, I *think* it's good news."

Laughing, Celine rose, helping Mila stand before throwing an arm over her shoulders. "You'll see," she said as they began to stroll back to the house. "It's going to be fun."

They reached the front gate and Mila stepped onto the sidewalk. "Glad I saw you back there as I was walking to the office," she said, giving a salute. "It certainly was an interesting detour. I'll let you know what Sebastian says."

"You're the best, Mila!" Celine called as she trailed away.

Her friend lifted her arm, waving as she continued toward her matchmaking agency.

Emitting a tiny squeal, Celine clenched her hands in front of her chest, praying to the goddess she hadn't made a mistake.

Chapter 3

Sebastian received the call from Mila as he was walking home later that evening. Lifting the phone to his ear, he grinned.

"Tell me some good news."

"You'll never believe this, but I found a woman willing to put up with you—for one night at least."

Chuckling, he slipped his hand into his pants pocket, happy she'd found a "date" for him. "Who is she? Anyone I know?"

"Nope. Her name is Anya and she requested to stay anonymous."

"Anonymous...how?"

"She agreed to be your gala date, but she wants to keep the mask on the whole time. It's the only way she'll attend."

Kicking a pebble in his path, he frowned as curiosity and a slight bit of disappointment welled within. "Is this personal? How can a woman I've never met hate me?"

"So he does have a heart," Mila murmured, causing him to scowl. "It's not personal, Sebastian. She lives at Astaria and has never heard of you. You have a clean slate. Don't fuck it up."

Relief coursed through him. "Okay. Is it strange to say I'm slightly excited to meet this mystery woman?"

"Not at all. I'm thrilled you're excited at the possibility of dating. Maybe after you and 'mystery girl' finish your date, you can focus on someone you actually have a chance with. Celine maybe?"

Sighing, he shook his head. "We've been over this, Mila. Celine is lovely but reminds me of a porcelain doll. She's the embodiment of 'seen and not heard.' I don't think I've ever heard her utter more than five words."

"Um, it's hard to speak to someone who rarely exists outside of his office. And have you ever tried to speak to her? You might be surprised."

"Look, I know you two are good friends, although I can't fathom what someone with your gregarious personality talks about with someone as mousy as Celine."

Her laugh wafted over the phone, causing him to scowl.

"What the hell are you laughing at?"

"You. I don't even feel bad anymore. I did for a while, but you deserve what's coming to you."

Baffled, Sebastian harshly rubbed his forehead. "I have no idea what the hell you're talking about."

"Oh, you will," she said, her tone mischievous. "Anyway, Anya will meet you promptly at seven in front of Lady Anne's Boutique in the main square. She's going to take you up on your offer to buy her a plethora of fancy gowns."

"Fine with me."

"You have to wear your mask the entire time, and she hers. That's the deal. Are we clear, Sebastian?"

"Crystal. Thanks for doing this, Mila. I owe you one."

"Just have fun and keep an open mind, okay?"

"I always keep an open mind," he said with a small pout.

The infuriating woman laughed so hard she snorted. Annoyed, he waited for the guffaws to abate.

"Are you finished?" he droned.

"Sorry, the 'open mind' thing threw me for a second. Have a good night, Sebastian. See you at the gala."

"See you there. Thanks again, Mila."

Clicking off the phone, he continued home as curiosity about his upcoming mystery date welled deep within.

"Well, he's as happy as a clam." Mila's voice chimed over the phone as Celine sat on her bed painting her toenails.

The phone was on speaker where it sat on her comforter, and she grinned as she drew the tiny brush over her pinkie toenail.

"He doesn't suspect anything?"

"Nope. I told him you were from Astaria and had never heard of him. So you can't indicate you know anything about him, okay?"

"Got it. I picked out this gorgeous dark green gown that's going to knock his socks off. I figured that fits with the whole Christmas theme, right?"

"Your guess is as good as mine. Who'd have thought we'd ever need to learn about the traditions of human heathens?"

Chuckling, Celine recapped the polish and reached for the clear setting gel. "I think it's exciting. A whole new species we're going to eventually integrate with. It's noble of Tordor and Esme to pave the path for us."

"It is. I mean, he gave up his kingdom to live with her in the human realm and slowly integrate the species. Talk about some true damn love."

Sighing, Celine rested her chin on her upturned knee. "Do you think we'll find it one day, Mila?"

"I sure hope so. On that note, I've got to dig through my closet and find something to wear on Saturday. It won't be as fancy as your outfit, I'm sure, but I still plan to knock a lady or two's socks off."

"You're going to look beautiful. You're so confident and genuine. It makes you absolutely stunning, Mila."

"Well, thanks for confirming you're the nicest person ever. Give Sebastian hell. He's going to meet you in front of Lady Anne's Boutique in the main square. As payment for your 'service,' he's also going to deposit a five-thousand-lira stipend in Anya's name for you to buy anything your heart desires."

"I don't need anything," Celine said, glancing toward her closet.

"I know, but the slightly twisted part of me makes him want to pay anyway."

Laughing, Celine wiggled her toes as they dried. "You're too much. If he leaves a stipend, I'll just give it to charity. Goddess knows many others need it more than me."

"You're a good egg, Celine. I wish more people knew the real you."

"So do I," was her soft reply as she ruminated on how others in the kingdom saw her. Meek. Biddable. Boring. Perhaps her luck was about to change...even if she were anonymous. "Sweet dreams, Mila. See you Saturday. Or should I say, *Anya* will see you Saturday...?"

Mila's chuckle wafted through the phone. "See you Saturday."

The phone went dark, and Celine plopped back on the bed, her golden hair splaying over the pillow. Yes, Saturday would be here soon enough, and she was determined to show the world she could be someone other than the woman everyone had already decided she was.

Chapter 4

The day of the gala arrived and Celine racked her brain for an acceptable excuse not to accompany her parents and brothers to it. When she didn't have a date for formal events, she always attended with her family. Of course, tonight, that was impossible.

Since Vampyres had self-healing abilities she couldn't feign sickness. But Vampyres still experienced occasional headaches and exhaustion, so she figured she'd use that excuse and hope her father believed her. She rarely missed formal functions since it was important to her father that she represent their family in public. But she also knew her father well, and he detested talking about anything personal—especially when it came to female issues. Snickering, she decided she'd lay it on thick and hope he took the bait.

"Father?" she called, entering his downstairs office.

Looking up from his desk, he smiled under his thick beard. "Hello, sweetheart. I thought you'd be getting ready for the gala."

"About that," she said, resting her hand on her abdomen and splaying it wide. "I was really looking forward to it, but I'm not feeling well."

Narrowing his eyes, he sat back, lacing his fingers behind his head as he studied her. "I'm sure it will pass. These things always do for our kind."

"Normally, I would agree, but you see...well, this is quite embarrassing to tell my father, but it's my time of the month, and my...uh...flow is heavier than normal—"

"For the goddess's sake, Celine," he interjected, scowling as he rested his forearms on the desk. "It's not polite to speak such things aloud."

"I know." Twining her hands in front of her abdomen, she continued, observing him as he grew more uncomfortable by the second. *Perfect.* "Some months are easier than others, but the cramping is terrible, and I fear it will get worse—"

"Fine," he said, holding up a hand and rising. Striding over, he slid his arm across her shoulders. "I can't hear anymore. It's not proper, dear. I'm sorry you're not feeling well. I'll let the royal family know you wished to attend but couldn't." Kissing her forehead, he frowned. "Now, please, no more talk of these private matters, okay?"

"Yes, Father," she said, bowing slightly to hide her grin. "Thank you."

"Feel better, dear." He patted her shoulder, effectively sending her on her way. "I'll tell you all about it tomorrow."

Pivoting, she breezed out of the room, thrilled her plan had worked. She would make sure to avoid her family at the gala since they were the only ones with a chance of recognizing her in her disguise.

Armed with her freedom—for one night at least—she returned to her room, counting the minutes until her family departed so she could head into the balmy night to meet Sebastian.

Sebastian straightened his bow tie in the mirror, ensuring it was perfectly aligned. Checking his cuff links, he took one last look at his reflection before reaching for the mask on his bed. It was white, which complimented his crisp white shirt underneath his tuxedo. Securing the elastic strap behind his head, he maneuvered it around his eyes and over his cheeks until it was firmly in place. Giving one last nod to his reflection, he turned to head downstairs and lock up the house.

His father had already left for the gala, his mother dashing on his arm in her red gown. Once he met his "date" in front of Lady Anne's, he was sure he'd find them in the grand ballroom at Valeria's main castle.

Striding down the sidewalk, Sebastian clenched his hands at his sides, wondering why he was nervous. It wasn't as if this were a *real* date. Both parties were completing a transaction. He would satisfy society's rules by having someone by his side, and the lady would get gobs of new clothes with the stipend he left at the boutique. A few hours of work with rewards for both.

Then why does tonight feel different?

He had no idea, but perhaps it was the mystery of it all. It wasn't every day he went on a clandestine date with a secret companion. Perhaps he was just reacting to the strange circumstances.

The main square was quiet as most Vampyres were already at the gala. Music wafted from the castle, faint and festive, as Sebastian approached the boutique. Focusing on the figure who slowly came into view, his breath caught in his throat as he studied her.

A long, forest green gown covered a tall body, willowy with slight curves. Long, black hair fell straight down her back, softly flitting in the breeze. Her skin seemed to glow in the moonlight, and his palms suddenly tingled with the urge to touch it...caress it...to see if it was as soft as it appeared.

She turned, facing him fully, and Sebastian felt a jolt in his solar plexus. Her ice-blue eyes shone bright, almost glowing under the stars, and he expelled a breath as he drew closer. Many Vampyres had blue eyes, but hers held the perfect twinge of mischief and innocence. Feeling his body harden, he halted when mere inches separated them.

"Anya?"

White fangs glistened as she smiled under her mask. It was made of elegant black lace and covered her from the tip of her nose to her eyebrows. Black eyelashes extended from those stunning eyes, and his heartbeat escalated as he waited for her to speak.

"You must be Sebastian."

Her voice was husky and slightly hesitant, giving him a small bit of relief. Perhaps he wasn't the only one who'd somehow lost control of his rapid heartbeat. Reaching into his pocket, he pulled out a small corsage.

"It's a poinsettia flower with festive green leaves. I passed a street vendor yesterday who was selling them for the gala and I thought you might like to wear it. If it doesn't clash with your dress," he finished lamely, wondering if he sounded like a dolt. Did men buy women corsages anymore? Hell if he knew. He'd lived for centuries and had no idea what modern dating traditions entailed. When he'd passed the vendor yesterday, he bought it on a whim, wanting to support a small business owner. It also prevented him from showing up empty-handed, but now he was doubting the decision.

"It's lovely," she said, spurring a relieved breath from his chest. "Will you pin it on me? Right here should do." She tapped the collar of her gown, and his eyes trailed to the place where the small swell of her breast rested underneath the silky fabric.

Nodding, he stepped forward, lifting his hand and reclaiming her gaze. "I need to lift the fabric a bit..."

"It's fine," was her raspy reply.

Gently gripping the fabric, he slid the pointed tip of the safety pin through, threading it until he could clasp it. Noticing the slight shake of his hands, he wondered when the hell he'd turned into a nervous schoolboy who couldn't retain his wits. Her skin flushed as he finished clasping the corsage, and he suddenly had images of licking the heated flesh as she pulled him close. Determined to control his reaction, he patted the corsage before stepping back.

"Looks perfect with your dress. You look beautiful, Anya."

One of her gorgeous eyebrows arched. "Even though you can't see my face? Who knows, I could be hideous under here." She pointed to her mask.

Chuckling, he extended his arm. "I don't think so. May I walk you to the gala?"

"Why, of course." She wrapped her arm around his, and they began the three-block walk to the governor's mansion.

"I can't thank you enough for agreeing to this," he said, smiling into her upturned face as they strolled. "I'm a council member and my life is consumed with work. I just don't have time to date."

"I understand. Mila was very clear you aren't interested in any romantic entanglements."

I wasn't...until I saw you standing in the moonlight...

Clearing his throat, he tamped down the inner dialogue. "And what of you? How is it possible none of the bachelors at Astaria snapped you up to be their date?"

"Men are a stubborn lot who only see what they wish to see. I can only assume I wasn't interesting enough to catch anyone's eye."

"Impossible," he breathed, inhaling her scent, which was an intoxicating mixture of roses and evergreen. Sweet and wild, both at once. It suited her perfectly.

Lifting those piercing blue eyes to his, she murmured, "I assure you, Sebastian, it is entirely possible."

He studied her, noticing the white flecks in the blue of her irises...feeling as if he'd stared into them before. As his eyebrows drew together, he asked, "Have we met before? You seem familiar to me."

Something flashed in her eyes, and for a moment he thought it was fear. But it disappeared as quick as lighting, and she straightened her spine. "I rarely leave Astaria, so I doubt it. My parents are aristocrats who decided not to attend tonight because they didn't want the hassle of taking the train to Valeria. Hence why I needed a date. I usually accompany them to formal functions, and didn't want to come solo."

"Well, I'm happy to be of service." He winked and regally circled his hand a few times in front of his waist. "How do you know Mila?"

"I reached out to her several months ago, informing her I would be open to dating but wasn't in the market for a serious relationship yet. Most of her clients are looking for something serious, so it never panned out. Until you," she finished with a cheeky grin.

Thanking the goddess for his fortuity, he vowed not to squander the evening. He had the entire night to talk to her, dance with her...and perhaps even kiss her if the moment felt right. As he gazed at her lips his shaft hardened in his tuxedo pants. He anticipated nibbling them as she moaned in his arms. Her tongue darted out to bathe them, coating the pink flesh with wetness that shone under the street lamps, and he almost groaned. Goddess, he wanted that tongue on his. *Tonight.*

"I'm honored to have you as my date, even if it's only one night and I can't see your face. Or perhaps I can convince you to remove the mask as the night progresses. I *have* been known to be stubbornly persistent. Mila says I'm extremely hardheaded."

Her laughter surrounded them, silky and low, and she shook her head. "The mask stays on. That was the deal."

"I know." He squeezed her wrist. "And I'll also deposit the money at the boutique on Monday. I'm a man of my word."

Her soft grin shot tremors of pleasure through his pulsing body. "I believe you are. Thank you, Sebastian."

They arrived at the mansion, Sebastian walking her up the red-carpeted staircase as the music wafted over them. Once inside, he said obligatory hellos to his friends and fellow council members, introducing Anya as his "friend." Eventually, they made their way to one of the bars in the corner of the ballroom, and he leaned his forearm against it.

"What would you like to drink?"

She perused the bar, gnawing her lip as she pondered. Mesmerized by the action, he didn't hear her when she replied.

"Sebastian?" she called, waving her hand in front of his face.

"Hmm? Sorry. What did you say?"

"Champagne, please."

"Yes, ma'am."

Drawing his wallet from his pocket, he pulled out a stack of liras and gave them to the bartender. "Please keep them coming, and you can keep what's left."

"Sir," the bartender said, counting the bills, "this is seven hundred lira. The drinks are only ten lira each and the proceeds go toward Prince Tordor's human immersion fund."

"I understand. Subtract whatever we have from the total amount and keep the rest as your tip. I already contribute heavily to the immersion fund and want to make sure you and your fellow bartenders are taken care of. You pool tips, right?"

"Yes, sir," he said, excitement lacing his tone. "That's very generous. Thank you." Depositing the money in the cash drawer, he poured Anya's drink before Sebastian ordered a beer.

Once they had their drinks in hand, Sebastian suggested they head to the balcony for some fresh air. Splaying his hand on the small of her back, he led them outside, craving one-on-one time with her so he could get to know her better.

Chapter 5

Celine clenched the glass, her knuckles white with nerves as Sebastian escorted her to the balcony. The heat of his hand sizzled against her back, and she wanted nothing more than to close her eyes and lean into his touch. But they were in public, and he had no idea who she really was, so that fantasy was quickly shooed from her thoughts.

For one moment as they were walking to the gala, he gazed into her eyes and she swore she saw recognition. But alas, he didn't recognize her, and for that, Celine should be grateful.

This is what you wanted, Celine. He's never taken the time to see you. Why do you think he would start now?

"How about here?" he asked, directing them to a secluded spot at the far corner of the sprawling balcony. Resting her forearms on the cool stone, she took a sip of champagne and sighed. "Never can go wrong with fancy champagne on a warm moonlit night, can you?"

"Never," he said, leaning on the balcony beside her. His fingers twirled the glass in his hands as they overlooked the manicured lawn lined with holly bushes planted specifically for the Christmas theme.

"Christmas happens in winter for humans in the Northern hemisphere," he said, "but I do enjoy the warm nights in our realm."

"Me too." Glancing up at him, she reminded herself to ask questions. After all, he was supposed to be a perfect stranger to her. "So, tell me about the council position."

Wrinkling his nose, he considered for a moment before shaking his head. "Usually, I love to talk about my job, but tonight I want to get to know you." His arm scooted closer to hers on the railing, the fabric of his coat brushing against her skin and making it tingle. "Why don't you want a serious relationship? I don't because of my work. What's your excuse?"

Laughing, she shrugged. "Aristocratic women have had the same role for centuries in our kingdom. Queen Miranda and Governor Evie are slowly changing that, but it takes time. I've always been raised to be a proper, refined wife, but honestly, that just sounds so *boring*."

"That it does," he said, chuckling. "If you could do anything, without the restraints of society, what would it be?"

Gazing wistfully at the sky, she released a slow breath. "This probably sounds ridiculous, but I'd like to train children on horses. I was quite fearful of horses when I was young, and we had a fantastic trainer who was extremely patient and helped me get over my fears."

"That doesn't sound ridiculous at all. It's quite noble."

"Not the way my father sees it," she muttered. "I want to teach children everything, not just riding. I think it's important they know how to muck out the stalls, clean the horses, feed them, and everything else. My instructor taught me all those things..."—she traced the balcony as the sad memories surfaced—"until my father realized. He fired the man on the spot because he was teaching me laborer's work. He was only supposed to teach me to ride. The other duties were to be left to the staff."

"Ah, I see." Sebastian's face was contemplative as he sipped his beer. "Old traditions of the Vampyre kingdom are deeply embedded, especially in the older generations. Your father probably thought he was protecting your aristocratic nature or some such nonsense."

Her eyes widened as she studied him. "You wouldn't have a problem with an aristocratic woman doing laborer's work...and making a living from it?"

Pursing his lips, he pondered. "I don't think so if it made her happy. Hell, Anya, our lives are long. If we're not doing want makes us happy, what's the damn point?"

Smiling, she lifted her glass. "Exactly."

Clinking their glasses, they gazed into each other's eyes as they drank.

Sebastian's eyes smoldered behind his white mask, causing her breath to hitch. Ever so slowly, he reached over and brushed the skin of her shoulder.

"A piece of pollen," he said softly, his fingers swiping her skin in a soft caress. "All gone."

His touch lingered as if he didn't want to pull away, and she felt the thrumming of her heartbeat in her throat. Struggling to breathe, she gazed into his deep brown eyes, wondering if she'd ever been in such close proximity to him. His musky scent filled her nostrils, and she fought the urge to close her eyes and savor it. Feeling her throat bob, she searched for something to say to break the heavy silence.

"My dear Anya," he said, lowering his hand and giving a formal bow. "I fear I cannot go another moment without dancing with you." Extending his hand, his fangs glowed atop his lower lip as he smiled. "Will you please do me the honor?"

Setting her glass on the ledge, she took his hand, nodding since her throat was too dry to speak. Sebastian had finally asked her to dance after all these years. Well, he'd asked *Anya*, but still, it was extremely special to her.

Knowing she would cherish every moment his body was pressed to hers on the dance floor, she followed him inside, her steps echoing in tandem with her rapid heartbeat.

∞

Sebastian led Anya to the dance floor, hoping she didn't notice the slight sheen of sweat on his palm. Her proximity was like a tuning fork; the closer she got, the more every cell in his frame seemed to vibrate. Leading her to the dance floor, he slid one arm around her waist and held up his other one.

"Is this okay?"

She nodded, the lower half of her cheeks flushing as she took his hand. Gently gripping her waist, he began to move. Forward...back...in the rhythm of the formal dance steps he'd learned as a child, while the band played in the background.

Anya matched him step for step, and he was impressed with her skills. "You're an excellent dancer."

"A must for a proper aristocratic Vampyre female, no?" She cocked a brow as they swayed.

"Absolutely. Still, I think I'd rather see how you fare mucking a stall. For some reason, I can't imagine it."

Tossing her head back, she laughed, exposing the line of her throat. Sebastian's fangs itched to touch her there...to scrape the delicate skin as she clutched his shoulders, begging for more...

"Well, my father owns our stables and I'm on strict orders not to go inside. The horse must be prepared for me by the staff so I can ride it without getting dirty." Sighing, her lips formed a slight pout. "It's so fun to get dirty though."

"I think I'd like to get dirty with you," he murmured before he could stop the silken words.

Her hand tightened as her lips fell open, slightly stunned. But Sebastian also saw the burning desire in her eyes, and a thrill shot down his spine that she felt their attraction too.

"Did I shock you, darling?" he asked, drawing her closer as their bodies moved in tandem. "I would apologize, but I think you liked it."

A stuttered breath left her lungs before she formed a slight grin. "I *did* like it," she whispered. "For someone who doesn't want a relationship, you certainly are a flirt."

"Only with women who will disappear at midnight, leaving me heartbroken and alone," he teased. "So, I need to take advantage of our time together."

Leaning into him, she rested her cheek on his chest, withdrawing her hand from his and sliding it around his neck. "I would like that," she murmured, pressing her body closer to his. "You can take advantage of me until midnight, Sebastian."

Gliding his arm around her waist, he spread both palms over her back, caressing it through the silken fabric of her dress. Pressing his cheek against her hair, he melded their bodies, marveling at how well they fit. Her lithe frame and subtle curves pushed against his firm muscles, and he almost sighed in contentment.

As they danced and he inhaled her fragrant skin, another aroma wafted toward his nostrils. Clenching his teeth, a muscle flexed in his jaw as he smelled her arousal. Vampyres had highly evolved senses, and males could inherently smell a female's arousal. It was extremely intoxicating, and his body jumped into action, ready to mate. His cock sprang to life inside his pants, and his heart hammered in his chest as he wondered if she would push him away.

He knew the moment she felt his rapidly swelling cock push against her lower abdomen. Inhaling a quick breath, her fingers tightened on the back of his neck.

"I'm sorry," he whispered, half-embarrassed and half-joyful she knew he was aroused. Sebastian was an extremely forthright man, and he had no desire to hide his attraction. Hell, he wanted nothing more than to kiss her before the night was over, so she might as well know he was viscerally attracted to her.

"Do you want to stop dancing?"

She shook her head against his chest, and his eyes narrowed at the feel of her hair along his jaw. For some reason, it felt coarser than he'd imagined. More synthetic in a way. Still, he reveled in having her pressed against him and felt the tension leave his muscles when he spoke.

"You must smell my arousal," she said softly. The skin of her neck turned a deep red, and he chuckled at her embarrassment.

"Thank the goddess the lights are dim and we're on the corner of the dance floor. Our bodies seem to have a mind of their own, although I'm not complaining."

"Me neither." Her arms tightened around his neck, and he took the cue, tugging her so close their bodies seemed to morph together. His erection stood proud against her stomach as her desire-laced scent surrounded them, and Sebastian held tight, wishing the night would never end.

Eventually, the band took a break and the lights were raised so Sofia could address the room. After completing the very difficult task of letting Anya go, he led her to stand with the other immortals so they could hear the speech.

"Thank you all so much for coming to our Christmas gala," Sofia said, lifting her wineglass to the gala attendees. "Christmas is a very special time for human Christians like me. I know you all worship Etherya, and I'm honored she gave her blessing to throw this fete."

"Plus, it allows me to show off my DJ skills," Heden said, throwing his arm around Sofia's shoulders and lifting his beer. "I have the coolest playlist. You all are going to love it—"

"Not happening!" Miranda's voice chimed from the back of the room.

"Jeez, Miranda, let a brother live a little," Heden said as the crowd chuckled. "I know you secretly love my playlists. I made one specifically for you and my brother to knock boots so you could have a new heir, and look how that turned out."

"You're *not* getting credit for this," Miranda said, rubbing her extended belly as Sathan's thick arm surrounded her, his expression morose at his brother's antics. "Although I think Sathan *did* develop an unhealthy obsession with human pop music thanks to your playlist."

"If I have to listen to Lizzo one more time, I'll burst my own damn eardrums," Sathan droned, squeezing Miranda's shoulder. "You created a monster."

"Okay, okay, *I'm* the one who likes pop music. Who knew? Lizzo's pretty badass, and it's catchy." She grinned at Sathan and scrunched her features. "Anyway, carry on, Sofia."

Laughing, Sofia continued. "To close, I'd like to remind you we have several stations you can swing by to learn more about our culture. I'm running one, and Evie and Arderin are too since they lived in the human world and have experience there."

Both women waved, flashing welcoming grins as they stood beside Miranda and Sathan.

"And now, I urge you to have fun and remember, if you walk underneath mistletoe, you have to kiss the person closest to you. Enjoy!"

The crowd gave a raucous cheer before dispersing, many heading to the various stations to learn about the Christmas story, the three wise men, Santa Claus, and more.

Turning to Anya, Sebastian asked, "Do you want to visit any of the stations?"

Biting her lip, a hint of mischief flared in her eyes. "I know we should, but is it terrible that I don't want to? We only have two hours before I walk back to the train, and I was having so much fun dancing. Maybe we can have another drink on the balcony and wait for the band to start again..."

"I'd love that." Extending his hand, he gestured for her to lead. "After you, darling."

She shivered slightly at the endearment, causing Sebastian's heart to *thunk* in his chest. Determined to whisper the tender word in her ear before the night was over, he followed her to the bar, enamored by the gentle sway of her hips in the stunning gown.

Chapter 6

After another round of playful and intimate conversation, Celine danced with Sebastian until the band played their last song. As the lights lifted and people began to exit the ballroom, she lifted sad eyes to her handsome date.

"Well, I guess that's our cue to leave. I was having so much fun."

"Me too." Hesitation lined his expression as he held out his hand. "Can I at least walk you to the train? I promise I'll be a perfect gentleman."

Nodding, she placed her hand in his, and they exited the mansion to the sidewalk. Setting a leisurely pace, Celine placed her arm in the crook of his, hoping to draw out her time with him as much as possible. How could she ever go back to real life where he ignored her? A small part of her wanted to rip off the wig and mask, grab his arms, and shake him.

"*Look at me*," she would plead as he finally understood it was *her*, the woman he'd been intent on ignoring for centuries.

But that was a fantasy for a woman more confident than Celine. Although she was proud of herself for her courage this evening, it only went so far. After years of rejection, she just didn't dare to take a chance. If he rejected her, she might not survive the emotional fallout.

So, she walked with him to the train, reveling in how charming he was as they chatted. When they arrived at the underground platform, she turned to face him, feeling nervous. Crossing her arms over her chest, she rubbed them, wondering if he would try to kiss her.

"I had a lovely time," he said.

"Me too. Thank you, Sebastian."

"Come, let's have a bit of privacy." After leading them to a secluded spot under some nearby trees, he reached into his jacket pocket. Pulling out a bundle of mistletoe, he flashed a grin as he held it over her head. "Would I be extremely cheesy if I stole this from the party so I'd have an excuse to kiss you?"

Breathing a laugh, she stepped closer, threading her arms around his neck. "You don't need an excuse, but it's very cute." Rising to her toes, she whispered, "Please kiss me, Sebastian."

His arm snaked around her waist as he tossed the mistletoe aside. Drawing her into his warm body, he slid his hand to her nape, supporting her as his fingers slid over the cap of the wig.

"Oh, I...uh...just got my hair done, so my scalp is very tender. Probably better to hold my neck."

A strange look crossed his expression before he nodded, sliding his hand down and cupping her neck. "Like this?" he murmured, moving closer.

"Like that," she sighed, thankful he hadn't realized she was wearing a wig.

Grazing her lips with his, he gently pushed them open before sliding his tongue over her top lip...and then her bottom one...

Celine groaned, her eyes closing as elation coursed through her frame. Spearing her fingernails into his neck, she urged him closer, her body shuddering at his low growl.

His tongue speared into her mouth, licking...tasting...as she tentatively touched her tongue to his.

"Yes, darling..." he rasped, sucking her tongue between his full lips...drawing her further into the kiss. "Use that sexy little tongue and kiss me back. Show me you want me half as much as I want you."

Whimpering with desire, she slid her tongue in one slow stroke over his, a small laugh escaping her throat when he cursed.

"Damn, woman," he groaned, nipping her lip with his fangs. "You're going to kill me. Do that again."

Feeling her confidence soar, she began to kiss him in earnest, sliding her tongue over his, moving her lips in tandem with his thick ones as he pressed his erection into her stomach. His tongue mated with hers, darting over every crevice of her mouth before he drew back and trailed a line of kisses over her cheek to her ear. Resting his mouth against the shell of her ear, he whispered, "Take off the mask, Anya."

"Noooo…" she moaned, her knees buckling when he licked the sensitive shell of her ear before gently biting the lobe.

"Please, sweetheart. This can't be the end. I need to see you again."

"I can't," she said, placing her palms on his chest but unable to push him away. "Only one night. We had a deal."

Lifting his head, his deep brown eyes searched hers, filled with lust and blazing regret. "I never should've agreed to one night. I didn't think this would happen."

Needing to break contact, she turned, resting her head in her hand. "Sebastian, I…oh goddess, this is a mess…"

His fingers trailed over the back of her neck as he brushed the long hair of the wig aside, placing it to lie over her shoulder. Replacing his fingers with his lips, he trailed soft kisses over the swell of her shoulder while her body shook with desire.

"You have a birthmark here," he murmured against her skin. A moment later, she felt his wet tongue glide over the mark above her shoulder blade. "I'd love to see your other ones, Anya. Perhaps you have one on your leg too." His hand trailed over her thigh toward the slit in her dress. "Or on your inner thigh…"

Wanting to sob in frustration, she halted his hand before it could slip under her dress. "I'm sorry," she whispered, wishing she'd never come up with the stupid scheme. Now that she'd kissed him, it would be impossible to stop pining for him. Furthermore, he was now infatuated with a woman who didn't exist. Cursing herself, she turned and placed her palms on his pecs.

"I had a lovely time, but I have to go. Thank you, Sebastian. I wish you all the best. Good night."

Turning, she tried to flee, but he grabbed her wrist, halting her. "Please, Anya, if you just give me a chance—"

A frustrated huff left her lips as she clenched her fist. "A chance? A chance?" Telling herself not to blow it, she tamped down the exasperated scream lodged in the back of her throat. "You're a fool, Sebastian, but I'm no better. This was a mistake. Good night."

Dislodging her wrist from his grasp, she turned and ran to the platform, disappearing down the stairs to the underground station as he called her name.

Called *Anya's* name.

Not wanting him to follow her, she ran to the bathroom, knowing someone as polite as Sebastian would never follow her inside. And then she waited...for what seemed like hours, but it was only minutes in the scheme of things.

Stepping toward the long mirror above the sinks, she took off her mask and wig, massaging her scalp as she set her blond hair free. Staring deep into her own eyes, her chin trembled as she realized she was doomed. Never would she forget the taste of Sebastian on her lips...or her tongue...or *in her mouth*...

Touching her lips, she licked them, savoring the taste of the man she'd loved since she knew what the word meant. Then she picked up her wig and mask and left the station. Her walk home was brisk since she wanted nothing more than to curl up in her bed and cry.

Once she got home, she snuck through the back door and tiptoed up the stairs. After washing her face and brushing her teeth, she slid into bed, knowing her family believed she'd been there all night.

"You never should've lied to them, Celine," she said, punching the pillow. "You never should've lied to *him*. Oh goddess, what have I done?"

Clutching the pillow close, she buried her face in the soft feathers and cried herself to sleep.

Chapter 7

Sebastian walked home from the train in a daze, confused by how things had gone so horribly wrong. One minute, he was involved in the most erotic kiss of his life. The next, Anya was pulling away and running to the station. After he'd recovered from the shock, he jogged down the stairs to find her. She'd all but disappeared, and he certainly didn't want to make the situation worse by seeking out a woman who was vehemently trying to flee, so he'd trudged up the platform stairs and headed home.

Once back in his father's opulent mansion, he slid into bed and settled in the darkness. Wondering how it had all gone wrong, he slid his hands under his head on the pillow as the ceiling fan whirled above.

"You should've never asked her to remove the mask, Sebastian," he muttered, furious with himself. "It was the one stipulation you agreed to, and you blew it." Rolling over, he punched the pillow, knowing he would get no rest as thoughts of Anya flitted through his mind.

∞

On Monday, Sebastian walked to work, noting the streets had been cleared of the Christmas decorations. They were disassembled and put away, vanished as effectively as his sultry night with Anya. Scoffing, a part of him wondered if it had all been a dream.

During lunch, he strolled to the boutique and opened a private account in Anya's name.

"Do you have her father's name, sir?"

"No," he mused as his eyebrows drew together. Citizens in the immortal world didn't use last names. Instead, they were referred to by their father's name. He was Sebastian, son of Astaroth. And Anya was the daughter of...well, he had no idea since he'd agreed to her anonymity.

"When she comes in to claim it, ask her what it's for. She'll mention the Christmas gala. I think that will be enough to identify her."

"Will do, sir," the owner said. "This is a nice stipend, and I appreciate your business."

Always happy to support a local business owner, he gave her a brisk nod before leaving.

Instead of heading back to his office, Sebastian trailed through town, ending up at Mila's office. Hell, he didn't even know his legs were carrying him there until his hand was on the doorknob. Turning it, he stepped inside as the bell rang above his head.

"Well, look what the cat dragged in," she said, threading her hands behind her head as she sat at the desk in the small office. "You look like crap."

"I can always count on you to bring my ego down a few notches," he muttered, lowering into the chair in front of her desk. Resting his palms on the smooth surface, he lightly gripped the wood. "I need to know how to contact her, Mila. Please."

"Wow," she breathed, leaning back in her chair and crossing her ankles atop her desk. "I can't believe it. You're interested in a woman. I'd almost given up hope."

"I don't know what it was about her." He circled his hand, leaning back in the chair and resting his forehead on his fingers. "Maybe it was the mystery of it all. I've never felt attraction like this. It was just...*easy* with her, you know?"

Mila squinted one eye as she bit the inside of her cheek. "I think you're right. The anonymity and lack of commitment allowed you to relax and be open. And once you were open, your attraction and intuition took over."

"Maybe," he said, rubbing his forehead. "I did feel relaxed with her. Bachelors in our kingdom are always on guard because meddling parents are trying to make bonding matches. Since that wasn't a possibility with her, I felt free."

"I'm glad to hear that, Sebastian, honestly, but I can't give you her identity. You know that."

Frustrated, he picked at a stray thread on the side of his dress pants. "I don't want you to break your word. It's just…" Lifting his gaze to hers, he tamped down the urge to plead for Anya's phone number…or her address…or anything that would allow him to locate her. "I think she might be my mate."

Arching her brows, Mila dropped her legs to the floor. Leaning forward, she rested her forearms on the table. "Sebastian, nothing would make me happier."

"But if I can't locate her—"

"You'll figure it out," she interrupted, holding up a finger. "You're a stubborn son of a bitch if I've ever met one, and if she's truly your mate, you'll find a way."

Sighing, he nodded, frustrated when her office phone rang.

"I hate to kick you out, but Mondays are busy here. Everyone who had a terrible date over the weekend wants to start fresh."

Standing, he ran his hand through his hair. "I'm going to find her, Mila. Mark my words."

As she reached for the phone he noticed the mischievous glint in her eyes. "I'm counting down the days until you do." Lifting the receiver to her ear, she shooed him away.

Determination welled in his gut as he exited her office and strode through the main square. Failure was not an option, and Sebastian would stop at nothing to find his mystery woman.

Chapter 8

Celine's phone rang promptly at 7 p.m. Monday evening. After her epic crying session on Saturday night, she'd woken up the next morning with a sense of firm resolve. She had made the decision to deceive Sebastian, and although she felt terrible about it, it had led to the only kiss she would probably ever share with him.

And oh, how magnificent the kiss had been. Celine had only been kissed by a handful of men in the past, and none of them came close to Sebastian's skillful ministrations upon her lips. Knowing she would treasure his taste and sultry words for years to come, she rose and reminded herself to buck up. She was a strong woman—stronger than many gave her credit for—and she needed to start living that way.

"Did I lose you?" Mila asked on the other end of the line.

"No," Celine said, putting the phone on speaker as she washed her hands. "I just came in from the stables."

Silence stretched as her friend contemplated. "Umm, I thought Handor forbade you from going inside the stables. Aren't your fancy servants supposed to do all the dirty work for you?"

"They're my father's staff, not servants, and I'm tired of not pulling my weight in my own damn life. I love horses and told the foreman I want full access to the stables."

"That's probably going to get him fired," she said acerbically.

"I won't let that happen. Anyway, what's up? I need to get ready for dinner with the family in a few minutes."

"Sebastian came to my office today. He wants to see Anya again."

Celine's heart nearly leaped from her chest. "What did you tell him?"

"That I wouldn't do it. But he's got that determined glint in his eyes, Celine. He's stubborn, so I'm not sure what's going to happen. Oh, and he left the stipend at the boutique in Anya's name."

Frowning, Celine decided to donate it as quickly as possible. Something about having a financial "transaction" between them didn't sit right in her gut. "I'll stop by tomorrow and give instructions on where to donate it. I bet it will buy nice gowns for several girls at Lynia and Naria who need dresses for their formal school dances."

"That's very generous, Celine."

"It's what any decent person would do."

"Well, that's the problem, honey," Mila said, breathing a soft laugh. "Some people just aren't decent. Okay, I've got to run, but I just wanted you to know Sebastian's sniffing around. Honestly, I hope he figures it out. I think he needs to know the woman who set his world on fire Saturday night was *you*."

"He'll never believe it," she said, her tone sad as she traced the porcelain. "He doesn't see me that way—"

"Then *make* him see you that way, Celine. Show him who you really are."

Sighing, she digested the words.

"Okay, gotta go. Bye."

The screen went dark, and Celine mulled over her friend's words. Gripping the edge of the sink, she stared at her reflection, allowing herself to feel her inner strength. She'd expressed it today when she told the foreman to give her full access to the stables. Could she go further and express it around Sebastian? For some reason, the thought was terrifying.

Deciding to shelve it so she could prepare for dinner, Celine eventually headed downstairs, distracted as she met her brothers for a pre-dinner drink in the den.

As the week progressed, Sebastian found himself walking past the boutique quite often. Although he told himself he needed fresh air and exercise, the truth was that he was hoping to catch a glimpse of Anya entering the store. If he could catch her when she went to claim the stipend he'd deposited, he could at least try to get her to agree to see him again.

As he strolled past the boutique after finishing his morning paperwork, he glanced through the window and noticed Celine settling up at the register. She was having an animate conversation with the boutique owner, who eventually bounded around the counter and enveloped Celine in a firm hug. Curious, Sebastian waited until they were finished, grinning at Celine as she exited the store.

"Oh," she said, pulling the door shut. "Hello, Sebastian." She pasted on a grin, although it didn't reach her eyes. "Fancy seeing you here in the middle of the workday."

"It's a nice day for a stroll, and I've realized recently I don't take enough breaks during the day." His eyes darted to the boutique owner through the window before returning to hers. "You two seemed to be embroiled in an exciting discussion."

"Oh,"—she waved her hand flippantly—"that was nothing. I was just checking on an order I placed for some gowns. I'm one of her frequent customers, so she dotes on me."

"Hmm..." was his soft reply as he studied her. Sebastian had known Celine forever, although he'd rarely made the time to speak to her alone. Why bother when she was born to be someone's aristocratic bonded mate and he had no desire to bond with anyone? Furthermore, his father had concocted some hair-brained scheme to set Celine up with Garridan, although it had backfired when he fell for Siora.

Studying the woman in front of him, Sebastian took a moment to actually *see* her. Yes, she was known as one of the most beautiful women on the compound, but had he ever really looked at her? Although she had blond hair, her eyelashes were long and dark. They extended above her ice-blue eyes, bracketing them so they shone in the sunlight.

As the silence deepened, her pale cheeks inflamed, the reddish flush extending down her neck as the pulse there thrummed. A small wisp of something sweet and airy entered his nostrils, and he inhaled, savoring the scent. It was one of roses and evergreen, so similar to Anya's...

"Well, I have to meet my brother at the coffee shop," she said, clearing her throat as she backed away. "It was lovely to see you, Sebastian."

Pivoting, she rushed across the street while he stood frozen on the sidewalk. Had Celine always had such an intoxicating scent? And why in the goddess's name was it so similar to Anya's? Deciding he was promptly losing his mind due to a longing for a woman he might never see again, he shook off the encounter and continued down the street.

By the next day, the curiosity was too much to bear, so Sebastian entered the boutique to ask the owner if his stipend had been claimed.

"Oh! Yes, sir," she said, excited as she held up some silky fabric behind the counter. "Your lovely recipient donated the entire amount to two girls' schools at Lynia and Naria. It will allow me to make thirty beautiful gowns for girls who couldn't afford them otherwise. May the goddess bless you both."

"That's quite generous," he said, taken by the gesture. "Did she request to leave me a message or note, perhaps?"

"Oh, I'm sorry, sir, but she requested to remain anonymous. She did say she had a splendid evening with you. She's such a lovely girl, our Cel—" Covering her lips with her fingers, the shop owner gasped. "Our *celebrated* donor."

Sebastian's eyes narrowed as he wondered if the woman was hiding something. "Yes, she is quite special. Thank you, ma'am. Take care."

Exiting the store, Sebastian strolled down the cobblestone sidewalk, wondering when his life had become a strange amalgamation of coded conversations and unrequited attraction. No wonder he'd never thrown his hat in the dating ring. The entire situation was quite maddening.

By Friday, after several sweat-soaked, sleepless nights dreaming of Anya, Sebastian decided he might not be cut out for romance of any kind. His thoughts were consumed with his mystery woman, and worse, last night he'd dreamed of Celine.

Sweet, quiet, biddable Celine.

It made absolutely no sense.

As he'd thrashed in bed, visions of Anya had plagued him: her gorgeous eyes and full lips, glistening under the moonlight as they stood in the secluded park by the train. But then her eyes had widened, those glorious eyelashes lifting as she removed her mask. Celine's face remained, her scent the same as Anya's...roses and evergreen...and he reached for her as she backed away, tears streaming down her cheeks as she cursed him for not knowing what was real...

He'd awoken with a gasp, struggling to breathe. After chugging some ice-cold water, he'd returned to bed, his thoughts consumed with the unmistakable knowledge his mystery woman and Celine shared the same addictive aroma.

When he finally did make it to work, he was distracted and could barely complete any of the projects on his desk. Deciding to take a walk, he strolled toward the main square, his heart leaping in his throat as Celine and her brother approached.

"Good morning, Xandor," he called, nodding before resting his gaze on his companion. "Celine," he softly murmured.

Her throat bobbed under the pale skin of her neck, sending a jolt of awareness to his shaft. Had her skin always been so creamy and smooth? What would it feel like to graze his fangs over it? To make her moan before he plunged them deep inside her pulsing vein...

Briefly closing his eyes, he wondered what the hell was happening to him. He'd gone from fantasizing about a phantom lover to fantasizing about Celine of all people. Someone he'd convinced himself he could never be interested in...

"Hello, Sebastian." The slight gravel in her voice seemed to wrap around his skin, caressing it like a feather that fell from the sky. As his heartbeat accelerated in his chest, he continued the conversation, attempting to maintain appearances.

"I hear you're going to be joining me on the council soon. Your father is excited to retire and proud to have you take his place."

"I'm ready to fulfill my duty," Xander said with a broad smile. "And perhaps it will help my little sister here finally find a mate.

She will now be related to *two* council members, one former and one current."

"Thank you, but I've done just fine without a mate so far," she said, swiping his arm off her shoulders. "And I don't need you or father to matchmake for me."

"Ah, our feisty sister. Many think she's timid because society taught her to act that way, but you should see her at home, Sebastian. Why, just yesterday I caught her washing one of our horses in the stable. Can you imagine? We have a staff of fifty, but she insists on doing laborers' work. It baffles the mind."

"The horse's name is Lucy, and she gave me a magnificent ride through the meadow," Celine said, crossing her arms. "I only felt it proper to give her a warm bath afterward."

Sebastian's gaze flickered to hers, covered with indignation as she scowled at her brother. A memory of the conversation he'd had with Anya about her wanting to work with horses flitted through his mind. Information slowly began to click together as his wheels churned like puzzle pieces that had finally found their match, solving the mystery he'd somehow already unconsciously known.

"Our altruistic sister," Xandor continued. "Why, the other day, I overheard her talking to Mila about a large donation she made to purchase gowns for girls on Lynia and Naria. First horse baths, and now this—"

Covering her brother's mouth with her hand, Celine hissed, "Will you shut up? You shouldn't eavesdrop on private conversations."

Chuckling, he removed her hand. "As I said,"—he cocked an eyebrow at Sebastian—"feisty as hell, although no one outside of our home truly knows. Such a shame."

"Oh, you're infuriating," she cried, stomping her foot. "I'm going to see Mila. You can have coffee alone since you're intent on mocking me."

Huffing, she pivoted and began walking down the street toward Mila's office.

"Celine," Xandor called, amusement in his voice. "Come now, don't storm away!"

She held up a hand, waving him off, and Sebastian thought she'd most likely flip him off if she weren't so proper.

"She's been crabby all week, ever since she was ill and couldn't attend the Christmas gala. Women," he muttered, rubbing his forehead, "am I right?"

Sebastian could only nod as the breadth of information rushed through him. Celine's scent was eerily similar to Anya's. She enjoyed bathing her horse in the stables too. She'd recently made a donation from the boutique. She didn't attend the gala on Saturday...

He hadn't even noticed she wasn't in attendance, but that was par for the course with Celine. He rarely noticed anything about her...until recently...until she'd *forced* him to...

Overwhelmed with the stunning conclusion his brain was quickly drawing, Sebastian struggled to catch his breath as the unshakable truth assuaged him: Anya *was* Celine.

"Are you okay, Sebastian?" Xandor asked, cupping his shoulder. "You look quite pale."

"I'm fine," he said, backing away and showing his palms. "Just a flush of heat from the sun. I have to get back to work, Xandor. Excited to work with you on the council. Take care."

Turning, he strode to the nearest park, seeking solace. Resting his palm on the firm bark of a tree, he inhaled several deep breaths, disbelief coursing through his frame.

"Why would she deceive me?" he asked, the words quiet and filled with equal parts anger and incredulity.

The chirping birds held no answer as he clenched his fingers on the bark. Desperate for answers, he did his best to quell the rage as he pushed away from the tree, striding from the park toward Mila's office, knowing Celine would be there.

After a week of sleepless nights and unsated desire, it was time for Sebastian to get some answers.

Chapter 9

Celine rushed inside Mila's office, closing the door behind her and sprinting to her desk. Placing her palms on the wood, she cried, "He knows, Mila! Oh goddess, he knows." Sinking into the nearby chair, she buried her face in her hands and tried to hold back the tears.

"Okay, okay," Mila said, grabbing a tissue and striding over to sit beside her. "This isn't the end of the world, Celine. After all, you had to know he'd eventually find out. Perhaps a small piece of you wanted that, hmm?"

Sniffling, Celine took the tissue and swiped her nose. "I didn't want him to hate me. At least in the past he was just indifferent toward me. Now that I've deceived him he's going to detest me, Mila."

"Don't jump to conclusions," she said, rubbing her shoulder. "He was pretty torn up about you when I saw him earlier this week—"

"That was about *Anya*, not me—"

"*You* are Anya, Celine. You told me you felt confident when you were able to be someone else, but it was always *you* inside. You need to be strong and show him you're the one he wanted the whole time."

"Oh goddess, this is a mess." Tossing the tissue into the wastebasket, she wiped her cheeks. "I should've just left him alone."

Arching her eyebrow, a knowing glint entered Mila's eyes. "I'm glad you didn't. I think it's finally time you ruffled his feathers."

Several loud knocks pounded on the door, causing them both to gasp.

Patting Celine's shoulder, Mila leaned down and whispered, "Give him hell." Stalking to the door, she pulled it open and said, "Where's the fire? I heard you the first time you knocked."

Sebastian breezed past her, fire in his eyes as he gazed at Celine. When he lifted his finger she noticed it shook with rage. "What the hell, Celine?" he asked, nostrils flaring as he stared her down. "I want answers!"

"Whew, he's pissed," Mila said, her eyes widening as she spared Celine a mocking grimace. "I'm out. Don't break anything in my office. I'll be back in an hour. Ta-ta!" With a breezy wave, she darted from the office, closing the door firmly behind her.

Sebastian focused on Celine, anger oozing from his large frame as he slowly approached. Rising, she backed away until her backside hit the desk. Unable to escape, she gripped the edge of the wood, wondering if she'd ever seen such emotion in his usually stoic expression.

Reaching her, he leaned forward, bracketing her with his arms as his palms rested on the desk. Small pants left her lungs as her body ached to press against his while simultaneously knowing she needed to retreat. Staring deep into his brown eyes, she waited, trapped as effectively as the rabbits her father snared for hunting.

"I thought I was going mad," he gritted, his face so close she could feel his warm breath on her cheek. "Every time I saw you...or *smelled* you...I thought of *her*..."

"I'm sorry," she whispered, shaking her head.

"And every time I dreamed of her, I began to dream of *you*..."

Lifting his hand, he touched his finger to her cheek. Inhaling a swift breath, she waited, wondering if he would strike her. His cheeks were flushed with anger, and rage simmered in his eyes. But she also saw a slight bit of arousal in the brown depths, jump-starting her body's reaction as she absorbed his nearness.

"Oh, no," he said, shaking his head, "I'm not going to strike you. Any man who does that isn't worth his mettle." Gliding his finger across her cheek, he caressed the corner of her mouth before slowly dragging his finger across her bottom lip. Desire surged to her core, and she felt a resulting rush of wetness as she grew slick between her thighs.

Closing his eyes, he inhaled, savoring the aroma of her arousal before lifting his lids. Softly caressing her lip, his fangs glistened as heavy breaths exited his lungs.

"I thought I'd never smell this arousal again...but here it is, smothering me in the most pleasurable way." Dipping his finger inside her mouth, he touched the wetness, setting her body on fire.

A whimper leaped from her throat as he softly moaned.

"Damn it, Celine," he whispered, rimming her mouth with his finger. "I don't understand any of this. All I know is that I'm furious...and that I want you so badly I fear I might explode if I don't kiss you..."

Desperate to show him she was sorry for her deception, she closed her mouth around his finger, drawing him inside as he groaned. Gazing into his eyes, she sucked him, gliding her tongue over his skin as he emitted a low growl.

"Goddess, Celine," he rasped, inching closer as he moved his finger between her lips. "Where have you been hiding all this time?"

She gently bit his finger, causing a rush of air to escape his lungs before he withdrew it.

"I've always been in front of you, but you've never seen me, Sebastian. *Never*—"

Pressing his body to hers, he touched his lips to her trembling ones, cutting off her words and stealing her breath.

"So you deceived me? Made me look like a fool?"

"I never wanted that," she rasped, drowning in his musky scent and the heat of his body. "I just wanted you to *see* me—"

His hand shot to her nape, threading through her thick hair and tugging so she was forced to tilt her head back. Caught in his grasp, she waited.

"Damn you," he murmured against her lips. "I can't decide whether I want to strangle you or fuck you, Celine—"

Unable to control her desperate need to taste him, she speared her tongue into his mouth. Sliding her arms around his neck, she perched on the desk, lifting her legs to wrap them around his waist. Strong fingers tightened in her hair as he pulled her against his body, his other arm snaking around her waist to hold her close.

Moaning her name, he began to kiss her in earnest, his talented tongue gliding over hers as she responded with ardor.

He tasted every crevice of her mouth, working furiously as his body grew even harder with arousal. Reveling in the feel of his erection between her legs, she pushed her mound against it, a fresh rush of slick coating her core when he groaned.

"Look at you pushing into my cock, Celine," he murmured, his tongue circling her lips as he dropped his hand from her waist to her thigh. His large palm slid over the silken fabric of her dress, inching ever so close to the slit that ran down the left side. "Do you want to feel it against you when there's nothing between us? What have you been hiding under all these formal dresses? Are you wet for me, sweetheart?"

Unable to control the undulation of her hips, she closed her eyes, pushing toward him as a stuttered breath left her lungs. In truth, she hated the formal gowns of the Vampyre aristocracy but usually wore them in public to please her father since he was deeply concerned with appearances.

"So greedy," he hummed, gliding his fingers past the slit to her inner thigh. Goose bumps appeared under his skillful hand as he caressed a trail to her mound. Resting his forehead against hers, he softly commanded, "Look at me."

Fear that he would laugh at her—or worse, reject her—coursed through her frame, but she pushed it aside and lifted her lids. Brown orbs glazed with lust stared back at her as he traced his finger over her wet thong.

"Such naughty panties for such a proper woman," he rasped, trailing his finger up and down the wet fabric. "You have everyone fooled, don't you, Celine?"

"I only want to be myself," she whispered, shaking her head. "Everyone else decided who I was before I got the chance."

"Such a waste," he murmured, sweeping the thin fabric aside to trace the lips of her core. "You've been hiding this sweet, slick treasure from me for ages, haven't you?"

Whimpering, she nodded. "I've wanted you like this for so long..."

"Like this?" he asked, rimming her opening with his finger. Saliva pooled in her mouth at the intimate gesture as he began to push inside. "Or, like this?" Gently probing, he nudged into her wet channel, a ragged moan escaping his lips as he pushed deeper...

"Like that," she whispered.

"Dirty girl," he murmured, nipping her lips. "Has anyone ever touched you here, Celine?"

"No..." Threading her fingers in his hair, she held tight, embarrassment swamping her at her lack of experience. "No one ever wanted to touch me there..."

"Fools," he rasped, slowly moving his finger in and out of her tight vise. "Every man on this damn compound is a fool, and I'm the biggest one of all." Drawing her into a kiss, his tongue played with hers as he impaled her with his finger. "Spread your legs wider," he softly commanded into her mouth.

She complied, elated at the pleasure that reverberated through his frame at her acquiescence. Drawing her bottom lip between his teeth, he gently sucked her as he inserted two fingers into her quivering body.

"Good girl," he murmured, pressing soft kisses to her lips as his fingers moved within. "Do you like that, Celine?"

"Yes...."

Gathering her wetness on his fingers, he trailed up her folds, burrowing under the hood of her mound to the spot filled with a thousand nerve-endings. "Have you ever had an orgasm?"

She nodded, unable to speak with his fingers against her deepest place.

"Who gave you the orgasm?" he growled, possession lacing his tone.

"Me. I'm the only one who's ever touched myself there...until now..."

"Thank the goddess," he whispered against her lips. "I thought I was going to have to murder someone."

A shocked giggle escaped her lips as she reveled in the possessive words. "I only ever wanted you to touch me there, Sebastian...*oh god*..."

His fingers made concentric circles over her swollen little bud, generating such pleasure she thought she might melt into a pool of lust in his arms. Digging her fingernails into his shoulders, she searched for a stronghold as he took her higher.

"First, you're going to come in my arms, Celine. Do you hear me?"

"Yes," she cried, her mouth falling open as he spoke the dirty words.

"Then you're going to tell me why you deceived me."

The pressure of his fingers increased, causing stars to appear behind her closed lids as she neared the peak.

Pressing his lips to her ear, he tenderly licked the lobe before nipping it with his fangs. "Come for me, naughty girl. Come, and I just might forgive you..."

"Oh...I...*Sebastian!*" Tossing her head back, Celine clutched his broad shoulders, squeezing with all her might as she dove head-first into the most spectacular orgasm of her life. Losing control, her body quaked and shuddered as Sebastian whispered words of praise in her ear. Cupping her mound, he held tight, offering support with his body as his other arm held her waist.

Sparks of pleasure jolted to every cell in her body, setting them aflame before pooling into tiny pulses of bliss. Small whimpers escaped her throat, laced with her unyielding desire for him as she gave herself to the only man she'd ever loved.

Sebastian held her until her quivers abated, continuing to place soft kisses on her ear and temple. Slowly regaining her wits, she lifted her head, opening her eyes but finding it hard to focus. His low-toned laugh surrounded her as he nudged her nose with his.

"Are you...*laughing* at me?" she almost squeaked. "Goddess, Sebastian, I'm already so embarrassed...please don't make it worse."

"Embarrassed you came?" he asked, eyebrows drawing together and his hand clenching her mound. "Why would you be embarrassed about that, darling?"

The endearment reminded her of their night together, and of how he'd showered tender words on someone who wasn't truly her. Feeling her heart crack, she lowered her gaze, unable to meet his eyes.

"Because you want me because you're angry and nothing more. I know what you think of me, Sebastian."

Tilting her chin, he reclaimed her gaze as tangible energy pulsed between them. Those limitless eyes darted between hers, seeming to contemplate before he slowly lifted his hand from her mound. Lifting it to his mouth, he glided his tongue over his finger, licking away her essence before moving to the next one.

"Tell me, darling," he rasped, eyes locked with hers as he licked her honey from his fingers. "Tell me as I taste your release on my fingers what I really think of you."

Mesmerized by his sensual actions, Celine could only watch as he licked every glistening drop from his hand. Then he stepped forward, aligning his lips with hers before plunging his tongue into her mouth.

He kissed her, languid and deep, and she tasted herself on his tongue. Breaking the kiss, he drew back and licked his lips, the gesture so erotic she felt a new rush of wetness at her core.

"You think I'm boring...and cold...and insignificant..." she finished lamely.

"Mmm..." was his sultry reply as he continued to lick his lips. "What else?"

"Damn you," she whispered, wishing she could release his shoulders but needing the stronghold to stay upright. "Stop mocking me!"

Cocking a brow, his lips curled into a sexy grin. "You deserve much worse than mockery, my dear, but I find myself unable to be angry at you right now. I'd take the win."

Exhaling a breath, the guilt rushed over her once more. "I'm sorry for deceiving you, Sebastian. Truly, I am. I hope you don't hate me."

"Hate is very far from the emotion I'm feeling right now," he muttered. "Most importantly, I'm wondering how in the hell I was so blind." Trailing his fingers over her hair, he gazed at her reverently as her heart pounded. "I knew your hair felt coarse that night...you wore a wig."

Biting her lip, she nodded.

"And I consider myself an observant person. Guess that's out the window."

Taking pity on him, she laughed and cupped his jaw. "I knew you wouldn't notice. It was me after all."

Sighing, he shook his head. "I'm going to need some time to process what an oblivious idiot I am."

"I'm just happy you're not still yelling. I've created a bit of a mess."

"I would argue we both have—"

The door to Mila's office swung open and Handor stepped inside. "Mila, have you seen Celine? I need her for—" Bristling, his mouth fell open as he observed their sensual position on the desk, Sebastian between his daughter's open legs as her skirt fell to one side.

"You son of a bitch!" he hissed, jabbing his finger at Sebastian. "How dare you touch my daughter before she bonds?"

"Father!" she cried, mourning the loss of Sebastian's warm body as he drew away. Repositioning her gown over her legs, she hopped to her feet and smoothed it over her thighs. "This is none of your concern!"

"None of my concern?" His face turned a thousand shades of red as his eyes threatened to bulge from his head. "Your one duty is to bond with a suitable mate, and I find you here, giving yourself to someone who hasn't promised you anything?"

"I'm sorry, Handor," Sebastian said, showing his palm. "I take full responsibility."

"Damn right you do. I demand you bond with her. If you have any honor, you'll set things right."

Alarmed at the escalation, Celine held up her hands. "Enough! No one is bonding with anyone. Everyone needs to calm down—"

"I agree, sir," Sebastian interrupted, appearing contrite. "I will bond with Celine."

"What?" she cried, not understanding how things had devolved so quickly. Of course, she'd always dreamed of bonding with Sebastian, but not if he was forced to do it. No—this was all wrong. He was supposed to fall madly in love with her before lowering to one knee and asking her to be his mate for eternity...

A slight bit of tension left Handor's shoulders as he warily eyed Sebastian. "Fine. We will have the ceremony next weekend. There's no time to waste since she is compromised."

"Compromised!" she exclaimed, stomping her foot. "I'm right here! Stop speaking as if I don't exist. No one is bonding next weekend—"

"Yes, sir," Sebastian said, "I am honored to have Celine as my bonded mate."

Ending the discussion, her father nodded and turned to leave the office. "Have your father contact me so we can work out the details, Sebastian. If I know Astaroth, he'll want to have the ceremony in his back yard to keep up appearances."

Scoffing at how alike their fathers were, Celine gaped at Sebastian. "Are you really going to let this happen?"

"You have no choice, Celine," her father said, his tone devoid of emotion. "I won't have a daughter so careless with her choices under my roof any longer. You can begin packing when you return home so your things are ready to move to Sebastian's home after the ceremony." With a final nod, he strode through the door, closing it behind him.

Swiping a hand through her hair, she stared open-mouthed at the door as Sebastian stood silent. Shaking her hands with exasperation, she approached him. "You can't be serious. This is madness, Sebastian."

Unreadable eyes lifted to hers, swirling with emotions she couldn't begin to decipher. "It's done, Celine. Let's make the best of it."

Sputtering, she slapped her palm to her forehead. "Make the *best* of it? Up until twenty minutes ago, you didn't even know I existed, and *now* you want to bond with me? This is absurd."

Raw emotion laced his features as a muscle ticked in his jaw. "As I stated, I was a fool. A fact I am now trying to remedy."

"From one night together where you didn't know it was me and one tiny moment of passion?" She gestured to Mila's desk. "Absolutely not. This isn't the way it's supposed to happen, Sebastian. We can't—"

Striding toward her, he gripped her arms, careful but firm. "Your father saw us in a compromising position, Celine. We have no other option." Lifting his hand, he splayed his fingers and leaned forward, speaking in a low growl. "And now that my fingers have been buried inside your sweet body, you're insane if you think I'll allow anyone else to touch you."

A disbelieving laugh escaped her lips. "You've had centuries to bond with me, Sebastian. *Centuries!*"

His lips thinned as he spared her a droll look. "My dear, I'm sure you know this, but men are often daft. I have no excuse except to say I'm a workaholic who never saw much beyond the horizon of my desk. A feat I wish to remedy immediately."

Feeling her chin wobble, she shook her head. "This isn't how it's supposed to happen. It can't happen this way..."

Confusion marred his features as tears formed in her eyes.

"Oh, you'll never understand," she warbled, pressing her fist to her lips. "Goddess, what have I done?" Unable to face him any longer—or to accept her inevitable fate—a sob escaped her throat as she pivoted to leave.

"Celine, please—"

"No," she said, shaking her arm from his grasp. "It can't happen like this. I won't let it. I have to speak to my father." Gathering her skirt in her fists, she burst through the door to try to talk some sense into the hardheaded man.

※

Once home, she begged and pleaded with Handor for hours to no avail. He was determined to bond her to Sebastian and complete his duty to find a worthy bonded mate. In that moment, she truly understood she'd never represented anything more than a brood mare and a burden to him.

Climbing the stairs on shaking legs, she threw herself on her bed and wept at the knowledge she was destined to bond with a man who didn't love her back and most likely never would. If he'd been granted the chance to court her after their passionate tryst on the desk, perhaps she could've wormed her way under his stoic exterior and carved off a small piece of his heart.

But, alas, she'd run out of time, and she would now become a duty and a burden to the man who'd never seen her and who now had no incentive to even try.

Chapter 10

Sebastian lowered to Mila's desk, perching on it as he rubbed his forehead. The past hour had quite certainly been the most eventful of his life, and he doubted there would ever be one to rival it. He'd discovered Celine's treachery, realized the woman he'd been obsessed with for the past week was one he'd known for centuries, shared an intimately erotic moment with said woman, and agreed to bond with her.

Yes, quite eventful indeed.

For someone as commitment-phobic as Sebastian, he should've been furious at Handor's demand he bond with Celine. And yet, as soon as the declaration had left her father's mouth, Sebastian had rushed to agree. Why? Contemplating, he rubbed his chin.

Because something changed last weekend, and you know it.

Narrowing his eyes, Sebastian accepted the very obvious truth. Something *had* shifted when he saw Anya—saw *Celine*—standing tall and regal in the moonlight. A piece of his heart that was locked away had been set free, and he'd become open to possibilities he'd never considered. Hell, he'd even told Mila he thought she was his mate. His friend's resounding smirk should've been yet another clue that his phantom lover wasn't a phantom after all.

Goddess, he was an oblivious fool.

"Well?" Mila asked, striding into the office. "Where's Celine?"

"I assume she's speaking with her father, begging him to end the betrothal we entered into."

Stopping short, Mila worked her jaw. "You're betrothed to Handor?"

"Funny," he said, his expression droll. "Handor burst through the door looking for Celine when we were...uh...compromised."

"Oh, wow," Mila said, eyes alight with excitement. "How compromised?"

Glancing at the desk, he arched a brow. "Pretty compromised."

"Ew," she said, striding toward the desk and shooing him away. "Do I need to disinfect something?"

Breathing a laugh, he shook his head. "I think you're fine. But it was comprising enough that Handor demanded I bond with her." Tilting his head, his features drew together. "And before I knew it, I agreed. In fact, I couldn't get the 'yes' through my lips fast enough." Lifting his gaze to Mila's, he swallowed thickly. "What the hell does that mean?"

"Oh, my dear friend," she said, approaching and patting his shoulder. "I think it means you've finally met your match. It's the only reason I agreed to her scheme. I saw the logic of you both shaking things up. You just needed a change of perspective to see what was in front of you both."

"Thanks for that, by the way," he muttered. "I feel like an idiot. How did I not know it was her?"

Lowering into the chair, she shrugged. "Celine was raised to blend into the background. To be a dutiful, biddable female. But times have changed, and she desperately wants the world to see her for who she truly is." Her lips formed a soft smile. "She wants *you* to see her that way most of all. I think Saturday was the first time you let down your walls and allowed that to happen."

Sitting beside her, he reclined in the chair as he pondered. "I should be pissed, and a part of me is, but another part of me is grateful she took the chance." Leaning forward, he rested his forearms on his thighs. "I've never felt like this, Mila. It's daunting...and also quite...magnificent."

"Well, you're welcome." Crossing her ankle over her knee, she shook her foot as she spoke. "Just remember, she's quite sheltered and has no way to survive on her own. It will take time to fully realize her potential once she's escaped from Handor's grip. You could be the one who helps her grow, Sebastian. You're so altruistic with our people, and you could show a bit of that consideration to her once you bond."

"I can," he said with a nod. "Although, she seemed...disappointed. I guess I thought..."

"Yes?"

"Well, she must have feelings for me if she concocted this scheme, right?"

Arching a brow, Mila muttered, "What do you think?"

Scowling, he asked, "Then why wouldn't she be happy to bond with me?"

"Well, let's see." Ticking her fingers, Mila said, "She's had feelings for you for centuries, which you completely ignored. She finally gathers the courage to do something about it and gets caught by her father doing the nasty with you. Her father demands you bond with her and a business transaction is made between you." Her features turned sardonic. "Did she have *any* say in the matter?"

"I..." Scratching his head, he frowned. "Well, not really. I just assumed she would find me an acceptable match. I mean, seconds earlier, she was moaning my name on your desk—"

"TMI," Mila interjected, holding up a hand. "You didn't even ask her, did you? No sweet words or romanticism at all."

"No," was his sullen reply as began to realize why Celine was upset.

Sighing, she shook her head. "Men. Every last one of you are idiots."

"I get it." Holding up a hand, he nodded. "She deserves better."

"She deserves *more* than better." Rising, she tapped his forehead. "Search your brain for how to do that, Sebastian. I think you could build an amazing life together, but you're going to have to figure out how to be a good mate."

Standing, he cupped her shoulder. "You're putting a lot of faith in a man who never wanted a commitment."

"Until now. Don't lie to yourself. She's under your skin. I've never seen you like this."

Unable to stop his smile, he nodded. "She's definitely under my skin. It feels good. I didn't expect that."

"Love and bonding are never duties or chores if you're with the right person. Look at your brother with Siora. He's completely besotted with her and happily so. That's how true love works."

Blowing a breath through his lips, Sebastian shook his head. "Avowals of love are still too terrifying to contemplate, but I'll admit, Celine has awakened something in me. I've never been a coward, Mila, and I want to pursue this."

"No, you haven't. Now go fix this mess you two created. Give her some romance, Sebastian. You can do it."

"I'm still half-pissed at you," he teased, holding his thumb and forefinger an inch apart.

"Good. Maybe you'll leave me alone so I can work." Shooing him away, she trailed behind her desk. "Gotta get back to it. Congrats on the betrothal. Byeeeee!" Lowering to the chair, she faced the computer and began to type.

Realizing he'd been dismissed, Sebastian left the office and headed down the sidewalk. Pulling out his phone, he called his brother.

"Hey," Garridan's deep voice chimed. "I'm about to head into training, but I have five minutes. What's up?"

"I think it's time I finally took possession of your key," Sebastian said. "I know you offered for me to move into your house now that you've moved to Lynia, but I never saw the need to."

"And now you do?"

Clearing his throat, Sebastian inhaled a deep breath. "Now I do. You see, I've recently become betrothed."

His brother must've been drinking water because a choking noise sounded over the phone before he broke into a coughing fit. Sebastian couldn't help but grin at his obvious surprise.

"Excuse me," he said after the coughing abated, "I must be hearing things. It sounded like you said you were betrothed."

"I am."

Garridan's palpable confusion emanated through the phone. "And who is the lucky lady?"

Grinning from ear to ear, Sebastian wondered if his brother would break into another fit of coughing at the news. "Celine."

Silence drifted between them.

"Garridan?"

"I'm waiting to hear the punchline. Don't get me wrong, I'd love nothing more than for you to bond with Celine. I always thought she was perfect for you, brother. But you barely ever noticed her. And believe me, we tried."

His eyebrows drew together. "What the hell does that mean?"

"Remember the fundraiser before the battle with Bakari? I offered to be her wingman to try to make you jealous. Of course, it didn't work because you spent most of the night holed up in your office working."

"My council work is important, Garridan."

"I know, but it won't keep you warm at night, brother. I wager Celine will be much better at that. Trust me. Having Siora at my side means more than any medal or promotion I've ever achieved."

"Aww," Siora chimed in the background. "He's so sweet. Hope he remembers that when I kick his ass in this drill we're about to start. Come on, no time to chitchat."

Sebastian heard a smacking sound, which he assumed was Siora placing a firm kiss on his brother's lips, before Garridan chuckled. "Goddess, I love her. Have to go. I'll bring the key to you when I'm done in a few hours. There are a few basic items left in the house, and I hope you'll decorate it and make it your own. I'm happy for you, Sebastian."

"I'll tell you the whole story when I see you. Let's just say there's a lot more to Celine than meets the eye."

Garridan's chuckle echoed over the phone. "It's finally time you figured that out. I like Celine immensely and will be honored to call her family. Well done."

"Don't congratulate me yet. She's not exactly thrilled. I'm going to need some pointers from you on romance and whatever else women like."

"Garridan!" Siora called in the background. "Get your ass over her and stop wasting my time!"

"As you can see, I'm no expert either," Garridan muttered. "But the best advice I can give you is to put her first. If you do that, she'll give you the world. Gotta go. See you later."

The phone went dead as Sebastian took his brother's words to heart. *Put her first.* Hell, he was an altruistic council member who put his constituents first every day. He certainly could do it with the woman who'd burrowed under his skin and turned his world upside down in a matter of days. She deserved nothing less, and as he strolled under the midday sun, he made a silent promise to give it to her.

Chapter 11

The next day, Celine was in the sitting room anxiously chewing her nail as she wondered if she would ever regain control of her own damn life. A knock sounded at the front door, startling her, and she trailed through the foyer before slowly pulling it open.

Sebastian stood on the other side, so handsome in his crisp white-collared shirt and dress pants. A few springy brown hairs peeked from beneath the shirt below his neck, and her mouth suddenly went dry as she had visions of kissing him there. Would the hairs tickle her lips as she went lower?

"Hi," he said, his tone warm as he smiled. "Are you busy?"

"Busy watching my life fall apart," she muttered, arching a brow. "Why?"

His smile deepened as his eyes roved over her face. "I'd like to show you something." Extending his hand, he waited. "If you're willing to come with me."

Narrowing her eyes, she studied his hand. "Aren't you supposed to be working? You *are* the most infamous workaholic on the compound."

Chuckling, he nodded. "I am, but I find something else...or rather, *someone* else, has captured my attention recently." Affection swam in his eyes as he shook his hand. "Please?"

Taken by his adorable grin and tender plea, Celine took his hand, closing the door behind her. They began to walk down the sidewalk, and she realized he was leading her to his home several blocks away.

"Where are we going?"

Evading her question, he surveyed her formal gown. It was a deep purple that highlighted her pale complexion. "You look very pretty today."

"Compliments will get you nowhere, especially since I've worn this gown a thousand times and you've never noticed."

His lips twitched. "I'm noticing now."

Huffing a breath, she remained silent, wishing she wasn't thrilled to be in his presence. In truth, it was wonderful to have his full attention after craving it for so long, but she'd be damned if she let him know that. He was no better than her father, trading her as if she were a baseball card between human teenagers. Just dreadful.

They arrived at Astaroth's home, and Sebastian led her down a private walkway to the house on the adjacent property. Garridan had lived there for centuries before he recently moved to Lynia to be with Siora.

"You're taking me to your brother's home?"

He didn't answer, leading her to the front door and inserting a key to unlock it. Drawing her inside, they walked down a long hallway to a living room with large windows, a couch, and a fireplace.

"As you can see, it's pretty sparse. Garridan only left a few items—the couch, some chairs, the bed." His eyes lit with desire. "But otherwise, it's going to need to be decorated."

"You're moving in here?"

Clasping her hands in his, he squeezed. "*We're* moving in here. If you agree, of course."

"I wasn't aware I had a choice," was her sardonic reply as she scanned the room.

"Celine, I'm sorry I didn't ask you. It was a precarious situation, and I reacted without thinking." Lifting her chin with his fingers, he gazed into her eyes. "And neither of us is perfect here, darling. If you recall, you deceived me. Quite viciously—"

"It wasn't vicious," she interjected, heart pounding from the warmth of his fingers. "I just...wanted to know how it felt to be near you and have you notice me," she finished lamely, dropping her gaze in embarrassment.

"Mission accomplished," he said, arching a teasing brow. "And I don't want our mistakes to linger between us. I'll forgive you for deceiving me if you forgive me for being an unromantic dolt and not *asking* you to bond with me."

Swallowing thickly, she pondered. "I don't want to bond with someone who doesn't want me, Sebastian."

A tender light entered his gaze as he cupped her jaw, slowly running his thumb over her cheek. "Your father has made his decision, Celine. He's determined we bond, and whether it's fair or not, you don't have any recourse. You're dependent on him and have no way to support yourself if we don't bond."

Tears filled her eyes as she silently accepted his words.

"But I can help you, if you'll let me. I have no wish to rob you of your independence. I want to help you gain it."

Her eyebrows drew together. "And how will I do that if we're bonded? My ownership will just transfer from my father to you."

"I have no wish to own you, darling." Glancing at the ceiling, Sebastian squinted one eye. "Except, perhaps, in the bedroom." Reclaiming her gaze, a naughty glint entered his eyes. "But we can discuss that later. For now, I want a partner. An equal."

Pretending her body wasn't thrumming from his "bedroom" comment, she toyed with her lip with her fangs. "An equal how?"

"I'll give you a stipend each month—yours to save and spend however you like. If you detest being bonded to me, eventually, you can take it all and leave."

A shocked laugh left her throat. "You're joking."

"I'm one hundred percent serious, my dear," he said, lifting a finger. "I hope this will assure you that bonding with me won't be quite as dreadful as you've decided."

Her gaze fell to his chest, roaming his crisp shirt as she mulled over his proposal. "You're still purchasing me in a way. But I guess I have no other choice." Clearing her throat, she battled the shyness that warred within. "And we'll be...intimate?"

Cupping her chin, he waited until she reclaimed his gaze. "Yes, Celine. You said you didn't want to bond with a man who didn't want you, but I'm pretty sure you were in Mila's office yesterday." Stepping closer, he pressed his body to hers. "I think it's quite obvious I want you, darling."

Her treacherous body strained toward his muscular one, reveling in the feel of his taut muscles and firm length against her stomach. Licking her lips, her knees wobbled at the flare of lust in his eyes.

"I want to bond with someone who loves me, Sebastian," she whispered.

Running his thumb over her lip, he formed a gentle smile. "I understand." Inhaling deeply, he slowly shook his head. "I don't want there to be anything but honesty between us. An avowal of love at this point would be disingenuous, and you deserve better than that, Celine."

A tiny crack shot through her heart.

"This is still very new, and I've been a confirmed bachelor for centuries. But..." Lifting a finger, he cocked his brow. "I'm willing to try. Give me some time. Let me earn you. I'm open to love, but I have a lot to learn. Maybe you can help me."

His expression was earnest as he softly caressed her jaw, and she knew in that moment she would never love another. He was offering her freedom and the chance to build a life with him. Moreover, he desired her and was blatantly honest. It was more than most women had in these circumstances, and if she opened her heart to him, perhaps he would do the same. Inhaling a huge breath, she opened her mouth and spoke the words that would cement her future.

"I would be honored to be your partner, Sebastian. It's a lovely offer. Thank you."

Relief washed over his handsome features as he palmed both of her cheeks. "Thank the goddess." Leaning forward, he brushed his lips over hers. "I'm honored to have you, Celine. Now kiss me to seal the deal."

Shivering from his command, she slid her arms around his neck, drawing him into a heated kiss. He moaned as his tongue glided over hers, sending a jolt of wetness to her core. Maneuvering his lips over hers, he spoke hungrily into her mouth.

"I can't wait to be inside you," he rasped, threading his fingers through her hair as he plundered her mouth. "I'll be a proper gentleman and wait until our bonding night, but know that I'm going to ravish you afterward, darling." Waggling his brows, he nipped her lip. "Maybe you should decorate the bedroom first."

Laughing, she glanced around the room. "The house definitely needs a lot of work."

"I'll leave that to you. It's your home now, and I want you to decorate it however you see fit."

Joy surged through her at the thought of owning something and putting her stamp on it. "Are you sure?"

"Absolutely." He pecked her lips. "Just nothing too pink. Otherwise, go for it."

"I like purples and deep greens...and a royal blue here and there. I'll figure it out. What's the budget?"

Arching a brow, he shrugged. "In case you haven't noticed, I'm the eldest son of an aristocrat who's richer than half the kingdom combined. I also make a good salary as a council member. So I say go for it. The sky's the limit."

Biting her lip, she grinned. "Are you placating me with decorating so I'll be amenable to you in the bedroom?"

"Why, Celine, you wound my heart," he teased, covering his chest with his palm. "And also, yes. Very much yes."

Giggling, she nodded. "I'll allow it. Oh, Sebastian, this will be fun! Thank you!"

His expression was reverent as he tucked a strand of hair behind her ear. "I like seeing you smile. I think I might have to buy more houses for you to decorate."

"Oh, stop." She swatted his chest as he chuckled. Licking her lips, she said softly, "I'm looking forward to our bonding night. I'd gotten to the point where I was afraid I was never going to lose my virginity."

His frame shuddered in her arms, and she glowed with the knowledge that he was viscerally attracted to her, even if he didn't love her. Although her gala-night scheme had unintended consequences, she was finally able to admit it had been worth it.

"Oh, it's as good as gone, darling." Leaning down, he pressed his lips to her ear. "I'm going to bury myself so deep inside you there will be no doubt who you belong to."

Shivering in anticipation, she clutched him, hoping she would be able to please him when the time came. He held her for a small eternity, whispering sweet words in her ear as they gently swayed. Accepting her future, she closed her eyes and vowed to ensure she did everything in her power to make him love her back.

Chapter 12

A week later, Sebastian stood in his father's expansive back yard under a white altar lined with flowers. The sun shone brightly above, and a bead of sweat dripped down his temple. After wiping it away with his sleeve, he stuck his finger between his collar and neck, attempting to create some space. Damn, but it was tight.

"Stop fidgeting," Garridan muttered behind him, causing Sebastian to glower. "You're going to be fine, brother. Deep breaths."

"You can skip the unwanted 'best man advice,'" he said, scowling. "Never in a million years did I think I'd bond first, but here we are."

"It's time, Sebastian," Garridan said, patting his arm. "You were hiding behind your job, just as I was hiding behind my position in the army before I met Siora. Your life is about to become so much fuller. I can't wait to see it."

The officiant—a well-respected retired councilman who was friends with Astaroth—cleared his throat, and Sebastian straightened his shoulders, facing the altar. As he waited for Celine to walk down the aisle, he begrudgingly admitted his brother's words were true.

For so long, he'd hidden behind his duty, telling himself it was noble. Yes, his job helped people, and he took immense pride in that. But he would be lying to himself if he didn't admit his life had become quite...hollow. A shell of the full life he promised himself he'd live one day but hadn't pursued in centuries. Somewhere along the way, he'd just accepted the status quo and forgotten to take the next steps.

His lips twitched as admiration for Celine surged within. She'd been quite stagnant too, but she'd taken it upon herself to try something different. Although he'd been shocked to discover she was his mystery lover, he admitted it had jump-started both their lives in a new direction. And for once, he was *excited* about something.

After so many years of wearing blinders, he was beginning to see Celine for the woman she was. Feisty and brave when she summoned her inner courage, but still innocent and sheltered in other ways. Thanks to Miranda and Evie, women in their realm were no longer background characters in aristocratic men's lives, and Celine would benefit from having a partner instead of a caretaker like her father.

Sebastian didn't know the first thing about relationships, but he felt they could grow into one together. She could relieve him of his habit of being a stuffy workaholic, and he could give her autonomy to make her own choices. Although he'd sworn he didn't want a bonded mate, he realized he was grateful to Etherya for the circumstances that had led him here. Yes, he was nervous, but that was normal for any man about to bond. But he finally understood what others had seen for so long: he and Celine were an excellent match.

Music emanated from the string quartet situated beside the rows of chairs, and he turned to face Celine as she glided down the white carpet. *Oohs* and *ahhs* emanated from the crowd as they rose, the guests' reactions reflecting the consensus: his mate was absolutely radiant.

She grinned at him from behind her veil, nervously biting her lip, and he winked as all remaining hesitation left his body. If he had to bond with anyone, he was grateful it was this gorgeous woman who embodied so much more passion and character than most would ever know. Hell, he'd overlooked her for centuries because he'd bought into the narrative everyone wrote about Celine. They were all fools—he the biggest one of all—but she'd pulled back the curtain and showed him her true essence.

She approached, kissing her father's cheek before he released her and sat in the front row. Taking her hands, Sebastian squeezed, resolved to do right by her and make the best of their circumstances. Turning to face the officiant, he held her hand as they recited the vows of Etherya in front of their friends and family.

∞

After a long day of dancing and celebrating, the last guests departed Astaroth's property and Celine lifted a hand to her mouth to stifle a yawn.

"Tired, darling?" Sebastian asked, sliding his arm around her waist.

"Yes. Bonding ceremonies are exhausting. I might have to stay with you forever just so I never have to do this again."

Chuckling, he kissed her temple. "I'm happy to hear one more reason you won't rush to leave me. It would ruin my reputation."

Wrinkling her nose at his teasing, she smiled as his parents approached.

"All the guests are gone, and we're heading to bed," Astaroth said, shaking Sebastian's hand before turning to Celine. "Thank you for finally convincing my son to bond." Cupping Sebastian's shoulder, he beamed. "I expect an heir soon."

"On that note, we're heading home," Sebastian droned. "I know it's been your greatest wish to see me bonded for centuries. Let's take the win and hold off on the 'heir' talk for a few months at least." Kissing his mother on the cheek, he faced Celine. "Ready?"

Nodding, she kissed his parents goodbye, thanking them for their hospitality as hosts, and slipped her hand in Sebastian's. He led them across the property to his home—their home now—and stopped at the front door. Pushing it open, he lowered, gathering her in his arms as she yelped. Chuckling, he carried her over the threshold before setting her on her feet.

"I messed up the proposal, but at least I can do one thing right."

Celine smiled at his thoughtfulness before slipping off her shoes and massaging her tired feet. "I can't wear those things one more minute. My feet are throbbing."

Approaching her, he slipped an arm around her waist. "I'm happy to relieve you of any clothing that is causing you distress, dear."

Her heart slammed in her chest as he gazed at her with lust-filled eyes. Tiny butterflies of anxiety fluttered in her belly, and she did her best to tamp them down. "How very thoughtful," she rasped.

"You have no idea," he murmured, cocking a brow. "But you will soon. Let me lock up and I'll be right up."

Nodding, she trailed up the stairs, entering the bedroom she'd begun to decorate days ago. After their conversation, she'd seen no reason to wait to start making the home her own. Plus, she'd known they were going to need the bedroom decorated for their bonding night, so she'd already spruced up the room with new bedding and furniture.

Sitting at the new vanity she'd purchased, Celine observed her reflection as she removed her earrings before starting to pluck the various pins out of her hair.

Sebastian entered the room, removing his jacket and tossing it onto the nearby chair.

"I did *not* purchase that chair to be a clothes hanger," she teasingly scolded. "I hope you're not one of those men who don't hang their clothes."

Grinning, he approached, lithe as a cougar as he slowly unbuttoned his shirt. "I'm afraid I've been a bachelor too long." Removing the shirt, he tossed it across the room to lie atop his jacket. "Perhaps you'll punish me for my transgressions."

Choppy breaths exited her lungs as she gazed at him in the reflection. "Perhaps."

She continued to remove the pins, shaking her hair so it fell loose and full down her back.

Placing his hands on her shoulders, Sebastian asked, "Do you need help with your dress?"

Swallowing thickly, she nodded and rose. Pushing the bench under the vanity, she presented her back to him. Sweeping her hair over one shoulder, she grinned over the other one. "The buttons are tiny. Let me know if you can't release them."

His deft fingers freed the tiny pearls one by one, and his skill sent shards of doubt through her frame. How many lovers had he been with? Did she have a chance of pleasing him since she had no experience at all?

After all the buttons were free, he pushed the fabric open, and a waft of cold air rushed against her back. Stepping forward, he traced his finger over the birthmark at the juncture of her neck and shoulder.

"I remember kissing this pretty mark the night of the gala," he said, his caress causing heat to flare in her belly. "I promised myself I would do it again one day."

Shuddering at his visceral words, she closed her eyes. "Sebastian..."

"Like this," he murmured, gliding his arm around her waist and aligning his front with her backside. Lowering his mouth to the mark, he tenderly kissed it.

Tilting her head, she allowed him access, loving the feel of his lips against her skin. He kissed her affectionately before lowering his hand to cup the mound of her sex through her dress. Burying his nose in her neck, he inhaled deeply.

"Goddess, Celine," he murmured, scraping his fangs against her neck as her knees buckled. "You smell so good. How did I never notice?"

"I think you have to be within several feet of someone to notice their scent," she teased, glancing at him in the reflection.

Lust flared in his eyes. "I plan to be wrapped around you all night, darling, so that won't be a problem." Stepping back, he slowly pushed her dress down her body so it pooled at her feet.

She stood before him, clad only in her strapless bra and thong, and fought the urge to cover herself.

"Oh no," he said, grasping her hand and leading her to the bed. "You're not allowed to cover one inch of flesh when it's bared to me." Turning her, his lips formed a salacious smile. "I want to see every part of you, Celine."

Tears welled in her eyes as the backs of her knees brushed the bed. She'd waited so long to be right here, but now that the time had come, nerves flared in her chest.

"Darling?" he asked, brushing a tendril of hair from her temple. "What's wrong?"

"I..." Swallowing thickly, she shook her head. "I have no idea how to please you. I've always hated my virginity, and never more than right now."

Compassion crossed his expression as he gently encircled her hand, drawing it to his swollen shaft underneath his pants. Celine caressed him, tenderly squeezing as he groaned.

Leaning forward, he nipped her bottom lip. "As you can see, I am sufficiently pleased."

A soft giggle escaped her throat. "But we haven't even started."

"The fun is in the buildup, dear. Would you like me to show you?"

Unable to reply, she slowly nodded.

"Good girl."

The words sent shivers through her frame.

"Lie down," he instructed, tugging her toward the bed.

Celine lay on her back, shimmying up the comforter until her head rested on the pillow. Fanning her hair to spread across the satin, she waited.

Sebastian placed the pad of his finger on her collarbone, trailing it down her body, over the fabric of her bra, and down her belly. Her skin quivered underneath as he placed his palm over her abdomen.

"I'm a bit dominant, if you hadn't noticed." His fingers caressed her skin, soothing her as he spoke. "I think you like it, judging by the way you respond to me." His hand drifted lower to play with the lacy hem of her panties. "But if I do or say anything you don't like, I want you to tell me. Do you understand?"

She nodded.

"Give me the words, sweetheart."

"I understand."

His lips curved into a sultry smile as he lightly tapped the hood of her mound several times. Celine squirmed on the bed, her hips arching to meet his hand, craving more.

"Goddess, you're so responsive. I love that about you, darling."

Celine's heart melted at the poignant words. Although not a declaration of love, they were caring and sensual, and they quelled a large portion of the doubt that simmered in her belly.

Removing his hand, he stepped back, eyes locked with hers as he discarded his clothes. Naked, he strode forward, and Celine couldn't help but study him. Small brown hairs covered his chest under broad shoulders, leading to a narrow waist and muscular thighs. His sex stood tall and proud from his body, reaching for her as it seemed to pulse in the dim light of the bedside lamp. His thighs brushed the bed before he palmed his length, sliding his hand back and forth as his breaths grew heavy.

"This is for you, Celine," he murmured, stroking his cock as he gazed into her eyes. "You already please me more than you know."

She lay frozen, mesmerized by his words and the erotic motion of his hand.

"There's nothing you need to do except let me love you, darling. Now, raise your hands above your head."

Dazed by his sultry tone, she lifted her arms, resting them on the pillow as his nostrils flared with desire.

Climbing onto the bed, he straddled her, his thick cock resting on her abdomen as his eyes darted over her bare flesh. Gliding his hands under her back, he unclasped her bra, lifting it in the air and shaking it.

"I'm going to toss it on the floor. Don't scold me."

Breathing a laugh, she shook her head. "I won't."

Winking, he tossed it to the carpet before placing his palms on her stomach. Desire marked his handsome features as he slowly slid his palms toward her breasts. Cupping the small mounds, he squeezed, groaning as he palmed her flesh.

"They're quite small," she said, biting her lip. "Sometimes I wish I were curvier like Mila—"

"You're perfect," he interjected, lowering to brush a kiss across her lips. "Now, hush and let me kiss you."

Celine licked her lips, preparing for the onslaught from his mouth.

Chuckling, he shook his head and placed his lips against her collarbone. "Not there," he rasped, trailing kisses over the valley between her breasts before veering sideways toward her nipple. "Let me kiss you here." Grazing the little bud with his lips, he gauged her reaction.

"Oh, *goddess*..." she whispered, watching her nipple grow taut and turgid as he grinned. "*Please*..."

Opening his mouth, he placed it over her nipple, drawing it inside as she squirmed beneath him. The wet warmth of his tongue washed over her, and she mewled, pressing into him.

"*Mmmm*..." he moaned, cupping her other breast as his mouth created the sweetest suction on her nipple. "Do you like that, sweetheart?"

"Yes!" she cried, clutching the pillow above her head, leaving her hands high as he commanded although she desperately wanted to clutch his hair.

"And how about this?" Extending his tongue, he flicked the taut nub over and over as heat flushed every cell of her skin. Drowning in pleasure, she purred, feeling the tingle between her thighs as wetness rushed to her core.

His tongue and fingers toyed with her nipples before he switched, kissing a path to the other breast and laving it with his tongue. He sucked and flicked her in an endless rhythm as his fingers toyed with the wet pointed nipple his mouth had abandoned. Writhing under him, Celine felt a burning deep in her belly.

"You're on fire for me, aren't you, sweetness?" he growled, sucking her nipple deep into his mouth as she squirmed. "Let me taste how much you want me. Goddess, I'm dying to taste you…"

His mouth placed wet kisses down her stomach as he repositioned himself between her legs. Hooking his fingers beneath the straps of her thong, he quickly tugged it off her quivering body. Cupping the backs of her knees, Sebastian placed them over his shoulders. Embarrassment swelled as he faced her deepest place, and her legs reflexively attempted to draw together.

"Oh, no," he commanded, pushing her thighs wider with his shoulders as he placed his fingers on her wet folds. "You'll bare this sweet pussy to me, Celine. Do you hear me?"

"Yes," she whispered, instinctively arching toward his mouth.

His sultry chuckle surrounded her. Drawing her folds open, he blew a long, warm breath over her core. Staring deep into her eyes, he asked softly, "Yes, what?"

Groaning, her back arched on the mattress.

"Don't deny me, darling. Follow your instincts. Your submission is addictive to someone like me, and so damn beautiful." Blowing on her center again, he waited. "Yes what, Celine?"

"Yes, sir."

His large frame shuddered between her legs, causing her to realize how much her submission pleased him. Understanding dawned as she comprehended that submission didn't mean lack of control. Instead, she suddenly felt drunk on her own arousal…and on the power she had to make him tremble with need. Pushing toward him, she offered herself, unabashed and unafraid.

A ragged groan escaped his throat before he lowered his head, nuzzling into her wet slit. Locking his gaze with hers, he licked a path from her slick opening, over her sensitive folds, to the tiny nub at the top of her sex. Overcome with joy, she closed her eyes, head falling back on the pillow as he loved her.

His deep murmurs of approval vibrated against her wet skin as he lapped up her essence, licking every spot on her core until she felt the orgasm looming on the horizon.

"Please, Sebastian. I need to move my arms...I need to touch you..."

"You're such a good girl to ask me nicely, Celine," he murmured against her wet folds. "You can move your arms, darling."

Whimpering, she lowered her arms, thrusting her fingers in his hair and clenching. Unbridled lust burned within as she drew him deeper, begging for more as he growled against her. Closing his lips over her clit, he began to suck...then flick...then suck once more...causing the engorged bud to swell even more under his intense ministrations.

"Oh god, right there," she crooned, spearing her nails into his scalp as he stimulated her clit with his tongue. "Oh...*Sebastian*...I'm going to come..."

He spread her folds wider, his mouth working the sensitive nub until her spine stiffened.

Giving in to the orgasm, she expelled a shuddered moan, her body racking with tremors as pleasure shot from the base of her spine to every cell in her frame. Riding the wave, she reveled in his words of approval whispered against her wet, ravaged core as he nuzzled into her. For so long, she'd dreamed of having Sebastian desire her. Finally, after so many centuries, he was hers. Reveling in her love for him, she tightened her thighs, hugging him closer as her muscles quivered.

His deep laugh reverberated against her, and she opened one eye, squinting down at him. Small quakes shook her frame as she gave him an incredulous look. "Are you really laughing at me? Seriously, Sebastian, you're going to give me a complex."

Running the tip of his nose over her wet folds and inner thigh, his lips formed a lascivious grin. "I'm sorry, sweetheart. You were squeezing me with your thighs and I had the fleeting thought I might be smothered by your sweet pussy." Kissing her mound, his grin deepened. "And I quickly realized that's the only way I want to go if I ever meet my untimely demise."

Huffing a laugh, she relaxed her legs. "I'm sorry. I didn't mean to smother you. It just felt so good." Heat flooded her cheeks. "Thank you."

Placing one last reverent kiss on her mound, he shifted, looming over her before lowering to align their bodies. Brushing a kiss on her lips, he shook his head. "You never have to thank me for making you feel good. We're bonded now, and it's my honor to give you pleasure."

Languid from her orgasm, she tenderly stroked his face. "I want to please you too."

Gliding his hand down her body, his fingers searched, finding her core and rimming her wet opening. Gathering some of her essence, he spread it all over her deepest place. The tender motions jolted her heartbeat once more as arousal flared deep within.

"Nothing pleases me more than to know I'm going to claim this sweet, tight pussy as mine." His tone was possessive as his hand worked its magic on her core. "That I'll be the only one who ever touches your gorgeous body."

Her fangs pressed into her bottom lip as she grinned. "Unless I leave you once I save up my stipend," she teased, undulating against his fingers as he emitted a harsh laugh.

"Try it," he murmured, lowering his lips to hers. "Once I claim you, I'm never letting you go."

Wrapping her arms around his neck, she opened her legs wider, allowing him to settle deeper between her thighs. "Promise?"

Gripping the base of his cock, he touched his sensitive head to her drenched opening, hissing as he rested his forehead against hers. Dousing his cock with her slick honey, he gazed deep into her eyes.

Celine held on for dear life as he began to push inside, inch by slow inch, the possessive glint in his eyes deepening with every small thrust. "Promise," he whispered, drawing her into a tender kiss.

Celine's lips toyed with his as she adjusted to the feeling of having him *inside* her. It wasn't uncomfortable, but with every jut forward she felt fuller. The small spark of nervousness she'd felt when he entered the room returned, and she stiffened slightly beneath him.

"Don't tense up, darling," he whispered, drawing her into a kiss as his hand found her breast. His fingers toyed with her nipple, sending renewed sparks of pleasure through her body, and she uttered a soft groan.

"That's it," he said, his hips undulating against her as he began to work his thick cock in her tight channel. "Feel me as I pinch these tight little nipples and claim every part of you."

The dirty words sparked a thousand fires deep within, and she moaned his name.

"Yes, sweetheart, there you are..." He circled his hips, the motion causing the head of his shaft to brush a place deep within that caused her to gasp. Brown eyes lit with desire as he watched her, moving his hips to hit the spot once more.

"Is that it?" he asked, jutting against it in small, rapid thrusts as she speared her fingernails into the skin at his nape. "Oh yes," he said, his lips curving into a sexy grin as he continued the maddening motion. "How does that feel, sweetheart?"

"Full...and amazing...and...*ahh*..." Unable to finish, she closed her eyes, her head relaxing into the pillow as she absorbed each pleasure-filled thrust.

"My naughty little virgin," he murmured, lowering his mouth to her ear and rimming the shell with his tongue. "You love taking my cock, don't you?"

"Yes!" Gripping his shoulders, every last ounce of strength left her muscles as she opened herself to him.

"Goddess, Celine," he gritted, teeth clenched as the pace of his hips increased. "I've never felt anything so tight around me... You're like a vise...it feels so good, darling..."

A cry escaped her lips as happiness flooded her. She wanted so desperately to please him and felt immense joy he was experiencing pleasure too. Wanting to pull him deeper, she squeezed her inner muscles, reveling at his shout of pleasure as he jerked above her.

"Dirty girl," he rasped, lifting her leg and wrapping it around his waist, opening her even more. "You're squeezing me. Do it again."

Celine clenched her inner muscles, closing around him before releasing and clenching again. Bliss contorted every feature in his handsome face as he cried her name, and Celine had the fleeting thought that maybe, just maybe, she could still make him fall in love with her. If they shared such a deep connection physically, surely she could transpose that to an emotional connection.

"Look at me," he commanded, drawing her from the serious thoughts.

Staring into his eyes, she squeezed him everywhere she could—his shoulders, his cock, his waist—and clutched him as he neared the peak.

"I need you to come again," he said, lowering his hand between their bodies. Finding her clit, he rubbed concentric circles on the engorged nub as he fucked her. "Please, sweetheart, come with me. I need you—"

Aching to kiss him, she pulled him close, inhaling his words as she drew him into a passionate kiss. His deep groans of pleasure echoed in her mouth as she slid her tongue over his. His powerful body trembled against hers, the ministrations of his fingers on her clit driving her toward another cliff. Surrounded by his warm body and sultry moans, she dove off the side, headlong into another orgasm, as his body bucked against her.

He surged inside her, filling her one last time before his head snapped back. Screaming her name, he began to come, his body jerking above her as he erupted. Grunting with lust, his hips jolted with every hot, pulsing jet he shot into her body.

Craving every part of him, she wrapped her legs around his waist, pulling him close as the hurried jerks of his hips turned to smaller shudders. Filling her with one last pump, he collapsed, his body half-atop hers as he rested most of his weight on his side.

Giggling, she ran her calf over the back of his hairy thigh as he huffed against her neck.

"Now who's laughing?" he mumbled.

"I was just thinking how considerate you were to only collapse halfway over me so you don't crush me. Still the proper, polite aristocrat, even in bed."

Lifting his head, he nipped her lips before breaking into a wide grin. "We're both creatures of habit, aren't we?" Resting his head on his fist, he traced the sweaty skin between her breasts, causing her to shiver.

"Yes, but knowing is half the battle." Lifting her finger, she arched her eyebrows. "We can help each other lighten up. I'll make sure you don't drown in paperwork, and you can help me become more independent...or worldly...or whatever I need to be so people don't think I'm a boring dimwit."

"I want everyone to think you're as boring as drywall so no one will realize how magnificent you are," he teased, chucking her nose with his finger. "You're mine, and no one is allowed to look at you."

Pride swelled at his words. "It wouldn't matter if they did. I only want you, Sebastian."

"Thank the goddess," he whispered.

They lay entwined, gently caressing each other, as their bodies cooled. Eventually, he ran his thumb over her lip.

"Are you okay, darling? I wanted to be gentle your first time, but I might've gotten a bit carried away." He cocked a satiated eyebrow.

"I'm fine. It felt good once I got used to the fullness. And the spot you found..." Overcome with embarrassment, she flattened her lips.

"Yes?" he crooned, cupping her breast and running his thumb over her nipple. "Did you like it when I hit that spot, Celine?"

Biting the inside of her lip, she nodded.

"Good. I'll make sure to give it *lots* of attention every time we do this."

Taken with his sultry expression, she finally let the realization wash over her that they were bonded for eternity. Well, as long as they could figure out how to make each other happy. He had offered her the option to eventually leave if she saved up enough money, but she doubted she would ever wish to do so.

"What is it?"

"I was just thinking about the future. We didn't discuss this—although we should've—but I have an IUD. I have for years because it regulates my cycle. Since this happened so fast, I know we're not ready to discuss children, but I want to be honest with you."

Disappointment washed over his features as her heart fluttered. "Sebastian?"

He pasted on a smile, although it didn't quite reach his eyes. "We should've discussed it, and I'm sorry we didn't. It's been kind of a whirlwind few weeks." He lifted a sardonic brow.

"It has. I think we should allow ourselves to be newlyweds for a while and settle into this. We have eternity to discuss these things."

"My wise little aristocrat," he said, plopping a kiss on her lips. "That we do." Glancing down, he eyed their bodies as he began to slip. "Don't move. Be right back." Extricating from her embrace, he padded to the bathroom, wetting a cloth before returning to her. Urging her to lie on her back, he spread her legs, wiping away the evidence of their loving.

As he stroked her with the warm cloth, his eyes lit with sated desire. "I love seeing you covered in my release. Goddess, sweetheart, it's so sexy."

Shaken by his desire-laden words, she bit her lip, watching him through half-lidded eyes. Once finished, he tossed the cloth in the hamper and turned off the bedside light as she crawled under the covers. He slid beside her, drawing her close.

Sprawling over his broad body, she rested her cheek on his chest, splaying her palm over his heart as it beat firmly beneath it.

"Good night, my naughty little mate. You're officially no longer a virgin."

Grinning, she ran her palm over the spiky hairs on his chest. "I'm not naughty."

Laughter rumbled as he squeezed her. "Oh, darling, you might've convinced everyone else, but I've seen behind your curtain. Now be a good mate and let me sleep. You tired me out."

"Yes, sir," she said, cuddling into him as she yawned.

He responded with a slap on her butt, causing her to beam as she snuggled against him. Wrapped in her bonded mate's embrace, she closed her eyes and inhaled his musky scent as she gave way to her dreams.

Chapter 13

Sebastian dove headfirst into building a life with Celine, often berating himself for the centuries he'd wasted as a proclaimed bachelor. He quickly realized his feisty, precocious bonded mate was his perfect match, and he inwardly declared himself the biggest dolt on the planet for overlooking her for so long.

For one thing, she was exceedingly generous and polite to the interior design staff she'd hired to decorate the house. Every time Sebastian came home he would find her working alongside them, painting walls or hanging wallpaper. A wealthy aristocrat like Celine could've chosen to be pampered in luxury for the rest of her days. Instead, she was content to help, wanting to stamp her mark on the work. Sebastian admired her greatly for it, and he also thought her adorable when he discovered her in the worn work attire.

"Look at you," he said, two weeks after their bonding ceremony when he returned home for lunch. She was dressed in baggy overalls with paint splotches covering her perfect features. Running his finger over her paint-soaked cheek, he grinned. "Who would've guessed our proper Celine is an avid house painter?"

"Oh, stop it," she chided, swiping his chest. "I want to help, and it satisfies my urge to make things perfect." Gesturing around, her eyes lit with excitement. "Do you like the color?"

Surveying the living room, he admitted it was gorgeous. The deep forest green complimented the wood floor and stone fireplace, and he knew she would buy furniture that only enhanced the colors. Sliding his arm around her waist, he tugged her close, brushing a kiss on her lips. He ached to do more—perhaps spread some paint to other regions of her stunning body—but alas, they were surrounded by workers, so he behaved himself.

"I love the color. Well done."

"You're home for lunch again," she said, lifting to her toes to kiss him back. "I thought you always ate at the office."

"I find I can't go more than a few hours without seeing you, darling," he murmured, nipping her lips. "What do you think that means?"

Affection swam in her eyes as she smiled. "That you're slowly losing your desire to be a workaholic. It's a miracle."

Chuckling, he ran the backs of his fingers over her cheek. "Perhaps you've cured me. If so, I'm exceedingly thankful."

Her delight at his words was palpable, and he reveled in her stunning smile. In truth, Sebastian was becoming quite addicted to his mate, and he found himself longing for her when they were apart. Never in all his centuries on the planet had he craved the company of another, but now, he admitted he was hooked. He couldn't imagine building a future with anyone else, and he silently kicked himself for giving her an out. Would the day come when she saved up his monthly stipend and decided to leave? The dreary thought brought him great discomfort, so he pushed it away every time it appeared.

When she'd told him about her IUD, he'd experienced a moment of such melancholy his throat closed as he'd caressed her soft skin. He'd never given much thought to children, but now that he was with Celine he saw no reason to wait. She would be an excellent mother, and the possessive part of him wanted to bear a child with her. To create something special that belonged only to them. A child they could love and cherish as they continued to build their future.

Did she want that with him though? Or did she see bearing his child as another tie to him? Perhaps deep within, she still felt as if he'd bonded with her out of duty. Perhaps Sebastian had used that as an excuse, but deep down he knew the truth: each day, he was falling deeper into the abyss for his bonded mate.

Sebastian had never been in love before, but he had the stinging suspicion that it felt a lot like what he was experiencing. The need to be near her constantly. The bliss he felt when she tossed back her head and gave a joyful laugh. The bone-deep arousal he felt every time they made love. It was all-consuming, and he finally began to comprehend what Garridan had tried to explain about his feelings for Siora.

The emotion he felt for Celine was encompassing. Although that frightened him slightly, he also wanted to push through the fear to other side, knowing the reward of building a future with her would be so much more fulfilling than the staid, boring life he'd lived for so long.

After all this time, he craved a future with a mate and hoped he could convince her to stay. To bear his children and build a life full of affection and joy.

As the weeks turned into months, Sebastian and Celine fell into an easy pattern. She focused on decorating the house while he performed his council duties. They attended the formal fetes and fundraisers together, Sebastian always so proud to have her on his arm.

One night, after a particularly stuffy fundraiser, they returned home and Celine proceeded to kick off her shoes in the foyer. Chuckling, Sebastian lifted her in his arms and carried her up the stairs.

"Why do you wear them if they hurt your feet, darling?" he asked, placing her on the bed and lowering beside her. Bringing her foot to his lap, he began to knead the swollen arch.

"Oh goddess..." she moaned, throwing her arm over her eyes as he massaged her foot. "That feels amazing." Squinting from under her arm, she gave a cheeky grin. "And I wear them because they're fashionable, of course. A prominent aristocratic council member must have an appropriately dressed female on his arm."

The corner of his lips curled. "I appreciate the sentiment, darling, but I prefer you without any clothes at all. I think you know that by now."

Heat flushed her cheeks as she bit her lip, adorable in the soft light of the bedside lamp. Rising, he slowly removed her dress, dragging it off her body along with her undergarments. Sebastian gazed at her, lust thrumming through his veins from her dewy skin as it glowed on the bed. Once he was naked, he straddled her, sliding his hands under her arms so her back rested against the headboard. After fluffing the pillows behind her to ensure she was comfortable, he balanced on his knees as he straddled her flushed body.

"Darling," he said, cupping her chin as his cock strained toward her. "I need to claim you here." He ran his thumb over her lips.

Doubt entered her eyes as her breaths grew heavy. "I don't know how. I don't want to do it wrong—"

A desire-laden laugh rushed from his lips. "Impossible," he whispered, inching toward her. "Just kiss me. I promise, anything you do to me feels good, sweetheart." He placed the sensitive tip of his cock on her lips, overwhelmed with how gorgeous she was as curiosity warred with doubt in her expression.

Finally, she took pity on him and opened those full lips. Seizing the moment, Sebastian slowly slipped inside.

Working his hips, he pumped into her wet mouth, overcome with how sexy she was as she stroked him with her lips and tongue. Those stunning ice-blue eyes locked with his, filled with desire and hope, and he chuckled as he caressed her cheek.

"It feels amazing. Just like that..." Increasing the pace of his hips, he fucked her sweet mouth, observing her confidence grow as she realized *she* was the one in control.

"Yes, darling," he rasped, placing his palms flat on the headboard to brace himself. She smiled around his cock, the little minx, causing the sensitive flesh to swell even more. "You have me in the palm of your hand. You always do. You know that, right?"

Lifting her hand to his sac, she gently squeezed as he groaned. Baring his fangs, he thought he might drown in the image of his sweet Celine sucking him as she caressed his most sensitive place.

"Naughty girl," he rasped, the base of his spine tingling as his climax loomed. "I smell your arousal. You're gushing as you suck me, aren't you, darling?"

She whimpered, nodding as she coated his shaft with her saliva.

Suddenly craving a deeper connection, he withdrew, sliding down her body and pushing her legs apart. Settling between her thighs, he thrust his hand in the hair at her nape, clutching as the sensitive head of his cock slipped through her essence.

"Open up to me, honey," he rasped, positioning himself at her core.

Wrapping her arms around him, she nodded. "I'm ready—"

Her back arched as he surged inside, claiming her as lust clouded his brain. Anchoring her by her hair, he thrust in strong, deep lunges, unable to control his need to possess her. Pressing his forehead to her neck, he inhaled her intoxicating scent as his hips worked her ravaged body. Aching to have all of her, he licked her neck, preparing it for his invasion.

"I need to drink from you, sweetheart," he rasped, overcome by the taste of her salty sweat on his tongue. Drinking from one's mate was a sacred tradition in Vampyre culture, and a threshold they hadn't yet crossed. "Please, Celine, I have to—"

"Yes," she cried, spearing her nails into his back. "Drink from me—"

Armed with her consent, he bared his fangs and thrust them deep into her vein. Her blood burst onto his tongue, coating it as he moaned. A thousand shards of pleasure shot to every cell in his frame as he consumed her, body and soul. Lost in her scent and spurred on by her sexy purrs, he fucked her, raw and deep, until she began to tremble.

"Oh yes...right there, Sebastian..." Her head fell lax on the pillow, baring her neck to him as her fingernails scraped his back. The little hellion was probably drawing blood, but Sebastian didn't care. All he could fathom was this moment, lost in his beautiful Celine as he loved her.

Closing his eyes, he emitted a deep groan, falling over the edge as the orgasm claimed him.

The walls of her tight pussy clenched, milking his release from his body as she shuddered below him. Locked inside her tight vise, he rode the wave, his lips still covering her pulsing vein as they experienced the high. His hips jerked, emptying the last of his release into her warm core, and he licked her neck, sealing her wounds with his self-healing saliva.

They lay entwined, sticky and sated, slowly caressing each other as they fell back to earth. She ran her nails over his scalp, the soft strokes infinitely pleasurable, and Sebastian felt the urge to say the three words he'd never said to another.

"I liked sucking you," she said, the words laced with a hint of shyness.

Lifting his head, he couldn't stop his sultry grin. "I liked it too."

"You did?"

Nodding, he caressed her jaw. "Darling, don't you know by now that I live for the moments you touch me? In any way, and for however long."

"My romantic Vampyre," she sighed, trailing her fingers over his back. "I never would've guessed."

Chuckling, he kissed her collarbone, understanding how special his romantic words were to her. Realization dawned that he needed to do more. Not just in the bedroom, but in their daily lives as well. Racking his brain, he tried to think of something that would show her. Not just with words or passionate lovemaking, but a real, tangible expression of how much she meant to him.

An idea slowly formed in his mind, and his lips curved as his wheels continued to spin.

"What's that mischievous grin for?" she asked, curiosity lacing her features.

"Nothing. I'm still high from being buried inside you, darling."

Biting her lip, she nodded. "Me too."

Feeling himself slip, he rose, cleaning them both before they crawled under the covers and held each other close. As she fell asleep in his arms, Sebastian stroked her hair, formulating the details of the gift he was going to give her. One that would show her he truly saw her, after all this time, and that there was no doubt his future belonged to her.

Chapter 14

Mila discovered Celine sitting underneath one of the oak trees in her expansive back yard. The branches offered shade from the sun, and she absently chewed her nail as her friend approached.

"No decorating today?" Mila asked, sitting on the spongy grass beside her.

"It's mostly finished," Celine said, staring off into the distance as she frowned. "I have a few small things left to decorate, but for the most part, the work is done."

"That's great. Why do you look miserable?"

Huffing a breath, she lifted her hands in an exasperated shrug. "Because after it's done, what the hell am I going to do?"

"Umm...I don't understand the question."

"I don't want to become a burden to Sebastian. Decorating the home has given me a purpose." She slowly trailed her palm over the grass. "Once it's done, am I just supposed to sit around all day and wait for him to come home? Won't that make me the simpering, useless female he always saw me as? What if he comes to resent me? Or worse, decides I'm the boring aristocrat everyone else thinks I am?"

"Wow," Mila said, leaning back on her palms. "There's a lot to unpack there." Pursing her lips, she contemplated. "First of all, I don't know why you're freaking out. Sebastian is clearly in love with you, Celine."

"Then why won't he say it?" she murmured, her lips forming a pout. "Sometimes, when we make love, I feel he's so close to saying it, but he never does."

"Have *you* said it? Sometimes men need a push, Celine. You know this better than most since your experience as *Anya* is what pushed him to finally acknowledge you."

Sighing, Celine's lips fluttered as she blew out a breath. "I'm afraid to say it first. Then he'll know he owns my heart." Staring at her friend, she almost choked on the emotion welling in her chest. "I don't want him to *own* me, Mila. I want us to be equals."

"Then tell him. He's not a mind reader, Celine."

"I know." Drawing her knees to her chest, Celine rested her chin upon them as she stared over the rolling hills. "I want to have his children...and build a family with him."

"Perhaps he wants that too. It's long past time you were a mother, Celine."

"But children will bind me to him even more. I don't want him to feel obligated to me."

"Well, you're bonded—"

"Yes, because my father forced it." Angrily shaking her head, she scowled. "But I want him to *choose* me. Is that too much to ask? Am I just being ridiculous?"

Sighing, Mila contemplated. "I don't know. He's not the most expressive man—"

"You should see him in the bedroom," Celine interjected, excitement lacing her tone. "Oh, Mila, he's so passionate—"

"Um, yeah, I'm all set." Mila held up her hand as Celine chuckled. "You two are still learning to communicate with each other, but now's not the time to hold back. You need to tell him what you want." Gazing into her eyes, her friend smiled. "Tell him you love him, Celine. I know you're afraid it will make him feel obligated to say it too, but maybe he's waiting for you. You won't know until you take the chance."

Tears burned Celine's eyes as she acknowledged Mila's words. "And what if he doesn't say it back?"

"Then you continue to save his monthly stipend and hope he gets his act together. If not, you'll always have the opportunity to leave down the road."

The thought of leaving Sebastian, whom she loved with every piece of her heart, was so distressing she pushed the possibility from her mind. "I can't accept that reality."

Rising, Mila wiped the grass off her backside before extending her hand. "Then make the reality you want, Celine. Come on—I need your help. I'm meeting a prospective new client at the coffee shop and want your opinion."

"Why do you need my opinion?" she asked, taking her hand and rising to her feet.

"Because, my dear," she said, waggling her brows, "I think I might want this one for myself. She plays for my team, if you know what I mean."

"Ohhhh," Celine said, clasping her hands under her chin. "I'd be honored to help you assess. Let me wash up, and I'll walk to town with you."

Hoping she could help her friend find love, Celine tucked her words deep inside, praying she could gather the strength to face her bonded mate and voice her true feelings.

Chapter 15

A week later, Celine finally summoned the courage to confront Sebastian. He'd seemed a bit distracted lately, sometimes rushing off to take important calls at odd hours of the day and night, and she was worried he'd begin to focus on work again now that they'd settled into their lives. She'd decided she would tell him she wanted to remove her IUD and start trying to get pregnant, hoping that would keep him focused on things at home now that the renovation was mostly finished.

When he breezed through the front door, Celine's heart leaped in her chest as she flitted around the kitchen putting the finishing touches on everything she'd prepared. He stepped into the room and broke into a wide grin.

"What's all this?" he asked, striding toward her and drawing her into a deep kiss. "Did you prepare lunch for me, darling?"

"Yes," she said, gesturing to the island countertop. "I prepared some Slayer blood and some food too. You've been working so hard lately I figured you deserved a treat."

"Have you been keeping tabs on me, dear?" Leaning down, he brushed the tip of his nose against hers.

"Well, you've just seemed a bit distracted with all the work calls..." She drifted off, not wanting to complain. "But I know your job is important. Our people are lucky to have you."

A tender expression crossed his features, and he nodded. "My work is important, but nothing is more important than you, Celine. You know that, right?"

Hating the tears that welled in her eyes, she worked her jaw, struggling to speak. "I...honestly, I don't know, Sebastian. I think we're still learning to communicate, and sometimes I'm not sure what to think."

His lips formed a sympathetic smile. "We are, and I appreciate how patient you've been with me." His fingers stroked her jaw as he spoke, his tone reverent. "I was a grumpy, lovelorn bachelor for way too long and never learned how to be romantic."

"I think you're doing a fine job."

Chuckling, he shook his head. "In some areas, perhaps..."—his eyes lit with desire—"but I know I could do more. In fact, I have something to show you." Stepping back, he extended his hand.

Curious, she placed her palm in his, following him as he tugged her toward the back door. He led her outside, past the tree where she'd had the discussion with Mila, and through a thicket of dense trees and brush. Eventually, they made it to a clearing with an expansive meadow that housed a large circular wooden fence.

"Garridan never used this piece of land, but it's part of the property, and I've finally commissioned it for use."

"Oh," she said, surveying the field. "What for?"

"As you can see, the workers I hired already built the horse corral." Pointing toward the side of the corral, he grinned. "And the stable can go there if that works for you."

Celine's heart began to pound as she struggled to comprehend what he was saying. "If you're building stables, you don't need my approval."

"Well, darling, since the stables are for you, I would rather have your opinion."

"For me?" she whispered.

"Yes, sweetheart." Encircling her wrists, he brought them to his chest. "I racked my brain to find something that would show you how much I love you, Celine, and that I *see* you. I remember you telling me you wanted that when you first turned my life upside down." He flashed a teasing grin. "I'm building you a stable, darling, where you can open an academy and train children to ride horses. My dear, you can muck out as many stalls as your heart desires."

A laugh escaped her throat as she spread her palms over his pecs. "You're building me a stable?"

"Yes. And the academy will be yours to run however you wish. It will allow you to build your own business so you're not so dependent on me." Leaning down, he nudged her nose with his. "I know you want your independence, Celine, and I have no wish to deny you that. I just want you to be happy. It's the only chance we have of building the future we want."

Tears ran down her cheeks as she stood frozen, awed by the immensely romantic gesture. Unable to form words, her arms snaked around his neck, and he drew her into a warm embrace.

"Don't cry, sweetheart," he crooned, soothing her as he rubbed her back. "This was supposed to make you smile."

"I'm overwhelmed," she said, drawing back to gaze into his eyes. "I wished for so long you'd love me back, but I wasn't sure you would ever see me as more than a burden forced on you by my father."

"A burden?" he asked, stroking her hair. "Goddess, Celine, you're the best damn thing that's ever happened to me. I was a shell of a man buried in work when you shook up my world. I'm so thankful for you, darling." Leaning forward, he rested his lips against her ear. "And you're so deliciously dirty in bed, my naughty little virgin."

Her cheeks reddened with embarrassment as she swatted his chest. "I'm not naughty, and I'm certainly no longer a virgin. You took care of that quite promptly after we bonded."

Tossing back his head, he laughed. "I certainly did, but you are delectably naughty, Celine. It's one of my favorite things about you."

"Sebastian," she whispered, tenderly stroking his face. "I love you so much. I've loved you for centuries. I'm so honored you finally decided to love me back. I want to give you babies and build a future with you if you want the same."

Cocking a brow, he murmured, "I'll agree on one condition. You *must* teach our children how to muck out stalls. I think I'll enjoy watching that very much."

"You devil," she chided, biting her lip. "Will you ever stop teasing me?"

"Never." He brushed a kiss over her lips. "How can I when it's so fun? Your cheeks turn the sexiest shade of red when I tease you, darling—"

Done with his tender chiding, she drew him close, cementing her lips to his as they shared a torrid kiss. Sebastian groaned, pressing his body to hers as their tongues glided over each other's, sending sparks of desire through her veins.

Gently breaking the kiss, she pressed her forehead to his. "Thank you for this." She glanced out over the meadow. "My own business where I can teach children and work with horses. It's a dream I never imagined would come true for someone like me, raised to be a boring aristocrat."

"'Boring' isn't even in my vocabulary when it comes to you." Gliding a hand over her hair, his eyes darted between hers. "I love you, Celine. Thank you for being patient with me."

"I love you," she cried, rising to her toes to peck his lips. "Thank you for seeing who I truly am."

Lowering, he swept her into his arms and began to carry her home. As he plodded across the yard, she rested her head on his chest, closing her eyes and thanking Etherya for her gorgeous, thoughtful mate.

Once they crossed the threshold of the back door, he set her on her feet and locked the door.

Glancing at the counter, her lips formed a sultry smile. "I have a feeling we're not going to be eating lunch for a while."

Hunger entered his gaze as he slowly approached. "Oh, I intend to feast...just not on the delicious spread you prepared..."

Arousal flared within as her mate approached, reaching for her with his broad, talented hands as she squealed. Rapt with joy, she pivoted, running from the room and bolting up the stairs.

His deep laugh followed as he trailed after her. "You know I'll have to punish you for running, right, darling?"

Throwing herself on the bed, she waited for her lover to arrive. He slowly approached, gazing at her with such adoration her heart threatened to explode in her chest. Extending her arms, she beckoned to him. Strong, stoic Sebastian, the only man she'd ever loved, and the man who finally loved her exactly as she was.

Enfolding him in her arms, she opened every last piece of her heart. Her skillful, soulful Vampyre loved her, slowly and passionately, whispering tender words as they cemented the future they would build for centuries to come.

Before You Go

Well, dear readers, Celine and Sebastian found their happy ending! I think Mila needs to find hers too. What do *you* think? Make sure to check out all of my books at **RebeccaHefner.com** and thank you for reading!

Did you know that Rebecca has an online store where she sells **signed books**, an Etherya's Earth **adult coloring book**, and more? Check out her website for more info!

Acknowledgments

Thanks to everyone who asked for Celine and Sebastian's story!

Thanks to Megan, Bryony, Anthony and Sarah for being part of my team and for making my books shine.

And thanks to every one of you who reads my books!

About the Author

USA Today bestselling author Rebecca Hefner grew up in Western NC and now calls the Hudson River of NYC home. In her youth, she would sneak into her mother's bedroom and read the romance novels stashed on the bookshelf, cementing her love of HEAs. A huge Buffy and Star Wars fan, she loves an epic fantasy and a surprise twist (Luke, he IS your father).

Before becoming an author, Rebecca had a successful twelve-year medical device sales career. After launching her own indie publishing company, she is now a full-time author who loves writing strong, complex characters who find their HEAs.

Rebecca can usually be found making dorky and/or embarrassing posts on TikTok and Instagram. Please join her so you can laugh along with her!

Also by Rebecca Hefner

Etherya's Earth Series
Prequel: The Dawn of Peace
Book 1: The End of Hatred
Book 2: The Elusive Sun
Book 3: The Darkness Within
Book 4: The Reluctant Savior
Book 4.5: Immortal Beginnings
Book 5: The Impassioned Choice
Book 5.5: Two Souls United
Book 6: The Cryptic Prophecy
Book 6.5: Garridan's Mate
Book 7: The Diplomatic Heir
Book 7.5: Sebastian's Fate
Book 8: The Solitary Protector

Prevent the Past Trilogy
Book 1: A Paradox of Fates
Book 2: A Destiny Reborn
Book 3: A Timeline Restored

Made in United States
Troutdale, OR
03/28/2025